Swiss Chocolate

D0905814

By James M. Weil

Swiss Chocolate
Copyright 2010 James Weil
All right reserved
First Printing January 2011

ISBN # 978-0-9824331-0-2

Written by James Weil

Cover by Windward Design

Edited by Heather Taylor

Published by Dailey Swan Publishing, Inc

Swiss Chocolate is a fictionalized memoir. Any
resemblance to real persons, living or dead, is
purely coincidental.

Dailey Swan Publishing, Inc
2644 Appian Way #101
Pinole Ca 94564
www.daileyswanpublishing.com

Acknowledgments

I would like to thank my friend and agent, Chamein Canton, who never stopped believing in me, even when I was riddled with self-doubt. She has been a wonderful friend. I would also like to thank my editor, Susan Mary Malone, whose brilliant editing helped me flush out the characters and story. She worked with me tirelessly to make the manuscript shine. Special thanks go to Ottavia Giorgi Monfort, whose words of encouragement and insightful critiques gave me the inspiration to keep going as I was writing the story. Her helpful knowledge of some of the finer points about Italian etiquette and cuisine gave the manuscript more credence. Finally, I would like to thank my father, whose continued generosity, kindness and understanding has helped me through some of my darkest moments.

Dedication

For my children, Andrew and Samantha

Chapter 1

I squirmed in my seat trying to get a glimpse of the Swiss Alps over my mother, whose great head of red hair all but obstructed my view. Her eyes were red from lack of sleep and her skin looked pale and drawn. "Stop leaning over me!" she snapped.

I sat back in my seat and scowled. Looking to my father for assistance was no use since he never stopped reading his book—a lengthy discourse on world affairs by Oxford Analytica—until the plane came to a complete stop at the terminal. In fact, he didn't say much the entire trip, he and my mother avoiding conversation whenever possible since we left New Jersey.

With less than an hour before our train left Geneva, we took a cab from the airport to the train station. At fifteen, not only was this my first trip to Europe, but it was also the first time I had heard French in everyday use. I had studied the language for years in school, and some of the words sounded familiar, but it all seemed so new. Besides, my academic career was horrible, and I never really studied my lessons well anyway. My father's French was passable, impressing me with his ability to converse with the taxi driver, even though his accent was awful.

The train station bustled with people and activity—people darting all around without concern, intent on their own agenda. Seeing an opening in the traffic, I sighed, smiled, tucked my ski bag over my shoulder, and reached down to grab my bags from where the cab driver had dropped them to join in the fray. Yet, to my surprise and grief, I could barely lift my suitcases. My mother and grandmother, having both been more excited about my going to boarding school in Switzerland than I was, had taken me shopping in New York to outfit me with appropriate clothing.

Brooks Brothers and Bloomingdale's had a very good weekend when my grandmother came to town, and now I was paying the price trying to lug all those clothes through the train station.

"Hurry up," said my mother, glancing back at me with scorn, as I hobbled along behind her beneath the staggering weight of my bags. At last we found a porter to help us and were taken to our train. There was something very old-world and romantic about taking a train through Switzerland. I had taken trains from where we lived in Rumson, New Jersey to New York, but those were just small, uncomfortable commuter trains. This one was stately and we had our own compartment that opened to a corridor along one side of the car. There were large plush seats with enough room for six people to be quite comfortable, so you can imagine how much room that allowed the three of us. Nevertheless, as before, my father read his book, my mother looked tired and gaunt, and I stared out the large single-pane window and dreamed of the adventures these rails must have had in the past.

My father had mentioned that the trip to Sierre should last about three and a half hours, winding through the canton of Valais in the southern part of Switzerland. From Sierre we were to take another train to Bluche where my school was located. I had no clue where these places were. My mother had shown me the brochure for the school. The pictures of the dining room looked more like a country club than a boy's dormitory, and the rooms seemed so European and different. But, and this is a big but, the school was located right next to a famous ski resort, and was included in the curriculum. I couldn't wait. I had thumbed through the brochure with disbelief, thinking that all my dreams had finally come true.

My cousins went to this same school when they were about my age. My uncle died in a train wreck when I was just a baby, and my aunt packed up her kids and moved to Switzerland to help

8

deal with her grief. She suggested I go to the school to help with my discipline problems, believing the Swiss Alps would be the perfect place to help stimulate my intellect. I had already been expelled from two private schools because of my miserable academic failures and rowdy behavior. Exasperated, my parents finally pulled me out of private schools altogether and sent me to public school. That was a disaster. The other kids hunted me on the playground relentlessly. Not being much of a fighter, I did my best to protect myself, yet I ended up on an almost weekly basis with my clothes scuffed, torn, and covered in blood. I was finally suspended for fighting and my parents decided Switzerland was my only chance at ever having a respectable academic career.

The train pulled out of the station shortly after noon. Before long, my mother dozed off, and my father, who sat across from me, put down his book and eyed me up and down. His pale blue eyes had a slightly hardened look. He had dark, wavy hair and boyish, full lips. He was a tall man— 6'2"—and his amazing good looks made him stand out wherever he went. His tweed blazer and grey slacks were his idea of casual dress. People told me I looked a lot like him, except I had my mother's thick, dark auburn hair, freckles and deep blue-green eyes. "You screw this up, and there won't be any more chances for you," he finally said.

"I won't screw it up, Dad."

"Your grades are worse than awful, and your behavior has been an embarrassment to this family. And don't think for a minute that you are being sent to the finest boarding school in Switzerland as some kind of a reward for your antics. In my book you are less than shit," he said, scowling at me.

My chest muscles tightened as I flinched from his words. When he talked to me that way I never knew if he might follow it up with a slap in the face—it wouldn't be the first time.

9

The truth was I didn't know if I was going to screw it up. Although a voracious reader, I always had a tough time with school. I read books way beyond my age level, but couldn't perform well in school to save my life. It baffled my teachers and parents, but their consternation didn't come close to my feelings of guilt for my underachievement. I took all the opportunities being raised in a well-to-do family handed me for granted, but going to school in Switzerland overwhelmed me with self-doubt and fear of failure.

Instead of answering him and possibly aggravating him further, I just nodded slightly, and then returned to staring out the window at the passing scenery. The leaves were beginning to turn, and I scanned the horizon for the snowy peaks I had imagined seeing, but there were only rolling hills covered with wheat and corn. I had expected to see a lot more mountains, and wondered if the Swiss Alps were simply an imaginary product invented by Hollywood. As the train gently rocked and my mother began to snore softly, she rested her head on my father's shoulder, and he went back to his book.

When we came upon Lake Geneva I thought we were at the ocean. Although the water looked relatively calm, it stretched as far as I could see. It was early October, and winter hadn't set in yet. The air was crisp, but the sun was bright and warm. Sailboats glided lazily across the water in the afternoon sun.

Eventually we left the lake behind us and the scenery was replaced with endless fields of grain. I didn't feel the altitude start to rise until we reached Montreux. The terrain gradually became rocky precipices that jutted out over the tracks. When we entered Valais I beheld the Alps rising before me like nothing I had ever seen. Their majestic, snowy peaks loomed in the distance, and I could hardly believe this was where I'd be going to school. My heart raced, and I sat up straight in my seat and gazed at the horizon. The entrance to the valley was mostly rolling hills where cattle grazed in greenish-brown pastures, but a little further up, the snowcaps glistened in the afternoon sun, and the train chugged away at the tracks, rising higher and higher to our destination.

As the air became thinner, my mother's snoring became more irregular. By now I was so tired it nearly hurt, but I was still too excited to even think about closing my eyes. My father finally drifted off to sleep as well, his last motion as he gave into the encroaching slumber was folding his book neatly on his lap.

Quickly growing tired of the snoring now coming in stereo, I left our compartment and walked about the train to get a fuller grasp of everything around me. While most passengers seemed to take the scenery in stride, I just couldn't stop gazing at the mountains rising on either side of us as we snaked our way though the little towns in Valais. Small villages clung to the sides of the mountain precariously, as if it could shudder slightly and shrug them off, like cattle shooing flies. Most of the towns were small, and the chalets were exactly as I imagined—just like the gingerbread houses we used to get during Christmas time. I found myself falling in love with the storybook landscape. When the mountains were not angry pieces of granite jutting out in all directions, they were steep pastures where cattle grazed. In some places grape vines clung to the ground, wrapped with twine—as if a great spider had spun a huge web on the side of the mountain.

I pressed my face against the window and watched in awe as the scenery rolled past when I saw the reflection of a man behind me. "The farmers wrap the vines this way to protect them from the frost after the harvest," said the conductor, winking at me. I was surprised at how well he spoke English. His blue cap sat upon a narrow, craggy face, and his bushy moustache covered the corners of his mouth.

"When do we get to Sierre?" I asked.

He took a pocket watch from his vest pocket, popped open the cover, and glanced at the face. "An hour and ten minutes," he answered, smiling as he closed the watch and slipped it back into his vest. "Is this your first trip to Switzerland?"

"Yes. I'm going to school here."

"Where?" he asked.

"*Ecole des Roches*, in Bluche."

"I've been there. It's a beautiful place. Lots of good skiing," he said, winking once more. He touched his fingers to the brim of his cap and tipping it slightly, turned and continued down the corridor, while I went back to gazing out the window, too excited about my new school to even imagine what it was like.

I went back to our compartment and watched my parents sleep. My mother's arm was curled around my father's, and he dozed quietly with his head tilted forward. I enjoyed watching them sleep; it was the only time they seemed almost happy together. As the train made an abrupt shudder on the tracks, my father awoke, cleared his throat, and looked at his watch. "We should be there pretty soon," he said.

"It's beautiful here."

"Just remember what I told you. If you screw this up you're finished."

"I'm not going to screw up, Dad," I answered with just a hint of defiance. The man would not let me even allow the moment of joy I was feeling. He eyed me with contempt and then looked out the window until boredom overtook him and he closed his eyes once more. How anyone could be bored by all of this I could not understand—maybe because I was seeing it with a sense of adventure, while he saw it as almost a chore.

The late-afternoon sun was sinking over the mountains when we reached Sierre. I expected to see a much bigger town, but it was tiny, with the train station nothing more than a single platform only slightly raised from the ground. My heart sunk. Sierre was a dumpy little town, with just a few modest shops here and there selling clothing and shoes.

My mother yawned as we stepped off the train; her thick red hair was pressed flat on one side of her head from where she had slept on my father's shoulder. She shivered slightly, and then gazed at the snowy peaks on either side of the valley. "What a beautiful country," she said.

"We still have a ways to go," my father said, picking up his bag.

"Is this where the school is, Dad?" I asked, looking around me, trying not to make my disappointment too obvious.

"No. We need to take the funicular up to Bluche. It's about an hour's ride up the mountain."

I hoisted my ski bag over my shoulder and grunted as I lifted my suitcases, and we climbed down the narrow steps off the platform and headed up the street until we came upon the funicular station. I had never seen such a contraption before. Basically a set of railway cars connected to either end of a thick cable, as one car ascended, the other descended. The seats were raised and tilted forward to compensate for the steep incline. We loaded all our baggage on the car and took our seats.

The funicular groaned as it left the station, causing my mother to sit straight up in her seat. "Absolutely beautiful," she said, looking out the window and smiling at me, trying her best to hide her nervousness.

"The conductor on the train told me the skiing is fantastic," I said, eyeing the snowy peaks far above us with excitement.

"This is no ski vacation, young man," my father said with the same commanding tone as before.

"I know, Dad," I said, staring out the window as the funicular creaked and groaned its way up the mountain. Although

13

early in the season, patches of snow covered the ground. Small, simple farmhouses sprinkled the landscape, while cow pastures—delineated by thin wire fences—stretched below us to the bottom of the valley. My ears popped as we ascended, and the air got colder.

Darkness had settled when we arrived in Bluche, and the evening air was now quite cold. The funicular station was pretty far from the school, and I struggled with my skis and suitcases as we trudged up the dirt path from the platform to a single paved road.

"Well, there's not much to the town," said my father.

"I wouldn't say that," my mother replied with a lilt in her voice. "I think it's utterly charming!"

I was simply too captivated by my surroundings to speak at all. We came upon the girl's dormitory, *Prés Fleuris*, a three-story stucco building, which looked more like a small hotel than a girl's school. Each of the windows of the dormitory rooms had black shutters, and a small balcony, enclosed by a low wooden railing, jutted out over the second and third floors. Next to it sat a little inn and restaurant. The classroom building was between the girls' and boys' quarters. Made from stucco and strong steel beams, it stuck out among the rustic surroundings as if it didn't belong there at all. On the other side of the street, overlooking the valley was a basketball court and a soccer field. Then at the end, next to my school, was *Auberge Petit Paradis*, which reminded me of an oversized Swiss chalet. My parents would be staying there the next couple of days before continuing their tour of Europe. Above the school, sprinkled among the trees, were some small chalets which seemed out of place in the pristine landscape, and that was pretty much everything there was to see.

After my parents got settled in their hotel room, they escorted me to my new school to meet the headmaster. The entrance looked more like some of the smaller ski lodges I had seen in the Catskills in New York. The words "*Les Roches*" were above the front entrance on a large wooden plaque. The building was cement with brown cedar siding—not as stately as some of the private schools I had attended, but it had its own European charm.

We entered into a flagstone lobby, and I peered at my surroundings, excited and nervous. A heavy glass door opened into one of the dormitories, with wooden lockers lining the hallways. I couldn't see into the rooms, but the dormitories looked comfortable. A long flagstone corridor led to the dining room on the left, and directly in front of the main entrance, a flight of stairs led to the basement. At the bottom of the steps were cubbyholes filled with slippers. To the right of the entrance were the administrative and Headmaster's office.

The headmaster, Mr. Davis, came out and greeted us. I was surprised to see he was quite short with bushy eyebrows and receding gray hair, and as he shook hands with each of us, mentioned he was from the U.S. I couldn't place his accent to tell from where in the states, but it was somehow comforting to know there would be some connection to my homeland. He quickly ushered us into his office and gestured to the chairs in front of his desk as he walked around the massive oak structure to take his place in his throne-like chair. On his desk was a file jacket with my name on it. His eyebrows bunched as he reviewed my transcript, revealing his knowledge that he was dealing with a problem student.

"How's your French, Mr. Smith?"

"It's okay," I replied.

"*Combien d'années avez-vous étudié le français, Monsieur?*"

I felt my skin flush and my cheeks prickle. I had no idea what he just said. He cleared his throat and looked over my transcript a little more. My parents said nothing the entire time, and beads of sweat dribbled down the inside of my arms.

"Well," he finally said, "Your grades are not the best, but according to some of the comments I've seen, you appear to have a certain aptitude for learning. We'll start you off in a lower level French class, and I think that with enough discipline we can make something of you."

The smile he may have presented outwardly did nothing to hide what to me was an obvious threat. My mother looked over at me and managed an encouraging smile, and my father just nodded knowingly. It was then I noticed that I had yet to see any of my soon-to-be fellow classmates. "Where is everyone," I asked, wondering if I might already be off to a bad start by even so simple a question.

"In study hall," he replied, smiling. "We have school Tuesday though Saturday. We ski on Sundays and Mondays to avoid the crowds, and on Wednesdays and Fridays we have half days to ski. Study hall is every evening from 5:00 to 7:00. Dinner is at 7:15 and lights out at 10:00."

I gasped; I really had died and gone to heaven. Half days to ski? I couldn't imagine having it so good.

"Why don't we get you situated in your new room," he said.

I was introduced to the house masters, or Internats as they were called, Roberto Meneghetti and his twin brother, Franco, who were assigned the task of showing my mother and I to my room while my father settled accounts with the bursar.

Both brothers were identical, but Roberto had a bushy moustache that nearly covered his top lip. "You're in Pavilion A," he said, leading us down a small corridor into the dorm. There were four people to a room. My bed was in the corner next to a large window that opened sideways, but a smaller window was framed within the larger one that could be opened for ventila-

16

tion. Posters of beautiful women wearing skimpy bikinis and ski-ers shushing through deep powder adorned the oak-paneled walls above each bed. All the other beds looked occupied, with various knick-knacks sitting on each of the nightstands.

Monsieur Meneghetti showed me to my locker in the hall-way. "Monsieur Smith, I expect you to keep this locker neat and tidy. We have locker and room inspections every Friday night. *Comprenez-vous?*"

"Yes," I replied. Now that I understood.

As my mother unpacked my clothes and put them in my assigned locker I found myself wondering who would be my room-mates. "This is a cozy little room," she said. "And the bed looks comfortable. You should be quite happy here."

"I think so, Mom. I'm very excited. Do you think my room-mates speak English?"

"I wouldn't worry about it, Dear. I'm sure you won't have any problems. But do try to concentrate on school. You have a fresh start, so do your best."

"I will, Mom."

Once finished with the unpacking, my mother and I watched my father through the glass window of the bursar's office as we waited for him to finish. The bursar was an attractive woman in her mid-thirties, and my father flirted with her, as he did with a lot of women. She was leaning over the desk, showing him a list of accounts, and he stared at her intently, trying to communicate his intentions with his eyes. But she acted as if she didn't notice and just continued explaining the list. As his eyes became more intense, he pursed his lips, and I could see he was becoming frus-trated by her lack of interest. In fact, I got the sense that she was becoming more perturbed than he. My father was not used to women resisting his charm. His tall stature, good looks, and boy-ish humor had a tendency to sweep most women off their feet.

My mother saw him in action as well, but she was so used to his behavior she seemed to take it in stride. What did he intend to do if the bursar responded to his advances? Would he have a two-day fling with her right under my mother's nose? The bursar looked over at my mother and me disapprovingly, and I looked away in shame. "Tell your father I went back to the hotel to unpack," my mother said, looking disgusted and angry. I continued waiting for my father, feeling awkward and embarrassed for being put in the middle of this uncomfortable scene.

The main door flew open and a throng of young boys came gushing in, all flushed from the cool night air. Everyone wore the same dark blue ski jackets emblazoned with the school emblem, an embroidered gold patch of the globe, and a thin gold stripe down each arm. Most of what I heard was French, but I also heard a fair amount of English as they talked excitedly about the upcoming ski season. I listened to their conversations with envy as they disappeared down the stairs, where each of them replaced their shoes with a pair of slippers from the cubbyholes, and then went to either their rooms or into the smoking lounge.

My father, having finally finished with the bursar, left her office, sat down next to me and said, "That woman is perfect for a good time."

I just looked at him confused. Why was he telling me this? To explain his behavior or to perhaps impress me? Regardless of the reason, I was not impressed, and didn't know how to react. My father had affairs before, but until recently I didn't really know what was going on or how to handle it. I often went with him on his trysts, and he usually asked me to tell my mother we had been playing tennis or went to the movies together, never to talk about how he truly spent his time.

"Why don't you have dinner at school this evening? I'm going back to the hotel to see about your mother," he said. I returned to my room and found three young boys gathered around my bed. Each of them was about my age, and they stared at me when I walked into the room. "What is your name?" asked the one with the round face and a Dutch boy haircut.

"Drew," I replied.

"My name is Axel. I was born in Norway, but I lived in New York with my mother for several years."

His English was perfect, but his Scandinavian accent gave his speech a slight lilt. Like me, he was a skinny kid and his clothes had a comfortable, disheveled look. His smile made his face seem even rounder, making him look almost Bohemian, as if he had achieved some sort of inner peace through knowledge and wisdom. He seemed mature for his age. The other two boys, Patrique and Laurent, were both from Paris and didn't speak much English. They seemed rather effeminate in their manner and dress, their wool trousers and cashmere turtlenecks almost too sophisticated for their age.

Axel took me downstairs to the television lounge, where a small snack bar opened at various times of the day, allowing us to buy cigarettes, candy, and sundries. Not far from the television lounge was the smoking area, where a group of boys puffed on strong French cigarettes, and talked excitedly about the upcoming dance. Tonight was the school's weekly *soirée*. Every Saturday night the girls from *Prés Fleuris* came to the school for a dance in the gymnasium, which was adjacent to the smoking lounge. Being the highlight of the week, all the young boys were freshly showered and had put on their best clothes. A few of the older boys were busy setting up the sound system.

Monsieur Meneghetti's voice boomed over the P.A. "*Allez à la salle à manger pour le dîner, s'il vous plaît!*"

"Time for dinner," Axel said with glee as everyone began to file down the hall to the dining room in pairs. The dining room looked more like a fine restaurant than a boy's dining hall. The room was filled with neatly set four tops, with the staff standing at the service station, waiting for us to sit. Since everyone had been pre-assigned a seat at the beginning of the semester, M. Meneghetti showed me to a table with an empty chair. "Drew, this is Stefan, Christophe, and Simon," M. Meneghetti said, gesturing with his hand. "Gentlemen, this is Drew Smith. He just arrived today." I shook hands with all three and sat down. As a courtesy to me they spoke English. They were a few years older than I.

Stefan, a tall, thin boy with straight dark hair was the first to address me. "Where are you from, Drew?"

"New Jersey. And you?"

"Both me and Christophe are from Basel. We grew up together."

"I'm from Lebanon," said Simon, the tallest of the three.

"Do you ski?" Christophe asked. It was plain to see where his interests lie.

"Yeah, actually, I've skied quite a bit in upstate New York and Vermont."

"And what is it like there?"

"Mostly icy and the snow is usually manmade. Sometimes the conditions are good, but not usually."

"Are you any good?" he continued, a gleam in his eye now evident.

"Pretty good," I replied, which I thought was a fair assessment of my skills. I could tell that Christophe was practically raised on skis and was much better that I. "Where do we ski?" I asked.

"In Montana," replied Christophe. "The slopes are right above us. What kind of skis do you have?"

"Atomic Compound Glass," I replied.

20

"Those are good skis," said Stefan. "Do you race?"

"I've never been in a race," I replied. "Are there a lot of races?"

"If you qualify, yes," replied Stefan. "Christophe is one of the top skiers in Switzerland. He competes all the time."

"I doubt I'm good enough to compete," I said, looking at Christophe in awe. He was tall and muscular with dark curly hair. I felt like a complete beginner in the presence of these boys.

"You will be surprised at how quickly your skills will improve," said Christophe. "We do a lot of skiing."

"Monsieur Davis told me. I can't wait," I said. "When does our ski season start?"

"In a couple more weeks," replied Christophe.

The wait staff brought our food to the table and we all dug in. Although the dining room was impressive, the food did not live up to the elegant atmosphere we were seated in, reminding me of the bland institutional food most private schools were famous for.

Shortly after dinner the girls from *Prés Fleuris* poured through the front door in a procession of laughter, smiles, and intoxicating scents. The boys helped them out of their coats as the young women filtered into the gymnasium where the music had already begun to play. Not knowing anybody, I stayed in the smoking lounge and watched. Somehow the French-speaking girls seemed completely off-limits to me, as if our worlds were so far apart that there could be no common ground between us.

At the end of the procession a small group of girls came down the stairs. They seemed different from the rest—okay, to be honest, as a group, they were homely. One had thick, dark eyebrows that nearly grew together, and the other seemed to be terribly depressed and withdrawn, but the last in the group I thought was the most beautiful girl I had ever seen. When I saw

21

her I felt a kind of fascination and desire that left me utterly speechless. She was dressed even plainer than the rest, but her features were anything but plain. Her deep, chocolate-brown eyes were filled with intelligence and compassion, and her strong chin gave her an almost masculine appearance. Her long, dark hair was parted in the middle and worn straight down. She seemed to be my age, but she was much more developed than most, and try as she might, she could not dress that down. Despite her obvious shyness, she walked with her shoulders back and with such perfect posture it looked almost regal.

When I saw her I didn't know what to do. She stood right next to me, and I couldn't move. I stuttered ever so slightly, looking for something to say, but then clamped my mouth closed out of fear of rejection. She noticed me looking at her and blushed—a deep blush filled with embarrassment—followed by a smile. Just then her friends whisked her into the gymnasium where they found seats in the far corner of the room in the shadows. I followed them and watched from across the room. They seemed disinterested in the other boys as they talked amongst themselves. Most of the other kids were dancing or talking in small groups, while I stood against the wall, too embarrassed to do anything. Finally, a tall, good-looking French boy walked up to the object of my fascination and asked her to dance. She nodded politely and followed him onto the floor. Damn.

"Are you having fun?" Axel asked as he walked over to me.

"Yes," I said, "but I don't know anyone."

"Don't worry," he said. "You have plenty of time to meet people. Come with me. I have something to show you."

He led me outside behind the dormitory where a group of boys were passing around a bottle of cheap red wine. "Drew, this is Dave, Chris and Robert," said Axel. "He just arrived today."

"How you doing?" asked Chris, a tall boy with soft brow hair.

22

"I'm doing okay," I replied. "It's nice to meet you all."

"Why are you here in the middle of the trimester?" asked Dave.

"I'm a bit of a problem child," I replied with a smile. "My parents thought going to school in Switzerland would help me become better adjusted."

Everyone laughed.

"Join the crowd," said Chris. "Let me guess. You were kicked out of school."

"More than once," I replied. "School sucks."

"Yeah, but you'll like it here," said Dave. "The skiing is phenomenal."

"So I've heard. I can't wait. What's it like?"

"It's nothing like the States," said Chris. "The slopes are wide open with no trees. There are dozens of trails. Where are you from?"

"I'm from New Jersey."

"I'm from New York. Where in Jersey do you live?"

"Rumson. It's in Central Jersey, by the shore."

"Never heard of it."

"It's a small town near Sea Bright."

"I've heard of Sea Bright," said Dave. "I'm from Philadelphia. This is my second year here."

"I have an uncle in Philadelphia. He once took me there. Nice city."

"What grade are you in?" asked Chris.

"I'm in tenth grade," I replied. "And you?"

"I'm in eleventh."

"What grade are you in, Axel?" I asked.

"Same as you," he replied.

"Then we'll be classmates," I said. I got the feeling that Axel and I were going to be good friends.

I began to feel more at home. So, we passed the bottle around, laughed like idiots, and talked about the upcoming ski season. Later, the bottle emptied and the group dispersing, I went back to the gymnasium. The dance was ending, and the last slow dance was being played—'Nights in White Satin' by the Moody Blues. I loved that song.

The girl I saw earlier was now back to talking with her friends in the corner, and I wished for the courage to ask her to dance, but the song ended and the lights came on. The girls were rounded up by the Internats and sent home. I finally got into bed and slept like a rock until breakfast was called the next morning.

My parents were leaving for Greece Monday morning. From there they were going to tour Italy and France before returning home. The night before they left we had dinner at a small, elegant restaurant in Montana, which was one town above us by funicular. M. Meneghetti ensured that I was wearing the proper dinner attire for an evening out—a blue blazer, gray slacks, white shirt, and the school tie of blue and gold stripes. My parents looked pleased when they came to pick me up. "Don't you look nice," my mother said, kissing me on the cheek. My father just stared.

Once seated, my father ordered a cheese fondue and a bottle of wine, and my mother ordered a scotch. When she had finished the first and was now ordering her second, I knew she would be drinking heavily this evening. "You be sure to write us, Dear," she said. Her hazel eyes were slightly glazed and her words were slurred. My father seemed not to notice.

"Your mother and I rode the *télécabine* up to the Glacier today. It's beautiful. You can see the entire valley from up there."

"Did you ski?"

"We did some cross-country, and it was quite an adventure, let me tell you. We must have trekked for at least ten miles," he said.

"I'll be lucky if my legs ever heal," my mother said with a snide sigh. She hated exercise, and my father was always trying to get her into physical activities. She tried to play mixed-doubles tennis with my father and their friends at our tennis club every weekend for a while, but hated it so much she threatened divorce if he forced her to play one more set. She was more content reading ancient history or trashy novels. More than anything she looked forward to returning to the ruins in Athens, and to see the museums in Paris and Rome.

By the time dinner was served my mother had finished her two cocktails and most of the wine and was having trouble getting the bread on the fondue fork, much less getting the fork into the pot. My father helped her casually, as if this were a common occurrence.

"We'll be sure to send you postcards from all the various cities we travel through," he said.

"That would be nice," I replied, squirming in my seat out of fear and embarrassment. I hated seeing my mother so drunk. She finally gave up trying to eat altogether and just sipped her wine.

"You make sure you study hard," my father said, as he pulled a piece of bread smothered with cheese out of the pot.

"I will, Dad."

"Make sure you do, you little prick," my mother said. I recoiled at her words. Her face was twisted up in rage, and her eyes were filled with anger.

"Why don't you eat some fondue, Martha," my father said, as he dipped a piece of bread in the pot and then put it on her plate.

"Fuck you, David," she said, rolling her eyes at him.

He simply laughed. I thought he was laughing because he was embarrassed, but then he filled her glass with more wine. My father finished his dinner casually, ordered a cognac, and smoked a cigar while my mother drank herself into a stupor. I simply wanted dinner to be over so that I could return to school.

My parents stopped to say goodbye the next morning. It was cold and gray and the wind swirled around us nipping my ears. My mother looked disheveled and tired, but made no mention of yesterday's events. I waited with them at the funicular station. My mother held on to my arm tightly to stay warm, while my father lectured me again about the importance of good grades. After what seemed an eternity, the funicular arrived. Quickly kissing my parents goodbye, I ran back to school as snow began to fall. This was the first major snowfall of the season, and my heart pounded against my chest with excitement. As I got closer, I could see a few of the other boys were already outside whooping and hollering with excitement, and without even stopping to catch my breath, I joined in the celebration. The snowfall and the upcoming skiing might have excited them, but for me it was much more than that. At last, I was free.

Chapter 2

Getting out of bed in the dark took some getting used to, but gradually I got used to the routine. Every morning after breakfast we all walked down the road from our dormitory to the classroom building. My hair, still wet from my morning shower, would be frozen solid before I was halfway there. We were on the western side of the valley, and below us the Rhone snaked its way between the great peaks that rose on either side. The snow, usually powdery and deep, crunched beneath our footsteps. In the early dawn the snowcaps on the other side of the valley were just dark, purplish cones that topped the mountains in the distance. Slowly the tips of the snowcaps turned red, as if they were hot pokers being superheated by some invisible source. When the snowcaps looked as though they were on fire, gradually they faded to orange, then yellow, and then pale white, until the sun popped up in the horizon, basking the entire valley in daylight.

I wanted to linger outside and watch the day begin, but we were always quickly ushered into class. The classroom building, Saint François, was three stories high, forcing us to scurry up and down the stairs between classes, barely leaving us time to socialize with the girls from *Prés Fleuris*. By this time the older boys had found girlfriends, and aside from the fact that half of us spoke French and the other English, it was like any other high school.

During those frantic moments between classes I would sometimes see the girl from the dance. After hearing the French boys talk about her in the dormitory, I found out her name was Alexandra Cavalletti, from Rome, Italy. Apparently she had the same effect on quite a few people; her eyes were so big and brown, and her smile was so captivating. Seeing her in the hallways made my body tightened up, and I became short of breath. One morn-

27

ing between classes I came bolting around the corner and ran right into her, nearly knocking her over. She had to put both her arms around my shoulders to keep from falling. "I'm sorry!" I said reaching out to her to steady her, only to realize I had placed my hand firmly on her breast.

Seeing my embarrassment, she put both her hands over mine and pressed it firmly. "It's okay. You haven't killed me—yet," she said in surprisingly good English.

"Uh— Drew, I'm really, I mean my name is Drew," I said, gently pulling my hand from beneath hers, feeling her nipple brush against my fingertips. She gave me a hint of a smile, and I wasn't sure of what she had intended, and wondered if she were as excited as I was.

"Hello, Drew. My name is Alexandra." Her voice was deep and melodic, with a heavy Italian accent, and I gazed into her dark brown eyes, stupefied by her beauty.

"Yes. I know. I saw you at the dance the other night."

I could see a faint spark of remembrance in her eyes and saw the corners of the mouth begin the slightest of upturning.

Of all the times for the damn bell to ring, it had to be that very second.

"It was nice meeting you, Drew." She said, but I was sure it was not the intended sentence.

"Perhaps we can talk again sometime?" I asked as my heart jumped.

"Perhaps," she replied, and hurried past me and on down the hall. I turned to see her glance back at me and smile, and then as she made the corner, disappear from view.

Never in my life had I felt such passion—my whole being throbbed with feelings I knew had existed, but had never experienced until now. The rest of the day the image of her face and the memory of my fingertips on her breast were the only things on my mind, and I could focus on little else. I fantasized about kissing her, and being with her in all manner of romantic interludes, some more innocent than others.

After school I saw her walking out of the building and nearly fell down the stairs trying to catch up. But before I could, she stopped to talk to a French boy named Philip Gaston, from Paris. He was older than I, and many admired him for his easygoing manner and charm. He reached out and took her hand, and their fingers momentarily entwined—almost naturally, as if I were watching an episode of Jacques Cousteau's underwater world where two sea creatures come together in a symbiotic mating dance. Her chocolate-brown eyes sparkled with playfulness as they looked into his, and I knew she had feelings for him. I felt like an idiot. This girl was way out of my league, but she had already stolen my heart.

I went back to the dorm and sat on my bed. A dull ache in my chest moved around my body. At times I felt it in my throat, and at others it lodged deep in my stomach. Without thinking I began to write. I let my emotions pour out of me in a poetic stream of consciousness about love and disappointment. I wrote for nearly an hour before Axel came into the room.

"What are you doing?" he asked. I simply handed him the sheaf of papers. He sat down and began to read. When he was finished he looked up at me and smiled. "This is good! Is this for a class?"

"No. I just felt like writing."

"You write well."

"Think so?"

"Yeah. Keep writing."

I had found an outlet for all the emotion that was pent up inside me. All the reading I had done over the years left a mark, and I had my own voice and something to say. I folded the papers neatly and put them in my nightstand, proud of my accomplishment.

A couple of days later M. Meneghetti called me to his office. "*Monsieur* Smith, you have a dentist appointment," he said, writing down an address on a piece of paper.

"I do?"

"*Oui, Monsieur.* Your parents have arranged for you to get your teeth cleaned. You will go to Montana directly after school. And make sure you are back in time for study hall, *comprenez-vous?*"

The last thing I wanted was to go to the dentist, but there was no arguing. Besides, my parents were not even around to argue with. The dentist did not speak English, but he still managed to get me into the chair and scrape my teeth for an hour. It was a hellish experience, and I was glad when my appointment was finally over.

I had some time to kill before I had to be back at school for study hall. Montana was a resort town filled with lots of small boutiques and restaurants where people came from all over Europe to ski. But it was during winter when the town really sprang to life. The sound of snow chains jingled merrily as people drove past, with their skis mounted on the roofs of their cars. Next weekend our ski season started, and everyone was looking forward to it.

Across the street, in a small *chocolaterie*, I saw Alexandra. I sucked in my breath and froze for a moment. Should I say hello or not? She stood at the counter, holding several large boxes of chocolate. Finding it odd that she would be buying so much chocolate, as well as being in Montana alone, I let my curiosity get the better of me and entered the shop. The sweet smell of cocoa permeated the air. In the back of the shop were some small tables where people sat drinking coffee and tea. As she saw me, she turned and smiled. "Drew, what a nice surprise! What are you doing here?"

"I had a dentist appointment. I was just walking around when I saw you through the window. How about you? What are you doing here?" I asked, trying to sound casual yet surprised.

"I had a doctor's appointment, and I offered to buy some chocolate for the girls at school. Have you had this chocolate before? This is the best *chocolaterie* in town."

How fortunate that we would run into each other like this. The Internats supervised us constantly, so a chance to be alone with her was like a gift from Heaven. Inside the glass case at the counter was an exquisite assortment of chocolates, all handmade and fresh.

"I've never seen anything like this," I said. "In America we buy chocolate bars in candy stores. But it's nothing like this."

"Oh, yes. When I was in New York I had some of that chocolate. It was dreadful," she said, scrunching up her nose.

"You were in New York?"

"Several times. I've traveled all over your country. My father spends quite a bit of time there on business."

"Really? What does he do?"

"He does many things, but his passion is horses. He breeds them and trades them."

"A horse trader," I said, suddenly envisioning her living on a farm in the south of Italy, with chickens, goats, and assorted barnyard animals. I was just at the point where we were in the hay loft together when her voice snapped me back to reality.

"Would you like to have a cup of tea with me?" she asked.

"I'd love to," I said, trying my best to contain my excitement about the prospects of spending time alone with her.

"Do you like dark or light chocolate?"

"Light."

"You must try some," she said.

She ordered the tea and some chocolate for me. Her French, although fluent, still had a heavy Italian accent, much like her English. I loved listening to her speak French, and wished I could as well.

When the lady finished tallying her purchase, she reached beneath the counter, and taking out a leather-bound book, asked Alexandra to sign. I tried to act casual about it, but I was quite surprised. Most of us were given a meager allowance each week for cigarettes, candy, and sundries, but it was never enough. Some kids were given extra money by their parents, and could afford to go shopping when they wanted, even eating out occasionally, but she was the first person I ever met who had an account at a chocolate store.

We took our tea and chocolate over to a little table and sat down. I opened my box of chocolate and put it in the middle of the table. She opened one of her own and took off her jacket. She was not tall, but she carried herself with so much grace and confidence she seemed that way. Her jeans and light-brown cashmere sweater revealed her well proportioned and very sexy shape. Her eyes were so expressive and filled with passion; they danced with a certain liveliness that only the truly brilliant possessed. I suppose that's what attracted me to her the most; I knew how bright she was, but she didn't need to compete.

I picked out a piece of light-brown chocolate; it was an explosion of flavor in my mouth. Seeing my surprised expression, she broke into joyous laughter.

"It's nothing like that horrible candy you get in America, No?"

"It's amazing," I replied, savoring the delicate taste of fine milk chocolate. "Where did you learn English?"

"At the American School in Rome," she replied. "My mother

insisted I learn English."

"Your English is excellent."

"No! It is horrible. My accent is terrible," she said, shaking her head.

"I love your accent, and you express yourself quite well."

"Thank you, you are too kind," she said politely, realizing she couldn't get out of receiving a compliment.

"Did you read American books at this school?"

"Quite a few of them," she replied, sipping her tea.

"Who's your favorite writer?" I asked.

"He is not an American. You probably never heard of him. His name is Gianni Celati. He's an obscure Italian writer from Naples."

"You're right. Never heard of him," I said, reaching for another piece of chocolate.

"You should read him. He's quite good. I'll see if I can find one of his books in English."

"I'd like that. Do you like to read?"

"I love to read."

Neatly folded in my jacket pocket was the bit of prose I had written the other night. How would she react if I showed it to her? Could she possibly realize I had written it because of her? I had nothing to lose, so I finally pulled the sheaf of papers out of my pocket and put it on the table. Looking at the pieces of paper before her, she raised one of her thick, dark eyebrows and pursed her lips.

"Tell me what you think of this," I said.

"Did you write it?"

"Yes."

She unfolded the papers and sat back in her chair. Her eyebrows knitted while she read, and I felt moisture building up on my palms. Once finished, she looked up at me and smiled, her chocolate-brown eyes filled with approval. "This is excellent! Really good!"

"Thank you," I said. I sat in my chair a little more smartly and wished I had more to show her.

"Do you write often?" she asked.

"No. I mean, I just started, but I read all the time."

"What do you like to read?"

"Fiction. I just finished 'Islands in the Stream', by Hemingway."

"I never read that book, but I enjoy his short stories."

"Which is your favorite?"

"I really loved 'A Clean, Well-Lighted Place'."

"I love that story too!" I said, ecstatic to find that we had so much in common. We talked for quite awhile about literature. She told me someday she would like to write, but hadn't written anything yet. I told her about where I came from, and how beautiful our town was.

We both had to report back to school for study hall. We packed up all our chocolate and I offered to carry her bag. It was heavy, and I wondered if she and her friends lived on the stuff. I started toward the funicular station, but she took my arm and led me in another direction.

"I know another way down to school," she said. "It will save us a lot of money."

She led me through the narrow back streets of Montana until we came upon the edge of the woods where a well-traveled path traversed its way down the mountain through the trees. The path was steep, and as we made our way down, it became hard not to break into a jog. The combined briskness of the air and our walk brought a flush to her cheeks, causing her to glow with a radiance that caused my heart to melt. Am I in love? I had never experienced anything like this. When I looked at her I felt only an

34

overwhelming desire to take her in my arms, but I kept thinking about Philip. Seeing that I was beginning to struggle with the bag of chocolate, she smiled and asked if she could carry it for a while.

"No, no. I'm fine," I replied. "But I wouldn't mind taking a short rest."

We found a log not too far from the path to sit on, and once I set the bag down, I began to work my fingers, trying to get the blood flowing through them again.

"Alexandra, are you going out with Philip?" I finally asked, trying to make my question sound casual.

"Do you mean is he my boyfriend?"

"Yes, that's what I'm asking."

"Yes. He is my boyfriend," she said. "Do you know Philip?"

"Not very well, but he seems like a nice guy."

I lied. He was always so well dressed—with silk scarves, wool trousers and handmade, English shoes. His father was one of the managing partners at Michelin, and his family had more money than they knew what to do with. He seemed so suave, but he was aloof with only a very small, elite circle of friends. To the rest, he wasn't rude; he just didn't associate with most of us. We didn't care—except that his crowd dated the best-looking girls in the school. Alexandra took my hand and pulled me up. "Come," she said. "We have to get back to school."

We headed down the mountain until we came upon Bluche.

"Thank you for carrying my bag," Alexandra said, relieving me of my burden.

"I had a great time."

"Yes, so did I. *Au-revoir*," she said, reaching up to kiss me on the cheek, as most Europeans would do. Not being used to this gesture, I momentarily froze. I smelled the sweet, herbal scent of her hair, causing a wave of passion to well up in my body. I wanted desperately to kiss her, but knew that it was out of the question; she was going out with Philip, and as much as I hated it, I would have to accept that fact.

"*Au-revoir*," I replied, heading back toward the dorm.

Axel was sitting on his bed writing a letter when I arrived. "Where have you been?" he asked.

"In Montana with Alexandra."

"Really!" he said, sitting up straight.

I recounted the entire afternoon for him while we ate some of the chocolate she bought.

"Be careful of her," he warned. "She is not for you. You need to find yourself a nice American girl."

He was probably right, but no matter how I tried, I couldn't get her image out of my mind. The memory of her touch and the way she smelled made me tingle, and my desire for her was so overwhelming I could think of little else. Study hall was called, and we gathered up our books.

Chapter 3

That long-awaited day finally came—our first ski day. On Sunday after lunch everyone put on long johns and ski pants. The ski jackets issued by the school seemed a bit light, especially considering how cold it was, but one of the older boys showed me how to dress—a cotton t-shirt, then a turtleneck, the school sweater on top of that, and finally the jacket. Beneath all those layers it was very warm.

We piled into the ski shed and changed into our boots, grabbed our skis, and put them on a waiting bus. The steep and narrow road snaked its way up the mountain without a single guardrail. Although fitted with snow chains, the road was solid snow and ice, and the bus skidded backward on some of the steeper inclines before finding traction and continuing. The road overlooked a steep ravine filled with jagged rocks, and it seemed to me the bus could never make it around the tiny hairpin turns on its way up the mountain. Axel laughed when he saw my knuckles turn white from gripping the armrests so tightly. "This is nothing," he said. "You should see the roads in Norway!"

Montana was just below the tree line, and not too far above town, the *télécabine* station sat at the end of a big parking lot. The *télécabines* reminded me of the gondolas on a Ferris wheel. Each one seated four people and was enclosed by a Plexiglas bubble with windows that opened on each side.

The ride up the mountain lasted nearly forty minutes. Axel and I sat quietly across from a German couple, spellbound by the view. The snowcaps across the horizon looked like giant pieces of lemon meringue, while far below us, little toy houses sat at the bottom of the valley. Parts of the Rhone were encased in cement barriers—locks that were flooded to allow occasional barges through. The trails were well packed—not quite the image I had of deep, virgin powder—but they were wide open without the crowds of people I was used to seeing in New York.

At the top an attendant opened the door of the *télécabine* and let us out. Quickly grabbing our skis, we looked out over the slopes. It was a beautiful, sunny day, but the air was thin and cold, making me a bit lightheaded. A few yards away, yet another gondola could take us up to the glacier *Plaine Morte*, but that was at least another twenty minute ride, and we were too impatient to wait that long. Axel mentioned that the conditions on the glacier were also unpredictable; one minute could be sunny and calm and the next one would be skiing through a snow squall.

I was so excited I could barely get my skis on, but then heard the satisfying snap when the bindings locked my ski boots firmly into place. I looked down the slope and felt butterflies in my stomach. "Ready?" asked Axel.

"Let's do it!" I replied. We started down the slope, and I could instantly see that he was a much better skier than I. His motion was fluid and natural, and he attacked every obstacle without flinching or slowing down. Not used to skiing so fast, I had a hard time keeping up, and soon realized the word stop wasn't in his vocabulary.

Axel was already halfway down a particularly steep part when he realized I wasn't behind him. I looked down the slope at the huge moguls in front of me, realizing I didn't have the skills to master them, and my knees went slightly weak. A group of girls from *Prés Fleuris* were at the bottom of the slope. Katrina, their Internat, was teaching them some basic techniques. A thin, severe woman in her early forties, her job was to make sure the girls remained ladies by constantly correcting the girls' behavior, and admonishing the boys if they became too physical. Nothing escaped her eyes. Alexandra was in the group. She was not a good skier, and watching her snowplow down the mountain renewed my confidence.

"Come on!" Axel called out at the top of his voice. "Just keep your upper body pointing down hill and use your knees to turn!"

All the girls looked up at me, leaving me no choice but to give it my best shot. I aimed my skis downhill and pushed. I didn't do so badly at first. I pointed my skis between the moguls and managed to make a few nice turns, but it wasn't long before I picked up so much speed I couldn't maneuver my skis fast enough. Instead of turning through the moguls I tried to go over them, which only made me go faster. Turning sharply into a mogul in a desperate attempt to regain control, one ski crossed over the other, flipping me into a perfect cartwheel. Thankfully my bindings popped instantly, and I slid head first down the slope on my stomach, skidding to a stop right in front of Katrina.

"Are you okay, *Monsieur*?"

"Yes. I'm fine." I said, looking up at her. My face was covered with snow, but the heat from my embarrassment probably melted it quickly.

"I suggest you take it a bit easier in the future," she said.

"You only live once," I said, trying my best to sound nonchalant.

"And you won't live at all if you don't exercise some restraint."

All the girls burst out laughing. I did my best to pick myself up with a modicum of dignity. Snow was lodged in every crevice of my clothing. Axel rounded up my skis and poles.

Alexandra smiled. "Are you sure you are okay?" she asked, brushing the snow off me.

"Yeah. I'm fine, just really embarrassed."

"Well, I haven't seen anything that graceful since I went ice skating last winter."

I laughed. She was really very kind.

"Alexandra, come along," Katrina said.

Axel helped me with my skis while the girls from *Prés Fleuris* snowplowed down the slope behind Katrina like a flock of ducklings following their mama.

Philip and his friends stood above us, watching the whole scene. Without a word they started down the mountain, twisting and turning through the moguls with ease. Philip was a good skier—not as good as Axel—but good nonetheless. They whisked by us quietly and disappeared down the trail.

"That was a friendly gesture," Axel said sarcastically.

"If he didn't like me then, he probably hates me now."

"I warned you," Axel said, shaking his head and frowning. "Alexandra is not for you. You two will never have anything meaningful in common besides heartache."

I looked at Axel quizzically. "Do you think she likes me?"

"Probably. But not the way you would hope. And even if she did, feelings have nothing to do with it. You are an American and she is Italian. You two will never bridge that gap."

"How can you be so sure?"

"I have lived in Europe most of my life. I know these things. Let it go. There are other girls."

"But why should the fact that we come from different countries stop us?" I asked.

"You don't know who she is, do you?" he asked, planting one of his ski poles firmly in the snow. "Her family practically owns most of Rome. Her father is one of the richest men in Italy. You will never be anything more than just a nice American boy for her."

Perhaps he was right, but her smile set me on fire, and seeing her face stole my breath away.

Axel eyed me and shook his head, "This is going to be a lot

of work." He started down the mountain.

Axel taught me a lot about skiing, and soon the two of us were shushing down the mountain with our hair on fire. I loved the thrill of hitting a jump just right—that moment when I reached the apex of my arch and flipped the back of my skis up in the air, propelling me another foot or so higher. Eventually I found my own style, and took pride in keeping my skis perfectly parallel, swinging my hips like a pendulum as I left a series of perfect S's down the mountain.

Something was inherently dangerous about fifteen-year-old boys on skis. Most of us were thrill seekers, and we craved going faster and jumping higher, constantly pushing ourselves, all the while challenging the laws of physics and gravity. The season wasn't without casualties. At least one or two boys or girls were laid-up with broken legs, sprains, or severe bruises. One kid broke his leg in three places. I'll never forget the day he was released from the hospital. He had metal pins embedded in his knees, and the doctors told him he could never ski again. I couldn't imagine something so horrible, but it came with the territory and was to be expected. Although the school kept very tight reigns on us, we were set free when we were skiing, and I could barely wait for our half days when the school let us loose on the slopes.

As the semester continued my studies improved slightly, mostly because of the rigorous discipline that was enforced in the classroom. But my imagination was so active I couldn't concentrate very well. I daydreamed through most of the lectures about my being a suave, sophisticated, yet slightly eccentric man who was always in command of any social situation. Sometimes my daydreams were so vivid I could actually carry myself outside of my body, as if the movie that was playing inside my head had somehow become real. People made fun of me because in some of my fantasies I placed myself in humorous situations with my friends and thought of funny conversations that would make me burst out into raucous laughter. My teachers thought I was daft. Axel knew what was going on, and he encouraged me to keep writing. I did, and as my writing improved, so did my imagination, which didn't help my studies much.

Most of my writing I kept to myself. I wrote angry, dark stories filled with angst and intrigue. I always showed them to Axel, and the ones I thought were better than the rest I sometimes gave to Alexandra. We didn't get many opportunities to spend time together. She spent most of her time with Philip between classes and at the *soirée's*. When I saw her alone I would say hello. She was always happy to see me, and would ask how the writing was going and looked forward to when I would give her my latest story. She always gave them back to me with wonderful comments and words of encouragement written in the margins. As much as I appreciated our friendship, when I saw her it was all I could do from reaching out to touch her; I wanted so much to be with her, but she remained a distant fantasy.

Chapter 4

The ski season ended just before Easter break. By then the conditions were not so good and most of us went up to the glacier where the air was a bit colder and the snow not so slushy. It was a long season, and I didn't complain about it ending. I didn't think it was possible to get sick of skiing, but I had done so much of it.

Axel invited me to his house in Greece for Easter. He couldn't stop talking about the island of Hydra, describing in detail the enchanting cottage where he and his mother lived. His father, a writer and musician, spent winters in Canada with a woman named Suzanne, and summers with Axel and his mother in Greece. Axel talked about his father's other woman often, saying she was very beautiful. How odd that he should have two women, but Axel didn't seem to have a problem with it, and according to him, his mother was okay with it as well, especially since his parents were never married in the first place.

Our plane landed in Athens late in the afternoon. We checked into a small hotel near the port for the night. The next boat to Hydra didn't sail until morning, so Axel showed me around Athens. Tiny shops that sold multi-colored strings of worry beads and evil eyes choked the narrow side streets, and old men sat in lawn chairs as their wives lured people into their stores. He took me to see the Acropolis. It was early evening by the time we got there, and the Parthenon was illuminated eerily with floodlights. I stood in awe of the great columns and looked out over the city. The view from the Acropolis was beautiful, and the lights below us twinkled in the darkness. As a boy I was fascinated by Greek mythology, and one of my earliest memories of my father was when he read me the story of Icarus and Daedalus. For me it was a sad story, and seeing the Acropolis reminded me of the time I sat in his lap, and he read me the tale of how Icarus disobeyed his father and flew too high, only to fall to his death because his wax wings were melted by the sun. I always felt that to be a very sad story. He told me his father had read him the same story when he was my age.

Later that evening we had a big fish dinner at a sidewalk café, and Axel introduced me to ouzo, a Greek liqueur that tasted like licorice.

"What do you think of Athens?" he asked.

"It's a beautiful city."

"Wait until you see the island," he said. "We are going to have a lot of fun. My mother has arranged for you to meet Austin."

"Who's Austin?"

"You'll see."

"I guess I will," I said, swallowing another shot of ouzo.

My head began to spin from too much alcohol, and I was tired from the day's travel. Axel and I went to bed early. We woke up late the next morning and had to run down to the port, barely making it to the boat on time. I felt a bit queasy from the alcohol, and hadn't slept so well. I had expected the weather to be much warmer, but the air was cold even if the sky was sunny. Tourist season didn't start for another couple of months, so fishermen and laborers packed the boat. People sat on the floor in groups and ate the smoked fish and cheese they had brought aboard. The smell made me seasick. Axel took the whole thing in stride.

We finally pulled into a semi-circle shaped port that was lined with small cafes and restaurants, and Axel pointed to an area high on a hill where his house was. Cars were prohibited, since the streets were narrow tiered steps made from cobblestones, which only donkeys and people could use.

Axel and I weaved through the narrow streets up the hill until we came to an unpainted wooden gate. He rang an old cowbell hanging next to the latch. A few moments later an attractive, blond woman opened the door and embraced her son warmly.

"You must be Drew," she said, kissing me on both cheeks. "Axel has written me so much about you!"

"How do you do?"

"Call me Marianne," she said. Her wispy blond hair was pulled back into a ponytail, revealing sharp blue eyes and a tanned face. She wore a printed cotton skirt, sandals, and an old sweatshirt. She looked just like I had imagined a Norwegian woman would. "Come in! Come in!" she cried.

We passed through a small courtyard filled with flowers and shrubs. A small Greek villa, the house was old and the walls were whitewashed and thick. The front door opened into a small kitchen with an old-fashioned stove where a big cast-iron pot was simmering something that smelled of fresh vegetables and spices. In front of the stove sat a rough-hewn dining table and six chairs.

To the left, a staircase with very narrow steps seemed to go straight up. Axel and I grabbed our bags and took them upstairs. I had to hold on to the steps with both my hands as I went up. Never in my life had I seen stairs that steep and narrow.

"You'll get used to the steps," said Marianne. "By the way, if you need to use the bathroom there is an outhouse in the back. And we don't have a telephone. You'll have to walk to town to call your parents if you need to."

"No telephone?" I asked, looking at Axel.

"My father hates telephones. You'll be sleeping in this room."

The small room at the front of the house had a bed next to the wall and a large trunk in front. In the corner was a small desk on which an ancient manual typewriter sat.

"This is where my father works when he is here," said Axel.

On the desk an old record album had a picture of Axel's mother on the back. She was wrapped in a plain white towel and sitting at that very desk in this very room. The room was exactly the same.

I was curious to hear the album, but they had no record player—only an old guitar standing in the corner. Axel explained that when his father was here he wrote poetry and books. Occasionally he would write a few songs, but he recorded most of his music in Montreal. Axel talked about his father quite often. He was so proud of him, but I didn't recognize his name.

Marianne called us to lunch. She had been cooking a lentil stew all morning, and the kitchen had an earthy, wholesome smell. The food was amazing. A long, long time had passed since I had tasted food that good. Axel's relationship with his mother was extraordinary. He talked openly with her about any subject. Axel had a girlfriend on the island that was much older and he was going to go see her tomorrow. He had talked about her at school, and sometimes she sent him perfumed letters and cards, which he would let me smell. She wrote in Norwegian, so I couldn't read the writing, but the scent made me delirious.

"Axel tells me you are a writer," Marianne said, breaking a piece of bread from a big loaf in the middle of the table.

"I like to write. It helps me relax."

"He tells me you are quite good," she said, smiling, the corners of her eyes twinkling playfully.

"I don't know if I'm all that good, but I enjoy it."

"Well, tomorrow I am going to take you to see Austin," she said. There was that name again.

"Who is Austin?" I asked. I was starting to get frustrated by this game.

"Austin is a friend of the family," said Axel. "You'll enjoy meeting him."

The next morning Axel, Marianne, and I headed over the hill to see Austin. When we arrived a big burly man with a huge mane of flaming-red hair that fell in great clumps into a matching beard greeted us at the door. His dungarees, plaid shirt, and suspenders gave the appearance that he had just walked out of the woods. I would have thought it perfectly appropriate if he had an axe slung over his shoulder.

"Marianne! How are you?" he asked.

"I'm Fine, Austin. This is Drew, the young man I told you about."

"Hello Drew," he said, his whole face breaking into a warm grin as his huge sweaty hand enveloped mine and he shook it furiously.

"Drew, we'll be back to get you in an hour," Marianne said, leaving me with no idea what was about to happen to me.

"Come on in, Drew," Austin said as he ushered me inside. A group of people was creating some sort of symmetrical design out of colored sand in the middle of the floor. Delicately, and without uttering a word, they poured sand onto the floor, carefully sculpting the design. Each person worked almost independently of the other.

"What are they doing?" I asked.

"They are creating a *mandala*," Austin replied.

"Will I be doing something like that?"

"Not just yet. Come with me," he said, redirecting me to another room. Scattered about the room was every kind of toy imaginable— soldiers, cars, dolls, balls, balloons, bottles, sea glass, and other assorted objects. Near the window was a large sandbox sitting on a table. To the left of the sandbox was a smaller table, and to the right was a big desk piled with papers and books. I looked around the room in wonder.

47

"For the next ten minutes I want you to take any toy you want and put them on the table next to the sandbox," said Austin.

"Any toy?"

"Anything that catches your eye," he answered, sitting down at a desk facing the sandbox.

I walked around the room and picked up little things I found interesting. After a few minutes I had amassed a large collection of toys while Austin watched silently.

"I think I'm done," I said.

"Good. Do you remember when you were a child how you played with toys in a sandbox?"

"You want me to get in the sandbox?" I asked.

"You can if you want," he answered, "but I want you to play in the sand with the toys. Just let your imagination go and have fun for an hour."

It sounded like fun, so I played in the sandbox quietly. I built an elaborate city. Actually, I played out the destruction of some imaginary empire—complete with a final battle scene and relinquishment ceremony. I took some wooden matchsticks I found on Austin's desk, stuck them in the sand, and lighted them to make torches for the ceremony. Austin took notes furiously the entire time. When I got to the part where I lighted the matches, he fumbled around his desk for his Polaroid and took shots of my work. He seemed quite excited. For me it was just play. When the hour was up he finally spoke. "Drew, do you know who Carl Jung is?" he asked.

I had heard Axel talk about him, but the way he described him didn't make much sense. "I've heard of him, but I don't know who he is."

"Carl Jung was a colleague of Sigmund Freud's. He believed that mankind is psychically linked by a Collective Uncon-

48

scious, and that the psyche manifests itself in symbols—such as when we dream. These symbols are what Jung called archetypes. While you were playing you were using these archetypes to express your inner self."

"And you can analyze me from how I play?"

"Partly, there is a lot more to it than that, but I got an immense amount of information from our session."

"What did you get?" I asked.

"Drew, do you have problems in school?" he asked, running his fingers through his thick, mangy beard.

"Yes," I replied, but that was no big secret.

"Do you find yourself daydreaming almost constantly? And are your daydreams so vivid they are almost real?"

Now he piqued my interest. My daydreams were becoming so powerful I couldn't control them. I could barely pay attention in class anymore, and it seemed I had the attention span of a housefly.

"Yes," I replied. "Is that wrong?"

"Wrong!" he boomed. "No wonder you are so unhappy! Drew, in all my years as a psychiatrist I have never met anyone as creative as you. The last place you should be is in a classroom. There are alternative schools for people like you. You will never do well in a traditional classroom environment. It's too structured. You need to be in a place where your creativity will be fostered and directed."

Perhaps he was right, but my father would have a cow. My mother might understand the concept—and even agree with it—but my father would rather die than see me throw my life away in some alternative-education program. I knew I was different, but I believed there was something wrong with me. Years of private schools and the disappointment of my parents convinced me of that.

"So what should I do?" I asked. Hearing this news made me slightly sick to my stomach. I never considered myself special.

"I'll talk to Marianne. She knows about some schools that would be good for you. You should continue working with a good therapist. I can send your parents a letter and recommend some good people for you."

Marianne arrived shortly after our session ended. Axel was still at his girlfriend's house, so I waited outside on the veranda while Marianne and Austin talked. Finally they came outside. "Are you ready, Drew?" She asked, placing her hand on my shoulder and smiling first at me, and then at him.

I thanked Austin and said goodbye, and Marianne and I headed toward town to do some grocery shopping. I felt dazed, and could barely focus on walking. Marianne took my arm. "What did you think of Austin?" she asked.

"That was one of the more interesting experiences of my life. Did he tell you what he said about me?"

"Yes, but we'll talk about that later. You seem upset."

"I'm just very confused."

"Don't worry," she said. "Life has a way of ironing out wrinkles."

She bought several bags of groceries at an outdoor market, and I strained under the weight of carrying them back to the house. I helped her in the garden weeding until Axel arrived late in the afternoon, with big red blotches covering his neck. Marianne didn't say a word, but Axel beamed with pride. She began cooking dinner while we sat in the kitchen and talked.

"Mother, I had sex this afternoon," he finally announced.

"Were you careful?" she asked.

"Of course!"

"Good," she said, kissing him on his forehead and tousling his hair.

Oh, my God! That was the last thing I would ever announce to my mother, who would have died if I told her something like that. I wanted desperately to find out more about his afternoon, but he seemed more interested in mine.

"So, how did it go with Austin?" he asked.

"It was interesting," I replied. I studied Axel carefully to see if sex had changed him in any way. He wore his hickeys like trophies. I was still a virgin. I began to think about Alexandra…I wished she were here to share these experiences with me.

"Austin had a lot to say about Drew," Marianne added.

"Really? Like what?" Axel asked, his big blue eyes dancing playfully.

"Tell him."

"Austin told me that I was too creative to be in a traditional school. He said I was one of the most creative people he had ever met."

Saying those words made me feel ridiculous. Creative people create, and I had never created anything. People enjoyed my writing, but I was no creative genius, and I began to mistrust the whole situation.

"That's wonderful!" Axel said. "But I knew how creative you are."

"Do you really think so?"

"Yes! And I don't think you will ever do well in school. You should be in a school for artists," he said. Axel told me he went to a Montessori school in New York. He loved it, but he wanted a more traditional education as he got older.

"My parents will never go for something like that," I said.

"I could talk to your parents," Marianne said. "Perhaps Austin and I can persuade them."

"You would do that?"

"We'll write them a letter and see what happens," she said.

After dinner Axel and Marianne took me out to the only nightclub on the island. Seated on a rocky precipice high above the port, it could only be reached by climbing some steps that had been chiseled out of the rocks. The harbor lay below us, and the lights from the cafés that lined the port splayed across the water. It was a small place, and hardly anybody was there. Axel said the place was packed in the summertime, but being early spring the only people on the island were fishermen and year-round residents.

We sat down at a table near the dance floor. Axel ordered a rum and Coke and Marianne just had bottled water. A brochure on the table for *Metaxa* brandy, produced in Greece, listed brandies starting from one star to ten, with each being increasingly expensive. I asked Axel about it.

"The number of stars represents the level of refinement," he explained. "One star is like drinking turpentine. Ten stars are the best."

I ordered a three-star brandy.

Occasionally some of the local fishermen got up and danced to Greek folk music with shot glasses filled with ouzo on their heads. As the tempo increased, they bent their knees and danced lower and lower to the ground, holding their arms out in front of them for balance. Everyone cheered loudly until the music ended, and then they removed the shot glasses from their heads and downed them in a single gulp without a drop being spilled.

Axel danced with his mother to a couple of songs. I watched. He was really a happy, easy-going boy who nothing seemed to faze. An excellent student, during study hall he made it a point to not sit near me so as not to be disturbed. Study hall was two hours of hell for me. I could not concentrate on my schoolwork to save my life, and learned to distract myself by writing poetry and prose. I was constantly in trouble with my teachers.

Perhaps Austin was right: I didn't belong in school, but I never pictured myself as an artist either. As much as I hated school, I also felt inadequate for not performing better academically, and I occasionally tried to focus on my studies, but always came up short.

The waitress came by and asked me if I needed anything. I had the bright idea to drink my way through all ten stars. I downed my drink and ordered a four-star brandy, and had nearly finished it by the time Axel and his mother returned. The alcohol made me feel warm and tingly, and I began to relax. Marianne took me by the hand and led me to the dance floor. I enjoyed dancing, and the music carried me away for a while. I could have danced most of the night, but Marianne wanted to rest.

When we returned to the table Axel offered to buy me another drink. I ordered a five-star brandy. My head started buzzing, and my muscles didn't respond correctly anymore.

"Axel, I don't know what to do about all this." I slurred.

"What do you mean?"

"I mean about what Austin told me."

"Mother, Drew doesn't know what to do about what Austin told him," Axel said.

"Drew, you need to get off your butt and do something with your creativity," she said.

Her answer did not make me feel any better. Now I felt as though I had some God-given gift I had to live up to. I finished my drink quickly and ordered a six star brandy, but could only finish half the glass. Stinking drunk, Marianne realized I was over the edge. The bartender had already cut me off, and she told Axel to help me home. Getting down the steps from the nightclub was hard enough, and the long walk through the port and up the hill was torturous, but getting up the stairs to my room was nightmarish. My feet did not seem

53

to fit on the steps, and Axel had to drag me up the stairs by my arms.

As soon as I got into bed, I needed to go to the bathroom. I would never survive the trip down the stairs, and if so, my chances of making it back up were slim. My only option was the window. I stood in front of a big window and pulled down my underpants. The windowsill was just below my knees, and as I began to relieve myself I leaned forward slightly to ensure I didn't pee on the floor. Suddenly, I lost my balance and plummeted over the sill head first into a shrub. The next morning, Marianne found me lying in her garden draped in her shrubbery and quite scratched up. She realized what had happened, and was not happy. If it were not for the shrub I might have died. I had also run up a large bar bill that I couldn't pay. My hangover was so severe I couldn't get out of bed the entire day. Alcohol wasn't for me.

I apologized profusely for what happened, and Marianne finally forgave me. Axel thought the whole thing was hysterical. Later that day she brought me some soup. "Feeling better," she asked.

My head pounded with a dull, aching pain. "I'll live."

"You were lucky. That was some fall," she said

"I don't remember it much."

"Let this be a lesson to you. Drinking is not cool."

Judging by what I was now feeling, I didn't know how my mother could stand the stuff. I wondered if people built up a tolerance to it after a while, but after what I had been through I didn't care to find out.

Axel and I spent quite a bit of time exploring the island. It was a quiet little place, and near the shoreline were tiny restaurants where we sometimes ate lunch with the local fishermen for not much more than a song. I enjoyed the wonderful dinners Marianne cooked, and was sad when it was time to go back to school.

It was a bright, sunny day the morning we left, and we sat together on a little park bench as the boat began to board. "Be sure to write," Marianne said, stroking the back of my head.

"Bye, Momma," said Axel, giving her a hug.

"Study hard and take good care of yourselves."

We boarded the boat and stood on the deck as it pulled away from the port. I watched Marianne wave to us, and wondered what she would write to my parents.

Chapter 5

The snow was nearly melted when Axel and I returned to school, and in warmer weather people spent more time outdoors. The mountains were transformed from blankets of snow to fields of green. Now that we were no longer skiing we were left more to our own devices. The French boys played football, and some coed sports resumed as well, but many of us sat in the grassy field next to the basketball courts and talked. Alexandra sat with her girlfriends while Philip played football. He was in an intramural league, so he was constantly off practicing with his friends.

Sometimes Alexandra and I took walks around the field together. We were never allowed to stray too far, but we had the opportunity to talk. I told her about my experience in Greece, and she agreed that I was very creative and that I had a wonderful way with words and loved the way I wrote. She also talked to me about Philip and his many mood swings. One minute he was happy and attentive, and the next, depressed and withdrawn. She asked if I had noticed anything about him that seemed different. Honestly I hadn't, but I didn't associate with him, so I wouldn't have known.

By the middle of May the weather was really warm. Alexandra tanned so easily and quickly her skin glowed. Seeing her in thin cotton tops and jeans made me crazy with desire. When I saw her in the hallway between classes I wanted to hold her in my arms. Sometimes I would walk with her in the afternoons after school, and I wanted to reach out and take her hand, but I could never bring myself to touch her.

Most weekends not enough activities existed to keep us busy, so on sunny days the school organized long promenades through the mountains. Everyone complained about the hikes, but I enjoyed them. At about 10:00 am the girls from *Prés Fleuris* joined us at the foot of our driveway. We'd start off single file up through the narrow back roads of Bluche, and then traverse verdant spring meadows still glistening with the morning dew, sprinkled with purple and white daisies, black-eyed Susans, bright-yellow buttercups, and deep-blue morning glories, through thick, woody areas filled with pungent pine smells, until we came upon a small clearing with a small lake in the middle of nowhere.

The kitchen staff had driven a truck to our destination beforehand and set up a barbecue. The smoky smell of cooking sausages lingered in the air as we played Frisbee, baseball, and other sports in the sun. Alexandra was usually with Philip on these outings, but on this occasion he was off at a football match against a neighboring school, so we sat together in the lush spring grass and ate lunch.

"Drew, I am very worried about Philip," she finally said.

"Why?"

"He's acting crazy! I don't know what to do," she said, her eyes widening slightly

"What do you mean?"

She moved a little closer to me and lowered her voice. "Please don't tell anyone this, but late last Saturday night, Philip climbed up on the balcony of *Prés Fleuris* and came into my room."

I was surprised he would do something like that, but after careful consideration I might have done the same to be with her.

"Did he get caught?"

"No. That's the thing. I didn't know he was there. I was sleeping. The window was open, and he could have woken me up, but he just sat on my bed watching me sleep."

"How did you know he was there?"

"Nausicaa saw him. She said she woke up when he came in through the window, but she didn't say anything because she didn't want to get us in trouble."

"How long did he stay?"

"Almost two hours."

"He didn't say a word to you?"

She shook her head and plucked a few strands of grass. "No. She said that after awhile he went back out the window and disappeared."

"Maybe he was afraid of how you might react," I suggested.

"I would have been happy to have seen him on my bed!"

Those words stung. The idea of her with Philip in her bed was painful, and I pushed it aside as if it would never happen.

"It's not just that," she continued. "I think he is becoming more unstable. He keeps talking about death all the time. Sometimes he is so carefree and gentle, but then he becomes dark and moody without warning."

"Have you talked to him about it?"

"I've tried but he keeps changing the subject."

"Does he know that you know he came to your room?"

"No. And I don't want to say anything," she replied. "I hope he does not do that again. I don't think I could handle it."

Without thinking I caressed her shoulder. She slipped her arm around my neck and pulled me to her. She kissed me briefly. I wasn't expecting it. I kissed her back, not knowing if I was kissing her correctly. I felt her tongue inside my mouth, so I put mine in hers. It felt so strange and wonderful, but I was slightly ashamed because there was so much saliva, and I was afraid I might be drooling down her chin. I pulled away gently. She smiled at me and squeezed my hand. I think she realized it was my first kiss.

I couldn't believe what just happened actually happened. I wanted more, but too many people were around.

"Drew," she said, "I like you a lot, but I don't want to hurt you. I'm still with Philip, and I should not be doing this with you."

"Do you love him?"

"I don't know," she replied. Her eyebrows crinkled up and she shook her head slightly. She cared for him—I could see that, but there was something else going on that I couldn't put my finger on.

"What do you feel about me?" I asked.

"Tenderness. When I am with you I feel tenderness," she said, caressing my arm. Her touch set me on fire. I pulled her to me and held her close. Her body next to mine made me melt, but I became short of breath when she slipped her leg between my own as she kissed me. A burning sensation swept through my body. Suddenly my body stiffened. I had my first ejaculation. I came without warning. I was breathless and embarrassed.

She held me gently and caressed my back. "Its okay, Drew," she said. I nestled my head on her shoulder and held her tightly. What was sex really like?

We headed back towards school around 3:00 pm, and the sun was still warm as we headed back down. Going home was almost as exhausting as getting there. Alexandra walked back with her friends, and Axel and I stayed by ourselves at the end of the line. I told him what happened.

"You really shot your wad when she kissed you?" he asked, his blue eyes wide with fascination.

"It was unbelievable. It just happened. I couldn't stop it," I replied. I had heard about boys having wet dreams, but I didn't think it was possible to have an orgasm just from kissing a girl. "What was it like your first time?" I asked.

"Nothing like that! Did she say anything?"

"No. She said it was okay. That was it."

"Did anyone see you kissing?"

"I don't know," I replied. "Probably."

I didn't care. Completely in love, I watched her walking with her friends at the front of the line, and wondered if she were talking about me. I'm certain her friends saw us kiss. How would Philip react when he found out? I wasn't afraid of him; he didn't seem like a bully, but this whole situation was getting overly complicated.

"I hope you know what you are doing," Axel said, shaking his head and frowning.

"I have no idea what I'm doing," I replied. "But it feels really, really good."

Axel simply laughed. He didn't say much more on the subject. I nearly floated the rest of the way down to school. Although my first orgasm left a big mess in my pants, it also made me more relaxed than I had been in years.

After dinner I went down to the television lounge. I missed American T.V. The television at school didn't get many channels, and they were all in French. My French had improved dramatically, and although it wasn't fluent, I could understand most of the conversations the other boys were having. I also tried harder than most of the other American boys to use the language. I loved listening to it—it was so rhythmic, and had its own cadence.

I practiced with the French boys whenever I got the chance. At first they made fun of me. That was to be expected; I butchered their language. Soon, however, some of the boys realized I was serious and that I wanted to learn. They corrected me when I made mistakes and were patient while waiting for me to find the words to express myself. I truly enjoyed learning the language.

The television lounge was a small room with some wooden chairs in front of a T.V. Not too many people were around—just a few boys watching the news.

60

"*Ça va, mecs?*" I asked.

"*Oui, ça va*, Drew."

I sat down and watched the news. America was in shock over the Nixon-Watergate scandals, and I watched the synopsis of the hearings in French. Europeans took these sorts of scandals in stride, but the Americans wanted blood, as if exposing the turpitude of our leaders made us feel superior to others.

Philip and two of his friends came into the television lounge. They stood in front of me without saying a word.

"*Bon chance*, Drew," said the boy sitting next me, as he got up to leave.

I stood up to leave as well. One of Philip's friends, Jean-Pierre Horter, a short, wiry boy, threw his foot into my stomach with so much speed and power it knocked me back a couple of feet. I tried to throw a punch at him, but he just moved out of the way. I felt my arm slung over his shoulder as he turned to his side, and then I was flying through the air upside down. I landed on my back, gasping for air.

"*Mais, qu'est-ce que tu fais, cochon d'américain?*" Philip asked.

I still couldn't breathe, so I couldn't move—let alone answer him.

He put one knee on my chest and leaned down.

"This is a warning," Philip said. "Stay away from Alexandra. She is not for you. Do you understand?" His eyes reflected a gentle resignation, and I knew that his heart wasn't into what he was doing. I almost felt sorry for him for a moment.

"Yes," I gasped.

With that the three of them left. I picked myself up off the floor and went back to the room. By now everyone had heard what had happened. Philip had no choice but to squash me, but it took two of his friends to do it. It also made me somewhat of a celebrity.

Axel knew something had happened when I got back to the room. When I told him he just laughed.

"This amuses you?" I asked.

"You just don't see the humor in it," he said.

"Obviously!"

"You are not supposed to come all over their girlfriends. You are not even supposed to talk to them. The fact that you have gotten this far with her amazes me. She must be really special," he said, rubbing his chin.

I looked at him like he had lost his mind. I just got the crap beat out of me by three Frenchmen, and he was laughing about it. Then I started laughing. I wasn't scared of Philip, but his friends terrified me. I could tell they really wanted to hurt me, and judging by the way Jean-Pierre fought, they probably could.

The next day I saw Philip and Alexandra talking outside class during morning break. Philip was talking to her with quiet, harsh tones, while she simply looked up at him with compassionate understanding. She wasn't crying, but she frowned, and her eyes were slightly moistened. I didn't want to see what was going on.

Later that morning I heard they broke up. The French boys gave me dirty looks in the hallways between classes, and the French girls just avoided me. The American girls all seemed suddenly interested in me, and the American boys made me a hero. This was getting me more attention than I wanted; even my teachers seemed to look at me differently. All I cared about was Alexandra.

I was afraid I was going to have to fight again, but during lunch I was left alone. The excitement of the big breakup had died down, and all that was left were the hurt feelings of all the participants. I could see Philip with his friends at his table. He carried himself well, but his face became stolid and his eyes slightly red. Our eyes met briefly, and for the first time he acknowledged my presence—certainly not with approval—but an acknowledgment nonetheless. I didn't feel sorry for him anymore, even though he was really hurting.

After lunch Axel and I walked back to school together. I kept fidgeting, and had the urge to break into a trot.

"So, now you're a heartbreaker. How does it feel?" Axel asked.

For a moment I wanted to punch him. "Not very good," I replied. "I don't know what to do next."

"Nothing," he said. "Let things happen on their own. Don't do anything."

It was good advice. When Alexandra first kissed me, I floated around in a fantasy world of romance, but now that people were hurt and I was put on the spot, I didn't feel so easy and carefree.

I saw Alexandra with her friends as we approached *Saint François*. Our eyes met briefly. She went inside without a word and a wave of pain shot through my body.

Axel grabbed both my shoulders and looked me dead in the eyes. "Don't do anything," he told me. "Leave it alone for awhile. Trust me when I tell you that you will be thrown out of school if you don't handle this correctly."

"What the hell are you talking about?" I asked, squirming beneath his grip.

"If you let this get out of control, then it becomes a matter of a young girl's honor. Just stay away and let things happen on their own. What will be will be. Forcing the situation will only make things ugly."

I still wasn't completely sure of what he was talking about, but his expression and tone convinced me of his earnestness. There was so much about Alexandra I didn't understand, but Axel understood so much. I heeded his advice and kept to myself.

Summer was nearly upon us, and the days became warmer

and longer. Seeing Alexandra in the hallways was painful. I wanted so much to simply walk up to her and start talking, but we kept away from each other. She didn't avoid me, but she would not approach me either. The semester would be over in a few weeks, and I felt as though I was letting go of the best thing in my life—as if I needed to do something quickly before it was too late. I spoke to Axel about it.

"It's not over between you two," he said. "She will come to you when she is ready."

"But school's almost over."

"Look," he said, looking up at me reassuringly. "You two have unfinished business. She knows how you feel. She will come to you. Trust me."

"I don't think I can stand it, Axel. I'll never forgive myself if I just let her go like this."

"It's not your choice. It never was."

"What do you mean?" I asked, frowning.

"She makes the rules, not you. You need to decide whether you want to play by them. Besides, what difference does it really make now? She's going back to Rome, and you are going back to New Jersey. By the end of the summer you will have forgotten all about her."

I knew he was right in my head, but my heart couldn't reckon with the logic. Axel put his arm around me. "You need a release," he said. "We're going out tonight."

"What do you mean going out? Where?"

"I have a surprise for you," he said. He took me up to the room and pulled a couple of large beer bottles from underneath his bed. "Tonight we are going to party!"

After lights out, Axel and I climbed out our window and ran into a nearby cow pasture with our beer bottles, where the Grinnel brothers, John and Chris from New Jersey, met us beneath a tree. The stars were thick and bright over the mountains, and summer insects were starting their seasonal mating symphony. The four of us sat and drank our beer.

John was a tall, good-looking boy who always seemed to find trouble. He had a good sense of humor, but his antics were a little too racy for my speed. He and another kid stole a couple of mopeds from Montana and rode them all the way down to Sierre. He said at one point they were going so fast the brakes started to melt, and he had to get off to pee on them to keep them from catching fire. Had he been caught he would have been thrown out of school. We were in the same class. His brother, Chris, was in a grade below me.

"So, Drew. What's going on with you and Alexandra," John asked.

"Nothing," I said. "Nothing is going on."

"Make a move on her," said Chris. "Summer is almost here. You won't see her again until the fall."

"In good time," I said.

In truth, I was scared now. Alexandra had somehow slipped from my grasp, and I could only admire her from afar. Approaching her might somehow upset the delicate emotional balance that existed between us. I remembered how it felt when we first kissed and that amazing feeling of my first orgasm. Since then I had learned to masturbate, and did so as often as possible. She was always the subject of my fantasies.

"I've got to pee," said Chris. He was a fat kid, and he struggled to his feet. He went off to the edge of the pasture while we talked about our summer vacations. I didn't have any real plans for the summer. I would probably spend most of my time playing tennis and going to the beach. Axel said he was spending part of the summer in Norway, and John was going to summer camp with his brother.

Chris let out a blood-curdling shriek. We all jumped to our feet and ran over to him. The farmers had put up a knee-high strand of electrified wire to keep the cows from wandering. Not enough electricity in it to do any damage, it gave you a nice jolt. Chris peed directly on it. He stood there frozen, his privates cupped in his hand, and his eyes wide as saucers. We couldn't tell if he enjoyed it or not, but we all laughed so hard we could barely stand up.

That Saturday was the last *soirée* of the year. Some of us wouldn't be seeing each other again. I had done everything I could to look my best. Alexandra stood near the punch bowl with her friends. A slow dance was playing—something somber and soulful in French. I had barely taken two steps toward her when Philip beat me to it. I just stood helplessly and watched as they talked briefly. She smiled as they exchanged playful banter, and then he took her hand to lead her to the dance floor. She wrapped her arms around him and burrowed her head against his chest, while he stroked her long, dark hair as they swayed to the music. At last I couldn't stand it anymore and went back to the room to hide my tears.

We had exams the last of week of school. We all exchanged signatures in our yearbooks. I did not give mine to be signed by very many people—just a few friends that were important to me. I didn't have the heart to have Alexandra sign it. I did, however, give my yearbook to my French teacher, M. Bianchi, to sign. I liked him; he had a good sense of humor. I had really learned a lot of French, and he told me on several occasions that my accent was excellent, even though my grades were not very good. When I gave him my yearbook he wrote something under his picture and handed it back to me with a smile.

It's a pity you are so lazy. Without commentary.

I was hurt by what he wrote. He was the only teacher I

really liked. Now I couldn't even show my yearbook to my parents. Exams were over and I began packing while Axel watched. He seemed sad. It wasn't like him.

"Are you okay?" I asked.

"I'm fine. Are you going to be okay?"

"Who me? Yeah, I'm perfectly okay. I'll miss you," I said.

"You'll see me again. Did you find Alexandra?"

"What?"

"She was looking for you earlier."

"Where?"

"Out front."

I ran from the room and out the front door, but she was nowhere to be found. To hell with it all. I ran down the road to *Prés Fleuris*. She must have seen me coming because she walked out the front door to greet me.

"Alexandra," I said panting. "I can't leave without talking to you."

"I wasn't going to leave without saying goodbye," she said.

"I'm sorry for what happened."

"It's okay, Drew. I have no regrets. I'm sorry if I hurt you. It was not my intention."

"It never is," I said, "But you did hurt me." My tongue took on a sharp edge. "Are you and Philip back together?"

"No. But my relationship with Philip has nothing to do with you. I am not in love with him."

"Are you in love with me?"

"I don't know," she said, frowning. "I am happy to have known you, but I don't know you enough to love you. We are friends."

I took her in my arms and kissed her. She kissed me back passionately. Katrina saw us and came running out the front door to separate us.

67

"I have something for you, Drew." She reached into her back pocket and handed me a letter. "I have to go. You will write me?"

"Yes, of course," I replied. She kissed me once more on the lips and went back inside.

The next morning a van came to drive some of us to the airport. I hugged Axel and said goodbye. I saw him from the back window standing and watching the van depart as we headed down the road towards Sierre. His downcast eyes were filled with sadness. I loved him like a brother.

Alexandra's letter never stayed in my pocket very long. Nearly my only entertainment during the long flight home, every so often I took it out and unfolded it gently. Her words, so carefully written, made me wish I had never gotten on the plane and gone to Rome instead.

> *Dear Drew,*
>
> *I am so sorry to have hurt you. The time we spent together was really wonderful, and I enjoyed getting to know you as much as I enjoyed reading your writing. I need to thank you for letting me have my space when I needed it most; it was difficult to handle my breakup with Philip and my feelings for you. I really, really hope we can continue to be friends.*
>
> *Please don't stop writing, Drew. You write in a wonderful way, and I would be happy if you would write to me if you like.*
>
> *Kisses,*
> *Alexandra*

Each time I read her words I remembered her kiss, and wished more than anything we could have had more time together.

Chapter 6

My first morning back I slept almost until 10:00—something I hadn't done in ages. At school we were always out of bed at the crack of dawn. When I awakened I looked around my room, happy to be back. After being away so long I had forgotten what it was like having my own space.

Summer had just started, and a soft, warm breeze wafted through the three French windows that overlooked our backyard, carrying the familiar smell of freshly mown grass. My mother had redecorated my room while I was away with a rust-colored carpet and wallpaper to match. She even cleaned out the ashes in my fireplace and replaced them with a big bouquet of dried flowers.

I put on an old pair of blue jeans and a t-shirt and padded barefoot down to the kitchen. My mother was out, and my father was at work. Lynn, our old housekeeper, a heavy-set black woman with salt and pepper hair, was in the kitchen doing dishes. "Well, look who is finally up," she cried out when she saw me. "How are you, Drew?"

"I'm fine, Lynn. How are you?" She had been with us so long she was almost part of the family.

"You know me, same as ever. Are you hungry? Why don't you sit down and I'll fix you some breakfast," she said, putting a frying pan on the stove. "What would you like?"

I thought of the most American breakfast I could think of. "Some bacon and eggs would be great," I replied, grinning as I felt my taste buds already going wild in expectation. "And maybe some toast if that isn't too much work."

"Nothing is too much for my little world traveler – bacon, eggs and toast it is. Lots of butter as always?" she asked, opening the refrigerator and taking out an armload of food.

"Yep," I said walking over to the kitchen table and sitting down. As the bacon sizzled in the pan, the spicy smell that permeated the kitchen made me feel like I was really home. Lynn hummed while she cooked, and I poured myself my first cup of coffee.

After refilling my cup, I was just setting down to eat when my sisters came bounding through the back door, wearing blue jeans and riding boots, and smelling musty like horses.

"Drew! Welcome home!"

One after another, all three kissed me on the cheek. Gretchen was the oldest in the family, and then came me, then Annie, and finally Julie. Each of them had thick, wavy red hair of various shades, and dark green eyes that were lively and playful. As I ate, we talked about my experiences in Switzerland. I told them all about Alexandra, and showed them her picture in the yearbook. They were so impressed by her beauty, and her Italian background intrigued them.

My oldest sister, Gretchen, didn't say much, but she thumbed through my yearbook with fascination. She stopped at the picture of my French teacher, read his words, and looked up at me and scowled. "Looks to me like you have been having too much fun," she said.

I hated him for writing that, and wished I could erase his words.

My mother's station wagon pulled into the driveway. "Well, hello children," she said, walking into the kitchen with a big smile.

My mother had changed quite a bit while I was away. Her eyes no longer had the same sparkle I remembered, and deep lines now engraved her face, but her dark, auburn hair was still radiant with only a hint of gray. "What do you kids want to do today? Go to the beach?"

Of course, we all said yes, so later that morning we piled into her car and she took us to the beach club. Although still early in the season, things were already in full swing. A light, steady breeze blew off the ocean, and low tide was coming as Sea Bright Beach Club's trademark green and white umbrellas flapped in the wind. A long, wooden boardwalk extended the length of the club.

The tables and chairs that lined the boardwalk were filled with women who came to cool off after their morning tennis games. The seating arrangements on the boardwalk had a definite a social order. The older women from more established families sat at the tables closer to the bar, while the newer families sat further down, nearer the barbecue area. We always sat somewhere in the middle, unless my mother felt like actually sitting on the beach with a group of friends.

I felt like I was on display as I walked down the boardwalk—the old ladies who sat near the bar eyed me disapprovingly. My mother referred to that stretch as murderer's row because of how she was scrutinized when she walked down to her spot. Near the dance floor, between the bar and the barbecue area, I saw Aunt Theresa. She was my mother's older sister—the one who moved to Switzerland years ago with her children after her husband died.

She looked a lot like my mother, only much taller and slimmer. An artist specializing in watercolor painting, she was well known around the area. I liked her work—it was elegant and soft. She painted landscapes of the *Naversink* River, and sometimes portraits for local families. Her work hung in many restaurants and office buildings around the area. She had a studio not too far from our house, although she lived across the river in *Naversink*. When I was younger she brought me with her to her studio and set me up with an easel and some paints. I tried to paint, but my drawings never came out right. I just didn't have any talent for

71

visual arts, but she never stopped encouraging me. Realizing I loved to read, she gave me books she thought I might enjoy. Her face lit up when she saw me. "Drew Dear! Come give your Aunt Tess a kiss," she said, her smile stretching across her tanned and freckled face.

"Hello, Aunt Tess."

"Tell me all about Switzerland," she said. "Is Bluche still a charming little cow town?"

I laughed. "Yes, it really is a cow town. It's funny to see the farmers herding their cattle in the middle of such a fine boarding school."

She wanted to know all about Montana—if certain shops were still there. She remembered the chocolate shop where I first talked with Alexandra. "When we were living in Montana, it wasn't considered such an international ski resort. I hear it has grown considerably."

"It seems to be growing. There are a lot of new buildings going up."

"Such a shame," she said. "Ten years ago it was nothing but a charming little ski community in the middle of cow pastures. I met some really wonderful people when I was there. How's your French, Dear?"

"It's good. It really has improved a lot. How's the painting going?"

"I've hit a dry spell. I need to broaden my horizons a bit. Despite the incredible beauty of this area I just don't feel as moved by it as I used to be," she said, putting on a wide-brimmed straw hat to shield her face from the sun.

"You're just becoming a bit jaded in your old age," my mother said with a wry smile. "Would you like a South Side, Tess?"

"Please, Dear."

My mother ordered their drinks. South Sides were one of

the things that made Sea Bright Beach Club famous. A unique concoction comprised of 151 rum, blended with mint and other ingredients, they encapsulated summer days at the beach almost perfectly. I excused myself to take a dip in the ocean. The waves were well formed and large, rolling into the shore with nearly perfect form. I couldn't wait to go body surfing.

By late afternoon, red blotches mottled my delicate, over-exposed skin, and I felt waterlogged from spending too much time in the ocean. Mother and Aunt Tess looked a little sauced by now. She asked me to round up my sisters and we started for home.

My father arrived at around 5:30 pm. Despite working all day, he always found time to do chores around the house, and he usually changed quickly out of his working clothes into a pair of old khakis.

Today, however, he asked me if I would like to play tennis before dinner, and of course, I said yes. I loved tennis almost as much as skiing. I ran upstairs, changed into my tennis whites, and grabbed my racquet out of the closet. I helped my father take the top down on his car—a dark green, 1968 Pontiac Firebird with a three-speed manual transmission, which he kept in mint condition. It attracted a lot of attention during the summer when he drove it to the beach, and I couldn't wait until I was old enough to get my license so I could drive it too. I loved the whining roar it made when he downshifted into a curve.

Sea Bright Lawn Tennis & Cricket Club, ensconced from public view by tall, thick hedges, sat right before the Sea Bright Bridge in Rumson. Several tiers of perfectly manicured grass courts stretched all the way up to the clubhouse, without a single divot or brown spot marring the courts. Dozens of clay courts surrounded the grass, where children under the age of eighteen played. Juniors were not allowed to play on the grass unless accompanied by adults, and I always felt so privileged when my father played singles with me on the grass. We never played during peak hours or on weekends—only after hours, before the courts closed for the evening.

My father wasn't a very good tennis player. Although tall and thin, his movements were awkward and mechanical, and he couldn't seem to hit the ball just right. His lack of athleticism didn't stop him from trying; he was always taking lessons to improve his game. Slowly it did improve, but he never really got good—I think he mostly played to be social anyway.

We played for nearly an hour. I tried my best to keep the ball within his reach, never hitting it so hard that he wouldn't have time to get his racquet into position for the return. More often than not we chased down the balls that were missed, but I enjoyed the opportunity to play anyway. My father finally decided it was time to stop. "Why don't we go down to the beach club and get something to drink before we go home," he suggested, putting away his racquet.

"Sure."

We jumped into his car and drove across the bridge. Only a few people came down to the beach at this hour to barbecue with family and friends. The sun sat over the Sea Bright Bridge like a big red ball, and a cool breeze blew off the ocean. All the umbrellas had been removed from the beach, and the chairs had been stacked neatly in their racks. My tennis shirt, damp with sweat, clung to my skin, making me cold.

We took our drinks and walked down the boardwalk. The men wore their traditional summer garb of bright pastel or plaid pants and polo shirts. I never understood how people could wear something so awful, but they all seemed so comfortable in their attire. I felt out of place in my tennis whites.

My father stopped at a table almost at the end of the boardwalk, away from everyone else. It was the Worthingtons. "Hello, David," a woman sitting next to her husband said.

Mrs. Worthington was attractive and busty, but her husband looked sickly and pallid. He hadn't shaved in days, and his eyes looked sunken and sad. He talked quickly and kept changing the subject without warning. My father and Mrs. Worthington seemed to politely ignore him and carry on a civil conversation on their own.

It didn't take me long to realize what was going on. I focused my attention on Mr. Worthington. He talked to me quite a bit about his car—an old Jaguar that he had for years. Of the two he was by far more interesting, and I remembered seeing his name engraved on several plaques adorning the walls of the tennis club where his grandfather was one of the founding members. Mr. Worthington had won several prestigious tournaments when he was younger, although I never saw him there anymore.

His wife played regularly in a doubles game each morning with a group of women. She was also a good player, but her high-pitched voice annoyed me. She bragged about their summerhouse on the Shrewsbury River. The house used to be on the beach in Sea Bright, but it was threatened to be washed out to sea as the beach eroded, so it was floated across the river on a huge barge and set at the river's edge, safely away from the capriciousness of the winter tides. The Worthingtons only came down to Rumson for the summer. During the winter they stayed in New York City where they had a comfortable townhouse on the Upper East Side.

It was time to go. My father and I said goodbye and started for home, thank God. Night was falling, and the breeze off the ocean made me cold.

"Dad, what's wrong with Mr. Worthington?" I asked, as we got in the car.

"He's manic-depressive," replied my father.

"What's that mean?"

"It means he has a severe chemical imbalance in his brain that makes him very high one moment and very depressed another," he explained.

"Was he always like that?"

"No. In fact, when he was young he was quite brilliant. He graduated from Harvard Law School near the top of his class."

"What happened?"

"They think it's hereditary. Nobody knows. When he reached his forties he started showing signs of the disease."

"Can they do anything for him?"

"He's on some pretty strong medication for his condition, but he doesn't take it when he should."

"Why not?"

"It's part of the disease. When he starts to become manic, he believes he's capable of almost anything, and refuses to take his medication because he doesn't want it to slow him down."

"Was he manic tonight?"

"No. I'd say he looked pretty depressed," my father replied

I thought about him a while. He seemed so gentle and reasonable, albeit a little eccentric. Behind all the sadness in his eyes was a lot of kindness, and I felt genuinely sorry for him.

It was dark by the time we got home. My sisters had already finished dinner and were playing upstairs. My mother sat in the kitchen, drinking a beer, waiting for us to come home. Her eyes looked slightly glazed.

"What took you so long?" she asked.

"We stopped down at the beach to have a drink," my father said.

"Who was there?" she asked, taking a deep swig from her beer.

"The Worthingtons."

"How is Robert doing? Is he still on his medication?"

"He seems to be doing fine," my father said.

"I'm going upstairs," she said, looking disgusted and angry. "I kept your dinner warm for you. It's in the oven."

We ate our dinner at the kitchen table in silence. My mother's drinking seemed to be getting worse, but no one ever said a word.

"So, you must be a pretty good skier by now," he finally said, breaking his silence.

"Yes," I replied. "I'm not as good as some of the boys that were practically raised on skis, but I've gotten pretty good."

"How about your French?"

"*Très bon! Je parle français toujours avec mes amis. Mon professeur m'a dit j'ai un accent excellent!*"

"Yes, your French has most certainly improved," my father said, "but your grades are still awful. I'd better start seeing some more improvement in that area."

"I'll try harder, Dad."

He eyed me contemptuously for a moment and said, "I got a strange letter from your friend's mother in Greece."

I gulped. "What's strange about it?"

"What's going on with you and her?"

"What do you mean?"

"Nothing is going on?" he asked, his eyes hardening. He pushed his tongue into the side of his mouth, and I knew he was angry.

"Dad, Marianne and Austin thought I should be in school for artists. That's all."

"Horseshit! You can forget it. We've sacrificed a lot to send you to Switzerland, and you're not going to piss away anymore opportunities."

I sat back in my chair quietly and played with my food, not surprised by his reaction. Throughout the years my father resigned

77

himself to the fact that I was academically inferior, and treated me accordingly. My grandfather on my mother's side simply thought I was an idiot, incapable of any kind of meaningful intellectual achievement. In fact, that was the generally accepted idea among everyone in the family.

After dinner my father said he was going out to help one of his friends install a new dishwasher. When it came to fixing things around the house there was nothing he couldn't do, but I knew he would not be installing any major appliances that evening. I went upstairs. Peeking into my parent's bedroom, I saw my mother was already asleep; an open beer can sat on her bed stand, and the television was still on. I turned off the TV and went back to my room.

My room was my haven, and in it I was able to invent whatever life I chose. I sat down and wrote Alexandra a long, passionate letter, describing in detail what it was like to be home. I missed her terribly, and my loneliness came out in my writing. The pain of seeing my mother drunk and my father distance himself from our lives had not really sunk in yet, but it came out in the words I used. By the end of the night I had written her a twenty-five page letter. Even I was a little surprised by how much I had written.

The next morning my mother drove me to the post office to mail my letter.

"That's quite a letter, Dear. Who's it for?"

"My girlfriend, Alexandra."

"You have a girlfriend?" she exclaimed, smiling with pride. "Tell me about her."

"She comes from Rome. She's beautiful, and speaks wonderful English."

"You must feel very strongly for her to write a letter like that."

"I do a lot of writing, Mom."

"Really? I had no idea you like to write. When did you start writing?"

"I don't know when I was in Switzerland. One day I just sat down and started writing."

"What do you write?"

"Stories, poetry, whatever."

"Will you let me read some of your work?"

"Sure, Mom."

I was a little hesitant. Most of it was really personal, but lately I had started writing things that were not centered around me and strictly from my imagination. Most of it was still dark and angry and filled with pain, but that was how I felt these days.

Later that morning I put together a small collection of my better stories and poems and gave them to my mother in an envelope. She promised she would read them later, and I rode my bike down to the tennis club. My father had enrolled me in the junior's tennis clinic for the summer, where every morning a group of kids worked on basic techniques with the club pro and his assistant. Every aspect of the game was drilled into us. That way, by the time most of the kids were old enough to play on grass, we would most certainly not be an embarrassment to the club.

I enjoyed the sessions, and took great pride in perfecting my stroke. The club seemed to push the doubles match on us for the social aspects of the game, but I much preferred playing singles. What I liked most about tennis was that it was just as much mental as it was physical. Superior technique was only half the battle; winning in tennis requires intense mental discipline and focus. I played a good game, but I wasn't great. The great players at the club had a perfectly natural stroke, and they made it look so effortless. Although I was fluid and fast, I was way too tense to be natural. No matter how hard I tried to relax and feel the racquet as simply an extension of my arm, I ended up using it like a club and pounded the ball across the net. When I hit a winner it was usually traveling at the speed of light.

After the morning lesson I walked up to the clubhouse. My mother was sitting with a group of women in one of the overstuffed club chairs, talking about their children and drinking lemonade. She was the only one not wearing tennis whites, and her blue jeans and t-shirt made her stand out. All in their mid fifties, they had dark tans and deep wrinkles from too many summers spent basking in the sun. Despite their weathered skin they were in excellent condition. Tennis was almost a religion for many people in Rumson, but I was surprised to see her, since she hated the game. I said hello to everyone.

"Hello, Drew," Mrs. Boyle said, a tall woman with long dark hair, who easily could have been a cover girl in her younger days. "Your mother was just telling us about your going to school in Switzerland. How do you like it?"

"I love it."

"My husband and I traveled through Switzerland a couple of summers ago. It's a beautiful place."

Just then, Mrs. Worthington approached. Years of tennis had given her shapely legs, and her tennis outfit was short and tight. As president of the Garden Club, she knew many people. "Hello Martha!" she cried in her shrill voice and waving as if she was trying to land a jet.

"Hello, Joan," my mother replied, forcing a smile.

"I haven't seen you in ages! How have you been?"

"I've been fine, thank you."

"Martha, Robert and I would like to have you and your family over for dinner this Saturday. Can you come?"

"Of course," my mother said, looking only slightly horrified at the thought.

"Wonderful. We'll see you then."

My mother and I headed back towards her car. She looked upset, although she did her best not to show it. "Your father would like to have lunch with you," my mother told me. "I'll take you to the factory to see him after you've gone home and changed."

"Okay, Mom," I replied, lifting my bike into the back of our station wagon.

I liked going down to the factory to see my father. My father, along with my mother's oldest brother, had started a small manufacturing business many years ago, making O-rings and gaskets for aggressive environment applications, such as high-pressure oil wells and fuel-injection systems. My uncle, the real brains behind the company, became an eminent polymer chemist and held several patents for some of the rubber compounds he invented, despite never having gone to college. My father handled all the financial and technical operations.

Once I put on a clean shirt and trousers, my mother drove me to Red Bank and dropped me off in front. The factory had recently been moved from a smaller location to a newer, larger building near the train station, which I hadn't seen yet. The new building extended almost the entire block, and looked so much more modern than the old place, with the company logo emblazoned on the front in big, bold letters — Browning Seals International, Inc.

Excited, I went through the double glass doors and was greeted by the receptionist, Arlene. "Well, look who it is! How are you, Drew?"

"I'm fine Arlene, thank you. Is my dad busy?" Arlene had been with the company since they first opened the door, often bragging that her employee number was three.

"He's in his office," she said, pointing to a row of big, glass windows lining the far wall where his was the last. He sat bent

81

over a large stack of papers, making notations and muttering under his breath.

I knocked on his door, and with only a grunt and a quick glance in my direction, he waved me in. Reams of computer print-outs were piled on the floor in stacks that seemed to defy balance, and the bookcases lining the walls of his office were filled with technical manuals all pertaining to how to program and set up computers. It was the first time that these new fangled machines were available to business after being almost exclusive to only the government and universities, and my dad wanted to get a jump on his competition. "Hey. Give me a few seconds and we'll go eat," he said, picking up a box of cards.

"What are those?"

"Punch cards," he replied. He took one out and held it up for me to see the little holes that perforated the slim pieces of cardboard. "You load these cards in the computer, and the computer reads the holes to get its instructions."

"That reminds me of a toy car you gave me once for Christmas. You make notches in the card to make the car go where you want."

My father frowned. He didn't appreciate the analogy. "Follow me. I'll show you the computer room."

I followed him to a small room where a brand new IBM System32 mainframe computer took up so much space there was barely room to walk. Lights flashed in a rhythmic pattern, accompanied by the occasional whirl of large spools of tape made the whole process look like something out of a science fiction movie.

"Why is it so cold in here, Dad?"

"The room is climate controlled. We have to keep it cold to make sure the computer doesn't overheat."

"How can you stand it?"

"You get used to it," he said. I watched him as he carefully loaded the cards into the computer.

"What happens if you drop them?"

"Then you have a big goddamn mess."

Once the cards were loaded, he pushed a series of buttons on the front panel and the computer made a racket as the cards were shuffled through it.

We left the factory to eat lunch at the Molly Pitcher Inn, one of the oldest restaurants in the area. My father ordered a lobster salad, and I chose a hamburger, still not able to get enough American food. While we waited for our food, my father talked about all the plans he had for the factory. I was proud of him. I remembered when he and my uncle first started the company. They nearly went under several times, but somehow always managed to keep the place going, either through creative financing or just hard work and good ideas.

After lunch my father drove me home. My sixteenth birthday was coming up, which meant I would be old enough to get my driver's license.

"Dad, will you teach me how to drive?"

"In this car? Hell no! I'll give you a few lessons in your mother's station wagon. But you don't get your license for another six months," he said, pushing his tongue into the side of his mouth.

"Don't you think I should be a least a little prepared?"

"That's what a learner's permit is for. Why don't you focus on improving your grades? Your final report card came. I'm disgusted with you."

His words came as a shock. Why didn't he mention anything before? "I've made some improvement, haven't I?" I asked meekly.

"C's and D's are not what I call an improvement. And some of the comments your teachers wrote about you — Jesus Christ!

One of them wrote that half the time he isn't even sure you are even paying attention. What the hell is the matter with you?"

He shook with anger. The muscles in his face contorted, and his pale, blue eyes were reddened slightly with rage. Ever since I could remember my father reacted the same way when report cards came. When I was younger he beat me with a belt because of my grades. On report card day I would cower in the back of my closet when my father came home. He would pull me out screaming and whip me until I nearly bled. When he became like this, I learned to keep as still as possible to avoid provoking him, and I cringed in my seat, trying to make myself less noticeable. I stared at the big houses as we drove down Ridge Road into Rumson, too scared to utter a word.

He dropped me off at home, talked privately and briefly with my mother, then went back to work. My sisters were out riding, and my mother sat at the kitchen table with a beer in her hand, talking to Lynn. Her eyes were a bit droopy, but she wasn't quite drunk yet. She smiled at me when I entered the kitchen. "I read your stories, Dear. You have a gift for words."

I sat down next to her. After what I just went through with my father some positive reinforcement would be nice. "You really liked them?"

"Yes. I did. You know, before I met your father I was a writer."

"Really?"

She nodded and took a swig from her beer. "I worked for a newspaper in New York. My editor loved the way I wrote. Back then journalists didn't go to college. They got apprenticeships and learned their craft from other writers."

"I didn't know that."

"Nobody in my mother's family went to college. My grandfather worked on Wall Street and lost a lot in the Great Crash of

84

'29, and couldn't afford to send any of his kids to school, even when Uncle Frank had been accepted to Princeton."

"How come you don't write anymore, Mom?"

"I got married to your father and started having you kids," she said. "Did I ever tell you how I met your father?" she asked, smiling.

"No. I don't think so."

"Your father was in the army and stationed at Fort Monmouth." The base is not that far from where we live.

"Is that where you met him?"

"No," she said. "It was in New York. He was dating my roommate at the time. I was working for the Post as a journalist. It was love at first sight and we were married six months later."

"What was it like back then?"

She looked up in the air wistfully and smiled. "It was nice," she said. "After your father got out of the army we lived in a tiny apartment in New York. We didn't have much, so I continued working while he went to Colombia University to get his engineering degree. In the beginning we had so much fun. Gretchen was born shortly after we were married, and then you came along. You were born in Mt. Sinai hospital at 10:34 am. I still have the original telegram wishing us congratulations from your Pada Michael." Pada Michael was my grandfather on my father's side. He died of an aneurism when I was five. I had some vague memories of him.

"You know, Dear, we almost lost you when you were a baby. You were so curious and began crawling at such an early age, you nearly crawled out the apartment window. I managed to grab onto your leg just before you fell."

The story of my near demise and my mother's heroism shook me up a little. I imagined myself as a tiny baby crawling out an open window, and how it felt when my mother grabbed my ankle just before I fell. What would it have felt like to plummet out the window of a tall building?

"What did Dad do for work back then?" I asked.

"He worked for an elevator company. His G.I. benefits helped pay for school. Your father had a lot of trouble in school when he was your age. He was expelled from Exeter, and then he dropped out of Brown University."

"Dad? But he seems so smart."

"He is, but his problems were a bit different from yours; there were some discipline problems when he was young. If it wasn't for me he probably wouldn't have finished college, and if not for your uncle Frank he would certainly not have achieved all this."

I fidgeted for a moment before saying, "Mom, sometimes I think I am really smart, but I don't do well in school. I don't seem to pick up things like other people do."

"Well, you are going to have to, Dear. Times have changed. You won't go anywhere without an education, so you are going to have to work harder. You have a gift for words. Use it. But don't neglect your studies."

"Okay, I won't."

She leaned over and kissed me on the cheek and I went upstairs. What she said helped me understand my father somewhat better, but I would have thought him to be more understanding, considering all that he had been through.

That weekend we all went over to the Worthington's for dinner. My mother didn't want to go, but my father insisted. My sisters and I sat in Annie's bedroom and could hear them fighting over it next door.

"I don't like that bitch," my mother said. "She's a pretentious whore."

"She is not," my father said. "They are nice people."

"Robert belongs in a hospital. He's a wreck! What can you possibly see in them? Or is what you see in her?" she asked my father. Footsteps interrupted a brief moment of silence.

"Look," my father finally told her. "Robert has squandered his entire fortune. They are about to lose their house. If we play our cards right we can buy that place for a song."

"This is what all this is about? A house? I don't want their goddamn house! I don't even want to go over there!"

"We're going. You said you'd go so you're going," my father said.

"Jesus, David. I married a heartless, goddamn vulture. You'd sell your own mother to the devil if you thought there was enough money in it. What the hell do you want with their house anyway? This one isn't enough for you?"

"You're the one that's always complaining that this one's too big. Their house is a lot smaller and it's riverfront property."

"Jesus, David. I think you have lost your fucking mind!"

My father just laughed. Gretchen decided we had heard enough and said we'd better wait downstairs in the kitchen. It wasn't the first time they had fought, although their fights always rattled us and made us feel as if we were one step away from becoming orphans. Later we all piled into my mother's station wagon and headed over to the Worthington's house. My sisters, not ones to miss an opportunity to wear their summer best, had nonetheless primped themselves reluctantly, wearing fashionable sun dresses made from the finest cotton and lace. They didn't want to go either, but my father wouldn't hear any of it.

The Worthingtons lived in an old, rundown Victorian house at the end of an isolated road near the Shrewsbury River. A few of the weather-beaten cedar shingles were missing or cracked, and the shutters were in disrepair, while gobs of ivy threatened to overtake the balcony overlooking the front porch. The grass hadn't been cut all summer, and thick patches of cattails completely obstructed the view of the river from the backyard.

Mr. Worthington's classic Jaguar sat crumpled in the driveway; the front end was squished up like an accordion. He stood next to the car with his shirttails out. His pants, more than two sizes too big, were nearly falling off, and he had tightened his belt to keep them up, bunching them at the waist. He looked like had hadn't showered in days.

"Hello, Martha," he said, ignoring my father. He held a drink in one of his pudgy hands, and smeared back his greasy black hair with the other. His hands shook, rattling the ice cubes around in his glass.

"Hello, Robert," my mother said dryly. "How have you been?"

"Never better! I was in a car accident a few days ago, but things are great otherwise," he cackled, reaching into his shirt for a cigarette.

"Hello!" cried a loud, shrill voice from inside the house. The front door opened and Mrs. Worthington came outside, adorned in a short sundress plastered with big, bright flowers.

"Hello, Martha," she cried, kissing my mother on the cheek. My father's eyes lit up when he saw her. She looked good, and even I took a double take when I saw her. "Hello, David!" she said.

We followed her inside. The house was even older than ours, and was unkempt and smelled musty. Despite the heat, it remained cool because the ceilings were so high, and the big trees and overgrown bushes that surrounded the place shaded it from the sun. Everything in the house was dark. The wood, the furniture, even the curtains were dark and drab.

We were seated in Mr. Worthington's study, the only room in the house that was remotely cheerful. Light streamed into the room, illuminating the bookshelves lining the walls. I studied his book collection carefully. His tastes were eclectic, and some of the titles surprised me. Most of them were French and American classics, but I saw quite a few modern writers as well. His law credentials hung unceremoniously in the corner, almost out of view. He didn't practice law anymore, although he still had a license. If he ever stepped into a court room he'd be sure to lose it.

Mr. Worthington talked a mile a minute about nothing in particular. He dominated the conversation. He talked incessantly about politics and foreign affairs, but couldn't focus on any single subject for more than ten seconds, and sort of free-associated the entire time. At first it was entertaining, but then it got to be annoying. My poor sisters and I sat politely and tried to follow his ranting while my father helped Mrs. Worthington make cocktails in the kitchen.

"Jason! Come down and meet the Smiths," cried Mrs. Worthington. The Worthington's had a son my age, but I never met him. "Jason!" she yelled up the stairs.

"Yeah!" replied a rough voice. A few minutes later an overweight boy with thick, shoulder-length, brown hair came down the front staircase. His full beard and moustache nearly concealed his face. Gretchen whispered to my mother he looked like an oversized version of Cousin It from the Addams Family TV show. Apparently he was some sort of genius, and was at the top of his class at Andover.

"Jason, I'd like you to meet the Smiths. This is my son, Jason," Mrs. Worthington said proudly.

He mumbled inaudibly through the introductions. He did not say hello to my father, but instead just nodded coldly.

"Jason, why don't you show Drew your room?"

He gestured at me with his shaggy head to follow him up the stairs to his room at the back of the house, which reeked of cigarette smoke. I gaped at his record collection, which stood on their spines in alphabetical order and took up an entire wall.

"My God!" I exclaimed. "How many albums do you have?"

"I'm not sure. I lost count. I have at least 3,000 here and another 1,500 in New York."

Most of his music was early British and American Rock & Roll from the 60s on up. Some of the bands I recognized, but many I did not. The opposite wall was packed with books. He seemed to read mostly history and political science, with very little of anything else that I could see. On a card table in front of a television set was some sort of board game depicting the Battle of the Bulge. The ashtray next to his bed overflowed with cigarette butts, as did the one on his card table. It didn't look like he left his room much.

"My mother told me you were going to school in Switzerland?" he asked, almost tentatively.

"Yes, that's right."

"What's that like?"

"It's fun. We do a lot of skiing," I replied.

"Hmm. It doesn't sound fun. It sounds cold."

"It's really not that cold. The air is pretty dry up there so you don't feel it so much." He studied me a minute or two, trying to get an angle on me, and then lighted a cigarette.

"Do you want to hear some music?"

"Yeah, sure." He pulled an album from his collection and showed it to me.

"This okay?" The band was called Small Faces. I never heard of them, but the album cover looked interesting. He played the music and sat down at his card table and went back to his game. I studied him for a moment, then feeling like an idiot standing there and having the feeling he would rather be alone, I excused myself and went downstairs to find Mrs. Worthington just finish-

90

ing giving my mother and sisters the grand tour.

"Most of this furniture has been in Robert's family for generations," she told my mother.

"Most of her furniture is ugly," Gretchen whispered to Julie.

Through the kitchen window, I could see Mr. Worthington outside with my father, pointing at something near the top of the house, while my father listened to him politely. My mother sat at the kitchen table and drank while Mrs. Worthington prepared a dinner of boiled salmon in a dill sauce. Her face looked strained from trying to keep her sense of humor.

Dinner was called and we all ambled into a big dining room where Mrs. Worthington had set the table with her best china. She called Jason to dinner at least twice as we all found our places. Finally she got out of her chair and yelled at him from the bottom of the stairs. "Jason! Come down for dinner!"

When he did not respond she went upstairs to check on him. "Oh, my God!" she yelled.

My father bolted up the stairs. "Call an ambulance!" he told her. She ran down the stairs to the telephone, and my mother ran upstairs to see what was wrong. I heard Mrs. Worthington tell the operator that her son had taken an entire bottle of Darvon and was throwing up on the floor. Mr. Worthington fumbled around the house, trying to be useful, but didn't seem to fully grasp all that was happening.

Within minutes the paramedics were carrying him downstairs in a gurney. His hair and beard were filled with vomit, and I couldn't tell if he was breathing or not. My father drove Mr. Worthington to the hospital in his wife's car, while Mrs. Worthington accompanied her son in the ambulance. My mother drove us home; her face no longer looked strained, but taking on a hard, angry look. We were all pretty shaken up.

"When I talked to him in his room he seemed okay, Mom."

91

"That whole goddamn family belongs in a loony bin," she said.

"I didn't like them," said Julie. "They were weird."

"And that house looked like something out of the Addam's Family," Annie added.

My mother laughed, but I knew inside she was starting to lose it. The whole situation was becoming more and more macabre. Why had my father gotten himself so mixed up with these people? My mother took us all to Barnacle Bill's restaurant, a small seafood joint on the river. Her sadness welled up behind her eyes, and she ordered drinks in lieu of dinner. I knew my parents' marriage was in serious trouble, and I felt an overwhelming sense of dread. I knew my sisters felt the same as well, and we ate our dinner in somber silence.

I heard my father's car downshift slowly as he pulled into the driveway, well after 2:00 in the morning. I opened the door of my room to greet him as he trudged quietly up the stairs.

"Is Jason alright, Dad?"

"He's in a coma. It's too early to tell if he's going to be okay. He took almost an entire bottle of his mother's Darvon." He smelled like her perfume, but my mother had long since drank herself to sleep and would probably not notice.

"I'm going to bed, Dad. Goodnight."

"Goodnight, Drew."

We didn't hear from the Worthingtons for a few days, and nothing was spoken about them. For awhile I felt hopeful, as if all this madness would simply pass. I wondered about what could have made Jason try to take his own life, and realized his family situation was even worse than ours.

My mother had given my stories to Aunt Tess. She called one day and asked to speak with me. Her excitement bubbled through the receiver. "Drew, your writing is wonderful! It's full of

92

so much grace. When I first read it I realized I was reading the soul of an artist."

"Thank you, Aunt Tess." Her words really made me feel good. She went on to recommend dozens of books for me to read, but my tastes were so different from hers, but I appreciated her sense of aesthetics nonetheless. She was much more visual than I was, and the more I wrote, the more I realized that my approach to the world was more visceral than intellectual.

"You keep writing, Drew. And be sure to give me some more of your work. I really enjoyed it."

"I will."

When I got off the phone my mother smiled at me proudly. "I think you found your calling," she said.

"I don't know, Mom. I don't how good I really am. It's one thing to write because you enjoy it, but it's quite another to try and make a living at it."

"Writing is a craft. You have to work at it. The best writers always started with talent, but it was hard work and perseverance that made them good. Writing is ten-percent inspiration and ninety-percent perspiration."

I thought about what she said. When I first started writing I just wrote what I felt. I didn't care if it was good. I wrote because I needed to express myself. It seemed to me that writing was a profession for intellectuals and artists, of which I never considered myself either. What would Axel have said on the subject? I sat down to write him a long letter about all that was happening and what it was like to be home.

Later that week I received a package from Italy. Alexandra sent me a big box of chocolates with a note.

Dear Drew,
I received your wonderful letter. It was beautiful. Thank you. I really,

really love to read your writing. You seem to get better each time I read you.

This summer my father took me to Marbella, Spain with him on one of his business trips. Have you been to the south of Spain? It's so beautiful there. The water is the most beautiful blue and always so warm. Now I am back in Rome for the rest of the summer. Rome is nearly a ghost town in July and August. Most people leave the city on holidays, and it is dreadfully hot, but my mother insisted I take some summer classes at the American School. It seems my English will never be good enough!

I hope things are well for you.

Kisses,

Alexandra

My sisters and I sat at the kitchen table that afternoon and ate some of the chocolate. Their reaction was almost like mine the first time I ate it.

"When you go back to Switzerland, can you send me some more chocolate?" Julie asked, her fingers and face covered.

"Sure," I said. "It's good, isn't it?"

"It beats the hell out of the crap we buy around here," Gretchen said.

"You should taste it when it's fresh," I said and told them about the chocolate shop in Montana, but my sisters were more curious about Alexandra.

"What does her father do?" Annie asked.

"He's a horse trader."

Both Annie and Julie perked up. Gretchen wasn't as passionate about horses as my two younger sisters, but she also enjoyed riding.

"Does she live on a horse farm?" Julie asked.

"I think she does. She's talked about her father's horses. Apparently he has a lot of them," I replied.

"Do you think we can go visit her?" Annie chimed in before I could finish my sentence, the excitement in her voice showing throughout her entire body.

I laughed. When Annie wasn't out riding she was in her room drawing pictures of them. Her drawings were good; she had real talent.

"If I go to visit her I think the last people I would want with me are all my sisters," I said smiling.

It was then that looking through the kitchen window, we saw Mom's station wagon swerving down the driveway. Gretchen went upstairs, but the rest of us waited for her to come in. She was so drunk that she nearly fell down the steps as she came in through the kitchen door. Her eyes were completely glazed over and they didn't seem to focus on anything in particular. Her face took on a hard, angry look when she was drunk, but now her face was contorted with rage. She noticed the box of chocolates on the table when she approached.

"Where did this come from?"

"Alexandra sent them, Mom," I replied. I had never seen her so angry.

"Are you fucking her?" she demanded.

I felt as though I had been kicked in the stomach. I couldn't believe my mother would accuse me of something like that. "Of course not!"

"Fuck you, you little bastard," she said, taking the chocolate and stuffing it into the garbage bin. I tried to wrestle the box away from her. She picked up the telephone receiver and began beating me over the head. "You are just like your goddamn father!" she screamed.

"Mom, stop!" I cried.

She managed to hit me across the jaw once, sending sharp pains through my head and neck. I tried to grab the receiver out of her hands, but she was a lot stronger than I thought, and the last thing I ever wanted was to grapple with my own mother. But she had me cornered, and she fully intended to beat me to death with the telephone. Whether by accident or design she kneed me full force in the groin and I doubled over. The pain was debilitating, and I saw my sisters watching the whole scene in horror. Finally I swung my elbow at her and clocked her cleanly across the jaw. She crumpled on the floor.

Julie and Annie knelt down beside her in tears. I thought I was going to vomit. My heart pounded wildly against my chest and my hands shook.

"Drew! What did you do to her?" Julie cried.

Mom lay on the floor grotesquely with her mouth open. She was breathing heavily, but didn't look seriously hurt. After about thirty seconds her eyelids fluttered, and she regained consciousness. She was pretty groggy, and didn't seem to remember what happened, only muttering something nonsensical.

"Annie, help me get her to bed," I said, pulling her off the floor. I put one of her arms around my shoulder and as Annie got on the other side we slowly walked her up the stairs with Julie following behind us in tears. Mom passed out as soon as we got her on the bed.

My mother became more and more evil each week, and it affected my sisters as much as me. Julie, the youngest, became more withdrawn—like a small, frightened animal. She would wake in the night screaming from nightmares, and during the day she cried as soon as Mom began drinking. Annie cursed and yelled at everyone, including Mom and Dad. Gretchen also became more withdrawn, but in a much more serious way. She turned to drugs to escape the situation, and on more than one occasion she got caught sneaking out of the house to meet with her friends, a bunch of hoodlums from Red Bank. I tried to wish it all away, as if it were really just a temporary thing that would pass eventually.

By the middle of July my mother began drinking so heavily I wasn't sure she would live through the summer. My father had all but disappeared from the family. Mr. Worthington had completely fallen apart and had to be hospitalized. He was flat broke, with the last of his money spent on some shady restaurant investment in New York. About the same time he was admitted, Jason came out of his coma and was finally released from psychiatric care, yet once home, he continued to mope around the house as if nothing happened.

One Saturday afternoon Dad called and asked to meet me at the tennis club for a quick game. I hadn't seen him for a while and was happy to spend some time with him. I waited for him on the club patio for nearly forty-five minutes, but he didn't show up. Was he at the beach and just forgot? Or could he be at the Worthington's? I rode my bike to their house and saw his car in the driveway.

Nobody seemed home when I entered the house. My father's tennis racket sat on the kitchen table, but he was nowhere to be found. I heard noises from upstairs, and went up to have a look. As I approached the Worthington's summer bedroom, I heard Mrs. Worthington whimper slightly, and then my father groan. I left unnoticed.

Not knowing what to do, I went down to the beach. Aunt Tess was sitting by herself at her usual place and she smiled as I approached. "Hello Drew! How's the writing going?"

The truth was I hadn't done any writing in some time. All that was happening was so overwhelming I didn't know how to express it. "Things are good, Aunt Tess," I replied, sitting down in the chair next to hers.

"How's your mother, Dear?"

"Mom? I guess she's all right. She's probably home."

"I saw your father down here earlier eating lunch, but I

don't know where he disappeared to."

I winced. She looked at me, her big, brown eyes glistening with concern. "Listen, Dear. Your mother and father are going through a rough time, but don't let it affect you. Keep your chin up. Your sisters need you to be there for them. I've got some sandwiches and fruit here. Help yourself," she said, offering me her lunch pail. I was hungry and I ate the sandwich quickly, realizing Mom had simply let us all sort of fend for ourselves.

As she started to pack up her things to go home, she stopped and smiled. "Grandma is having us all over for dinner this Sunday. I'll see you then," she said, kissing me on the cheek. "Be strong."

"Thanks. I replied as I stood up for her.

Most of the beach goers had already started packing up their tanning oils and towels. I started home on my bicycle, and just as I was peddling over the bridge, the warning bells sounded and the gates closed, signaling that the bridge was about to open. I leaned against the railing and watched a tall sloop approach. Its sails were down, and a small outboard powered it through the swift current beneath the bridge. Handsome, young couples in bathing suits waved to us from the deck. Across the river, I could see the top of the Worthington's house through the tall trees. The attic windows were open, and sitting shirtless on a towel on top of one of the dormers was Jason, reading. I was sure my father was over there, and anger rose up in me. Tired of the way my father treated us, I wanted to have it out with him.

I rode my bicycle down their long street and dropping it in their driveway, I went inside without knocking. Mrs. Worthington was cooking dinner and looked up at me with surprise. "Hello Drew. What are you—"

"Where's my father, bitch!"

"What? He's not here. He left."

98

"How long has this been going on?"

"What are you talking about? Your father and I are just friends," she said, doing her best to look hurt and surprised.

"Fuck you, you stupid whore! Stay away from my family!"

Storming outside, I jumped on my bicycle and peddled home. Part of me regretted what I had just done, and yet I was relieved. Until then I never realized how much I resented my father, but nonetheless, I was glad he wasn't there. I didn't see my father when I got home; instead, my mother was lying on the couch with a beer can resting on her chest. She turned when I walked in. "Where the fuck were you?" she slurred.

"I was at the beach."

"I need you to go down to the market and buy me some more beer."

"Buy your own beer," I said, going upstairs and locking myself in my room.

Later that night when my father came home, I was in my room sitting on the bed and listening to music when he burst through the door angrily, splintering the lock off the wall and shutting off my stereo violently. "Who the hell are you to say something like that to my friends!" he yelled. His body shook with rage and his eyes were wild. I backed away from him in fear. "Who the hell are you to upset a nice lady like Mrs. Worthington with something that's not even true!"

"Don't you listen to him, Drew! Every word you said is true," my mother said standing in the doorway in her nightgown, looking nearly sober.

"It is not," my father said. "All he did was upset a very nice woman."

"You mean a very nice relationship," my mother said.

"Bullshit!" my father said, his voice quaking with anger.

"Fuck you, David! I want a divorce," she said, leaving the

99

room. My father followed her down the hall. Their door slammed and lots of screaming and yelling flooded the house. Finally my father ran down the front stairs, and starting his car, he left the driveway, his tires squealing as he pulled out of the driveway. My body shook as I sat down on my bed, and I wondered if my parents were through. Part of me never wanted to see him again; he was so brutal and mean. But another part of me loved him dearly, and desperately wanted his love and approval. Fat chance I'd ever get that now…

The next day we went to my grandmother's house without my father. My grandfather greeted us at the door just as always. He kissed all the girls and firmly shook hands with the men. A short man with thinning, red hair, his eyes reflected his cantankerous nature, and he had a habit of looking away during conversations. I avoided him when possible. My mother didn't drink the whole day; I guess the shock of losing her husband temporarily sobered her up. She had made a big deal about how I stood up to him, and that I was becoming such a fine, strong man, but I still felt rather shell shocked.

Once everyone got settled in a bit, my grandfather asked me to take a walk with him in the yard, and I obediently obliged. We walked down the steep yard below the dogwood trees almost to the edge of the property, where the holly trees clung to the edge of the riverbank, overlooking the wide and peaceful Naversink River.

"You know, Drew, I always liked your father," he said finally. "We had our problems at first, but I think he's a good man. I hate to see your parents end up this way."

"I'm not happy about it either, but that's the way it is."

"That's what I want to talk to you about, Drew. I don't want to see your parents split up."

"What do you want me to do about it?"

"I want you to get them back together," he said. "It's your responsibility to see that they don't split up."

"How's it my responsibility? I don't think it's such a good idea they stay together. They don't get along at all anymore."

His face contorted with disgust. "For some reason, I expected more out of you."

He turned away from me and started for the house. He could be such a mean, old bastard. We never spoke about it again.

After dinner Aunt Tess announced she was going to Rome for a month to renew her portfolio. My heart leapt into my throat. I wished so much to go with her.

"Tess! Drew has a girlfriend in Rome," my mother said with a sly smile.

"Is that right, Drew? What's her name?"

"Alexandra. Alexandra Cavalletti," I said.

"Did you meet her in school?" she asked, grinning.

"Yes. She's taking English classes at the American School for the summer."

"Does she live in the city, or on the outskirts somewhere?"

"I don't know," I replied. "Probably on the outskirts. Her father is a horse trader."

"A horse trader," barked my grandfather. "What kind of man is a horse trader?"

"No worse than a stock trader," my grandmother replied, and my grandfather muttered something under his breath. I chuckled. She could be really funny at times.

"Tess, why don't you take Drew with you for a couple of weeks," my grandmother suggested.

"That's a marvelous idea," my mother said.

"No arguments here!" I added, my smile now stretching all the way across my face.

"I think I could fit that into my plans for a week or two, as

101

long you don't complain about being on your own, since I'll be mostly working."

I can visit with Alexandra! I couldn't believe this was happening. All my dreams were coming true. I wished I could tell Axel about this new development. All three of my sisters scowled at me with total contempt.

"Why does he get to go to Europe while the rest of us are stuck here in this hell hole," Gretchen muttered.

"My sentiments exactly," my grandfather replied, sipping at his demitasse.

"Now, Roy, hush!" my grandmother said.

Being the only boy in the family had its benefits, although I felt bad for my sisters. Things were going to get rough around here.

"Don't you guys worry," my mother told my sisters. "I have a little vacation planned just for us," she said.

My mother talked animatedly about her plans to rent a summer cottage in Martha's Vineyard for a couple weeks. My sisters smiled and looked hopeful, and I felt better about going to Europe without them. Actually I really didn't care; I was going to Italy to see Alexandra, and could hardly wait.

Chapter 7

I stepped off the plane and nearly choked on the heat blast, pulling at my shirt to keep some air between the fabric and my skin. How could anyone stand this? We caught a cab from the airport to our hotel. August in Rome was stifling, and I squirmed in my seat, wishing the cab was air-conditioned. We arrived just after lunch, and noticing all the shops were closed, I thought it was a holiday. However, Aunt Tess explained they close for siesta at 1:00 and reopen at 5:00. The idea seemed so humane, especially in this heat.

Our hotel was almost in the city center, near *La Sapienza* University, on *Via dei Volsci,* not far from the train station. My room overlooked the courtyard of an old church, which, according to my aunt, was built in the fifteenth century. I could see the bell tower from my window.

"Aunt Tess. This is beautiful!"

She smiled at me and stroked my cheek. "There is nothing like Italy to bring out your deepest passions and artistic tendencies. I've always considered the Italians to be the greatest artists in the world. It's a shame their culture has been twisted up by so much bad politics over the years." She began unpacking all her camera equipment and paintbrushes.

"Are you here to paint or take pictures?"

"Both. I use the brush to capture the essence of what I want to paint and fill in the details from photographs. As much as I'd like to I can't stay here forever."

"What are you going to paint?"

"Whatever catches my eye. I'm going to try my hand at some of the offbeat architecture on some of the charming side streets that weave through the main thoroughfares. Some of it is so charming and utterly fascinating. Drew, I'm exhausted. I'm going to lie down for a bit before dinner. Italians usually eat at about 8:00 or 9:00. Can you wait that long?"

"I think so."

"Why don't you take a walk around the area," she said, patting me on the cheek and giving me a kiss.

I took the elevator down to the lobby. Lots of maps of the city and brochures for guided tours sat in racks near the front desk, and when I spoke to Alexandra, she promised me the grand tour of Rome. I couldn't wait to see her. Should I give her a call? She told me she'd get in contact with me once we got settled, but I didn't want to seem too eager.

A strong blast of heat hit me when I left the comfort of the hotel—a dry heat, and not quite as strong as it was earlier. Most of the shops were still closed, but people were about. I walked down the street in awe. The architecture was so ornate and magnificent, but it was the people that fascinated me the most. Italians looked so much more fashionable than Americans. Young men, not much older than I, strolled down the street arm in arm. They wore shiny leather shoes with fashionably high heels. Their pleated pants were held high on their waists with thin leather belts. The fruity, sweet smell of their cologne wafted toward me as they walked by, and I felt out of place in my corduroys and t-shirt. I'm sure I stood out like any American would.

The women all seemed so exotic and beautiful. The Mediterranean types had such beautiful, olive-colored skin and thick, dark hair. Some had dark green eyes—like cats—and were so beguiling.

Hearing Italian spoken in the street fascinated me. I understood nothing, but could discern specific words. Some of them were very similar to French and even English, but for the most part I was lost.

I walked up *via Tiburtina* toward *Città Universitaria*. The Coliseum stuck out of the horizon in the distance, and I couldn't wait to get a closer look, as well as seeing some of the cathedrals I had read so much about in school. No wonder Aunt Tess loved it here.

I walked pretty far, not going anywhere in particular. As the day ended, the heat subsided a bit, and people began filtering out of their homes into the street. Shops opened their doors for business and the city came alive. Even New York City on a Sunday morning was not quite as deserted up until this moment. I headed back to the hotel. Aunt Tess was sitting in the lobby, reading a magazine.

"You have a message, *Signore*," the concierge said, handing me an envelope. Handwritten on fine stationary; it was a formal and polite luncheon invitation from Alexandra's mother. A car would be sent to collect us tomorrow afternoon at 1:00 pm. I showed it to Aunt Tess. She showed me how to reply, and I handed it back to the concierge.

"*Grazie, Signore*," he said, handing the envelope to a bell-hop.

"Did you bring a proper jacket, Dear?" Aunt Tess asked.

"I brought a blue blazer."

"We have time to take care of those details later. Are you hungry?"

"I'm starving!"

"We're having dinner with an old American friend of mine in from Switzerland. You'll enjoy her. She paints wonderful night-club scenes."

We took a cab to a small restaurant near *Piazza Santa Maria* in *Trastevere*. Evening was falling when we arrived, and the street lamps illuminated the *piazza* with a soft, warm glow. Local artists and craftsmen were packing up their wares—pottery and paintings

105

in the back of trucks and cars. The restaurant was small, smoky, dark, and crowded. We stood near the bar at the front of the restaurant. Most everyone wore blue jeans and t-shirts, or cotton skirts with open sandals.

"Tess! Oh, my God! Tess!" a woman from the darkness somewhere cried out, and soon came running over. "It's been ages! It's so good to see you!" she said, giving my aunt a big hug.

"How are you, Christa? You look wonderful! Are you still giving these Italian men a run for their money?"

"I think so," she replied. "Half of them don't know when they are coming or going." The two of them cackled like school-girls when they laughed.

"Christa, I'd like to introduce you to my nephew, Drew. Drew this is Christa."

"It's nice to meet you, Drew."

"You too," I replied, shaking her hand.

Her blond hair and blue eyes gave the impression she had just walked off the beach in Southern California, and her faded jeans were stained with oil paints. Her smile all but glowed in the darkness. No wonder Italian men chased her around so much. We were showed to our table.

"So, I have set up a space for you in my studio, and tomorrow I'm taking you to an art-supply store to get you whatever you need," she said.

"I don't need much. I didn't bring an easel. I just couldn't bear the thought of lugging it around the airports."

"I have one you can use. You should count your blessings you work with watercolors. The price of good oil paints has sky-rocketed here. I had to give up smoking and drinking just to afford to buy paint."

"Well, at least you have your vices in order," Aunt Tess said.

"Are you a painter Drew?" Christa asked.

"Drew is a writer," Aunt Tess said. I blushed. I didn't consider myself a real writer, even though I liked the attention it brought me.

"A writer!"

"Drew has a girlfriend here," Aunt Tess said, crinkling her nose and winking at me. "We have a luncheon date tomorrow afternoon."

Again I blushed.

"Where does she live?"

"*Il Castello Baronale di Collalto Sabino*," Aunt Tess said with a grin.

Christa's eyes widened slightly, and her mouth dropped open. "What's her name?"

"Alexandra. Alexandra Cavalletti," I replied. I liked saying her name, and I realized I was beginning to incorporate some of the singsong nuances from the Italian I heard being spoken around me. "Do you know her?"

"Oh, I know of the family," she said.

"Really?"

"Yes. Have you been to their home before?"

"No, why?"

"Well, let's just say they live in a beautiful place I think you'll enjoy."

I was curious about her reaction. She seemed surprised when Aunt Tess told her where Alexandra lived, and then I remembered what Axel told me about her father, and wondered about who her family really was.

The conversation turned to books and art. Christa, using her flawless Italian, ordered food for all of us, and we drank lots of wine. My aunt spoke it surprisingly well, but was not conversational. It had been a long day, and now with Aunt Tess and me beginning to get drunk, we took a cab back to the hotel.

The next morning Aunt Tess examined my clothes. "The jacket will do, but don't you have a decent tie?"

"I have to wear a tie?"

"I would highly recommend it. You do want to make a good impression."

She took me to a small men's shop and we picked out a nice tie and some new shoes. Aunt Tess bought a basket of flowers to present to Alexandra's mother. "You never show up to somebody's house empty handed," she explained.

I felt pretty spiffy. That afternoon, a uniformed driver greeted us politely and helped Aunt Tess into a waiting car. I got in beside her, and we started for Alexandra's house. Butterflies fluttered around in my stomach, and I couldn't decide if I was excited or scared. I expected Alexandra and her parents to show up; I certainly wasn't expecting a chauffeured limousine.

We headed east on a big highway towards *Tivoli*. The congested city soon became countryside and rolling hills, covered with golden wheat fields and colorful vineyards. Gradually, the rolling hills became steeper. We traveled for at least forty minutes before exiting the throughway and heading toward *Collalto Sabino*, with the car weaving up a narrow road through a small village. A medieval stone castle sat at the top of the mountain, surrounded by an imposing wall.

"Aunt Tess, is this where we are going?" I whispered.

She squeezed my hand. "Don't worry. Just be yourself and you'll be fine."

The driver stopped the car inside a big wooden gate and let us out. The surrounding mountains loomed in the distance, while below us small villages and farmland stretched all the way back toward Rome. The air was much cooler up here, and smelled of farmland and cattle. I looked up at the almost impenetrable walls towering high above us in amazement, expecting to see soldiers walking among the parapets. We were led to a large cobblestone courtyard. Before us were two sets of stone steps leading up to two great wooden doors. Going up, the door opened and a uniformed servant asked us in. Alexandra and her mother were standing in the foyer. Alexandra wore a simple white dress made from fine linen, with a delicate pattern embroidered down the front and a smile. "Hello Drew!" she said, walking quickly over to me, taking my hands and kissing me on both cheeks. "Drew, this is my mother."

Signora Cavalletti was a pretty woman, with dark, wavy hair and brown eyes like her daughter's, but other than that, they didn't look so much alike; her mother was taller and her features were sharper. Her dress looked conservative, but she seemed very well mannered and kind.

"How do you do?" I asked. "This is my Aunt Theresa."

Aunt Tess handed her the basket of flowers. "Nice to meet you both," she said.

"Please, come in. My husband will join us shortly. He and my son are on their way back from Rome," she said, leading us into a cozy salon with matching divans.

The inside of the castle didn't look anything like the exterior. The tall, stone walls and parapets seemed so foreboding when we approached, but once inside the atmosphere was luxurious and warm. Each room we passed had a fireplace. I tried not to show my surprise. Alexandra sat next to her mother on the divan across from us. She smiled at me teasingly every so often, but not so her mother would notice. Aunt Tess did, I was sure. I was nervous around adults to begin with, but to be in a place like this with my girlfriend's mother made me sweat, and my shirt became damp beneath my blazer.

"*Signora*, this is a beautiful place," Aunt Tess said. "Has this castle been in your family long?"

"Thank you. Call me Isabella," she said. "Yes. My husband inherited it several years ago from his brother. It was in terrible condition. We spent a fortune restoring it."

"It's beautiful," I repeated, not knowing what else to say.

Mrs. Cavalletti looked over at me and smiled. "So, tell me, Drew. How do you like Switzerland?"

"I love it there."

"It's too cold," Alexandra said, shivering and rubbing her arms.

"Alexandra told me she treated you to your first taste of Swiss chocolate," her mother said, smiling. Her eyes had such a friendly twinkle in them.

I laughed. "I'll never look at chocolate the same again," I said. "And neither will my sisters, once I gave them some from the box you sent me. Thank you, Alexandra."

"You're welcome," she said. "I'll make sure to send you home with some more."

"Alexandra, why don't you show Drew around," her mother suggested.

"Sure, Mom. Would you like to see the castle?" she asked.

"I'd love to," I replied.

Alexandra stood up and motioned for me to follow. Mrs. Cavalletti smiled at me as I excused myself politely, and my aunt nodded at me and winked. My tension eased a bit when we left the room.

Alexandra eyed me with concern. "Are you okay, Drew?"

"Yes, I'm fine. I'm just a little intimidated by my surroundings. You didn't tell me you lived in a castle."

"Oh, please, it's nothing. Anyway, almost every American who comes here has just about the same reaction," she said, caressing my arm. Her touch reassured me. "Let me show you around."

The castle was horseshoe shaped. We went down a spiral, stone staircase to the first floor. I never saw so many rooms. On the ground floor, a *tavernetta* with a small kitchen opened into a flagstone patio, overlooking the valley. Next to it was a large auditorium, which seemed out of place.

"My father uses it for various reasons," Alexandra explained. "But it's also used for tours."

"Tours?"

"Yes. We have to open the castle to the public a few times per month to allow people to see the history. It's the law here."

"Doesn't that invade your privacy?"

"You get used to it," she said with a sigh. "Besides, we try not to be here on those days anyway."

She took me back up to the second floor where a large billiard room was on one end of the horseshoe.

"We have a billiard room," I told her. "The table is an antique. It's all hand-carved mahogany with crocheted pockets. Do you play?"

"Not very well. My brother likes to play. Maybe you and he could play sometime."

As she showed me the library my face lit up. I looked out the big windows over the valley. The surrounding mountains were covered with grapevines, which workers carefully pruned in the afternoon sun. Here the light flowed into the room generously, illuminating the leather-bound books with a soft, golden glow. The wall moldings and ceiling coffers were hand-carved with exquisite detail, and a large table with four chairs sat near the middle of the room.

Alexandra smiled at me and caressed my arm. I had a feeling this was one her favorite places. I studied the books that lined the shelves. Many of them were museum pieces—first editions

111

of rare books in French and Italian, and some English books as well. I imagined myself toiling away for hours in this room, writing great works of fiction.

Alexandra slipped her hand around my waist and kissed me gently. I kissed her back—deeper this time. She responded by holding me tighter, and we could both feel my excitement rising. She just smiled.

"We'd better move on," she said, taking my hand.

She showed me the rest of the rooms on that floor before making our way back to the salon where Aunt Tess and her mother were sitting, chattering away like old friends. My erection still hadn't died down completely, and it stuck out to one side at half-mast. Her mother noticed and shook her head as my cheeks became hot from shame and embarrassment. It was then we heard a man's footsteps clomp up the stairs.

"Finally! Your father is here," she said to Alexandra.

A tall man with gray hair came into the room, his presence not only filling where we were, but nearly the entire castle. In his early seventies, his wavy, gray hair was combed toward the back of his head, revealing a nicely shaped forehead and soft, brown eyes. He had a broad chest, and his strong physique bulged through his summer suit.

"Well now, it seems we have visitors," he said in a booming, cheery deep voice punctuated by just a hint of an Italian accent.

"Giorgio! I had nearly given up hope that you would be done on time to be back here to meet our guests. I'd like to introduce you to Theresa Cox and her nephew, Drew Smith."

"Hello," he said, as he walked over to us, kissing my aunt's outstretched hand. He had such an easy smile and handsome face it was impossible not to like him. I rose to my feet. "Drew," he said, turning to me and giving me a firm handshake. "I've heard a

112

lot about you. Alexandra tells me you are quite a writer."

"Thank you, Sir," I said. "The pleasure is all mine."

It was then that Alexandra's brother, Claudio, walked in. While not as tall as his father, he was probably the most striking young man I had ever seen. His features were so delicate and beautiful he looked as though his face was something carved by Michelangelo. He had dark eyes like Alexandra's, but without the sparkle. Although polite, he had an air of quiet broodiness that dampened his good looks. Nonetheless, he fascinated me.

Lunch was called, and Alexandra's mother showed us to the dining room. The table was set with fine china and silver, with the fireplace filled with fresh flowers for the summer. Once seated, white-gloved servants poured us wine. I noticed that Alexandra's family name graced the label.

"Is this wine from your vineyard?" I asked.

"Yes," her father said. "I hope you enjoy it; it's one of our best vintages."

"Well, then, I'd like to make a toast," Aunt Tess said, raising her glass. "Here's to meeting you all and to being in Italy."

"It's a pleasure having you," said Alexandra's mother.

I was not used to having wine with lunch. I took a small sip from my glass; it was a light white wine, slightly chilled.

"So, you are a painter," her father said to Aunt Tess as the white-gloved servants brought out the first course—*prosciutto e melone*. It looked delicious. I took my cues from my aunt, never picking up any of the utensils until she did. This worked out well, although I felt as though Alexandra's mother was scrutinizing my table manners. Her father seemed to take everything in stride, and his easygoing manner put me at ease.

"Yes. I do watercolor. I'm here to broaden my horizons a bit after having spent the last few years painting landscapes where I live."

"And where might that be?"

"A town called Naversink, in New Jersey," Aunt Tess said.

"Naversink?" he exclaimed, beaming. "I know it well – that's where they have that annual steeplechase at Haskell's Estate."

"Why, yes! You've been to one of those?" Aunt Tess asked, clearly surprised by his answer.

"About two years ago. John Haskell brought me along. What a marvelous time."

"We call it the hunt meet. It's an annual tradition in those parts. How well do you know the Haskell's?"

"He's a big client. I've done a lot of business with him. The man sure loves his horses," he said, shaking his head and smiling.

"Isn't that marvelous!" Aunt Tess said. "It's such a small world! Do you come to the States often?"

"Most of my business is in the States."

"Have you been to Rumson?" I interjected myself into the conversation, hoping it would not be considered rude.

"I think so. Isn't that where they have that tennis club with all the grass courts?"

"Sea Bright Lawn Tennis & Cricket Club."

"That's right. I've been there."

"Really! Do you play tennis?"

"I enjoy a game now and then. You know, we have a court here on the grounds. Perhaps you can join us sometime this week?"

"I would love to," I said, happily, and then, "Do you play, Alexandra?" I asked turning to her, but not seeing her sharing in my exuberance

"I try," she said as not much more than a whisper and looking down at her plate.

"She plays a good game when she sets her mind to it," her father said as he put down his fork and gave her the same glance I have seen from my own father many times.

The white-gloved servants cleared our plates and the second course was brought out—*cotolette alla milanese con patatine fritte, fettuccine al pomodoro fresco e basilica e insalata mista.*

"Claudio, Drew has a billiard table," Alexandra said beaming.

"Is that right?" Until now her brother hadn't said a word.

"Your billiard table is beautiful," I said, "Ours is very old, the slate needs to be replaced, and there are also a few rips in the felt."

"Are you any good?" he asked, his eyes narrowing.

"I've been known to sink a ball or two."

"We shall play after lunch then," he said with such a flourish he knew I could not refuse.

"Thank you. I'd enjoy that," I replied, hoping I hadn't just been hustled.

"Tell me, Drew. What does you father do?" Alexandra's father asked, thankfully changing the subject.

"He's in the O-ring business."

"O-rings? What's an O-ring?" Although his English was excellent, he had a few gaps in his vocabulary.

"They are the little rubber O's that you would see in faucets and cars," I replied, making the sign of an O with my thumb and index finger.

"Oh!!!" said Alexandra. Everyone laughed.

"I understand that you deal in horses."

"Mainly, yes."

"Where do you keep them? I didn't notice any stables."

"We don't keep them here. We have a few for pleasure, but the main stables are closer to Rome. Do you like horses?"

"My mother and my sisters love them, but I'm not such a good horseman. We grew up on a small farm before moving to Rumson."

"But you can ride."

"Yes."

"Well, then. I'll take you to see the stables sometime this week. Alexandra loves going there."

"That would be great," I replied. Actually I hoped he didn't expect me to ride. I didn't like horses; they seem so unpredictable and mean. I had been kicked, bitten, and thrown from so many of them I didn't see the point anymore, even though I appreciated their beauty. I'd much rather take my chances on a pair of skis—at least with them I was in control.

Lunch took most of the afternoon. Aunt Tess chatted with Alexandra's parents about art, literature and politics while Alexandra and I flirted subtly. For desert we were served *macedonia di frutta* and *a crostata*. I was stuffed.

We retired to the main salon for coffee. Alexandra and I were considered too young to drink any, even if I enjoyed a cup or two in the mornings. The salon was huge; it probably also served as a ballroom. At the end of the room a small couch and some comfortable chairs sat near an open window, overlooking the valley. Above the couch was a gigantic painting depicting the Parting of the Red Sea. I stared at the painting with fascination. Moses stood in front of the ocean and gestured with his arm, and the water rose on either side, making a path. Aunt Tess saw me gazing at the painting and smiled. "That was created by a famous Italian artist, Luigi Garzi."

"I am impressed," Alexandra's mother said.

"It used to be at Metropolitan Museum of Art," said Aunt Tess. "It was always the first piece that caught my eye whenever I walked into the Rococo Collection."

"It was on loan to them," Alexandra's mother said tersely. "It was actually one of my ancestors that commissioned Garzi to paint it." Her sudden change of tone was surprising.

116

"Well, I think it looks even more spectacular here," Aunt Tess said.

"It is time for our game now," Claudio announced.

"Sure," I said, hoping for more of an invitation than what sounded like a shootout.

"Excuse us," he said and I followed her brother down to the billiard room.

"I'll rack," I offered, putting all the balls on the table.

"What do you want to play?" he asked as he picked up what was obviously his favorite cue stick and applied the chalk diligently.

"Stripes and solids."

"Stripes and solids?" he asked with a smirk I was quickly learning to hate.

"That's where you try to get either all your stripe balls or solid balls in before the other person does. After you finish all your balls then you hit the eight ball in."

He nodded. "Ah, yes. I know that game. Would you like to break?"

"No. Go ahead," I replied. After racking the balls I stood back and watched him carefully line up the cue ball and take his shot. The balls scattered across the table, sinking both a stripe and a solid.

"Why don't you go to *Ecole des Roches* as well?" I asked.

"I go to school here in Rome," he said, taking aim at the two ball sitting near the corner pocket. He hit the ball hard, and the cue ball stopped dead after sinking the ball in the pocket. He was good.

"At the American School?"

"No. I go to a commercial school. I am studying agriculture."

"Why agriculture?"

"My father thought it would be useful. We have a lot of land to manage."

"Are you older or younger than Alexandra?"

"I'm two years older."

Claudio studied the table carefully. Winning in billiards was all about controlling the cue ball. Making a great shot meant nothing if you couldn't make the one after. Although he was good, he hit the ball too hard, which left him somewhat open to chance when it came to his next shot. "Do you have any brothers?" he asked.

"I have three sisters—one older and two younger," I replied.

He finally missed his shot. My turn. The table was wide open. I had a nice run, and I sank five balls to his three.

Realizing I could easily embarrass him on his own table, he buckled down and focused. He sank all the easy ones within his reach, but a cluster of balls near the middle of the table still needed to be scattered before they could be sunk. His only shot was to bank one of the balls into the side pocket, which would break up the cluster. If he made the shot he would be sitting in a very good position; if not it could be the end of the game. He bent his head down in concentration and hit the ball hard. It zinged off the cushion and went straight into the pocket.

"Great shot," I said.

"Thank you," he said, as if I were telling him something he already knew.

He sank two more balls before coming to the eight ball. It was not an easy shot. He missed. I had two balls left before the eight ball. My only shot was a long, difficult one. I took a deep breath, lined up the cue ball, and tapped it gently; it rolled steadily across the table, knocking my target into the pocket.

"Who's winning?" Alexandra said, walking into the room.

118

"Claudio," I replied. My next shot was easy and I tapped the ball in without difficulty. The cue ball lined up perfectly with the eight ball for an easy shot into the side pocket. Game over.

"Nice game," I said, extending my hand.

"Indeed," he replied with a tone that let me know he was not accustomed to losing.

"Would you like to play another?"

"No, thank you. I have some things to do before I return to Rome with my father."

With a quick, shallow bow, Claudio left and Alexandra turned to me and smiled. "Are you having fun?" she asked, caressing my chest.

"Yes. Lunch was amazing. Do you eat like that everyday?"

"Normally…maybe not as much, but we eat well."

"How do you manage to stay so beautiful?"

"Just lucky, I guess," she said, pulling me to her.

She leaned up against me and kissed me. Her hips pressed against my own, and her hands sent waves of pleasure down my back as she caressed me. Kissing was becoming my favorite pastime. Her breath became heavier as she leaned against me. Slowly I explored her body with my hands. Too scared to do anything brazen, she let me caress her breasts once. We pulled away from each other at the same time, as if we both knew we had better stop before we made each other crazy. Her eyes were wide and filled with desire. She held me close and squeezed me tightly.

"Drew. You have the most wonderful lips."

"Really?"

"Yes. I love the way you kiss."

"I love the way you kiss."

We kissed again briefly. I could hear the adults coming down the hall.

"My parents are giving your Aunt a tour of the castle,"

119

Alexandra said.

"Are there any secret passages?"

She laughed. "Maybe we'd better join them."

We followed her parents through the castle while her mother talked about its history. The castle was built in the early Fourteenth Century and had been largely restored to its original condition, with some minor modifications to make it more comfortable. She talked about all the families that owned it throughout history, and how it came to pass into her husband's hands after the death of his brother. The castle enjoyed a rather peaceful history, with the exception of one unfortunate event in 1861, when it was sacked by robbers and the entire family beheaded; the children's heads were carried about the town on large pikes.

We took a short walk through the garden. Behind the castle, obscured from view by hedges and tall pine trees, was a swimming pool nestled in the hillside. From here the entire valley stretched below us, and the afternoon haze gave the horizon a soft, pastel look. Not far from the pool was a grass tennis court. The grass wasn't as short and springy as the grass courts at home, but it was beautiful and well maintained. I looked forward to playing on it.

Time to go. Alexandra and her mother agreed to pick me up tomorrow morning and take me sightseeing around Rome. We thanked our hosts and were taken to the car. Alexandra gave my shoulder a quick caress as I got in, and Aunt Tess smiled at me tenderly, but her eyes were a little misty.

"Is something wrong, Aunt Tess?"

"No, Dear. Everything is fine," she said. "Alexandra is a wonderful girl," she added. "She has a real natural beauty and intelligence that's simply captivating."

"I think so," I replied with a sigh.

"Her father is quite a man—one of the few Italian aristocrats still surviving in this day and age."

"I liked him. What did you think of her mother?"

"I am not sure what to make of her. She is more of a lady of the house than anything else, but she seems to have a good handle on things. Her brother seemed a bit of an odd sort. What did you make of him?"

"He doesn't talk much, but he seemed nice enough."

That evening we just had a simple dinner at the hotel. Before going to bed, I sat down and wrote Axel a long letter about the day's events, describing in vivid detail where Alexandra lived. I knew he'd be happy for me, and I wished I could see the look of surprise on his face when he read my letter.

Alexandra phoned early the next morning to tell me she and her mother would be in Rome at about 10:30 to pick me up. Aunt Tess and I had a simple breakfast together consisting of cappuccinos and croissants before she left to meet Christa to get art supplies and scout areas of interest for painting.

While waiting for Alexandra I sat in the lobby and wrote a letter to my parents. I was deep in concentration when I felt a kiss on my cheek and she plopped down next to me.

"Good Morning," she beamed.

"And to you as well."

My God in Heaven, she was more beautiful than ever. She wore a light sundress, and her tanned legs were so shapely and smooth. Without thinking I put my hand on her leg and caressed her thigh. She sucked in her breath and sat up straight when I touched her. "Let me put this letter away and I'll be ready in a flash," I said, blushing.

"Take your time," she said, putting her arms around my neck and kissing me on the ear. I didn't realize the ears were so sensitive. Her lips against my earlobe gave me an instant erection.

I noticed the concierge looking at us and was suddenly

121

embarrassed. "We'd better get going," I said, rushing out the words so quickly even I had a problem understanding what I said. "Why don't you wait here a second and I'll put this stuff away."

As I stood, her eyes found my erection bulging in my pants, and she tried to stifle a smile. I wondered if she knew what she did to me, and sometimes did it on purpose.

"Take your time," she said, her face cherry red from blushing.

I took the elevator up to my room, found my camera, and waited a few minutes for my erection to subside. Should I change into a heavier pair of pants? I didn't want her mother to think I was only a life-support system for my penis—even if it were true. I decided not; I didn't want to keep them waiting, and I didn't want to be too hot.

"I'm ready," I told her when I got back down. The air was stifling when we left the hotel. Alexandra didn't seem to mind the heat, but I found it oppressive. Her mother waved us into the car. "Hello, Drew," she said.

"*Buongiorno, Signora*," I replied.

"Very good!" Alexandra said.

"I've been studying a book Aunt Tess gave me on basic Italian."

"What would you like to see, Drew?" her mother asked as we got into the car.

"I am at your disposal," I told her. "Why don't we start with the five-dollar tour and we'll take it from there?"

"Five dollars!" Alexandra said. "You Americans are so cheap!"

"It's just an expression," I said and she smiled.

"Alexandra! Mind your manners," her mother said. "I think we should start with the Coliseum. You will enjoy that."

She told the driver our destination, and we started through

122

the morning traffic. It was not so heavy this time of year. Alexandra, sitting close to me, caught me glancing at her breasts and smiled. She was not like many of the other girls I knew. She seemed really curious about her sexuality, and she didn't try to hide it as if she were ashamed. The Coliseum stood out in the middle of the city like the erection in my shorts. This was going to be a difficult day.

The driver dropped us off in front of the Coliseum. The ancient ruin stood almost 160 feet high. I was amazed that people could build such a magnificent structure so many years ago.

"I have shown this monument to so many people and I never grow tired of it," Alexandra said.

"It's gorgeous!"

"It held more than 50,000 people and there are eighty entrances. It really is a remarkable bit of engineering—even by today's standards. What's really amazing is it only took eight years to build."

"And God knows how many slaves," I replied.

As we entered the Coliseum I imagined the thrill of being a spectator coming to watch the gladiators fight in the afternoon sun.

"Let's start from the top and work our way down," Alexandra's mother suggested.

We climbed the marble steps to the top tier of the structure and looked down upon the arena filled with stone cells and an aisle going down the center.

"They kept the fighters and animals in those cells," Alexandra explained as she pointed to the bottom of the arena. "The floor was made of heavy wood planks and sometimes they removed it and flooded the cells with water to simulate naval battles."

From here I could see most of the ruins on *via dei Fori Imperiali*. The glory that was once ancient Rome. I gazed out over the monuments in wonderment, speechless at the beauty I saw. *"Quamdiu stabit Colyseus stabit et Roma; quamdiu cadet Colyseus cadet et Roma; quamdiu cadet Roma cadet et mondus,"* Alexadra's mother said.

"What does that mean?"

"It's a famous Latin quote. It means: While the Coliseum stands, Rome shall stand; when the Coliseum falls, Rome shall fall; and when Rome falls, so shall the world."

"And the Coliseum still stands," I replied. Interesting that so much importance would be placed on a monument built for the sole purpose of violence. More than 10,000 people had died in that arena, and who knew how many animals, yet it was probably the most celebrated ancient monument in Rome.

We spent most of the morning exploring the structure—from the catacombs to the emperor's seats. Despite the heat I was full of energy. Alexandra tanned every moment she was in the sun. Her skin took on a deep, bronze color that glowed in the sunlight, while I was beginning to burn.

"I need to get out of the sun," I finally said.

As we left the Coliseum and walked toward the car, the chauffeur was waiting outside patiently, and I noticed he was carrying a gun under his jacket. Seeing me notice the firearm, Alexandra said, "Italy can be a dangerous place for a family like ours. The politics here is not always pleasant."

I thought it best not to comment, but wondered if she were in any danger, or if her family was just being overly cautious. Her mother said something to him in Italian, and he walked several steps behind us as we headed towards the *Tempio di Venere e Roma.* Alexandra and her mother paid him no mind, but I couldn't stop thinking about his gun. I wasn't used to being shadowed by an armed bodyguard.

Via dei Fori Imperiali was filled with so many antiquities that it was impossible to see them all in one day. In fact, everywhere I

124

looked some interesting piece of history or art beckoned my attention. Rome had an elegant quality that left me speechless—even the more modern buildings blended with the antiquities with an aesthetic genius I had never seen before.

Alexandra's mother led us down a narrow street to a small restaurant on a shady *piazza* where we sat under a huge tree. I was thankful to be in the shade. The back of my neck prickled from being overexposed to the sun, and my face felt a little hot.

"You need to put some cream on," Alexandra said, reaching into her bag. Her mother ordered a bottle of Bernulli. I never had it before but it was refreshing.

"It comes from Sicily. Mr. Bernulli is a friend of the family. He has a son about Alexandra's age," her mother said, seeing how I was enjoying my drink.

Alexandra handed me the cream and I put some on my face while she spread some on my neck and I tried to decipher the menu.

"I'll order for everyone," her mother offered.

"That would be great, thank you," I replied, since I was afraid I might end up ordering a large tractor with a side of kittens.

"So, what did you think of Rome so far?" Alexandra asked, her smile stretching all the way across her face.

"It's spectacular. I really love it here, even if it is like being in the middle of a baked potato."

Her mother laughed. "You have come during a bad week. It's really not this hot all the time."

"Only the entire month of August," Alexandra said, fanning herself with her hand. "Most people don't come here in August. It's good in a way because the city is not so congested with tourists."

"Things just sort of worked out that way," I said, suddenly

thinking about my parents. I found myself staring at the ground with sadness, wondering if my father was gone from our lives for good. Alexandra picked up on my mood swing and looked at me with concern. It was amazing how perceptive she was at times; at others she just sort of lived for the moment.

"Are you okay, Drew?"

"Yes, I'm fine," I said, managing my best smile. In fact, I was really happy; probably the happiest I had been in years. "I'm really hungry. We really did a lot of walking."

"And you have seen so little," Alexandra said. "Most tourists come here for three days and say they have seen Rome, but that's impossible. There is just too much to see."

"Yes. It's probably not like going to New York. There is a lot to see, but it's not as rich in culture or history as Rome is."

"There is nothing like New York for shopping," her mother said with a smile.

"Didn't you once mention that your family owned Bloomingdale's?" asked Alexandra.

"I don't think they owned it. My grandmother's sister married the president of Bloomingdale's. He was responsible for bringing all the foreign boutiques into the department store. In fact, he does a lot of business in Italy."

"I know Bloomingdale's," her mother said looking wistful. "They have a big department store on Fifth Avenue."

"I think so," I replied. "Every year my grandmother takes us shopping there for school clothes. My sisters all look forward to it."

"I don't like clothes," Alexandra said, frowning.

I was tempted to follow that up with something witty, but decided against it. Her mother, however, could not let it go. "What do you mean, you don't like clothes?"

"I mean that clothes are not that important to me. I love

jewelry and art, but I don't get excited about clothes."

"But you are not a tomboy," I said, as if I were making a general statement about her character.

"No. But I don't mind getting my hands dirty either. I think I would have made a good man." Her mother shook her head and sighed.

"What a waste of a wonderful woman that would have been," I said with a smile. Alexandra burst out laughing and squeezed my arm. Her mother frowned at me. I don't think I was winning a lot of points with her. I got the feeling Alexandra didn't often live up to her mother's expectations, even if she were as nearly perfect as perfect could be.

Lunch was good. We had *penne* in a light cream sauce with sun-dried tomatoes and a salad. Alexandra and I chatted about school and the ridiculousness of some of the more archaic policies, mostly concerning the stringent rules governing girl-boy relationships. On this subject her mother listened with quiet amusement, although I was willing to bet that she agreed with most of the policies. After lunch we headed back toward the car. I was tired from too much sun, and it was time for them to head home.

"Tomorrow my father and I are going to pick you up early to take us to see the horses," said Alexandra. Although I relished the thought of spending the day with Alexandra, the thought of seeing the horses didn't excite me at all. I thanked them for a wonderful day and left. I was really tired, and I went up to my room and slept the rest of the afternoon.

The hotel operator awakened me at 7:00 the next morning. Having some experience around horses, I thought it best to wear a pair of jeans and a t-shirt and forget about the heat. Aunt Tess went out and bought me some sunscreen after seeing my burn, and I stuffed the plastic tube in the pocket of my jeans.

We got down to the lobby just in time to see a car pull up to the hotel and Alexandra get out. Aunt Tess and I went out to greet her.

"Hello!" she said as her father popped out behind her.

"Hello, Theresa. How are you?" he asked.

Aunt Tess and her father chatted for a few minutes while Alexandra and I talked about horses. "Are we going to ride?" I asked.

"If you want to."

"We'll see—"

"Are you afraid of horses?" she asked, looking surprised.

"I'm not afraid…it's just that they can be pretty unpredictable."

"Well, you have to show them who is in control. Point! Once they know who is in control they will do what you want."

"You are probably right," I sighed, remembering what someone told me about animals being able to smell fear. I knew it was true because they seemed just as uneasy around me.

We said goodbye to Aunt Tess and headed toward the outskirts of the city. I thought we were heading back to the castle, but the road we were on was not as wide.

"This is the farm," Alexandra said, gesturing toward acres and acres of wide-open land and some cattle.

"Where are the horses?"

"The horses are up further. This is where we let the cattle graze. We have eighty heads of cattle," her father said.

"That's a lot of cattle. Do you sell them too?"

"No, we use the milk to make cereal for the horses."

Alexandra said, "In Italy we have two types of farms — *scuderia Fonte di Papa* and *allevamento Fonte di Papa*. A *scuderia* is where they run the horses and the *allevamento* is where they breed them. We do both."

It was then that scores of horses ran through the pasture in

128

waves, darting and weaving from side to side as if at the whim and mercy of the wind, while others lazily grazed the grass in the morning sun. I could understand why people loved them so much; they were filled with so much power and grace.

We turned onto a dirt road and headed toward a long, wooden building with a high, shingled roof where the stables were housed. Ceiling fans spun slothfully on each side. The stables looked so new and clean. Further up the road were a small farm-house and a group of buildings where the farmhands stayed.

"How many horses are there?" I asked.

"About 150," Alexandra said and smiled.

While most of the horses were running in the pasture, some grazed in an enclosed paddock. Behind the stables, in a small paddock shaded by a great beach tree, a young man in blue jeans and a cowboy hat was training a colt. The horse was wearing a halter with a long, leather strap. The man stood in the center of the paddock, holding onto the strap, while the colt trotted evenly in a circle around him. He encouraged the horse gently in Italian—an Italian cowboy. I chuckled.

"What's funny?" Alexandra asked, seeing my bemusement.

"Seeing an Italian in a cowboy hat."

"That's Vincenzo. He's the best trainer in all of Europe. He spent many years in America with the some of the top breeders, working with their horses."

He coaxed the colt into a perfect trot. His concentration was total, as if they were one. The car stopped and we got out.

"Alexandra, I have some work to do. Why don't you and Drew take a couple of horses and look over the farm?" her father said.

"What type of horse do you want?" she asked.

"A tame one," I sighed and smiled softly.

"I meant English or Western."

129

"Oh, English—sorry."

I had never ridden Western. My mother taught us all to ride English style. She spoke to a young boy, and within a few minutes, he brought us two horses. Hers was black with a white diamond on its nose, and mine was tan with a dark mane. The boy saddled our horses and I watch mesmerized as Alexandra popped into the saddle gracefully. I looked at my horse hesitantly —obviously a mare with a bit of spirit. I stroked her muzzle and then grabbed hold of the saddle. My foot didn't go into the stirrup very easily and I struggled a bit, causing her to become nervous and take a step or two backward.

"Easy girl," I said, beginning to break into a sweat while Alexandra watched patiently. This time I managed to get my foot in the stirrup and hoisted myself up. I didn't fear horses after all, only a morbid fear of heights. Sitting so high up on the back of an animal that could easily run thirty miles per hour only intensified my fear. I also feared falling, which seemed natural to me, considering the circumstances. My horse stomped and reared a bit, and as she moved, I gripped with my knees, which made her even more uneasy.

"She really is a well-mannered horse," Alexandra said. "Just relax in the saddle a bit and you'll be fine."

I eased the pressure on my knees and took a deep breath. The insides of my thighs were cramping up. A long time had passed since I had been on a horse, and as I relaxed, so did the horse. Alexandra nudged forward toward the gate at the end of the paddock, and my horse followed, with me diligently bouncing along.

Gradually I became more comfortable in the saddle, and let go of my fear a little when breaking into an easy trot as we left the paddock and headed down a narrow trail toward some trees at the end of the pasture. I remembered the riding lessons my

130

mother gave us on how to post during a trot. Alexandra looked so natural in the saddle and made riding look easy, but I just couldn't get the rhythm right, and continued bumping around in the saddle like a sack of potatoes; at times it was painful. The hills, although soft, became more frequent, and we stopped on a ridge overlooking a shallow valley filled with wheat and assorted grains that seemed to stretch on for miles.

"All this land belongs to us," she said beaming with pride.

"I'm impressed. Is it all farmland?"

"Mostly. Further south we own some very famous vineyards. The wine you had was from there."

"Is it true the women take off their shoes and squash the grapes with their bare feet?"

Alexandra laughed. "They still might in some places maybe, but we don't do that anymore. We have machines." She laughed once more; I hoped it wasn't at me.

It might have still been fairly early in the morning, but I could already feel the sun beginning to scorch me, and put on generous amounts of sunscreen. Alexandra seemed to soak up the sun like a sponge. "Follow me," she said. "I know a nice place to go to get out of the sun."

She trotted her horse across the ridge and down a narrow path toward a clump of trees. As we entered into the valley we broke into a canter. Cantering was easier for me than trotting. I just lifted myself out of the saddle slightly and held tightly to the mane. Speed didn't bother me, although I had seen people get thrown from their horses when they would shy away from a jump or other obstacle. There were no obstacles here, and I enjoyed the feel of the wind on my skin as we sped across the terrain toward the trees.

We slowed down and as Alexandra went up a steep grade into the woods, I followed as best I could behind her. In a little clearing was a small, seemingly unoccupied villa with an old fashioned stone-walled well, complete with a bucket hanging from a crossbeam and everything. The valley stretched below us, and I saw the farm in the distance. I felt as if I were standing in some painter's landscape. My aunt would love to be here to capture this I'm sure.

"This house has been in my family for years. It was built in the fifteenth century," she said.

"Does anyone live there?"

"My father sometimes stays here with my mother when they want to get away."

"Really? That's kind of romantic," I said, smiling.

"I think so. My parents are so formal, but sometimes I catch them flirting with each other like teenagers. It's kind of cute."

"My parents spend most of their time avoiding each other," I said, frowning.

"I know a lot of parents like this. I find it so sad."

I just shrugged. "Thanks, but after a while you get used to it. Your father is so much older than your mother. Does that ever bother you?"

"No. Not really. He's a very strong man and nothing seems to slow him down. I know they still enjoy each other quite often."

She laughed as she saw first my puzzled look, and then the change in my expression as what she meant sunk in.

"Oh! Well, then… I hope to be that strong when I am his age," I said.

"Come," she said, dismounting. "Let me show you around."

She held my horse for me while I slid off the saddle. The inside of my legs hurt, and I limped. She laughed when she saw me walking. "You're not a bad rider, but you need to learn how to relax. Horses are for pleasure, not for pain."

"I'll try to remember that later tonight when I'm soaking in the tub."

We hitched our horses next to the well and pumped some fresh water into the attached trough. Alexandra found an old-fashioned key hidden in the knothole of a tree and opened the door. The place was small and comfortable. The flagstone floor was adorned with various throw rugs, and the walls covered with colorful tapestries. A simple wood table stood in the kitchen, and a large, stone fireplace was against the center wall with a couple of comfortable chairs in front. A wood ladder led to a loft.

"How often do they come here?"

"Not that often. Mostly in the fall and winter."

She showed me around. The kitchen had been modernized a bit, and was well outfitted. It looked as though someone came to clean every so often. She led me up to the loft and opened the French windows on the far wall, letting in a nice cross breeze. I could see why her parents liked coming here to get away; the atmosphere was easy and comfortable. Except for the occasional rustling in the trees, hardly a noise was heard.

The big bed was covered with a thick goose-down comforter, and the sheets looked cool and soft. Alexandra walked up to me and caressed my arms. I put my arms around her and kissed her.

"I like you, Drew," she said as our lips parted. "You are a sweet and tender boy."

"I like you too. You are different from most girls. You seem so fearless and open. I love your honesty."

She kissed me gently and pushed me onto the bed, and as I lay on my back she straddled me. Without a word she unbuttoned her shirt and undid her bra. I watched in amazement, and could barely believe what was happening. I cupped my hands around her breasts; touching them made me more excited than I thought possible. She lay down beside me and we kissed—a deep

133

kiss that made me feel like I was almost a part of her. After a while she helped me take off my t-shirt, and I held her next to me, caressing her soft skin. I knew she felt as awkward and inexperience as I, but it felt so good it didn't matter. As I kissed her breasts, her hand moved between my legs, and as our excitement grew we rolled around the bed until she suddenly stopped and sat straight up, her eyes were wild with desire.

"I am a virgin, Drew."

"So am I."

She looked at me with her mouth slightly open and one eyebrow raised, and then got off the bed, unbuttoned her pants and slipped them off. Her legs were shapely and beautiful. She stood over me and began unbuttoning my fly. As she worked her way down my whole body throbbed with excitement. I helped her pull them off and we lay on the bed next to each other in our underwear. Almost instinctively I got between her legs and we grinded our hips together as we kissed. After a few minutes I felt her pulling off my underwear.

"Wait! We can't do this," I said, rolling off her.

"Not to worry," she said, opening the drawer of the nightstand. She held up a box of rubbers and smiled.

It was mid-morning by the time we were finished. Covered with sweat, we drifted into sleep briefly, both of us happy and comfortable in each other's arms.

Alexandra stirred first and tenderly kissed me awake "We'd better get going before they come looking for us," she said.

I could imagine the look on her father's face if he found me in bed with his underage daughter, and my subsequent slow and painful death. I wanted to spend the rest of the day with her in bed. Her legs and arms were wrapped around me tightly and her body was almost glued to mine. Her demeanor in bed was so different from how she was in public. She was almost childlike in bed, but in public she comported herself with so much dignity and grace it was impossible to imagine she was so passionate. I held in my arms tenderly, happy to have had the opportunity to see both sides of her. As I pulled myself up she put her arms around my waist and pulled me back down. We made love quickly one more time.

We rode back another way—through open fields with tall grass. We ran almost at a full canter until the stables came into view and then slowed to an easy trot. I could see Alexandra smiling as she watched me ride. I finally found my rhythm, and my fear of riding was gone.

"I'll race you to the gate," she said.

Jabbing my heels into my horse, I took off like a bolt of lightning. Alexandra was right beside me as we approached the gate. Her father watched us bolting across the field and smiled.

"You must have ridden pretty far," he said.

"Yes, Papa. Almost to the vineyards."

"Did you enjoy yourself, Drew?"

"Yes, Sir. Very much so," I replied. If he only knew how much.

He looked up at me and smiled. Could he tell what happened? Parents had a sixth sense about these things. We dismounted and walked our horses over to the stable.

"We are going back to Collalto for lunch," he said once we rejoined him. "Afterward I'll drop you both off in Rome to do some sightseeing. Your mother will pick you up at the Spanish Steps at 6:00."

"Yes, Papa," she said as I felt her hand on my butt and she gave me such a squeeze that my hips suddenly lurched forward. Thank God her father didn't see.

We left the farm and headed for the castle. Lunch was not quite as formal as the last time since there was only Alexandra, me, and her parents. I still felt a little out of place. I couldn't get used to being waited on by servants. Lunches at our house consisted of whatever we could find.

Despite my discomfort, Alexandra and I exchanged playful glances. Her mother noticed the change in our interaction, and her expression became increasingly serious. Her father seemed to be having a good time, giving the impression he really liked me.

"Drew, going out of the paddock you looked pretty stiff, but coming back you seemed to be enjoying yourself more," he commented. Alexandra blushed slightly.

"I normally don't like horses when I first get on them. But today I think I have come to terms with my fear of them."

"That's wonderful," he said. "What do you think did it for you?"

"Alexandra," I replied. "She showed me how to relax in the saddle, and then I just found my rhythm. After that I just applied everything my mother taught me about riding."

Alexandra looked at me with an impish grin, and I felt my face flush.

"Is your mother a good horsewoman?" he asked.

"When she was young, yes. She used to ride in all the local foxhunts. She was also a champion jumper. All my sisters have been blooded."

"Blooded?" her mother asked, looking surprised.

"That's when the blood of the fox is smeared on your face after your first hunt to show your accomplishment."

"It's a disgusting tradition," Alexandra said.

"I don't think they do it anymore. In fact I think they let the fox go after they catch it."

"I take it then that you were never blooded?" her father asked.

"No Sir, I've never been in a hunt."

"Do your sisters compete as well?"

"No. They just ride for fun. My sister Annie loves horses more than anything in the world. When she's not riding she paints pictures of them, and she's really pretty good."

"Then artists run in your family," her mother said.

"I don't know about that," I said. "My mother was a journalist, and my aunt is a painter, but I don't think we are a very artistic family." I remembered that my grandmother had studied fine art at Vassar. She never used her skills, and from what I understood she was quite good. Why didn't she paint anymore?

"Drew, your writing is beautiful," Alexandra said. "If you keep writing the way you do you will be famous someday."

"Do you really think so?"

"Yes, I do. She said. "Your writing is so vivid and full of passion. You remind me of a famous Italian journalist that everyone loves so much because his words have the ability to touch everyone."

"I do?" I asked, wide-eyed.

"Yes. Your style is so simple and elegant, and reading your descriptions is like watching a movie. They literally jump off the page at you."

Alexandra had never lavished so much praise on me, and she hated compliments. Her words made me feel blessed. It was then I realized I had fallen so deeply in love with her it would last the rest of my life. Her parents suddenly became silent, and I did my best to keep from blushing out of shame and embarrassment.

After lunch we dropped her father off at the farm, and then Alexandra and I continued to Rome. We sat in the back of the car together with our hands entwined, and the chauffer kept checking on us in his rearview mirror to make sure we weren't doing anything inappropriate. I doubted we would get many opportunities to be alone again. The way her mother looked at me when I said goodbye made me feel like a common thief just caught and on his way to jail.

"What do you want to see, Drew?" she asked.

"I don't know. I've seen a lot of the ruins. I'd like to see some art."

"I know just the place. We'll go to the Vatican."

The line to get into the Vatican Museums took nearly two hours, but it was well worth the wait once we climbed the great spiral ramp to the museum floor. Every square inch of the Vatican galleries were covered with spectacular frescoes, tapestries and paintings, and I could not understand how anybody would not appreciate such an enormous gesture to mankind. The Gallery of Maps and the Library caught my interest the most until we entered the Sistine Chapel.

I had seen some beautiful churches, but nothing compared to the Sistine Chapel. The rule of silence there was moot for me because I was speechless by Michelangelo's genius. His frescos were the most amazing art I had ever seen by any human being. We stood quietly and gazed at the walls and ceiling for several minutes while throngs of people squeezed past us.

As much as I appreciated the immense beauty, the atmosphere was filled with so much religious supplication it almost suffocated me. I never knew how to behave in a church. I had long since rejected Christianity, but always felt guilty about it. My mother's family was Episcopal, and my father's family was Jewish. We were brought up Episcopalian, and every Sunday my father forced us to go to service where he was an usher. I don't know why he'd want to be an usher, or why he'd want to go to church at all. My mother insisted it was only so he could get into the good graces of the local society.

After spending at least four hours in the museum I was

beginning to get a headache from too much stimulus, and my neck was growing sore from looking up at the ceilings all afternoon.

"Let's get out of here," Alexandra whispered. "Too much Catholicism makes me nervous."

"I'm ready when you are."

We left Vatican City and went to a small bar to get something to drink. Alexandra ordered a bottle of water and a *panino* for me.

"That was an amazing experience. Never in my life have I seen so much beautiful artwork," I told her. "What are your feelings about the Church?" I knew her family was Catholic, but they seemed pretty liberal.

"It's stupid. So many poor Catholic countries are kept in poverty because of the policies of the Church. Their issue on birth control really makes me mad."

"Do you believe in God?"

"I don't know," she said, shaking her head and frowning. "Life is filled with so much beauty. It had to come from somewhere, but I don't accept the Christian version of God. If there is a God I think He'd be much more elegant."

"I've felt that way since I was thirteen," I said. "When I was in Sunday school, all the lessons we learned just sounded like silly fairy tales to me. I was always so amazed when all the other children just accepted what they were told as fact."

"That must have been difficult for you."

"No, not really… I asked a lot of questions, and spent a lot of time with our priest having one-on-one discussions about God and religion, but he never convinced me. The one ingredient that made it all work was faith, and I just never had it. It's funny how they all finally gave up on me and left me alone. Most of them don't even talk to me anymore."

139

"The same thing happened to my father. He used to go to church everyday with his mother, but when he was old enough to make his own decisions he stopped going, and lost a lot of friends."

"He doesn't seem any worse for it."

"He's not, and neither am I," she said. "I have a lot of friends who live their lives according to the laws of the church, and some of them are the unhappiest people I know."

I was happy she shared my views. It was a sore issue with some of my friends, and I had learned to hide my views on religion before they turned into heated discussions or even arguments.

"We'd better get going," Alexandra said, looking at her watch. We took a cab to the Spanish Steps where her mother was going to meet us. Alexandra sat between my knees on the step below me and I held her in my arms. She caressed my forearms while we talked about school. Now that we were a couple it was going to be a really interesting semester for both of us, and I looked forward to it more than anything in the world.

Her mother's car finally appeared, and I was dropped off at the hotel.

"I will call you later, Drew," Alexandra said, her eyes filled with tenderness.

I squeezed her hand gently. "Thanks for everything." I wanted so much to kiss her goodbye, but with her mother there I thought better of it.

Later that evening Alexandra called. We didn't talk long, giving me the impression she didn't like telephones. She invited me to Collalto tomorrow afternoon for lunch and tennis. Her father would pick me up at the hotel at 1:00, and I went to bed feeling so much joy I wasn't sure how I'd ever get to sleep.

The next morning Aunt Tess and I sat in a small café near the hotel having a breakfast of cappuccinos with fresh bread and jam. I was becoming addicted to cappuccinos.

"Aunt Tess, what do you think would be an appropriate gift for me to get Alexandra?"

"A gift should always be appropriate for the occasion," she said. "What did you want to express?"

"I'm in love," I blurted out.

Aunt Tess pursed her lips and eyed me seriously a moment. "Well, for someone your age it shouldn't be anything too extravagant. Does she feel the same way?"

"I'm pretty sure she does. If not, I know she has strong feelings for me."

"Why don't you write her a poem?"

"I'm always writing her poems," I replied. "What if I got her something simple—like a plain gold locket with an inscription?"

"That's a good idea. I'll tell you what. After breakfast we'll go shopping and see what we can find."

Aunt Tess and I inquired about jewelry stores with the hotel concierge. He recommended a small shop not far from the hotel, and we set off through the streets to find the perfect locket for my first love. The heat finally broke, and the air seemed a bit softer. It was a nice day for tennis.

The jewelry store was small but nice. The *padrone* spoke good English and was very sympathetic to my request. He showed me some gold lockets of varying shapes and sizes, but the one that caught my eye was different from the rest. Small and heart shaped, it was weaved from gold leaves that looked like rose petals. It was very delicate and beautiful.

"What do you think of it?" I asked Aunt Tess.

"It's lovely," she said. "I'm sure she would adore it. How much is it?"

The price was well out of my range, but Aunt Tess offered

to pay for it in return for some lawn work on the riverbank when we got back. I agreed, and the locket was wrapped in tissue and put in a velvet box.

"Would you like an inscription?" the *padrone* asked.

"Please" I replied, handing him a piece of paper with the inscription I wanted.

"Very good, *Signore*. When do you need it?"

"I'd like it this morning, if possible."

"Give me two hours. I will do the inscription myself."

Aunt Tess headed off to the studio, and I went back to the hotel to write a letter to Axel. So much had happened, I wrote nearly ten pages. Putting on a nice pair of pants and a clean shirt, I packed my tennis clothes in a small travel bag and walked back to the jewelry store.

When I entered the *padrone* nodded politely and showed me the locket. The inscription read: "*Ti amerò sempre* – Drew". I will love you always – Drew. I used the book Aunt Tess had given me to find the words in Italian.

"Would you like it gift-wrapped?" the *padrone* asked, tucking the locket neatly back into the box.

I thought about it a moment and declined since the box itself was beautiful enough. Slipping it into my pocket I headed back to the hotel to find Alexandra's father and brother already waiting.

"Hello, Drew," said *Signore* Cavalletti.

"Hello," I replied, shaking their hands. "Sorry I'm late. I was running an errand."

"You are right on time. Hop in and we'll get going."

Claudio sat in the car quietly while his father talked about the horses, occasionally nodding attentively. He seemed like a nice, easy-going boy, but I couldn't make heads or tails of him. He didn't show his emotions at all. He seemed bright enough, but his lack of interaction was out of character with the rest of the family.

"Alexandra tells me you went to see the Vatican yesterday. Did you enjoy it?" *Signor* Cavalletti asked.

"Yes. I did. Now I know where all the good art is kept."

He burst out laughing.

"The Vatican owns a lot of treasures. A lot of it is not even open to the public," said Claudio.

"I can believe that. I've heard that the Catholic Church owns more real estate than any organization in the world," I said.

His father nodded. "The Church is a very powerful organization, but its influence has been declining in recent years. There seems to be a general rebellion against some its policies."

"That might be true in America and Western Europe, but in many third-world countries the Church is still a very powerful," Claudio added.

"And that will probably always remain true," agreed his father.

Father and son talked about religion and politics. Claudio was well schooled on the subjects. His father was so full of energy and life he almost enveloped you in it while Claudio was more reserved. Although not meek, he was simply reticent, and kept me guessing about his character.

We arrived at the castle well before lunch. When we walked inside I saw Alexandra waiting by the door. She looked pretty, wearing a simple cotton skirt with a white blouse.

"Hello!" she said.

"Hi," I said. "What have you been doing all morning?"

"Reading mostly." The soft tenderness in her eyes and her gentle smile made me want to take her in my arms, but her father and brother being so close prevented that from happening. I put my hand in my pocket and fingered the little felt box, wondering when would be the best time to give it to her. "Take a walk with me," she said, putting her arm in mine.

We walked though the garden past the swimming pool and tennis court to where a little wooden swing was hanging from a tree. The mountains loomed across the horizon, and the little villages below us lay dormant in the afternoon siesta. Alexandra leaned against me with her hand entwined with mine. She smelled as if she had just gotten out of the bath.

"Alexandra, I have something for you," I told her finally as I pulled the little box out of my pocket and held it for her to see.

"Drew! You didn't have to do that!"

"Open it," I said, handing it to her.

She took the box from my hand and opened it slowly. She blushed when she looked inside. "It's beautiful!" she said, holding it up.

"There's an inscription," I said, opening the locket for her.

She read the inscription and kissed me. "*Ti amo anche Io*, Drew," she said, wrapping her arms around me.

I helped her with the chain. It looked good on her, and I kissed her lightly. We walked hand-in-hand through the garden, laughing and talking about nothing in particular. As we approached the castle, her mother walked quickly toward us.

"Alexandra, I need to talk to you," she said. She noticed the locket around Alexandra's neck and frowned. "Please excuse us, Drew."

The two women went inside. Philip stood at one of the big parlor windows, looking down upon me. What the hell was he doing here? Alexandra and her mother talked to him briefly, and they disappeared. I waited patiently in the garden. Several minutes later Alexandra came down.

"I'm so sorry, Drew," she said, teary eyed.

"I saw Philip here. What's going on?"

"I don't know what he's doing here. It's as if he has lost his mind. I think he might be on drugs. I've never seen him look so bad."

"How did he get here?"

"He took a plane from France. His parents didn't know where he was until now. My mother just got off the phone with his mother and she is coming to get him."

"But why did he come here?"

"He says he's in love with me and can't live without me."

"He came all the way here to tell you that? I thought you two had settled your relationship."

"So did I, but I guess things are not settled in his mind. Drew, I think he's in serious trouble, he looks terrible."

Tears dribbled down her cheeks. "What can I do to help?" I asked.

She put her arms around me and held me tightly. "I'm sorry to do this to you, Drew. Things are complicated. It's best you go back to Rome until we deal with this problem."

She was right, but the last thing I wanted was to leave her. "Should I leave now?"

"It's probably best," she said, taking my hands.

I followed her into the castle to see Philip standing in the parlor talking with her father. Alexandra was right; he looked awful. His skin had a funny, grayish color, and his eyes were sunken and bloodshot and the veins in his forearms were discolored and stood out. He had lost a lot of weight, and his clothes hung on him loosely. He turned and looked at me, and I saw the hurt and desperation in his eyes. Alexandra took me down to the courtyard.

"Alexandra, I think he needs a hospital. He looks like he's been shooting heroin or something."

"That's what my father thinks. Drew, I am sorry for this," she said again.

145

"It's not your fault. Call me at the hotel later," I said, kissing her quickly and getting into the car.

I had lunch by myself at the hotel. I wasn't in the mood to do any sightseeing, so I sat in the lobby and did some reading. I would be leaving Rome in a couple of days, and I hated to leave under these circumstances.

Aunt Tess came back late that afternoon. I was happy to see her; I needed to tell someone about my day.

"How did Alexandra like the locket?" she asked when she saw me.

"She loved it," I replied.

"I knew she would. It was really lovely."

Once she was settled I recounted the entire story of Philip and she listened attentively.

"Well, Dear. These things will happen," she said. "I'm sure she's not happy about it either. Give her some space to work this out, and you two can pick up where you left off."

Late that night Alexandra finally called. "Are you okay?" I asked.

"I'm fine. Are you all right?"

"Yes, of course. How is Philip?"

"Oeuf, he's a mess! I don't know what happened to him. He and his mother just left. It was quite a disaster. His mother pleaded with me and my mother for me to take him back."

"You're kidding, right?"

"No. She insisted that when we were together he was happy, and his problems started when we broke up."

"You can't take responsibility for that. What did your mother say?"

"My mother asked me if I wanted him back," she said, but her words didn't sink in at first.

"Why would your mother ask you that? The guy was a mess."

"Because he comes from a very important French family, and it would be good for everyone if we could work things out."

"But you don't love him."

"No. I don't. And that's what I told them."

"So then, it's finished. You have nothing to feel bad about. I'm sorry it happened."

"I'm sorry too. It really upset me to see Philip like this. He's a really a nice boy. I don't know what happened to him."

"I've seen a lot of kids get messed up on drugs. Some people just can't face their own pain and they turn to drugs to deal with it."

"It's such a waste," she said.

"There is nothing you can do. People make their own choices."

"Drew, I didn't get a chance to thank you properly for the locket. It's beautiful."

"I'm glad you like it," I said. "I got the impression your mother didn't like it so much."

"My mother is very Italian and traditional. She doesn't think it appropriate that young boys give young girls such extravagant gifts."

"Then she'd probably die if she found out what happened yesterday."

Alexandra laughed. It was good to hear her laughter again, finally. "You are a very funny boy. There are three things I love about you. The way you kiss, the way you write, and the way you make me laugh."

"Only three?" I asked.

"Well, you also have a beautiful ass," she said, almost in a whisper.

Now I was laughing. "Tomorrow is my last day in Rome. Will we see each other?"

147

"Yes, of course. Is there anything special you would like to do?"

"I wouldn't mind seeing your parent's villa again, but I'll leave it up to you."

Again she laughed. "I'll call you in the morning," she said. "Goodnight."

That night I went to bed wondering what drove Philip over the edge. Was he really that much in love with Alexandra? I felt truly bad for him, yet deep inside I felt partly responsible, but I was also desperately in love with her, and could really understand how he felt if I were in his shoes.

The next morning Alexandra and her mother came to give me a tour of Rome, driving to different monuments and museums. Her mother would never leave me alone with her—even for a second. It didn't matter. We would be seeing each other at school in just a few weeks. Nonetheless, we exchanged playful caresses whenever her mother wasn't looking, and I even got to kiss her once when her mother excused herself to use the bathroom after lunch. I had a grand time. At the end of the day, Alexandra told me she would go with me to the airport to see me off.

The next morning Aunt Tess, Alexandra, her parents and I went to the airport. Aunt Tess was going to stay in Rome to continue working a few more weeks.

When my flight was called her father shook my hand at the terminal. "It was a pleasure meeting you, Drew."

"You too, Sir. Thank you for everything. I really enjoyed myself."

"Goodbye, Drew. Perhaps we will see you at *Ecole des Roches*," said her mother.

"I hope so," I said, shaking her hand and kissing her on both cheeks.

Aunt Tess patted me on the cheek and kissed me. "Give

148

my regards to your mother and father, and be sure to kiss your sisters for me."

"I will, Aunt Tess."

Alexandra stood next to me quietly until now. I turned to her and smiled. "Well, then. I'll be seeing you in a couple of weeks," I said.

"I hope so," she replied. She put her arms around me and kissed me briefly. Her father smiled, and her mother frowned.

"This is for you," said Alexandra, handing me a shopping bag filled with chocolate.

I laughed. "You and your chocolate! Thank you," I said, kissing her briefly.

My flight was called again. "Goodbye, everyone!" I said, turning to board my plane. I floated all the way down the terminal to my seat—being in love had to be better than any drug ever made.

Chapter 8

My arrival home was worse than I thought. The plane landed just after 11:00, and I expected at least one of my parents to be at the airport to greet me. I waited in the terminal nearly two hours before realizing nobody was coming. They had forgotten me. Dinner consisted of some of the chocolate Alexandra had given me, and then, digging deep for the courage I would need, I called home. After several rings my mother answered the phone. She sounded drunk. Nice to know some things never change.

"Who the fuck is this?"

"It's Drew, Mom. I'm at the airport. Can someone come get me?"

"Can't you hitchhike?"

"Mom! I'm in Long Island. I can't hitchhike to Rumson from here!"

"Call your father."

She hung up. I stood there flabbergasted, not knowing what to do. I wasn't even sure where my father was, much less how to get in touch with him. Taking my best guess, I called information and asked for the Worthington's number.

Jason answered.

"Jason! Is my father there?"

"Who is this?"

"It's Drew. Drew Smith."

"Hold on a second," he said, putting the phone down. A few minutes later I heard my father's voice on the other end. He sounded sleepy.

"Dad! It's Drew. I'm at the airport. Can someone please come get me?"

"I'll send a car," he said and hung up.

An hour later a limousine drove up. The driver was holding a cardboard sign with my name on it. I introduced myself to the driver, and we started the long drive home. I sat in the back of the car silently, still in disbelief that my parents were through. I thought about Alexandra and her family, and realized how lucky she was. Her parents were so gentle and loving, and I wondered what that would be like.

The house was a mess when I got home. Dirty dishes were piled in the sink and the kitchen floor caked with dirt. My guess was that Lynn no longer worked for us. Exhausted, I left my bags on the kitchen floor and flopped into bed. Just a few more weeks of this and I'd be back in Switzerland.

I awakened the next morning to the sound of my sisters fighting in the next room, so I went to see what all the commotion was about. Julie and Annie were having a tug of war over a pair of pants, with Annie winning.

"What the hell is going on here?" I asked.

Annie let go of the pants, and Julie flew backward into the closet, causing Annie to laugh hysterically and Julie angry enough to spit. "Keep the fucking pants, you stupid bitch!" she yelled, throwing them on the floor.

She stormed out of the closet and went over to one of the heavy, French windows, yanking it open with such force it ripped right off the wall. I had heard about people having superhuman strength during moments of crisis, but I didn't know it also applied to anger. A lot must have happened the week I was away. Julie tried to balance the window on her shoulder and arm, but she couldn't hold it by herself. I ran over to help. A careful examination of the screws and frame proved that it was solidly mounted. She just ripped it off the wall with sheer force. She wrinkled up her little eyebrows, and then tears welled up in her eyes.

"Don't worry about it," I told her. "This is easily fixed. The glass isn't broken. All it needs is a little wood putty and some screws." She finally began to cry. Her sobbing was so deep it broke my heart.

Annie came over and hugged her. "It's okay, Julie. Everything is going to be okay," she said.

What horrors awaited me downstairs? My mother was in the kitchen pacing the floor with a beer can in her hand while on the phone with one her friends. Her hair was uncombed and she wasn't wearing makeup, showing the deep circles under her eyes.

"When did you get back?" she asked, scowling at me.

"Last night."

"How come you didn't stay with your father and his whore?"

"I don't like whores," I replied. The bag of chocolate and my suitcase still sat on the kitchen floor where I left them last night. Considering how she reacted the last time she saw chocolate, I thought it best to get it out of sight. "I'm going to unpack. Nice to see you, Mom," I said, going upstairs.

Now that I had a chance to see the house in daylight, I saw what a mess it really was. The study was strewn with papers and magazines, and there were dirty clothes thrown all over the furniture. Someone must have had a fit about doing laundry. I leafed through some of the papers. It looked as though my mother had started writing again, but none of it made much sense. Most of it was poorly typed poetry filled with spelling mistakes and obscenities.

I went back upstairs to my sisters' room and gave them several bars of chocolate.

"Weren't you guys going to Martha's Vineyard?" I asked.

"Does it look like we've been anywhere nice?" Annie asked, snarling at me with disgust.

"Has Dad been around at all?"

"No. He came by to get some clothes. That's it," she said.

"Where's Gretchen?"

"Who the fuck knows? Did you have fun in Italy?" she asked.

I was almost ashamed to tell her how much fun I had. "I had a great time."

"Did you see the horses?" Julie asked, excited.

"Yes. She has a lot of horses. I went riding one day at her farm."

"What's her house like?" Annie asked, suddenly interested in my trip.

"You wouldn't believe it if I told you. She lives in a big castle outside of Rome."

"Is she a princess?" Julie asked, her eyes filled with wonderment.

"No. I don't think so. Her family is just very rich. They have a swimming pool and their own grass tennis court. They also own a lot of farmland around Rome."

"You must have had a great time," Annie said, her voice filled with envy.

"I did. I saw a lot of beautiful art. Rome is filled with beautiful art."

"So, is she your girlfriend now?" Annie asked, continuing her grilling.

"Yes, she is most definitely my girlfriend now," I replied, putting my hands in my pockets and smiling.

"Well, I hate to burst your bubble," Annie said, "but it looks like you won't be going back to Switzerland."

I gasped, and then nearly choked on my own breath. "What are you talking about?"

"I heard Mom and Dad talking about it. Your grades are so bad that Dad doesn't think you should go back, and what your teacher wrote about you in your yearbook didn't help."

"What? You've got to be kidding, right? How did Dad get my yearbook? It was hidden in my room."

Neither of them said a word. I didn't believe it, and I went downstairs to find Mom. She had left, and I sat down in the kitchen in despair. This wasn't happening. I looked around at the dirty dishes and the grime on the floor. My whole world was coming apart.

Later that day my mother returned. I went down to the kitchen to talk to her, but the glazed look in her eyes showed she had been drinking. She reached into the refrigerator and popped open a beer. "What the hell do you want?" she asked.

"Nothing," I replied, going back to my room. I thought about calling my father at work to ask him about it, but I was afraid to hear what he might say. Later that night his heavy footsteps echoed up the stairs, and my heart raced when he came towards my room. I sat up straight on my bed when he entered.

"Did you have fun in Italy?" he asked.

"I had a great time," I replied, describing in detail all the wonderful art and monuments I saw. He listened quietly, but I knew he didn't really want to hear about my travels.

"Well, I'm glad you had fun. I have some bad news for you," he finally said. "Your mother and I are getting a divorce, and things are not going well financially. The gas crisis has really hit us hard and we've had to lay off a lot people at the plant. I'm not going to be able to send you to Switzerland next year."

I looked at him for a moment and blinked. "Dad, my grades are getting better. I know what I'm good at now. I know how to do better in school."

"Fine. You can apply what you know in public school. You're going to high school here next year."

"Dad. Please, Dad. Please don't make me go to public school here," I begged.

154

"You'll be starting in the fall. Your mother and I have already enrolled you," he said. "I'm sorry, but that's how life goes."

He left my room and I sat on my bed too distraught to react to what just happened. Finally I got up off my bed and walked over to the fireplace and looked at all the little knick-knacks I had collected over the years on the mantle. I thought about Alexandra, and all the times we were not going to have, and couldn't imagine what it was going to be like not to have her in my life anymore. I thought about Axel, and what he would have said about the whole situation. I thought about my father, and wondered why he needed to punish me so harshly. And then I began to sob. I sobbed so hard I had to hold on to the mantle to keep from collapsing on the floor. I sobbed until my gut began to ache, and when I couldn't sob anymore I went back to my bed and slept.

The next morning I saw my mother before she had a chance to start drinking. She was making a half-hearted attempt to clean the kitchen while on the phone. She tried to wipe the stains off the counter with a dirty rag, which only smeared them around and made things worse. When she got off the phone, she sat down at the table and gave me a smile.

"Mom, why can't I go back to Switzerland?" I asked. "I'm not doing that bad."

"Who told you can't go to Switzerland?"

"Dad told me last night."

"That bastard," she said, scrunching up her eyes. "He's just trying to weasel out of his responsibilities. He doesn't even pay your tuition, your grandmother does."

I was surprised to hear this news, but then my grandmother controlled all the money in our family with an iron hand. Her money was a big secret, and we were never allowed to discuss it. Money was a dirty word in our family.

"Do you want to go back to Switzerland?"

"More than anything in the world," I said. "My entire happiness is there."

"You are going to have to improve your grades you know."

"I will, Mom. I promise!"

"Fine, I'll talk to your grandmother and see what I can do."

I was so ecstatic I couldn't contain myself. I threw my arms around her and gave her a big kiss on the cheek. My world was saved.

I didn't see my father for a few days after that. He didn't come around much anyway, and when he did, it was only to pick up things he needed or to talk with my mother. Most times their discussions were simply heated arguments behind closed doors. Mom asked us if we wanted to stay in the house, and my sisters all said no, but I had mixed feelings. I loved our house, even if it was filled with unhappy memories. My mother could not have kept the place up by herself, and in the end I knew it was best to sell.

One evening I was sitting in the kitchen by myself having a bowl of cold cereal for dinner when my father walked in looking angry. "Where's your mother?" he asked, his eyes feral with rage.

"She's out," I told him meekly.

I could see there was something really bothering him. Finally he walked up to me, grabbed my cereal bowl, and threw it in my face, covering me with milk and Cheerios. "Why the fuck did you ever tell your mother about me and Mrs. Worthington?" he yelled.

I shot up out of my chair, picked up my cereal bowl, and heaved it at him as hard as I could. He ducked, and the bowl shattered against the kitchen counter in a splash of tiny shards. He chased me around the kitchen table a few times until I ran out the back door. He could never catch me, but I if he did…I waited

156

in the back yard until I heard his car start and saw him leave the driveway.

After that I didn't see him until a few days before it was time to go back to school. We didn't talk about what happened. In fact, I never told anybody about it. He gave me his usual speech about the importance of getting good grades, and I promised to do better. This time I meant it. I think I finally figured out how to get through school, and I looked forward to giving it a try. Beyond that I couldn't wait to see Alexandra again.

Chapter 9

The first thing I did when I got back to school was look for Axel, since he had not returned any of my letters, but he was nowhere to be found. I asked everyone if they had seen him or knew if he was coming. Nobody knew anything. I finally asked M. Meneghetti.

"*Monsieur* Jenssen will not be attending school this year," he said.

I swallowed back my disappointment. "Do you know why he's not coming back?"

"No. I'm sorry, I don't."

Later that day I saw Alexandra walking with her friends toward the little convenience store at the hotel Petit Paradis. "Drew! How are you?" she said, putting her arm around my waist and kissing me on the lips.

Her friends smiled and all the other boys looked at me with envy. She was wearing the locket I gave her, and I reached for it gently and held it in my hands. "I'm so glad to see you," I said, holding her tight.

"Are you okay?" she asked.

"Axel is not here. He's not coming back."

"I'm sorry," she said. "Do you know where he is?"

"No. I've written him so many letters, but he never wrote back."

"Why don't you give him a call?"

"I'd like to, but they don't have a telephone. His father doesn't believe in them."

"I'm sure he is fine," she said, wrapping her arms around me and giving me a hug. Her body next to mine gave me a warm feeling, and I wondered when we'd find a chance to be alone again. She smiled at me wryly and gave me a gentle squeeze.

"What ever happened to Philip?" I asked.

"I don't know. I never heard from him again. I will see you at class tomorrow?" she asked, kissing me gently on the cheek.

"Of course."

School was going to be fun this year, but I missed Axel. I was assigned a room with three Frenchmen. I liked the French, even if many American kids had problems with them. I didn't know where the friction came from, but an invisible wall existed between us that could not be overcome.

"*Ça va,* Drew?" asked my new roommate, Luc De Maurier, a skinny kid with thin, blond hair and eyes that crinkled up in the corners. He was liked by everyone. He was one of the boys who saw the fight with Philip last year.

"*Oui, ça va bien, merci,*" I replied.

We talked for quite awhile. He knew Philip. My French, although rusty, came back quickly. Philip was in the hospital and would be taking a year off from school. Apparently he got himself involved with the wrong people and started doing heroin. By the end of the day everyone knew about it, and his drug problems were discussed among the boys as if it could have happened to any of them. I was somewhat of a celebrity, and rumor had it that Alexandra and I were the reason for Philip's dreadful fall. I hardly knew the guy, but remembering his emaciated body, pale skin, and discolored veins made me feel bad about what he was going through. I could certainly understand how breaking up with Alexandra would have destroyed his world, although I couldn't understand what could be so awful about his life to drive him to stick a needle in his arm.

Nothing about school had changed much. The only real difference was that it wasn't all so new to me now. I knew what to expect, and looked forward to it. I recognized most of the boys, and there were a few new faces as well.

"How are you, Drew?" asked a tall boy standing behind me. It was John Grinnel, the juvenile delinquent from New Jersey who used to steal mopeds from Montana.

"I'm good, John. Nice to see you. How was your summer?"

"Summer was good. I hear you went to Rome," he said grinning.

"How the hell did you hear about that?" I asked.

"Stuff gets around. So are you and Alexandra dating?"

"Yes, we are dating. Have you stolen any mopeds lately?" I asked.

He laughed. "It's still early in the season," he replied. "Listen, a few of us are going up to Montana after school tomorrow. Why don't you come along?"

"Sure. I'd love to."

That night I wrote Axel one more letter before giving up. Not knowing what happened to him made me crazy. I wrote him in detail about what it was like to be back at school and how much I missed him. Regardless, I went to bed filled with hope and great expectations for the coming year.

After breakfast we all tromped down to *Saint Françoise*. Alexandra stood outside, waiting for me with a big smile. I wouldn't see much of her; our classes were different. The only time we'd get to talk would be during morning break or briefly after school and, of course, during *soirée*. Finding time to be alone with her would be difficult since our activities were strictly monitored.

"Good morning," she said.

"How are you?" I asked, kissing her gently on the cheek.

"I'm fine. Any news of Axel?"

"None, but I had a long talk with Luc De Maurier. He told me Philip is in the hospital, and will be taking a year off from school."

"Yes. I heard something like that from one of the girls. I'm not sure if I should send him a note."

"Why would you do that?"

"He's a nice boy, and I feel bad for him."

"Trust me, the last thing either of you need is to have old wounds reopened. Maybe later when he is doing better you can write him, but now is not the time. What he needs most is peace and time to heal."

She raised an eyebrow and smiled. "You are a very wise boy," she said, wrapping her arms around me the way she usually did. I melted. I also got really excited, and began to realize how overactive my sex drive was. Time to go to class; I kissed her deeply before we went inside.

As we broke from our embrace, she took a deep breath and shook her head. "We need some time alone."

I knew that better than she did, and my mind raced with schemes about how we could get away together.

My first class was algebra, which was probably my worst subject since my brain turned to mush the minute I saw numbers. Remembering Alexandra's words about time alone didn't help much. I did my best not to think about it, but my erection pounded against my thigh all morning. It was becoming unbearable. Finally, I couldn't take it anymore and excused myself to go to the bathroom. I unzipped my pants and ejaculated as soon as I held myself in my hand. Not wanting to make any noise, I nearly passed out from holding my breath. I came all over the wall. Embarrassed, I flushed the toilet and wiped down the stall. That's when I heard laughter from the other side.

"Drew, *qu'est-ce que tu fais là?*"

"Nothing. I'm taking a leak."

"Are you sure?" asked another voice. Two boys were in the stall, and they were both trying to contain their laughter.

161

"What are you guys doing there?" I asked.

"Shush! Not so loud," said one. I popped my head over the stall and saw Luc sitting on the toilet, and another boy standing next to him, holding a pipe. A greenish-brown substance partially wrapped in tinfoil was sitting on Luc's knee.

"Do you want some *merde*?" asked Luc.

"What do you mean shit?" I asked.

"Hashish," the other boy said giggling.

"Maybe later," I replied. I thought the two of them were crazy. Who in his right mind had enough gumption to do drugs in the bathroom? It was bad enough if I got caught in here masturbating, but I wasn't crazy enough to smoke hash during class. I quickly washed my hands and left.

I felt better when I got back to class, and found myself able to concentrate. Whenever my mind drifted I would try to remember the concepts the teacher was explaining by associating them with words. It seemed to work, and I discovered that my thought process was much more abstract than logical. I thought in pictures that I created with words. Although this technique was marginal when it came to math, it worked really well when I got to my history and social studies classes, and I found myself able to remember facts much better.

By morning break I was euphoric about my newfound empowerment, and felt as though I could even do well in school. I told Alexandra about my discovery.

"That's wonderful, Drew. I really hope you do well this semester," she said. Alexandra always got straight A's. I don't think she even realized how smart she is.

"All the girls are curious about you," she told me.

"Really?" I had noticed that girls seemed to like me, but I was always too unsure of myself to act on it. "What did you tell them?"

"Oh! Why do you want to know?"

"You brought it up!" I said smiling and shaking my head.

"I told them that you are a very tender, sweet boy, and that you kiss really, really well," she said, wrapping her arms around me again. The feel of her body next to mine made me want her more than anything in the world.

"Let's go outside," I told her, taking her hand. We had fifteen minutes before going back to class. Many people stood outside and puffed on cigarettes frantically before being called inside. We walked over to the fence by the football field. The late September air was still warm. The trees hadn't turned yet, but summer was over. I liked this time of year; the air was filled with excitement of dramatic change. In just a few weeks the mountains would be covered in snow.

Alexandra leaned her back against my chest, and I held her in my arms. Sierre lay below us, stretching eastward along the Rhone. Little villages sprinkled the mountainside, and farmers herded their cattle into greenish-brown pastures to graze in the morning sun. The other side the valley was steeper, and snowcaps topped the highest peaks. Near the top, just below a huge snowcap, a tiny village clung to the mountainside like moss to a tree. It looked as though it would topple over the side at any moment, and I wondered why it didn't. Life didn't get much better than what I was feeling at that moment. I really loved it here.

"I'm going up to Montana after school with John Grinnell and some friends," I said.

"That sounds like fun. What are you going to do?"

"I don't know. Mess around. Can I get you anything while I'm there? Do you have enough chocolate?"

"You can never have enough chocolate," she said, laughing.

"I'll stop and get you some."

163

"You don't have to do that," she said, reaching up for a kiss.

"It's my pleasure, as is this" I replied as our lips met.

Katrina called us back to class and we all filtered back into *Saint François*.

After school John, a new boy named Martin, and I took the funicular to Montana. Martin was a husky kid with blond hair and blue eyes. He needed to buy some skis and boots, so we went to Rinaldi's, a small ski shop in the center of town where all the latest skis were on display. My parents had bought me new equipment last year, but I eyed the latest K2 skis with envy. Everyone was talking about them; they were the best skis on the market. Martin bought a pair and some boots of equal quality. The bindings he chose were top of the line. I wondered if his abilities would live up to the equipment he chose.

Afterward we went to a small wine shop where we each bought a couple bottles of beer.

"I know a place where we can drink these," John said

"I need to make one stop first," I said. "I promised Alexandra I would get her some chocolate."

"Oh, isn't that sweet!" John said with a big grin.

The *chocolaterie* smelled just as delicious as I remembered. I picked out an assortment for her and a few pieces for us. The lady behind the counter wrapped it in a nice box and tallied up my order. Alexandra had an expensive habit, with the bill taking up almost my entire allowance for the week.

We headed down the path toward Bluche. Some afternoon hikers were coming up the trail—mostly older couples enjoying the beautiful, fall weather. They nodded politely as we walked by with our beer bottles clanking in our bags.

"Follow me," John said, heading off the trail toward a grassy knoll where some boulders sat. We climbed on top of one of them and John pulled out his Swiss Army knife and opened our bottles. I didn't enjoy beer that much; it left a funny taste in my mouth and filled me up too quickly, but John and Martin swigged at their bottles eagerly while I tried to keep up.

"I have a surprise for you guys," John said, taking off his boot. He pried off the heel with his knife. The inside had been hollowed out and was stuffed with little balls of tinfoil.

"What the hell is it," Martin asked, frowning.

"Hashish?" I asked, my guess coming from what I saw in the bathroom earlier that day.

"You got it," John said, grinning.

"Where did you get it?" Martin asked, the excitement in his voice and mannerism more than obvious.

"I got it this summer in Florida. I smuggled it through the airport in my boot."

"You're nuts! What if you got caught?" I asked.

"Do I look like a drug smuggler?" he asked, hammering the heel of his boot back on with the butt of his knife. He took a small pipe out of his pocket, and cutting a piece of the hash off the ball, placed it in the bowl. He lighted a match and sucked on the pipe until the little piece of hash began to glow, then he drew on the pipe for several more seconds. Finally he held his breath for as long as he could before exhaling a huge cloud of sweet-smelling smoke.

"Do you want some?" he asked, handing me the pipe, which I just looked at tentatively. It smelled good. I thought back to when I once saw Gretchen smoke it with some friends in the barn. She told me it was fun. Her eyes were red and she seemed to be laughing a lot.

"I'll try it," I said, taking the pipe and putting it to my lips.

"Just inhale as much smoke as you can and hold your breath," he told me. He lit the pipe again and I drew in the smoke.

It expanded in my lungs quickly and I began to cough. Never in my life had I experienced such a rasping feeling in my throat, and I chugged on my beer bottle to quell the burning sensation while John and Martin laughed hysterically.

Martin took the pipe and had no problems. Obviously, he had done this before. I didn't feel anything from my first toke. John took his turn and then handed me the pipe.

"Do you want to try again?"

I was more hesitant this time, my lungs still sore from my last attempt. "All right," I said finally, not wanting to be the odd-man-out.

I took the pipe once more and held it to my lips. This time I didn't inhale so hard. Again I felt the smoke expanding in my lungs, but managed to hold my breath. As I exhaled I felt a bit lightheaded, but still didn't feel anything remarkably different. My mouth felt a bit dryer, but I didn't feel high. We passed the pipe around at least four more times. Gradually as I felt more and more light-headed and when John's voice became sort of an echo, I realized I was stoned.

"Wow!" I said.

John looked at me and laughed and then I began to crack up as well. At first it was simply giggles at the idea of being stoned, but then it turned to raucous, uncontrollable laughter. I laughed so hard I didn't even know what was funny anymore and still couldn't stop. I must have laughed for more than ten minutes before it began to hurt. Being stoned was fun. John said everyone cracked up the first time they got stoned.

When my laughter finally subsided, I reached into my bag and pulled out some chocolate. It tasted so sweet and delicious I couldn't stop eating, and eventually I forgot about my beer and just ate the chocolate. By the time I realized what I was doing most of it was gone, with only a few pieces left in the bottom of the box.

"Oh, shit!" I mumbled through a mouth filled with the delicious morsels.

"What's the matter?" John asked, grinning.

"I ate all of Alexandra's chocolate!"

He began to laugh as Martin reached in and took the remaining pieces. Now nothing was left but crumbs. I didn't have enough money to get some more, and we had to be back at school for study hall.

Alexandra was waiting for me in front of *Saint François*. By now I wasn't as stoned and really wished I had some chocolate to give her. But more than that, I prayed she didn't notice I was high. I knew she would not approve of me being stoned. Alexandra took my hand when she saw me. I tried to avoid her eyes, afraid that she would see how bloodshot mine were. But I always gazed into her eyes; they were one of the things I loved most about her.

"Drew, is there something wrong?" She cupped her hand around my chin and forced me to look at her. Still, I avoided her eyes.

"No," I said. "I had too much to drink up in Montana. I'm not feeling very well."

She put her hand to my cheek and stroked my hair. "Then maybe you should go lie down."

"No, I'm fine," I said, taking her in my arms. "I'm sorry."

"Why should you be sorry," she said, pulling away from me.

"Because I bought you chocolate and we ate it all."

"Oeuf! Don't worry about that. How much did you eat?"

"It was a lot."

She laughed. "That's probably why you are not feeling well. What did you drink?"

"Just a few beers," I told her.

"Did you drink a lot?"

"Three bottles."

She looked up at me frowning, her dark eyebrows bunching together with concern. Given what she had been through with Philip she'd be horrified if she knew the truth.

We were called to study hall, with the boys in one room and the girls in another. As soon as I sat down I felt dead tired, but I forced myself to do my homework. I managed to get through my lessons, elated when study hall finally ended—at least the day wasn't a total wash. Although being high was fun, I had a splitting headache by the time dinner was called, and afterward went back to my room and slept all the way until morning.

During break I looked for Alexandra but she was not around. I asked her friend Laurence where she was.

"Katrina called her out of class this morning," she told me. "She had some kind of family emergency."

"Family emergency? Is everything all right?"

"I don't know," Laurence said. "I'm on my way back to *Prés Fleuris* to see if she is okay. I'll let you know."

I paced nervously outside *Saint François* for her to show up. Finally the two of them walked up the road toward me. Alexandra was holding back her tears, and looked scared.

"What's going on?" I asked. I had never seen her with tears in her eyes, and it hurt me to see her so broken up.

"It's my father," she said. "He died this morning."

"Oh, my God! I'm so sorry," I said, taking her in my arms. She wrapped her arms around me and began to cry. I felt her sobbing against my chest, and I thought about her father and how much I liked him. He was a great man. Alexandra was going back to Rome that evening to be with her family. She'd be gone a week.

Before study hall I walked her to the funicular station, carrying her suitcase and waiting with her on the platform. She was no longer crying, although she still seemed pretty dazed.

"Are you okay?" I asked.

"I'll be fine," she said, leaning up against me.

I put my arm around her and held her close. Her eyes, normally so bright and filled with passion, now reflected deep sadness, and I stood next to her on the platform, wishing I could do more.

When the funicular arrived I put her bag in the car.

"I love you," I told her, and kissed her goodbye.

"I love you too," she said. "I'll speak to you soon."

I stood on the platform and watched the car descend. I wished I could go with her, but knew that wasn't possible. When the car had all but disappeared from view, I turned and headed back toward school.

In Alexandra's absence I buckled down and concentrated on school. All my teachers noticed my improvement, with the exception of my French teacher, M. Bianchi, whom I refused to forgive for what he wrote in my yearbook—even if it were true, he had no right to write it.

Despite him my French improved daily. Living with three Frenchmen forced me to learn; I spoke enough French that they refused to use English when I was around. Sometimes I felt a little lost, but day-by-day I picked up more words.

One morning Luc handed me his newspaper. "The best way to learn a language is to read a good newspaper."

"Why?"

"Because the language is simple and very correct. Once you can read a newspaper without problems you can move on to books and magazines."

That made sense. My mother always said that good journalism was the purest form of language. When I first started writing she showed me how to edit out unnecessary words, always striving for the clearest way to express a thought. She hated adjectives, but I loved them. I wanted everything I wrote to have color and life. Nonetheless, every morning Luc gave me his newspaper, and I spent an hour or two looking up words I didn't know and learning about the intricacies of French politics.

Later that week I got a call from Aunt Tess who was back in Rome finishing up her tour of Italy.

"I just called to see how you are getting along, Dear."

"I'm fine, Aunt Tess. Did you get a lot done?"

"It was a productive trip. I think I have a whole new series going. How's Alexandra?"

"Her father died a few days ago. She's back in Rome."

"Oh, my God! Dear, that's terrible! I'll give her mother a call and see if there's anything I can do. How is Alexandra taking it?"

"I don't know. She seems to be doing okay, but I know she's very hurt by it all."

"I would imagine. I'll give you a call tomorrow and let you know how things are going."

"Thanks, Aunt Tess."

Thank God she called. Not being able to help drove me crazy, and Aunt Tess was really wonderful in these situations. She always knew just what to do—always seeming to find the right words.

That night I waited so impatiently for her to call that I sprinted down the hall when M. Meneghetti summoned me to the telephone.

"How are you Aunt Tess? How's Alexandra doing?"

"I'm fine, Dear. Alexandra is okay. I stopped by their place this afternoon to offer my condolences and to help out with whatever I could. She has plenty of family around, so she's doing okay.

She sends you her love."

"How's her mother doing?"

"Well, she's taking it kind of hard. It's difficult to lose a husband. Listen, Dear. I was planning to leave Rome tomorrow but I am taking a train to Switzerland with Alexandra this Saturday. We should be in Switzerland Sunday night."

"That sounds wonderful."

"I'll talk to you soon."

That Saturday was the *soirée*. Not having Alexandra there felt strange, so I danced a couple of songs with Laurence, but when I saw John and Martin, I excused myself to say hello.

"Drew! What's going on?" asked John. His eyes were droopy and red from being stoned. How did the Internats miss it? A lot of hash was floating around the school these days and quite a few boys looked stoned. John said that's how it was at the beginning of the semester until everyone had exhausted their supply.

"I'm doing okay, John. How are you feeling?" I asked.

"I'm feeling fine," he said, his grin spreading all the way across face, making him look stupid.

Martin looked even more stoned. At least John's eyes were partly obscured by his glasses, but Martin had pale skin with big, blue eyes and the whites of them were now almost crimson, his pupils dilated way beyond normal.

"Take a walk outside with me," John said.

We left the gymnasium and walked through the smoking lounge to the courtyard outside. The air was cool, but not quite cold. A few boys sat on benches with the some of the girls from *Prés Fleuris*. All the girls wore light, wool sweaters or were wrapped in shawls. They watched a lively ping-pong match two boys were having on an outdoor table made from concrete.

John pulled me off to the side. "Want to get high?" he whispered.

Alexandra was not around, and I remembered how much fun it was last time.

"Sure! But where?"

"Follow me."

We went behind the dormitories to a grassy hill, appropriately dubbed Strawberry Field, which stretched almost all the way down to Sierre. We walked through the tall grass down a shallow embankment to join another group of boys. Luc was among them. We sat down.

"So, who wants to smoke some *merde*?" John asked, unwrapping one of his little balls of hash. Luc pulled a small brick of his own stash from the pocket of his jacket. John's was a blondish color, but Luc's was dark brown with faint, red streaks coursing through it.

Two pipes went around the circle at once in opposite directions. Every time I exhaled another pipe was passed to me. Before long I was too stoned to know where I was. This wasn't like the first time I got high; this time I was completely disconnected from the world around me. I seemed to be floating, while strange noises buzzed around in my head.

"Drew, are you okay?" John asked, smiling at me.

I looked at him, but his outline was hazy, and I wasn't sure he was real. "I think so."

"He's fine," I heard someone say. "He's just stoned."

Everyone laughed. I lay back in the grass and looked up at the sky. The stars blinked back at me. At times they were sharp points of light, as if someone had pricked a piece of black velvet with a pin, and others they were big splotches of light, like Van Gogh's timeless painting. Every so often I waved my hand in front of my face just to feel the movement of my arm. The music from the *soirée* drifted down to us slowly across the field in waves. I could almost see them. It was all very strange.

Something tapped at my shoulder.

"Drew, let's go," John said.

We got to our feet and went back to the *soirée*. Everything seemed a bit cloudy and disconnected. I could have sworn M. Meneghetti looked at me funny, and I ducked inside the gymnasium to hide. Although I didn't have any drugs, I didn't want to get involved in any imbroglios surrounding them. The music pulsated through my body, and I stood against the wall and watched people dance.

After *soirée,* Luc and two other boys were sitting in the headmaster's office. M. Meneghetti and M. Davis were talking to them. They all looked very serious and one of the boys was crying. It was late for M. Davis to be here, and I knew something was wrong. John pulled me into the Pavilion, took me down to his room, and shut the door. "Luc has been busted."

"How?"

"*Monsieur* Meneghetti caught them red-handed in Strawberry Field."

"When?"

"Right after we got back," he replied. "He stayed out there too long. Meneghetti noticed they were gone and went looking for him."

"What's going to happen to him?"

"He'll probably be thrown out of school," he replied.

I shuddered at the thought.

Just after lights out Luc came back to our room. I was half asleep when he came in, but woke up just as he got into bed.

"Luc, what happened?"

"I got busted," he said matter-of-factly.

"But what's going to happen?"

"I have to leave school tomorrow."

"I'm sorry, Luc. I'll miss you."

"*C'est la vie*," he said quietly as he rolled over on his side.

That morning M. Meneghetti helped Luc and the two other boys pack before breakfast. They were put solemn-faced in the school van and driven to the train station before most people knew what happened. I didn't have a chance to say goodbye. After breakfast I came back to the room and saw Luc's empty bed and some loose papers on the floor. He left me his morning paper neatly folded on my nightstand.

Throughout the day everyone talked about what happened. John kept a low profile, not making many comments about the affair. Most people knew he was in Strawberry Field last night, and a few knew I was out there as well. I didn't fear my involvement getting back to M. Meneghetti; I had no drugs, and had no intention of buying any. I feared people associating me with them, and I dreaded what would happen if it got back to Alexandra. She would never understand.

That evening after study hall I waited impatiently for my aunt and Alexandra to arrive. Aunt Tess called shortly after dinner. She was staying at Petit Paradis, the hotel across from school, so I went to see her. Her tan face had a few more freckles, and she smiled at me when I walked into her room. In the corner were thick cardboard tubes filled with her rolled-up paintings.

"Aunt Tess! It's so good to see you!"

"You too, Dear," she said, giving me a kiss on the cheek. "How are you making out? You look a little tired. Are you getting enough sleep?"

"Yes. I'm fine, Aunt Tess. I stayed up late last night. How's Alexandra?"

"Alexandra is doing fine. She's a strong girl. Listen, Dear, I want you to go easy with her. Her mom is not doing so well."

I frowned. "What do you mean? Is she okay?"

"Well, she's not taking the death of her husband too well."

174

"I still don't know what you mean."

Aunt Tess took a deep breath and leaned forward in her chair. "When her father died, her mother locked herself in the bedroom with him for nearly five days. She wouldn't let anybody near him."

"Why would she do that?"

"Sometimes people mourn in loopy ways. That was her way of dealing with her pain."

"Is she okay now?"

"The jury is still out. Her father was a police captain, and the *Carabinieri* wanted to give him an official funeral, but her mother refused to let him be buried." She paused a moment and ran her fingers through her hair nervously. "It got to be pretty tense."

"Is she crazy?"

"I don't know if she's crazy. I think she's blinded by her loss, and people can sometimes do crazy things under those circumstances. At any rate, Alexandra has been through a hellish week; so when you see her tomorrow, go easy on her. She might be feeling out of sorts."

"Of course I will," I said, sitting up straight. "Poor Alexandra. Was she completely broken up?"

"She's upset, but we talked for quite some time on the train. She's got a good head on her shoulders. She's a very courageous young lady."

"How's her brother doing?"

"He seems to be doing okay. It's tough to lose a father, but he has his father's composure."

"Was her poor father finally buried?"

"He wasn't given the official burial the *Carabinieri* wanted, but there was a small family service."

"Did you go?"

"No. It was a private, family service. I didn't think it appropriate."

Aunt Tess talked a bit about her travels through Italy; how she stayed mostly in the South and fell in love with Sicily. She opened up a couple of tubes and spread her work on the bed for me to see. Her paintings were mostly street scenes of old *piazzas* and buildings, filled with interesting angles and reflections. Her work was good, and it seemed to be getting more interesting. I liked the way she played with light and reflections, giving them more prominence than the subject she painted. Even if her work wasn't abstract, it had an abstract quality that made it unique. I especially liked her paintings of Taormina in Sicily. The narrow side streets she depicted were filled with small villas draped with flowers.

Aunt Tess said she would be going home Tuesday morning, and that she'd take Alexandra and me out to dinner Monday night. That was the best part about parents and relatives coming to visit—you got taken out to dinner, getting you away from the blandness of the school's food. Most everyone felt the same way, so having parents in town made you the most popular guy in school; getting an invitation out to dinner was more valuable than a week's worth of pocket money.

The next morning Alexandra was standing outside *Prés Fleuris* with a group of friends. Her brown eyes had that lively look in them again. She smiled when she saw me. "Good morning," she said, taking my hand.

"How are you?" I asked, kissing her gently.

"I'm fine. Things are okay."

"I'm glad." I stroked her long, dark hair. It was still slightly damp from her morning shower, and her cheeks were flushed. We didn't have time to talk as the Internats called us to class.

"I'll see you at break," she said, kissing me quickly and going inside. I watched her as she went up the stairs to her first class, not looking at all like she had been through the ordeal Aunt Tess described.

My morning classes dragged on slowly, and I couldn't wait for morning break. The minute the bell rang I bolted down the stairs out front. A few moments later I saw Alexandra emerge from the building and we walked over to the fence by the football field. It was becoming "our" spot. I took her hand and we leaned against the fence. The sun was bright and warm, and it felt good on my face.

"How is your mom?"

"Oeuf! She's a disaster. Did Aunt Tess tell you about it?"

"Yes. I'm sorry. It must have been hard. Is she going to be all right?"

"I think so. She loved my father so much. Too much, I think."

"I know the feeling," I said without thinking.

Alexandra frowned slightly, and then caressed my arm.

"You must miss him," I said.

"You have no idea. My father had so much *joie de vivre*. He really, really enjoyed life. I will miss him terribly," she said. "Your aunt was really an angel. You are lucky to have someone like her in your life."

"Aunt Tess is really sweet. She takes care of me. She really likes you."

"You've been through a lot yourself. She told me about your family problems. You never told me your parents split up."

I looked down at the ground and shuffled my feet. "I was going to tell you, but it's hard to talk about it."

She put her arms around me and held me close. "Drew, you can tell me about things that hurt," she said. "It's not a crime to feel pain."

I held her tightly and burrowed my face in her hair. Slowly I began to cry—softly so that others would not notice. I cried because of my sadness, but also at the thought of how much I loved her. I held onto to her tighter, scared to let go, even more scared not to.

"I love you, Alexandra."

"I love you too," she replied. Her eyes were moist with tenderness and care. I kissed her briefly. She wrapped her arms around me and kissed me back. She leaned up against me and I could feel my passion building. She broke her embrace.

"Do you have any idea how much I want you?" I asked.

"Probably as much as I want you."

"What are we going to do?"

"I have a plan," she said. "Did you bring your tennis racket?"

"No. Not this semester. It's almost winter."

"Do you know anyone who has one?"

"I could ask around."

"Tell *Monsieur* Meneghetti you are going to play tennis after school with a friend. I'll bring Laurence with me and we'll sneak away for a bit," she said.

"Great plan!" The tennis courts were far enough away from school where we wouldn't be watched, and the weather was still warm enough to not arouse suspicions.

After school I asked around for a tennis racket, finding one from one of the younger kids. I changed into some sweatpants and a t-shirt and headed off to the tennis courts. They were down the road past *Prés Fleuris*, well out of sight from the football field where most everyone else would be. By the time I got there, Alexandra and Laurence were already hitting the ball back and forth. Her father was right. She wasn't a bad player. She didn't hit the ball very hard, but she placed it well and was fairly consistent. Laurence was equally as good. Alexandra was wearing a short

178

skirt and a thin t-shirt. Her legs were muscular and had perfect shape. Laurence blushed when she saw me.

"Would you like to play?" Alexandra asked, smiling.

"No thanks. I'll just watch."

The two of them had a nice rally going. They tapped the ball back and forth to each other at least four or five times before Alexandra missed a shot.

"Are you ready?" she asked.

"Ready for what?"

She just shook her head and laughed. Of course I was ready. I helped them pick up the balls and put them in the can, and as Alexandra put her racket in a big canvas bag, I noticed a blanket at the bottom.

Behind the tennis courts was a grassy hill leading down to a cluster of pine trees. Laurence sat at the top of the hill with a book while Alexandra and I disappeared into the trees. She spread the blanket on some pine needles, sat down on the blanket, and then took off her underwear. The air was thick with pine smells, and I inhaled deeply as I unzipped my pants.

"I don't have any protection," I said, suddenly feeling very disappointed.

"I've got some," she said, sitting up on her knees and reaching into her bag.

"You do come prepared."

"Yes, I do," she said, ripping the corner off the package neatly. We held each other close and kissed deeply until both of us were ready.

"Did you have an orgasm?" I asked, when we were finished.

"Yes. It was wonderful," she said, smiling.

"I wonder if we made a lot of noise."

"Probably, but nobody can hear us."

"I bet Laurence could," I replied with a chuckle.

She laughed. "She's a good sport. We'd better get going."

She got off me gently. I pulled off the rubber and buried it under some pine needles. Watching Alexandra putting on her panties gave me another erection, and I pulled them back down.

"Who knows when we'll get a chance to do this again," I said. She laughed and reached into her bag for another rubber.

Laurence turned bright red when she saw us coming up the hill; her book was perched on her knees and she smiled. She looked behind her and shook her head, her eyes filled with fear.

"Katrina is coming this way," she whispered.

"Bye. I'll see you tonight," I said, kissing Alexandra quickly and disappearing back into the trees. I ran through the woods and beyond the football field to the edge of Strawberry Field. Making sure nobody saw me, I headed back to school. As I went down the pavilion to my room I saw John.

"Where you been?" he asked.

"Playing tennis."

"With whom?"

"Alexandra," I replied quietly.

"Well, that explains the smile," he said.

"Shush! I don't want anybody to find out we were together. You know how paranoid they are."

"Don't worry. Nobody is going to find out."

"I'm not so sure. Katrina came by the tennis court."

"So? What's the big deal? You were just playing tennis."

"Not quite. We were coming out the woods."

"Oh!" he said, raising his eyebrows and pursing his lips. "Did she see you?"

"I don't think so. Laurence was waiting for us. She warned us Katrina was on her way and I bolted."

"Yeah, that would have put you in tight spot," John said.

"God, I really hate the way they constantly watch us. It makes it impossible to have a normal relationship. They must think we're all idiots and the first thing we'll do if we're alone with a girl is get her pregnant."

"What did you expect? Did you want them to hand out condoms with our pocket money?"

"Now that's what I like about you, Drew—creative thinking and insightful problem solving. At least they could give us a little room to develop healthy, normal relationships. Wouldn't you like to take Alexandra out to dinner once in awhile?"

"They'd have to give me more pocket money."

"You're an idiot," John said, laughing.

"No, I know what you mean," I said. "I would just like to spend an afternoon alone with Alexandra in Montana. There's no way they'd ever let us go out to dinner by ourselves."

"In the meantime I guess we'll just have to sneak around like thieves trying to explore our desires."

I laughed. "I'm going to take a shower before study hall. Speaking of dinner, my aunt is taking me and Alexandra out tonight."

"Lucky man. Have fun!" said John.

I had just a few minutes to shower before study hall. On my way down to the shower I realized I had forgotten my tennis racquet, and hoped Alexandra had grabbed it before she left. I doubted Katrina knew I was there because I would have heard about it by now. No wonder the school was so paranoid. Given the opportunity I'd want sex at least three times a day.

Alexandra was waiting for me outside when study hall was over.

"Did Katrina suspect anything?" I asked.

"I don't think so. She asked me what I was doing. I told her we hit a ball over the fence and I went to look for it."

181

"What about my tennis racquet?"

"I have it. I'll give it to you tomorrow. If the weather is nice maybe we can play another game," she said, putting her arms around my waist.

"I'm always up for tennis," I said, kissing her. "Aunt Tess and I will pick you up at 7:30. Is that okay?"

"I'll look forward to it. See you then," she said, giving me a quick kiss.

M. Meneghetti inspected my clothes carefully and straightened my tie. "*Monsieur* Smith, you will be in the company of two ladies this evening, so I expect you to be a gentleman. *Comprenez-vous?*"

"*Oui, monsieur.*"

"*Alors,* have fun. Be back by 10:00 sharp," he said.

Aunt Tess was waiting for me in the foyer. She smiled when she saw me. "Don't you look handsome," she said. "My, word! It's been years since I've seen this place. It really hasn't changed all that much. Your cousin Roy wasn't much older than you when I brought him here. Back then they didn't have an English section. Both my kids had to learn French the hard way."

"They were fortunate. Sometimes I wish Mom and Dad had put me in the French section."

"Aren't you a curious one? Most kids would scream and yell about being forced to learn a new language."

"I like learning French."

She raised an eyebrow and smiled. "That wouldn't have anything to do with Alexandra, would it?"

"I don't think so. I just think it's a beautiful language."

"It is a beautiful language. It's probably the most elegant of all the Romance languages. Shall we go get your date? We don't want to keep her waiting."

We walked down the road to *Prés Fleuris*, the air around us crisp and cool. She knocked on the front door and Katrina let us in.

"*Bonsoir, Madame et Monsieur.* I will call Alexandra," she said. This was the first time I had been inside *Prés Fleuris*, and as the young women walked by casually and greeted us, I felt as though I were standing in the middle of the forbidden zone. The accommodations at *les Roches* were much larger and nicer. Alexandra came down the stairs looking more fashionable than usual in a suede skirt and a wool sweater.

"Hello, Sweetheart. It's nice to see you," Aunt Tess said as she kissed her warmly on the cheek.

"You too," Alexandra said. Seeing them greet each other with so much familiarity made me smile. Alexandra and I waited in the foyer a moment while Aunt Tess spoke French with Katrina. Her French was perfect, and I was a little surprised to hear her speak it so well. I had always associated her with home, never expecting her to be so worldly.

We took the funicular up to Montana. The lights of restaurants and nightclubs glowed in the darkness, and people walked arm in arm through the streets. Normally we weren't allowed out of the dormitory at this hour, and I felt privileged to be able to see the town at night, especially with Alexandra.

"We're going to a little restaurant I used to frequent with friends when I lived here. I hope it's still as good as I remember."

Alexandra smiled at me and put her arm in mine. The restaurant was small. A fire burned brightly in a big, stone fireplace at the end of the room. The tables were elegantly set with fine china and silver, and the chairs looked plush and comfortable.

An older man in a tweed blazer and a bow tie looked up at us and smiled. His handlebar moustache curled at the ends. "Tess! It's so good to see you again after all these years!" he said as he kissed her on both cheeks.

183

"How are you, Frédéric? It's nice to see you too. I'd like to introduce you to my nephew Drew and his friend Alexandra."

"Come, I have a table for you by the fireplace. It's been so many years. How are your children?"

"They're fine. Shelly is off traveling around the world with friends and Roy is living out in California."

"And how goes the painting?"

"It's going well. I keep at it," she said and smiled as we walked past a small watercolor painting of the valley that hung on the wall.

"Aunt Tess, is that yours?"

"You have a good eye," said Frédéric. "Your aunt painted that years ago. She gave it to me just before she left Switzerland."

"It's beautiful," Alexandra said.

"I'm surprised you still have it," Aunt Tess said, smiling. "It's amazing how much the valley has changed. It's been too many years."

"Yes, it has," Frédéric said, shaking his head and pursing his lips. I knew from the glint in his eye that he and Aunt Tess had a romantic connection with each other. We were shown to our table—a little four-top by the fireplace, and the warmth from the flames felt good on the backs of my legs. Frédéric helped Aunt Tess with her chair, and I helped Alexandra with hers. He handed me the wine list, but I had no idea what to choose.

"We have an excellent Beaujolais," he recommended, turning the page for me and pointing at a reasonably priced wine.

"Not too sweet?"

"No, it's a nice, dry wine."

"Is everyone okay with red wine?" I asked, and they both nodded. "That would be fine, thank you."

"Excellent, *Monsieur*," he said, winking at my aunt.

A few minutes later a waiter presented me the bottle and

opened it. He handed me the cork. Remembering what my father taught me, I squeezed the cork to make sure it wasn't too dry and smelled it for traces of vinegar. It smelled earthy and somewhat heady. The waiter poured a little in my glass, and I swirled it around as I had seen my father do and took a sip. It tasted good.

"*Merci, Monsieur*," I said as the waiter filled our glasses.

"You have a birthday coming up, don't you Drew?" Aunt Tess asked after taking a sip.

"November 24th."

Alexandra smiled and tapped me with her foot under the table. "I was wondering when your birthday was."

"I'll be sixteen. When is your birthday, Alexandra?"

"In April. April 19th," she replied.

I made a mental note of it, hoping I wouldn't forget.

"You two make a very cute couple," Aunt Tess said. "It's sweet to see such young, innocent love."

"Thank you," Alexandra said, blushing.

The waiter brought our menus. I ordered a steak, not knowing when I would see a decent cut of meat again, Alexandra ordered the chicken, and Aunt Tess had a shepherd's pie.

"Do you think you'll make it to the States anytime soon?" Aunt Tess asked, breaking off a piece of bread.

"I don't know," Alexandra said. "I used to go to the States quite often with my father, but since his death, everything is so different."

"How old is your brother?"

"He's seventeen."

"He seems like he has both feet firmly on the ground. I'm sure he'll step into his father's shoes and help your mother deal with her loss."

"I hope so," Alexandra said, pursing her lips and glancing downward. "It's a lot to manage."

"I would say so," I added. "Is there anybody who can help your mother run the farm?"

"I don't know," she replied, picking up her water glass and taking a small sip. "Vincenzo knows quite a bit about the horses, but I don't think he knows the business like my father."

"What about your mother?" Aunt Tess asked, her eyes reflecting concern.

She shook her head slightly, causing her long, dark hair to cascade across her shoulders. "My mother knows nothing about horses. I don't think she even likes them, so I don't know what's going to happen with the farm."

"What about the vineyard?" I asked.

"Oh, the vineyards are not such a big problem. Claudio could easily oversee that. We have someone who tends the grapes and the winemaking."

"I wouldn't worry too much, Sweetheart," Aunt Tess said, squeezing her hand. "Things have a way of working themselves out for the best. Give your mother a little time to pull herself together and I'm sure things will be fine."

"I really hope so," Alexandra sighed. "I love the farm, and going there with my father will be one of the things I'll miss the most."

"It's hard to lose a parent, especially at your age. But you have your father's strength of character. I can see it in your eyes. You'll get through this just fine," Aunt Tess said, reaching over and smoothing back her hair.

My steak was cooked perfectly. Alexandra and I ate happily while Aunt Tess talked about what this area was like when she lived here. According to her, most of Montana wasn't here yet, and all the fancy stores had not been built. She claimed to have skied often when she was young, which I had trouble imagining since she didn't seem very athletic at all.

186

Alexandra and I had an *aperitif* after dinner, and Aunt Tess had a coffee.

"Tell you what, why don't I give you kids some time alone while I catch up with Frédéric at the bar," Aunt Tess said, as she collected her coffee cup, walked over, and sat down next to him on a stool. I watched as he offered her an *aperitif*, and they smiled and laughed.

Alexandra put her hand over mine. "I'm having a wonderful time."

"Me too. It's a shame we can't do this more often."

"I know. Winter will be here soon, and then the only time we'll get to see each other is between classes and at the *soirée*." The thought made me want to cry. I didn't know how we were going to get through the semester. She squeezed my hand. "Don't worry," she said. "There are always solutions to problems."

"I hope so. On top of everything else we have to contend with being separated by snow and ice."

"It's amazing what you can do in a *télécabine*," she said, running her foot up the inside of my calf. She bit her lower lip as she smiled at me, and my imagination went wild. Now I couldn't wait for ski season to start.

Frédéric had a waiter bring us some strawberry shortcake for desert with a note saying it was his gift of sweets for the sweethearts. Alexandra and I both waved and smiled our thanks as we dug into the mountainous dessert.

"Drew, have you done any more writing lately?" she asked between mouthfuls.

"Not too much. I've been really concentrating on school."

"How is school going?"

"Good. My grades have really improved. I might even get a B in Algebra this semester," I said, scooping a piece of moist cake into my mouth.

"That's wonderful! I hate math," she said. "Everyone thinks I'm so good at it but I really hate it."

"You're good at everything. You have perfect grades."

"School is not everything," she said, shaking her head.

"It is to my father."

"Fathers always want what's best for their sons," she said.

"That's why I'm working so hard in school this semester."

She cocked her head and raised an eyebrow. I recognized the look, and knew what was coming.

"When did your parents split up?" she asked, putting her fork down on her plate. She would not be happy until this was on the table.

"This summer. They finally split this summer, but it was a long time coming."

"Are you okay with it?"

"I suppose so," I said, leaning back in my chair. "They're probably better off. They really don't get along at all anymore."

"How are your sisters handling it?"

"The same as me—the best they can. It's not an easy situation for any of us. Why do you ask?"

"Because I care about you," she said, squeezing my shoulder. "You've also changed a bit since I saw you in Rome. Then you were really happy and carefree, and you talked all the time about your writing, but now you seem to be carrying so much weight on your shoulders, and I haven't seen any writing from you. You used to write all the time."

"I'll start writing more once I've got a handle on school. I can't let my grades slip. My father will kill me."

"School is important, but I want you to be happy." She leaned over and kissed me on the cheek.

Thank you," I said, reaching for her hand. Even if I wanted, I couldn't explain what I was going through so she could understand, but I was truly grateful she was there for me.

Aunt Tess came over to the table with a big smile. "Are you kids almost ready? It's time for me to get you back to school."

"What time is it?"

"It's almost 9:30"

"We'll never make it back by 10:00!" I said

"Yes, you will," Frédéric said, walking up behind her. "I'm driving you back to school."

Frédéric drove a small Peugeot. Aunt Tess sat in the front and Alexandra and I sat in the back. I held her in my arms and we exchanges soft kisses in the darkness.

"Aunt Tess, what time are you leaving tomorrow?"

"Early in the morning, Dear. We probably won't be able to see each other."

Frédéric weaved his car down the winding road to Bluche and passed right by the entrance to my school where he pulled his car over to the side.

"Thank you for dinner, Aunt Tess. It was a pleasure meeting you, Frédéric. Thank you for the ride," I said, getting out of the car.

Aunt Tess got out of the car as well and gave me a big hug. "Study hard and take good care of Alexandra."

"I will."

"I'll see you this Christmas."

She got back in the car and they drove down the road towards *Prés Fleuris*. Tonight was really wonderful, and I wished she could stay a few days longer.

October crept up on us quickly. Most of the trees had already turned and were beginning to lose their leaves. The air grew colder, and we all waited with excitement for the first snowfall. Alexandra complained more about the cold and became more concerned about her mother as time progressed. Behind the

189

sparkle in her deep, brown eyes lurked a hint of sadness.

One day after class I walked with her to *Petit Paradis* to buy some things she needed. She told me during break she spoke to her mother the night before as she put her arm in mine and sighed. "Drew, she's really crazy. She tells me she wants to sell all the horses to a meat company."

I stopped and stood there silent for a moment. "She can't be serious."

"She is. She said she can't handle the farm and doesn't know anything about horses. Her solution is to sell them for dog food."

"But can't she sell them to another farm?"

"She says there are too many horses and nobody wants to take them all. For her this is a quick, easy solution."

"What about Claudio? Can't he stop her?"

"She won't listen to him. She won't listen to anyone. The entire estate is under her control."

"But there has to be somebody in the family that can stop her."

"Drew, there's nobody. She won't listen to anyone. She's going to destroy everything my father built," she said, finally bursting into tears. Her body shook as she cried, and I held her in my arms. I couldn't imagine what her mother was like right now, and wished I could do more, but watching my parents rip their own lives to shreds taught me very little could be done. I simply held her in my arms and hoped to ease her pain.

"Let's call Claudio tonight and see if there is anything we can do," I told her.

"When?"

"Right before study hall. He should be at home, right?"

"Yes, I think so."

"We'll call from the phone in the lobby at *les Roches*. M. Meneghetti won't have a problem with it."

She leaned against me and kissed me softly. "Thank you, Drew," she whispered.

"It's 3:00 O'clock. Let's do something fun. What would you like to do?"

"Get into a bed and sleep," she said, holding me tightly and burrowing her head against my chest. Dark circles were under her eyes, and her face looked drawn and pale, her cheeks streaked with tears.

"Well, that's an option we don't have, unless we can manage to rent a room in a hotel somewhere."

She looked up at me and laughed. "You won't be happy until you've had me in your bed an entire night all to yourself."

"An entire night? How about an entire week," I said laughing.

"Why does life have to be so painful?"

"It's just how life is," I said as I held her tighter, realizing her problems were just beginning.

"Drew, I'm really tired. I'm going back to my room to take a nap. I'll meet you here at 4:30 and we'll call Claudio."

"Okay. Sleep well," I said, kissing her on the forehead. She walked slowly down the road to *Prés Fleuris* as if she were an old woman returning home from a hard day's work. I knew she'd feel better after a nap. Whenever things got too much for me, sleep always helped.

I felt dry inside. A co-ed volleyball game was being played next to the football field, but I wasn't feeling social. I thought about trying to write, but just didn't seem to have any good ideas at the moment. I went back to my room to dig out something to read. Alexandra had given me a collection of Hemmingway stories, so I sat on my bed and opened the book. Hemmingway always seemed to take me away, and I got halfway through "The Snows of Kilimanjaro" until my eyelids felt too heavy to stay awake.

I woke up at around 4:30, and went out to the lobby to wait for Alexandra and as she came down the driveway toward me, she looked rested and was smiling.

"Did you sleep well?" I asked.

"Like a rock."

"Are you ready? The phone is right over there." I pointed to a small, wooden booth. She got in and dialed the phone while I stood next to her and held her hand.

"*Pronto? Ce Claudio, per favore?*"

She spoke to her brother in Italian. As the conversation progressed her voice became louder, and her eyebrows knitted in anger. When she finally hung up the phone, her face was red from rage, and her dark-brown eyes looked intense.

"What happened?" I asked.

Shaking her head and narrowing her eyes, she said, "Claudio is not going to do anything."

"Do you mean he can't or he won't?"

"He told me it's none of my business and not to interfere in Mother's affairs."

"But doesn't he realize how much is at stake?"

"Yes, of course, but he's just going along with her so she won't be upset."

"I'm sorry," I said, stroking back her hair.

She took my hand and pursed her lips. "That's not all. He told me she wants to get rid of the vineyards."

"That's insane! Why?"

"She can't handle the business and doesn't want to take responsibility," she said, slumping into the little wooden seat.

"But I thought Claudio could handle it."

"He could if he wanted to, but he won't go against her."

"So what's going to happen to them? How do you get rid of vineyards?"

192

"I suppose she could sell them. Our label is worth quite a bit. It's famous in Italy. But that would mean selling a substantial bit of land."

"Doesn't she have any idea what she is doing? I have never heard of such a thing!"

"A lot of my father's friends have tried to reason with her, but she won't listen. She only wants to destroy everything my father has built."

"But what's going to happen if she does all this?"

"I don't know," she said, shaking her head. Her eyes drooped slightly at the corners, and she bit her lip. I knew how scared she was.

"I'm sorry, Alexandra. This is really awful. If there is anything I can do you know I will."

"Thank you, Drew," she said, squeezing my hand.

M. Meneghetti's voice boomed over the P.A. Time for study hall. Alexandra waited for me while I ran back to my room to get my books. She carried herself well considering what she was going through, giving me the feeling that she was not simply going to accept her fate and spend her time moping. When we got to *Saint François*, she put her arms around me and held me close for several minutes.

"Drew. We need to have sex," she finally said. My penis responded before I could.

"Right now?" I asked incredulously.

"Soon. I want to feel you inside me."

If Philip could sneak into her window, then so could I. "Tonight after lights out meet me on your balcony. We'll climb down and go to Strawberry Field."

"What time?"

"We have to make sure everyone is asleep, so eleven-thirty should be okay. If I don't show up it's because I can't get away."

"Perfect. I'll see you tonight."

"I can't wait," I said, kissing her deeply. She slid her hand down the front of my pants and caressed me gently before we broke our embrace. I was ready to explode.

That night after dinner I planned my escape. My room was at the end of the hall and was at least fifteen feet off the ground which made climbing out the window impossible. I went downstairs and looked around the bathroom. The windows were pretty high and they tilted in, not leaving much room to get out. It could probably be done, but getting back in might be a problem.

I could easily get out through the window in John's room. I found him in the smoking lounge and waved him outside.

"What's up, Drew?"

"I need your window tonight," I whispered, looking around me to make sure nobody was near.

"Hot date?" he asked, smiling.

"How did you guess?"

"How do you think I get to see Julie? Tell her to go to the far side of *Prés Fleuris* to climb down. It's easier. Do you want some party favors?"

"You mean hash?" I asked wide-eyed.

"No. I mean rubbers. Alexandra would kill you if she caught you with that stuff."

"Where did you get rubbers?"

"At the drug store in Montana. I had Simon buy me a box."

"Yeah, I'll take some just in case we need them."

We went back to his room where he pulled a lockbox from the drawer of his nightstand and opened it.

"Here take these," he said, handing me a couple. "Maybe we should double date sometime."

"That would be weird."

"Why? We could trade partners," he said with his usual grin.

"You're disgusting!"

He laughed and cracked open the window. "You see the tree over there?" He asked, pointing out the window. "Just inch along the ledge and grab that branch. From there you're home free."

"What about your roommates?"

"They're cool. I'll let them know somebody may come in the window tonight."

After lights out I waited in my bed quietly until 11:15. Without a sound I grabbed my clothes and got dressed, then slipped into John's room and opened his window. The night air was cool and cloudy. I swung through the tree branches to the ground, and then ran down the road in the shadows toward *Prés Fleuris*. Alexandra was waiting on the balcony, wearing a pair of jeans and a sweatshirt and carrying a small backpack. She waved, and then swung her leg over the balcony railing and climbed down silently like a commando. I didn't expect her to be so agile.

"Hello," she whispered, kissing me. I grabbed her hand and we ran across the street toward the football field. The grass was dewy and the evening mist dampened my hair.

"Where do you want to go?" I asked.

"Let's go back to where we were by the tennis courts."

"That's perfect. I like it there."

We weaved through the shadows and trees until we came upon our bed of pine needles, surprised to find it still intact. Alexandra opened her backpack and took out a thick, wool blanket and spread it on the ground, and then dumped the remaining contents on the blanket—chocolate bars and rubbers.

I held them in my hands like jeweled trinkets. "Where did you get all these?"

"It's part of my inheritance."

"I'm glad to see you carrying on your father's legacy."

"Someone in the family has to. Do you want some chocolate?"

"Sure."

We sat on the blanket facing each other, and she unwrapped one of her chocolate bars.

"Are you okay?" I asked.

"Yes, I'm fine. Tomorrow I'm going to call my aunt and see if I can get her to do something about my mother."

She handed me a large piece of chocolate. The sweet, delicate taste lingered on my lips, and bits of hazelnut crunched in my mouth. "I'm sure this is all just temporary insanity. Your mother will snap out of it."

"I don't know. When my father died, my mother tried to act like nothing happened. She took us out shopping for cakes as if she didn't have a care in the world. At first she seemed so normal, but my aunt warned us to be careful because she knew there was something wrong."

"My mother can act really crazy sometimes, especially when she drinks, but she's not always like that. Maybe your mother just needs a little more time to get hold of her senses."

"I hope so, Drew. I'm really worried," she said, leaning her back against my chest. I rubbed her shoulders and kissed the back of her neck. She took a deep breath and sighed.

"Drew, do you love me?"

I wrapped my arms around her and squeezed her tightly. "Alexandra, I didn't know it was possible to love someone so much. I love you more than anything in the world."

She lay back in my arms and sighed. I slipped my hands around her waist and caressed her tummy. She broke off another piece of chocolate and put it in my mouth, and then lay back on the blanket and pulled me to her, our kisses tasting sweet and syrupy from all the chocolate. It was too cold to take off all our

196

clothes, but we slipped out of our pants. We made love gently in the dewy mist.

She came before I did, and we lay on the blanket with our legs entwined around each other, eating bits of chocolate and snuggling to keep warm in the moist night air.

"Drew, what's going to become of my family?"

"Why do you ask?"

She snuggled a little tighter against my shoulder. "I don't know if I can deal with all this. If my mother gets rid of the horses, I don't know how we'll survive."

"The vineyards won't be enough?"

"Not with our expenses. She's really out of her mind. So many friends have offered her help, but she won't take it."

"God, I'm sorry, Alexandra. It must be so hard."

"You have no idea," she said, wrapping her leg around my hips and pushing against me. "I think about what she's doing and get so angry because there's nothing I can do."

"You need to talk some sense into your brother. He's the only one who can really do anything."

"I've tried, but he won't listen. It's like he wants her to destroy everything."

"I don't get it. Is he scared?"

"I don't think so. He just won't go against her."

I ran my fingers through her hair, and she rocked herself against me. It was getting late. "We'd better get going before the sun comes up," I said.

Dawn was just around the corner. We started packing up our things. I saw flashlights in the trees. "Someone's coming," I whispered, my heart racing with panic.

We ducked beneath the bough of a tree, doing our best to hide. It was too late to run, and I knew we were caught. Whoever it was must have heard us because the lights suddenly shone exactly in our direction. We huddled against the tree, too scared to make a sound. Before we were even aware of it happening, M. Meneghetti and Katrina towered over us, their flashlights blaring in our eyes.

M. Meneghetti simply shook his head and sighed, and Katrina glared at us with contempt.

"Goodnight, Drew," Alexandra said, kissing me. Katrina escorted her back to *Prés Fleuris*, and M. Meneghetti took me back to his office where M. Davis was waiting. He scowled at me as I sat down in the chair in front of his desk.

"You better hope she is not pregnant, Mr. Smith," he said.

"We were careful."

"You were stupid. You were doing so well in school. Now you are finished."

"You are throwing me out of school?"

"Consider yourself expelled," he said, coldly. "Your plane leaves tomorrow morning early. I'll be driving you to the airport tonight. Take what you can; the rest of your belongings will be shipped to you."

As I returned to my room to gather up what I could, I wished I could at least have a chance to say goodbye to Alexandra, but there was no chance of that happening. I loved this place, and fought back my tears as I packed my bag. The thought of not seeing Alexandra again broke my heart, and part of me couldn't believe this was happening. M. Davis drove me to the airport in the middle of the night. We didn't say anything to each other, and I struggled to get a good look at the passing scenery through the darkness, realizing I wouldn't be seeing it again for a long, long time. When we arrived I picked up my suitcase and left without saying goodbye.

My father didn't say anything when he picked me up at the airport, and the ride home was equally tense. It took some time to get through the traffic and head down the New Jersey Turnpike, and as we passed the acrid smell of the oil refineries in Elizabeth he finally looked at me with clear contempt. "Boy, you really fucked this one up," he said.

I didn't answer. Instead, I focused on the blinking lights that topped the smoke stacks in the darkness. As we drove over the Raritan Bridge he told me I would be going to public school. I didn't speak until we finally picked up the Garden State Parkway and headed toward the shore.

"You know I love her, Dad."

"Well, you won't be seeing her again anytime soon. That's for sure."

We didn't speak the rest of the way home, where he simply dropped me off and left. I stood in the driveway and just stared, afraid to go inside. I felt like ashes. Most of the house was in darkness, with only the kitchen lights showing anyone even still lived there. After what felt like an eternity, I picked up my suitcases and headed for the door.

Chapter 10

Summer had just begun and my reality got stranger with every passing day. My sisters and I sat around the Worthington's table, waiting for dinner to start. Jason stayed in his room, refusing to eat with us. Occasionally he sauntered down the backstairs with a cigarette in his mouth to get a cup of coffee. He always wore dirty, faded blue jeans and an old t-shirt, and looked even more depressed and withdrawn. None of us wanted to be there, and the atmosphere was tense.

As soon as dinner was served, Mr. Worthington walked in. His eyes were wild and he could barely stand still. He looked as if he hadn't slept in days, and his five o'clock shadow made him look like a vagrant who had just wandered off the street. He jabbered about what a wonderful summer he was having, and how he never felt happier. We all just stared at him, wondering what possessed him to go back there in the first place.

"I figure it's about time I got into shape again," he announced suddenly, and then took off running laps around the outside of the house.

Mrs. Worthington tried to pretend nothing was wrong. Every few minutes we'd see him running past the dining room widow, huffing and puffing with a big smile on his face. I felt terrible for him.

After about five laps, he finally came back inside covered with sweat. He smelled awful; the exercise had flushed all the alcohol out of his system, and it percolated through his pores. He reached into his shirt pocket and lighted a cigarette.

"Robert, what are you doing here?" Mrs. Worthington asked, disgusted.

"Since you asked, Madame, I'm here to claim my house,"

he said heaving and coughing.

"Robert, get out!" she said.

"No. It's my house. I think it's best you all leave."

The two of them started arguing, and my father took us home. I couldn't believe he was leaving us for this madness. On the way, he told us jokes and laughed as if nothing at all was wrong.

Our house had been sold late last spring, and moving day was coming up fast. We began packing up the house. Where would we put all the furniture? My father was over more those days, clearing out his belongings. I was happy to see him away from Mrs. Worthington. Normally everything we did together had to include her, giving me the feeling that he was forcing us to accept her, but none of us did.

We began moving in the beginning of June. Since my father didn't want to pay a mover, we rented a van and moved by ourselves. He and I loaded most of the furniture while my mother and sisters made endless trips with carloads of boxes. The move took most of the day. Furniture was piled into the house anywhere we could put it.

I thought for sure my mother would buy a house in another town, but instead she bought a place down the street from the tennis club, well within walking distance from where my father now lived. Any other person would want to move as far away as possible, but she moved even closer to her pain. I still remember the day she finalized the deal. Julie and I were sitting in the study amidst piles of boxes when she came home cheerful and full of smiles. "Do you kids want to see our new house?" she asked.

We drove down Rumson Road toward Sea Bright. Just before the Sea Bright Bridge she made a right turn; had she made a left she would have headed toward where my father now lived.

As she continued down the street, the houses became smaller and smaller until at last she stopped the car in front of our new house.

"Here we are kids!" she said, getting out of the car.

The lot looked to be the size of a postage stamp, but the front porch was spacious and shady, and as we all walked up the brick walkway, my mother was already talking about the patio furniture she was going to put there.

She opened the front door, and directly in front of us a couple of steps led up to the main staircase, while on the other side of the landing another couple of steps led to the kitchen. It was an odd layout that was probably necessitated by lack of space.

The living room was pretty large, and it had a small fireplace, which immediately gave me a bit of hope—at least we'd be able to enjoy the warmth of a fire on cold winter nights. A set of glass doors opened into the dining room, which was surrounded by windows on two sides, with a set of double French doors leading to small, cement patio in back. This part of the house was charming, and I could see why my mother liked it so much.

The kitchen was dank, dirty and really needed work. The cupboards were painted black and the floor was covered with a hideous, dark-green outdoor carpet. Toward the back of the house was an addition with a separate entrance and a tiny bathroom. The room had possibilities, and both Julie and I were thinking the same thing when we saw it—we'd have a place to escape to when my mother started drinking. I prayed my mother didn't try to claim it as her study.

My bedroom was so small I didn't think there was enough room for my bed. Even worse, the room was too small to have an actual door open into it, and the hall was too narrow to have one open out, so an old curtain was hung in its stead.

My mother saw my disappointment. "It's not so bad, Dear. You'll live like a monk." I just looked at her blankly.

All of us would have to share the bathroom, and I could foresee major fights in the mornings. Julie's room wasn't much bigger than mine, and she gasped in disbelief at her tiny, new space. Gretchen and Annie were lucky to be in boarding school.

After seeing the place, I dreaded moving and wondered if I should just take off and never come back, but I had no money and needed to finish high school. I looked around at all the furniture and boxes piled in the driveway with sadness. By late afternoon most of the major pieces of furniture had been moved, and my father and I sat in the driveway resting. I was tired, and my shoulders hurt. That evening I helped my mother and sisters move furniture around until the place was livable. Some furniture just didn't fit, so we stuffed it in the garage.

We had a couple of weeks before we had to be officially out of the old house, so I spent a few days rooting around the empty rooms looking for odds and ends that may have been left behind. I walked through each room remembering the times we had. Life would never be the same. This was the house I grew up in, and now it was gone.

As part of the separation agreement, my father continued paying the beach club dues for my mother and us. He asked me if I wanted to continue going to the tennis club, and of course I said yes. It was the only really fun thing left to do in the summer. He didn't look happy about it, but I knew this would be my last year there and I wanted to enjoy it.

Living so close to the beach club and tennis club was convenient. On weekday mornings I saw Mrs. Worthington with her usual tennis group. We didn't have a lot to say to each other; in fact, we made a point of avoiding each other as often as possible. She didn't spend much time at the beach during the week, preferring instead to work in her garden after her morning tennis game.

On weekends she came down to the beach with my father to have lunch. They sat almost at the very end of the boardwalk now, and my mother sat on the beach with the rest of the divorcées. Whenever they ran into each other there was always a tense moment as they exchanged a few nasty words. She once told me that being a divorced woman in Rumson was probably the worst thing that could ever happen to you, but if that were true, I couldn't understand why she chose to stay.

That summer my mother insisted I take a typing class. I thought she was crazy, but she told me that if I wanted to become a writer I'd need to learn how to type. When summer sessions started at the high school, I was the only man in a room filled with women. At first the keyboard intimidated me, and I couldn't make sense of the jumble of letters that sat in front of me.

The teacher understood my embarrassment, taking a little extra time to show me how to hold my hands on the keyboard. Each morning for a month I pounded out typing exercises until I could bang out at least forty words per minute without a single mistake. At the end of the session my mother asked my father to bring her an electric typewriter from the office. He brought over an IBM Selectric, and we set it up in the little addition, which had become the television room and study for Julie and me.

What used to be our kitchen table became my desk. My mother bought me a ream of writing paper, and I put in on the table next to the typewriter. Forcing me to take typing lessons was the best thing she ever did. I stayed up late almost every night, hammering out short stories and poetry. Having a typewriter made me feel more like a real writer, and my writing seemed to flow better. At times my mother had moments of lucidity and great kindness, but those moments only occurred when she was sober. More often than not she was drunk.

Summer was ending. I looked forward to school just for a change in routine. I hadn't heard from Alexandra since I left Switzerland, and I wondered how she was doing. My parents forbade me to contact her again, but I missed her kisses and how she felt in my arms. That night I typed a long letter about my summer. I held nothing back, recounting all that I had been through. The next morning I rode my bike to the post office in Sea Bright and mailed it, along with a collection of some of my more recent stories.

By summer's end I had written quite a few stories, and my writing had improved dramatically. I began to explore point-of-view, and dialogue came more naturally. I shared my work with Julie. Although only twelve, she could relate well to my work, and always had good criticism. I struggled with every word I wrote, never sure about whether it was the right one or not. I began reading other writers, studying their styles to see how my writing measured up. When I began reading Saul Bellow and John Updike I got discouraged, but I kept writing.

Aunt Tess had been away most of the summer at an artist's retreat in Vermont, finishing her series on Italy. She showed up early one morning on her way back from church. My mother wasn't up yet, and I was sitting in the kitchen, drinking a cup of coffee when she walked in unexpectedly and kissed me on the cheek.

"How are you making out?" she asked cheerfully, pouring herself a cup of coffee.

"Fine. It's good to see you."

"Where's your mother?" she asked, sitting down next to me.

"Sleeping."

"Have you heard from Alexandra since your debacle in Switzerland?"

"Not a word."

"Well, it's probably for the best. I never told you how sorry I was about what happened. I felt so awful because I knew you really shot yourself in the foot over that one."

I was too hurt to look her in the eyes. "I'm sorry it happened. I miss her."

"Well, try not to think about it. You start your senior year at high school, isn't that right?"

I nodded and took a sip of coffee.

"Well, it's a good school as far as high schools go. Roy finished his last year there when we came back from Switzerland. Try to keep your head down and do the best you can."

"I will. How's the painting going?"

"Really well. This new series I'm working on has great potential."

"That's great, Aunt Tess. I'm sure it'll be beautiful"

"Thank you, Dear. Now be a Saint and go wake your mother for me."

I went and called my mother, and before long, the two of them sat in the kitchen having coffee. I could tell by her demeanor Aunt Tess was disappointed with me, and I felt sad and ashamed. I locked myself in my study to do some more writing.

My senior year of high school finally began. Being a senior had certain privileges; for instance, the senior wing had a comfortable lounge where we could relax between classes and play music. I walked into the lounge my first day of school and sat down by myself. People sat together at tables, studying or talking. Others relaxed in overstuffed couches and chairs. Their faces looked familiar, but having begun the last semester more than halfway through the year, everything was such a blur, and I didn't know anyone. Everyone looked so vibrant and happy; I felt as if I didn't belong.

The following week my guidance counselor wanted to see me after homeroom. All seniors had to declare a sequence—college preparatory or vocational. My Counselor was a short man with a pointy nose and thinning hair. "Drew, how are you? My name is Mr. Dexter."

"Hi."

"Well, let's see," he said, looking through my file. "You spent some time in Switzerland. How was that? Fun?"

"It was amazing."

"I'll bet. You are lucky to have such a wonderful experience."

"I think so," I said, smiling.

"Well, your grades are not very good, Drew. You've gotten mostly D's and F's throughout most of your high school career."

"I did well my last year in Switzerland."

"Yes, I can see that. And from what I have heard your French is excellent, but you are going to have to do a whole lot better than what you did last semester if you expect to graduate. If it weren't for your grades from Switzerland we probably would have held you back a year. What's going on, Drew? Is everything okay at home?"

"Everything is fine."

He pursed his lips. "So, what sequence are you going to declare?"

"College prep."

"Are you sure about this, Drew? College is not for everyone, and we do have some excellent vocational programs here."

It never occurred to me that I wouldn't be going to college, and to hear my high school guidance counselor question my ability to even get into one made me angry.

"I'm going to college. I didn't end up in this hellhole to become a goddamn grease monkey!"

207

"Watch your language with me, son," he said, glaring at me, his face reddening slightly.

"I'm going to college!" I repeated, storming out of his office and slamming the door.

I went out to the park and found a group of potheads who just ignored me when I sat down. A fat kid with scraggly hair I heard was running for class president always had pot. "I'd like to score an ounce of weed," I said.

"Thirty-five bucks," he told me. I reached into my pocket and pulled out a wad of bills—nearly my entire allowance for the week. He counted out the money, reached into his book bag, and handed me a rolled up baggie. I opened it and smelled the weed. It didn't smell like very good quality.

"Thanks."

I got up and walked to the convenience store around the corner to buy some rolling papers. I had about twenty minutes before class. I went back to the park by myself and rolled a thin joint. The weather was beautiful. I lay back on the pick-nick table with my shirt opened and got stoned by myself.

Time for algebra; I felt rather conspicuous when I sauntered into class, and got the feeling everyone was looking at me. I tried to follow what the teacher was explaining, but was way too stoned.

"Mr. Smith," said the teacher. I heard him call my name, but for some reason I couldn't respond. "Mr. Smith!" he said again.

"Yes," I finally replied.

"Can you please complete this equation for us on the board?" he asked, holding up a piece of chalk. I looked at the board blankly. I had no idea what he was talking about. "Today, Mr. Smith."

I got up out of my chair and took the chalk from him.

Everyone watched me, and a few people snickered. I looked at the equation on the board; I had no idea how to solve it. "I can't deal with this," I said, going back to my desk.

"With that sort of attitude you will go nowhere in life," he said.

"At least I won't be here," I said, gathering up my books.

"If you leave this class I'll make sure you won't be back," he warned, his face screwed up in anger.

I sat back down. Throughout the rest of the session I stared out the window, wishing I hadn't gotten so stoned. I felt as though I were throwing my life away. When the bell rang I gathered up my books and started to leave.

"Hold on a minute, Mr. Smith. I want to talk to you," my teacher said. I waited for him by the door. Once everyone left, he motioned for me to sit down in front of his desk. "What's going on, Mr. Smith?" he asked, looking into my eyes. I was sure he could tell I was high.

"Nothing is going on."

"Look, I know all about your history, and I know you are capable of doing the work, but if you don't pass this class you are not going to graduate. If I were you I'd buckle down."

"What do you know about my history?"

"I know you were thrown out of more schools than I would care to admit, and I know you come from a broken home. I know that a broken home makes for an unhappy kid, and I know that you are pretty unhappy right now. Does that about sum it up?"

"Pretty much."

"Well, Mr. Smith. We all face hardships in life; how you choose to deal with them defines your character. You are digging your own grave. You can keep digging and eventually lie down in it, or you can pull yourself out. The semester has just begun, and your grave is already pretty deep in my book. So, what's it going to be, Mr. Smith? The choice is all yours. Your homework assignment is to think about that."

"Is that all?"

"That's all, Mr. Smith."

I hurried out. I was really screwing up. The problem was I couldn't seem to stop. I decided the only way to get through the year was not to be stoned during school.

As I walked down the hallway a group of kids looked at me and laughed.

"Stoner," a tall, lanky kid called out. I kept walking. I ate lunch by myself in the cafeteria. Almost nobody went to the school cafeteria because the food was so awful, but it was cheap.

After lunch I went to my English class, the only one I looked forward to. My teacher, Mr. Vargas, took a liking to me. A thin man in his mid-forties with a goatee and moustache, his trademark was polyester leisure suits. By most standards the wide collars and polyester material was considered tacky, but he seemed to wear them well. He had quite a collection, and wore a different color nearly every day. Not only was he the head of the English department, but he also ran the drama department as well. His classes were lively; he presented his material in a theatrical manner which helped to keep my interest.

Most of the books we were covering I had already read, but I didn't mind; literary criticism came easy for me, and I enjoyed analyzing the characters. As seniors we were required to hand in typewritten manuscripts. Most people struggled with the assignments, but I blew through the first couple of papers with ease. If nothing else I was determined to get a decent grade in English.

After school I went home and locked myself in the study. I had started a new story about my parents and their divorce. I wrote most of the afternoon and well into the evening. I finished writing just after midnight, and held my manuscript in my hands proudly, feeling the weight of the paper. My story was nearly twenty pages—the most I had written so far. I read through it carefully, looking for grammatical errors and breaks in the flow. I marked up the areas that I wanted to revise, and then smoked a joint and watched T.V. It was nearly two in the morning when I finally went up to bed.

My mother dumping a pot of cold water on me awakened me the next morning.

"Get up!" she screamed.

"What the hell are you doing?"

"It's almost 9:00! Get your ass to school!"

"Did you have to throw water on me?"

"I tried to wake you three times, but you didn't get up!"

"Oh, shit!" I had already missed homeroom, and my morning algebra class was about to begin. I threw on a pair of pants and a t-shirt.

"Mom, can you give me a ride to school?"

"Hitchhike. I'm not a taxi service."

I ran downstairs, grabbed my books, and ran out the door. School wasn't that far and the morning traffic was busy enough I could get a ride quickly. I ran across the road and stuck out my thumb. The fifth car that passed me pulled over to the side of the road. The woman who stopped was nice enough to give me a ride all the way to school. I ran to my class and opened the door out of breath.

"Mr. Smith, you are wanted at the principal's office," my teacher said.

"Now?"

"Right now."

I shut the door and headed toward the main wing. This year was not starting off well. I entered the office and told the gray-haired lady at the front desk my name.

"Have a seat, Mr. Smith. The principal will see you in a minute."

I sat in my chair fidgeting, not knowing what to do with myself, so I pulled out my manuscript and began to read. I liked the story; it read well. I had rushed the ending a bit, but all in all I was happy.

"Mr. Tyndall will see you now," the receptionist told me. She opened a little gate and led me down a short hallway to the principal's office.

The principal looked like a football player, with a stocky, strong build and thick blond hair that he wore in a crew cut. Purple and white pennants adorned his walls. "Have a seat, Mr. Smith," he said.

I sat down in front of his desk. My file lay open on his desk in front of him. Was it going to follow me around like a ghost the rest of my life?

"Mr. Smith, I've been receiving complaints about you. Your attendance has been awful. You cut a lot of classes, and you are consistently late for school. Mr. Dexter told me you cursed him out and stormed out of his office. Is that true, Mr. Smith?"

"No. It's not true. I did not curse him out personally. I lost my temper, but I did not curse him out."

"Mr. Smith, verbally abusing anyone on our faculty is completely unacceptable. Your classroom attendance alone is enough to warrant serious disciplinary action. So, you tell me, Mr. Smith. What should I do with you?"

I hated when they asked me that question. No matter how I answered it would never be good enough, so I just looked at him blankly.

After a few seconds he shook his head. "Well, Mr. Smith, I'm going to give you a week of detentions. If your behavior

212

doesn't improve I'm going to have to suspend you. No more missing classes and no more coming late to school. Do you understand?"

"Yes, Sir."

"Fine," he said, writing me out a detention slip. "You start today. If you miss a single detention you will be suspended for two weeks."

I took the paper from him and left. A week of detentions wasn't bad; at least I'd have a quiet place to do my homework. Every day after school I reported to detention, and managed to get through the rest of the week without further incidents. Because Algebra was my worst subject I focused on that first, making sure I got my homework done before doing anything else. I may not get into Princeton, but at least I wouldn't be held back.

Later that week I received a small package from Alexandra. The return address was in Lausanne. It contained a few bars of chocolate and a letter. Julie was in the study with me when I opened the package, happy to receive some of the rich chocolate.

Dear Drew,

Thank you for your letter and stories. (Typewritten! So formal!) It's been so long since we have spoken and so much has happened. Collalto was sold last month to an historical society called Quattrostelle, and we moved to a comfortable, old house closer to Rome. It was really hard moving out of the castle. It's been in our family for generations, and I'm so sad it's gone.

My mother sold the horses last spring. I cried like an idiot the whole time while they were being herded onto trucks like heads of cattle. It was so awful. Some sympathetic friends bought some of the better horses, but the rest were shipped off to slaughter. It broke my heart. Such beautiful animals; such a waste.

Just before we moved she had the vines burned to the ground. I couldn't believe it. All those wonderful vines cut down and burned. My poor mother

213

has destroyed a fortune, and I don't think she knows what she's doing anymore. She's really lost her mind.

I am going to a girl's school in Lausanne called Ecole NouvelleDe La Suisse Romande. The school is beautiful, but it doesn't have the charm that Prés Fleuris and Ecole des Roches had. At least I don't have to deal with Katrina and Monsieur Davis!

You letter hurt me a lot, Drew. I am very, very sorry for you. I didn't know things were so bad for you, but you are strong and smart. I know you can handle the situation and come out on top. Please, Drew, if things get too bad, think of me and the wonderful times we had. Try to get through your year of high school, and then you have the rest of your life to decide how you want to live.

Your writing has progressed so much over the summer! I was shocked at how good it has become in so little time. I know the writing is good for you, and it helps you express your pain, so just write. Write and write and write. Don't stop until you feel good again, and remember, I am always your dearest friend.

Much love and many kisses,
Alexandra

I held her letter in my hands and felt tears welling up in my eyes; I would have given anything to see her again. I showed it to Julie and she caressed my arm when she finished reading. "Drew, you two will always have a special bond," she said.

I rested my head on her shoulder. "I miss her so much."

"You'll see her again someday. I'm sure of it."

"Do you really think so?"

"Yes," she said, crossing her arms, her sharp, green eyes filled with confidence. "A bond this strong will never be broken."

"I can't believe her mother did all those things," I said, shaking my head.

"The poor girl! Her mother sounds like a real lunatic."

214

I broke off a piece of chocolate and put it in my mouth, the sweetness reminding me of the last time Alexandra and I were together. I wasn't sure if I should laugh or cry.

"Do you want to get high?" I asked.

"You have pot?"

"Sure do," I said, reaching into my pocket.

Julie and I went out to the garage. She was scared Mom would catch us, but I reassured her it was safe because Mom never went into the garage. I rolled a nice, fat joint and let her light it. After a few tokes, Julie's eyes were filled with panic, and she turned white and began shaking. "Drew, I think Mom is going to die," she said, her voice quavering slightly.

I looked at her in shock. "Why would you say that?"

"Look at the way she drinks. Nobody can drink that much and survive."

"Julie, Mom is not going to die. She's a tough, old woman. She'll survive."

She suddenly burst into heaving sobs, collapsed on the ground, and gripped her knees tightly to her chest and rocked back and forth. The fear in her eyes didn't seem reasonable.

"Julie, it's going to be okay," I told her, getting on my knees and taking her in my arms. She sobbed harder. I didn't know what to do. I held on to her tightly while she cried. After a few minutes she put her arms around my neck and leaned against me. Her sobbing turned to short inhalations and low sighs. She was still shaking.

"Let's get out of here. Why don't we take a walk to the park," I suggested.

I helped her off the floor and wiped her tear-stained cheeks. We walked up the street, past the Episcopal Church, to a small park where there was a swing set and little play area for toddlers at the foot of the Sea Bright Bridge. Julie looked pretty dazed. I pushed her gently in the swing while she talked about her friends. She sounded better, and I sat down in the swing next to her. "Julie, what happened before?"

"I don't know. All of a sudden I just got really scared."

"Well, you scared the hell out of me. Are you okay now?"

"I'm better... Drew, what's going to happen when you graduate? I don't think I can stand being here by myself."

"Maybe you can go to boarding school. We all went. I don't know why you shouldn't."

"I asked Mom about it a while ago. She said no."

"Really? How come?"

"I don't know. She just said something about me having to stay home and help her take care of things."

"I don't think you should stay here. I think you should talk to Dad and see if you can go to boarding school. Mom will drive you crazy if you stay."

"Fuck. Can we not talk about this now?" she asked, angrily.

I stopped, knowing she might lose her temper and turn on me like a wild animal.

"I have a little bit of money. Why don't we walk to Sea Bright and get some pizza?"

"Okay." she said with a disconsolate sigh.

We walked over the Sea Bright Bridge. Sea Bright looked like a ghost town in the winter; the crowds of people that normally choked Ocean Avenue during the summer were gone. The beach clubs were boarded up and locked down. Anniello's Pizza shop was a favorite spot for teenagers in the summertime, but in winter the place mostly survived on its delivery business. Julie and I entered and sat down.

A short, Italian man from Naples, Anniello had a strong accent, and whenever I saw him, was always unshaven and wearing his kitchen uniform. "What can I get for you?" He asked.

"Can we have a couple of plain slices, please?"

"*Certo*," he replied.

"*Grazie*."

"You speak Italian?"

"No. Not really. I had an Italian girlfriend, and I spent some time in Rome, but I only know a few words.

"Ah," he said, nodding at me. He went and got our pizza for us and we ate in silence. The sky over the ocean became cloudy, and I saw rain on the horizon. Julie seemed happier after eating. After finishing I got up to pay the check.

"How was everything?" he asked.

"It was good, thank you."

He looked me over a moment or two. "Listen," he said. "I need someone to help out here at nights and on weekends. How would you like to learn the pizza business?"

"Sure! I'd love to. How much does it pay?"

"I'll start you off at five dollars an hour, and then we'll see what happens by the summer. Do you have a driver's license?"

"Yes."

"On weekends I might need you to help out delivering pizzas. It gets pretty busy on Saturday nights."

"No problem."

"When can you start?"

"Is tomorrow, okay?"

"I'll see you then," he said, shaking my hand.

Julie and I left the shop and headed toward the bridge. I was happy to have a job and some extra money. The wind had kicked up and as the storm clouds rolled in off the ocean, and droplets of rain pelted my skin. It began to pour just as we got to the front porch.

My mother was sitting in the kitchen when we walked in; her beer can sat in front of her, and the ash on her cigarette dangled precariously. Somehow it never fell off, but sat there until she was ready to tip it in the ashtray. Her eyes were glazed and looked sad. We tried sneak around the kitchen through the living room to our study, but she saw us. "Where the fuck of you been?" she yelled.

"We were in Sea Bright, Mom," I replied.

"Julie, you lazy, little bitch. If I ever come home and find this kitchen like this again I'll ground you for a month."

"I'm sorry, Mom," she said, hurrying into the kitchen.

I followed. The kitchen wasn't all that messy. A few dirty dishes littered the sink and counter, but it wasn't a complete pigsty. I unloaded the dishwasher while Julie rinsed the dishes and wiped down the counter.

"What the hell were you doing in Sea Bright," she asked, popping open another beer.

"We went and got some pizza. I got a job there after school," I replied.

"Doing what?"

"Making pizzas and helping out with deliveries."

"It's about time you got off your lazy ass and did something with your life."

Julie and I finished cleaning the kitchen as quickly as possible, and then went to our study and locked ourselves in. In a couple of hours my mother would be too drunk to deal with at all. Julie sat in front of the T.V. and worked on her homework while I revised my manuscript and ate some of the chocolate Alexandra sent.

The next day after school I walked down to Sea Bright to start my new job. Anniello gave me an apron and showed me how to fold pizza boxes which I stacked on top of the oven.

Around 8:00 pm it started to get busy. Anniello kept a big pot of boiling water on the stove, and showed me how to measure the pasta and immerse it in the boiling water in a strainer, then put the cooked pasta in a tinfoil container and cover it with sauce. I enjoyed it. He told me I had a flair for cooking.

On a particularly busy Saturday night, Anniello asked me to help out with deliveries. He gave me the keys to his car—a Volkswagen Rabbit. He loaded up the passenger seat with six pizzas. They were all going to the same address in Rumson, which happened to be a girl in one of my classes at school. I drove down a long, dark street not far from the one where I grew up. The house was an old brick mansion that stood in the shadow of some big pine trees. Music blared from inside. I picked up the pizzas and held them on my shoulder as I rang the doorbell.

A young girl opened the door. She was holding a beer mug, and I saw a keg just inside the door. "Did somebody order pizza?" she called over the din.

"Yes!" called a voice from the back.

A tall boy came to the door—one of the potheads I knew from the park. He looked stoned. He was about 6'1", and he and his friends always wore their button-down Oxford shirts with the tails out, as if they were making some sort of political statement.

"So, you are delivering Pizzas now?" he asked.

"Yes. The total comes to twenty-seven dollars," I said.

He took the pizzas from me and set them down. "Hold on a second," he said, shutting the door. The door lock clicked shut. I waited on the stoop a minute, not knowing whether he intended to do what he had just done. Finally I rang the doorbell again. He opened the door. Everyone was eating pizza.

"Where's my money?" I asked.

"Fuck off," he said, and started to close the door. But before it closed, I managed to wedge my foot in the jam.

"You owe me money, asshole!"

"What was that?" he said, taking me by the shirt collar and

nearly picking me off the ground with one arm. He punched me hard in the nose. My head snapped back and the pain shot through my head. He threw me off the stoop onto my back and shut the door. Laughter came from inside. My nose was bleeding hard.

I wiped the blood from my face with my shirtsleeve and drove back to Anniello's.

"*Dios mio*! What the hell happened?"

"I got rolled," I replied.

"What do you mean rolled?"

"They took the pizzas and beat me up."

"Bastards! Where's the check and my keys?" I handed him both. "Watch the store while I'm gone. This won't take long."

He jumped in his car and took off. Anniello's wife gave me some ice in a dishrag and held it to my face. I felt more humiliated than anything else.

Anniello returned a half hour later. "Little pricks! They won't ever fuck with me again."

"What did you do?" I asked.

"I broke the fucking door down and told them to pay me or I'd beat the shit out of all of them!"

"You're crazy, Anniello," his wife said.

"Maybe so, but they won't ever mess with me again."

I could imagine him smashing through the door and demanding his money. Despite his size he was afraid of nobody, and I wished I could be more like him. I hated confrontation, and was a terrible fighter; I just didn't have the heart for it.

"Why did you let those guys treat you like that?" he asked.

"I didn't. The guy who hit me was built like the Jolly Green Giant."

"You're talking about that big, dumb bastard with the dark hair?"

"Yeah, that's him."

220

"I walked right up to him and told him if he didn't pay me I'd rip his nuts off and cook them on a pizza." I laughed as he continued. "Next Thursday come early. I'm going to teach you how to defend yourself. Otherwise those bastards will never leave you alone."

Next week at school, the pothead who hit me came up to me. I thought I was going to have to fight him again, but instead he held out his hand. "I was pretty wasted. I didn't know what I was doing," he said.

I shook hands with him reluctantly. The last thing I expected was an apology, but I still didn't like him or his friends.

That afternoon after English class Mr. Vargas asked me to wait behind. I stood by his desk, wondering if were going to get another lecture, but once everyone had left, he turned to me and smiled. "Drew, your writing is pretty advanced for someone your age. Where did you learn to write so well?"

"I like to write. I spend a lot of time doing it," I replied, never expecting to hear anything so positive.

"What do you write?"

"Short stories mostly. Sometimes I write poetry, but I like writing fiction."

"What kind of stories do you write?"

"Mostly about stuff that happens in my life. I don't know. I get all kinds of ideas and just start writing."

"Would you mind letting me read some of your work?"

"No. Not all. I'd like to get your feedback. I write all the time, but I don't know if it's any good or not."

"Well, I'd be happy to read some," he said, smiling.

"I'd appreciate that, Sir."

That night I went through my most recent stories. The one I just finished was too angry, and I didn't want to reveal too much about my family problems, so I picked up a story about Axel and

221

me, and my first encounter with Austin in Greece. I had put a lot of work into describing my surroundings and how my world was changed through our single meeting. I put the story in an envelope, and the next day, handed it to him after class.

"I hope you enjoy it. I wrote it this summer," I told him, nervous about how he'd react.

"Thank you, Drew. I'm sure I will."

That Thursday I went to work an hour early. Anniello took me to a little fenced courtyard behind the restaurant. "When I was a boy I had to fight everyday. I was smaller than the other kids, but I wasn't going to take any of their shit. Here, stand like this," he said, planting his feet firmly. "Now hold your fists up in front of your face." He took my hands and showed me how to keep my guard up. "No matter what, never drop your hands. First thing you need to learn is how to block a punch."

He had me throw a couple of straight punches at his face. He moved deftly out of the way and parried each of my attacks.

"Now you try," he said, throwing a couple of punches at me. At first I closed my eyes and swung wildly at his arm.

"If you close your eyes you are going to get hit. No matter what, keep your eyes open. And don't swing at my arm; just move my fist out of the way gently, like this," he said, demonstrating the movement.

Slowly I began to pick up the technique, and I began to get better at blocking his attacks. He increased his speed and varied his punches more. When I missed a block he'd smack me in the face and I wanted to smack him back.

"Don't be angry. It clouds your judgment. Each time you get hit learn from it, and don't let it happen again. If you get angry that just means you are no longer in control."

After an hour we stopped to go to work.

"You did well. Tomorrow I will teach you how to punch and kick."

"Kick?"

He jumped straight in the air and spun around. His foot whizzed right past my nose. I was stunned. "What the hell was that?"

"That was Tae Kwan Do. I am a second-degree black belt."

"You're kidding! I never would have guessed. Where did you learn that?"

"In Italy when I was a young boy. Like I said, I had to learn to defend myself at an early age."

"Will you teach me?"

"I will teach you if you promise not to use it for anything but self-defense."

"I promise."

"Good. Tomorrow we practice again. Now start making the sauce. Later on I'm going to show you how to mix the dough."

We went inside, and I felt a new respect for Anniello. What he was like in Italy?

After school the next day I went almost immediately to the pizza shop. Anniello was watching wrestling on T.V. Giant men with bulging physiques pretended to beat each over the head with chairs. They spent a lot of time throwing each other around the ring.

"This is all bullshit!" he said.

"It looks to me like they're knocking each other silly."

"You believe this garbage?" he asked, laughing at me. "Come. I'll show you what real fighting is about."

Anniello picked up a huge gym bag and we went outside. He showed me how to stand properly to minimize my vulnerable areas. Then he showed me how to punch, always remembering to pull my punch back to keep myself protected. He showed me how to give my punches snap without hyper-extending my arm and to use my hips for power. Finally he put on a couple of over-sized mitts and had me throw simple combinations at them—jab, jab, cross—jab, jab, cross. Occasionally he would swat at my head to ensure my guard was up.

"Never drop your hands," he told me as he moved around me in a circle, changing directions without warning. "Plant your feet before you punch; otherwise you will be off balance."

Finally, he showed me how to throw a front kick.

"Pick your knee up before you kick. Wherever you point your knee is where your kick will go."

He showed me how to flex my foot forward and pull my toes back, so that I hit with the ball of my foot. He had me practice kicking in the air several times, always adjusting my technique to get more power and speed.

"When you go home tonight, practice this kick in slow motion. Try to get your knee as high as it will go, and when you extend your leg lock it out and hold it for ten seconds. When you retract your leg, go back the same way. Do at least fifteen of those each night before going to bed, and your kicks will have power and control."

The following day after English class, Mr. Vargas asked me to stop by his office between classes. I knocked on his door. His office was stuffed with books, and he was sitting at his desk correcting papers.

"Come in, come in," he said, motioning me to a chair next to his. I sat down nervously. "I read your story, Drew. It was quite good. You have talent."

"Thank you, Sir," I replied, blushing.

"I especially liked your use of imagery, but you are a little heavy with all the similes. It's not necessary to be poetic all the time."

"What do you mean?"

"Here," he said, going through my manuscript, underlining sentences every couple of pages. "All these sentences have a simile used to express an idea. Similes are great tools when used sparingly, but sometimes it's better to simply express your thought and let the reader create the image for himself."

What he said made sense, but I enjoyed pushing my creativity through the use of language. "Isn't it the job of the writer to create an image for the reader?" I asked.

"Yes, it is, but you have to let the reader do some of the work for himself; otherwise the writing grows tedious. You have an ear for dialogue, but watch your colloquialisms. It's one thing to hear it spoken, but it's taxing for the reader if they see it on paper all the time."

"What did you think of the story?"

"Overall the story was pretty good. You built up tension quickly and your resolution was believable. Did you actually have this experience in Greece?"

"Yes, I did. Two years ago. My best friend took me to see this man. The experience changed me quite a bit."

"I could tell by your descriptions. They were very colorful, but there were times when I wanted more. You like to focus on your characters more than their surroundings. Sometimes the reader needs to feel the environment he is in as much as the character."

"It's true. I tend to be lazy about describing things. I like to cut right to the heart of the matter."

"That's what they call a minimalist approach. It's effective, but it can also alienate your reader. You have the ability to paint a scene quickly without too many words. Use it, just don't abuse it," he said.

"Thank you. I will, Sir."

225

"It's my pleasure, Drew. Do you have any more stories?"

"I have a few. Would you like to see some?"

"Absolutely, bring them in. I'm always happy to help a budding young writer," he said, patting my knee.

I jerked my knee away. "I'm just finishing a new story. It's more than twenty pages. It's my longest piece yet. When it's done would you mind reading it?"

"Not at all. Bring it in. And keep up the good work," he said, smiling.

I felt better than I had in months. During class I pulled out my manuscript and read though the places he marked up. His critique was good, and I wished I was at home to put it into practice.

After school I walked down to Sea Bright a little lightheaded. With all the negative feedback I had gotten from my teachers in the past, it was nice to hear something positive for a change. Anniello gave me a big smile when he saw me.

"You look different today. What happened?"

"Nothing, things are just going better," I replied.

"Good. Get my bag and come outside. We're going to work on some new drills today."

A canvas heavy bag hung from the fence.

"Did you practice your kicks?"

"Yes, I did."

"Good. Today we are going to learn a new kick, and then we'll work some combinations on the bag."

He showed me how to throw a wheel kick. "Pick your knee up and turn your hip over like this," he showed me. "Then flip your leg out keeping your toes pointed. You strike with your instep," he said slapping his foot. He had me throw them in the air at first.

It was painful. Then we worked some combinations with

the focus pads. Afterward he had me throw twenty front kicks and twenty wheel kicks against the heavy bag. The workout was harder than before, and at the end I was gasping for air.

"You are out of shape," he told me. "Try to jog two or three miles in the morning if you can. It will clear your head and help your wind."

The thought of getting up in the morning to run did not appeal to me in the slightest. I had enough trouble getting up for school.

"Is it supposed to hurt so much in the hips?" I asked.

"The pain is good for you. Your body is just not used to moving like this. You need to stretch. Follow me," he said, sitting on the ground and spreading his legs apart. I followed the best I could, but wasn't very limber. "Tonight practice your front kicks and wheel kicks in slow motion. Do ten of each kick without putting your leg down, and then switch legs. Afterward stretch lightly the way I showed you. Don't stretch too hard."

"Okay," I said. My legs and lower back were a bit sore.

"Let's get some strength in your body."

He held my feet down on the ground by pinning them between his knees. Each time I sat up I had to punch the focus pads. Afterward we did twenty-five pushups. At the end of it I felt as though I were going to throw up. I lay on my back, devoid of any energy.

"Come on, Drew. It's time to go to work. We are going to have a busy night." I helped him pick up his gear and lugged the bag inside. "You're doing well," he said, patting me on the back. "Just keep doing the exercises I showed you and soon you'll start kicking like an expert."

I stuffed his bag beneath the steel counter and pulled out what I needed to prep for tonight's business. I liked watching Anniello make pizzas, pounding out the little balls of dough into small circles on the counter and then tossing them in the air, spinning them until they fit perfectly on the pans. He let me try throwing a couple, but I kept tearing the dough, and they always came out lopsided.

"You are not ready to throw pizzas yet," he said.

That night after work I practiced my kicks. Doing the wheel kicks in slow motion was especially painful and made my hip flexors burn. The next morning I got up early to run. I put on a pair of sweat pants and a sweatshirt.

"Where are you going?" Julie asked, as I headed toward the front door.

"Running."

"Can I come?"

"Sure," I said, surprised but happy to have her company.

We set out down Shrewsbury Drive. November was creeping up fast and the morning air was crisp. We were both out of shape. We headed up Naversink Avenue to Ridge Road. After the first mile or so I began to feel good, and realized running got me slightly high. Julie didn't enjoy it as much, but she kept up well.

"Are you okay?" I asked.

"I'm getting a side split."

We walked the rest of the way home. I told Julie what Mr. Vargas said about my writing.

"I think someday you'll be a very successful writer," she said.

"I hope so. I don't know what else to do with my life. I am barely getting through school."

"I'm not doing much better."

"What is it about our family? How come none of us can do well in school? Are we all just stupid?"

She squinted slightly and shook her head. "None of us are stupid. Look at what we have had to deal with! How can we focus on school? Don't you remember what it was like just trying to stay warm in the old house?"

"At least Mom's house is warm. What is it about Dad and heat? He doesn't even heat his own house properly."

"He's just cheap," said Julie. "He was always like that. He's always talking about how broke but he is, but he's always off on vacations with Joan. He's a fucking prick."

My mouth dropped open, and then I laughed. I had never heard her express her anger toward Dad so explicitly.

Later that day I rewrote my story, being careful to remove unnecessary similes and adding descriptive paragraphs to give the story more texture and color. When it was completely done I gave it to Julie. I thought it read even better than before, but I was anxious to see what she thought.

"I'll read it tonight while you are at work," she said.

Anniello and I sparred in the little fenced courtyard behind the restaurant. His kicks were fast and accurate; mine were slow and clumsy, but my timing improved. I was also getting better at blocking. I had to wear thick boxing gloves when we sparred, but Anniello used his bare hands. When I dropped my guard he would give me a sharp rap on the head with the back of his knuckles. It stung.

Learning karate was nothing like what I watched on T.V. Anniello made it look easy, but only after years of training. The guys on T.V. who took a few lessons and were suddenly black belts were all baloney. I could barely kick above my waist, and when I tried to get my kicks any higher I lost my balance. Once I slipped and fell on my back.

"It's not necessary to kick high," said Anniello. "You can do a lot of damage kicking someone in the knee or the thigh."

"Anniello, shouldn't I get some kind of belt?"

"What do you need a belt for? I'm not teaching you

229

traditional karate; I'm teaching you self-defense. If you want to learn traditional karate I can recommend a good school. Do you want to go to school for it?"

I rubbed my chin lightly. "I don't think so, Anniello. Besides, my parents wouldn't pay for it."

"Your parents are rich. Why wouldn't they pay for it?"

His commentary surprised me, and I suddenly realized what my history teacher meant when he said perception is ninety percent reality. Since my parents had split up I no longer considered us rich.

"My father is rich, but I don't ask him for anything. My mother has barely any money at all."

"My father died when I was five years old, so it was just me and my mother. Growing up without him was tough, and I really wished he had been there at times."

"I'm sorry, Anniello."

"Ah, it's okay. Just remember your father loves you the best he knows how."

"Thanks." I knew what he said was true, but would he have still said it if he knew my father?

We had a busy night. I spent most of it driving around delivering pizzas. I liked deliveries because of the tips. The extra money really helped since my mother spent most of the money on booze and we ended up buying a lot of our own groceries.

I woke up late the next morning to find my mother sitting in the living room, reading my manuscript. Luckily, she hadn't started drinking yet. "I found this on your desk. Do you mind if I read it?" She was already five or six pages into it. No point in denying her now, and besides, I was curious to see her reaction.

"Please, go ahead."

I went into the kitchen to get a cup of coffee and sat down in one of the overstuffed chairs across from her to watch her read. Her eyebrows fretted as she turned the pages, and her eyes reflected deep sadness. Her face had changed so much in so little time. Her hair was no longer neatly coiffed, and it had turned almost white. Deep wrinkles engraved her face, and she looked really tired. She read quickly with intense concentration, blowing through the entire manuscript without stopping. When she was done she looked up at me and smiled. "My, God! We've all been through some hell, haven't we?"

"I would say so."

"This is really good. You have really captured a lot, and your writing has improved so much."

"Thanks."

"How's school going, Dear?"

"School?" She hadn't asked about school since I started in high school last Christmas. I just assumed nobody cared anymore. "School is going okay. I'm getting by."

"Well, do the best you can, Dear, and keep writing."

"I will."

She got up and went into the kitchen. I heard the spray of a beer can opening, and I finished my coffee quickly and went upstairs to dress. Why my story didn't upset her was beyond me since most of it was about her and life with a drunk.

The following day I stopped by to see Mr. Vargas. I knocked on his office door.

"Drew!" Come on in."

"I just wanted to give you this," I said, handing him my manuscript.

"It's heavy," he said.

"It's twenty-three pages long. I've been working on it all summer."

"Harmony House. It's a catchy title. I'm guessing there's not a lot of harmony in this house," he said, winking at me.

"Not a whole lot," I said.

"I'll look forward to reading it. Thank you."

Julie was in the kitchen doing the dishes when I got home from school. She banged the dishes around angrily and scowled.

"What's going on?" I asked, helping her gather up dirty dishes from the table and counter.

"Not a fucking thing," she said.

"Is Mom on a rampage again?"

"I don't know," she said, throwing the dishrag on the floor. "You know what? Why don't you just fuck off?"

"Goddamn it! I won't have you screaming and cursing like that in my house," my mother said as she came into the kitchen to get another beer. Her eyes were not completely glazed over yet, but the scowl on her face displayed her rage. There were only three beers left, and it was still early in the day.

"Drew, go down to Sea Bright and get me some more beer," she said.

"Where's your pocketbook?"

"I don't know. Find it." she said, taking a deep swig from her beer.

I found it sitting on the dining room table. I took out her wallet and opened it. "Mom, you're broke."

"You have a job. It's about time you started chipping in around here. You can buy the beer."

"You want me to buy your beer? No. I won't do it. If you want beer I'll go get it, but I'm not going to pay for it."

"Listen, you little prick! This is my house, and if you want to stay in it you can start contributing!"

"Contribute? I buy all the groceries. If it weren't for me, Julie and I would starve to death! You spend all the money on booze!"

"Get the fuck out of my house," she screamed.

"Where the hell am I supposed to go?"

"I don't give a damn. Go to your father's house."

"Fine, I'm leaving," I said, turning away in disgust.

I went upstairs and threw some clothes in a bag. I had nowhere to go, but I knew she would forget all about it by tomorrow. In the meantime, I was sure he would take me in for a night.

I walked over to his house. Darkness had fallen by the time I got there. Joan answered the door when I knocked. We went into the kitchen where she was busy preparing dinner.

"Your father is not home yet," she said.

"I can see that. I need a place to stay tonight. Mom threw me out of the house."

"Well, I'm sorry, Drew, but you can't stay here."

"But you have a huge house with lots of empty rooms. All I need is a place to sleep for one night."

"Don't you have any friends you can stay with?"

"No, I don't," I said. She continued making dinner, and I just looked at her with contempt. "You know, just forget it. I'll find somewhere else to go."

I walked down to Sea Bright. I couldn't believe that woman, and the more I thought about her the more I hated her. I went down to Anniello's.

"Drew, what are you doing here? You don't work until Thursday."

"I came down to visit and grab something to eat," I said, sitting at the counter. The place was empty; a couple of kids having just finished eating some slices and left.

"What would you like to eat? My wife made delicious lasagna. You want to try some?"

"That sounds good, thanks."

Anniello cut a big piece from a tinfoil-baking pan and put it in the oven as I helped myself to a Coke. He served me the lasagna in a baking dish with some bread. It smelled good and I was hungry.

"I've been running, Anniello."

"Yeah? That's good. Have you been doing your exercises?"

"Every night."

"How's school going?"

"School's all right. I'm getting by okay."

"Getting by? You're a smart guy. You should be doing better than getting by. What do you want to do when you get older?"

"I want to be a writer."

"A writer! What kind of writer?"

"I want to be novelist."

"It's a tough field, but if you sell one or two good books you are set. What about journalism? You could work for a newspaper."

"My mother was a journalist. Journalism sounds interesting, but I don't think it's for me. I'd rather be a fiction writer."

"You are an artiste!" he said, gesturing with his hand.

I laughed. "I'd like to think so. I spend enough time doing it."

"Really? What have you written?"

"Lot's of short stories. I'd like to try to write a novel, but I don't think I'm ready yet."

"Are you going to let me read one of your stories?"

"Of course, Anniello. I have just the story in mind. It's about my girlfriend in Rome."

"Yeah, sure. Let me read it. I'm no expert, but I'd like to see what you write."

I finished eating and sat in the kitchen with Anniello and watched T.V. I didn't want him to think I had nowhere to go. I figured I'd wait around until about 10:30 and start home. My mother would be asleep by then and I could slip back in the house. She wouldn't remember what happened.

234

When I arrived home all the lights were out. The front door was locked. It was unusual—we never locked the front door. I went around to the side door. She had locked that one too. I tried all the windows but they were closed tight.

"Bitch!" I muttered. There was no way in. I thought about banging on the door, but if I woke her up there would be hell to pay. I decided to sneak into my father's house. It would be cold, but at least I'd have a roof over my head. I walked across Rumson road and down Ward Avenue in the darkness. There were no streetlights, and the house was almost all the way at the end.

I tried the kitchen door but it was locked. The front and back doors were locked as well. I was getting discouraged. I didn't want to wake them after the words I had with Joan, and the thought of walking all the way back to my mother's house was just too exhausting. I thought about calling Aunt Tess, but I would have had to go back to Sea Bright to use a payphone, and I was too tired.

I found an old tarpaulin near the side of the house that covered the woodpile. It was heavy and smelled musty, but would keep me warm. I carried it to the back porch and fell asleep in one of the big, wicker chairs.

I woke up the next morning with my father standing over me. "What the hell are you doing here?"

"Mom threw me out last night. I had nowhere to go."

"You could have knocked. We would have given you a bed."

"I stopped by last night before you got home from work. Joan said I couldn't stay."

"Shit. Come on inside and get cleaned up while I make you some breakfast. Do you want to take a shower?"

"That would be nice."

"Let me go talk to Joan," he said, going upstairs.

I waited for him down in the kitchen a few minutes. Joan

235

came downstairs. She mustered a smile, but didn't look very pleased to see me. "Hello, Drew. Why don't you get cleaned up and we'll have breakfast together? Here's a clean towel."

I went upstairs and got in the shower. My body ached from sleeping in the damp cold and the hot water felt good. Afterward I went downstairs and joined my father and Joan in the kitchen to find they started on a health kick. My father had lost a lot of weight, but he looked good. It had been ages since I had seen a breakfast this good. We each had half a grapefruit and scrambled eggs. Joan had started baking her own bread and heated us up a couple of thick slices that we ate with fresh strawberry jam. After we ate, my father drove me home.

"Don't ever feel you have to sleep outside in the cold. If something like that ever happens again you can stay with us," he said, his voice filled with remorse.

"Thanks, Dad," I said, getting out of the car. "And thanks for breakfast."

He drove off to work, and I headed for the front porch. He could be so unpredictable. I guess the thought of having his children sleep on his stoop in the cold was too much for him. My mother didn't say anything to me when I went inside. I simply said good morning and went upstairs to get my books.

That morning I saw Mr. Vargas in the hall. He asked me to stop by his office when I had some free time.

"Did you read my story?" I asked him, fidgeting.

"Yes, I did. That's what I wanted to talk about," he told me. "Your story was good."

"Thanks. I'll drop by later."

"Talk to you later, Drew," Mr. Vargas said, winking at me and walking away.

"Stoner," said the tall, skinny kid who had harassed me once before.

"Blow me, gear head."

He pushed me so hard I lost my balance and slammed into the wall.

"You got something else to say to me?" he asked, standing over me with his fists clenched.

"Yeah, you're even dumber than you look," I replied, getting to my feet. A crowd of people quickly gathered.

"Why don't we settle this outside?" he asked, as his friends circled around me like a pack of dogs.

"After you, dickhead," I said, gesturing towards the door.

As we went across the street into the park, the crowd followed. We faced each other in the grassy field in front of the senior parking lot and everyone formed a circle around us. We both removed our jackets, and he started dancing around me like a boxer, except his hands were down and his stance was open.

He came at me with a wide punch. It was nothing like the punches Anniello and I had practiced—straight punches with speed and power—instead it was slow and sweeping, as if in slow motion. I didn't need to block it; I ducked underneath. His arm swung over my head, exposing his ribs. I punched him hard in the side and followed up with a strong wheel kick to the back of his knee. His leg buckled and he winced in pain. As he dropped to the ground I wrapped my hands behind his head and drove my knee into his chin. He flipped over on his back, unconscious.

The fight was over in less than ten seconds. Everyone looked at me in shock. One of his friends knelt beside him to help while I simply picked up my jacket and left. The knee to his face was probably unnecessary; he was finished when I took out his leg, but I was angry and wanted to hurt him as much as possible. He'd survive.

After that people nodded at me politely in the hallway. I was still regarded as a freak, but was now a bit of a mystery, with them wondering where I learned to fight so well. A few guys asked if I had studied karate. I said yes. It didn't make me more popular, but it gave me some respect.

That afternoon I went to see Mr. Vargas. He waved me in and smiled. "Have a seat," he said.

"Thank you, Sir."

"Well, I've read your work carefully," he said, patting my manuscript. "It's quite a story."

"What did you think?"

"I noticed some improvements in your style since the last time we spoke. It's a powerful story, Drew. I'm assuming it's based on real events."

"Most of it."

"It's not a publishable story. It's too angry. The writing is filled with too much rage," he said, clenching his fists and shaking them in the air for effect. "I think it's good you write about these things, but eventually you will have to let go of the anger or your writing will never progress."

"I have to write what I feel."

"And it's good you do that, but if you hold on to the anger too tightly it will eat you up."

I stared at the ground. I knew it was unnatural to be so angry all the time, but it seemed beyond my control.

"Drew, your writing has great potential. If you want to talk about what's going on at home I'd be glad to listen," he said.

"I've pretty much said it all in the story."

Mr. Vargas pursed his lips. "Tell you what. Let's see how well you write when you're not focusing on your anger. I want you to write me a story about something pleasant in your life. I know it sounds ridiculous; life isn't always pleasant, but I want you to focus on something happy that made you feel good."

"Why?"

"For the discipline. I want to teach you that your anger does not need to be your only motivation for writing."

"Okay. When do you want it?"

"There's no deadline. But tell you what. Why don't you get me a first draft the week after Thanksgiving?"

Thanksgiving was only a week and a half away. The story I had started about Alexandra and me was perfect.

"Okay, it's a deal."

"Good. I'll look forward to seeing it," he said, handing me back my manuscript.

I worked on my story each night after work. It was not an angry story, although I found that I became enraged when I thought about what happened to Alexandra and me.

The rest of the week I worked on my story. I was happy with the results, and gave it to Mr. Vargas.

"This is a bit different for me," I told him.

"Is it happy?" he asked, smiling.

"Happy as a clam," I replied, laughing.

"I probably won't have a chance to get to it until after Christmas. I have a lot coming up with the school play. We're doing Macbeth. You're going to come, aren't you?"

"Sure."

"Good! We need all the support we can get."

Later that week I bought a couple of tickets for the play on Saturday night and Julie agreed to go with me. Half the school was there with their parents and we just sat in the back and watched the performance. The acting wasn't great, but the sets were well done and the performance was pretty good for a high school play.

Christmas was strange. Gretchen and Annie were home on Christmas break. My mother did not have enough beds, so Gretchen and Julie slept at Dad's house, coming by on Christmas

Eve for dinner. Both of them looked tired and sick when they came through the front door.

"Fucking Dad!" Julie said, unbuttoning her coat and throwing it on the couch.

"What's the matter?" my mother asked.

"He won't turn on the heat! It's freezing in that goddamn house."

"I'll bet it's nice and warm where he sleeps," I said.

"It really isn't that warm anywhere in that place. I think he has something against heat," Julie said angrily.

"He has two furnaces. Didn't he turn the other one on?" I asked.

"He said he turned it on last night before we went to bed but it takes awhile for the heat to come up," said Julie.

"He probably turned it on but he kept the thermostat down so low it didn't make a difference," my mother said sarcastically.

"Why the hell can't he heat the house for a week when his kids are at home? It's not like the heating bills are going to kill him," Gretchen said.

My mother just laughed. "Your father and I fought for years over the heat. He put a lock on the thermostat because I kept turning it up when he wasn't around."

"He's fucking sick," Gretchen said. "I don't think I can stay there. I'll die of pneumonia."

"I'll talk to him," my mother said. "Would you like some coffee?"

"I'll make it, Mom," Gretchen said, going into the kitchen. "Say, where's the tree?"

"It's in that box. I can't deal with a live tree anymore."

"You got a fake tree?" Annie asked, looking inside the box with disgust.

"Yeah, I got a fake tree," my mother replied. "If you don't

240

like it you can go have Christmas at your father's house."

The tree was in three sections. Julie helped me put it together. It looked real, but without the pine smell. We all made jokes about how tacky the tree was while putting on the decorations. It didn't look so bad when we were done. My mother made a roast beef with Yorkshire pudding. She cooked well when sober, and dinner was good. By the time dinner was finished she was pretty sloshed. Gretchen and Julie decided Dad's house was just too cold, so I let them have my bed and I slept on the couch.

We opened Christmas gifts after breakfast, and then the four of us walked over to Dad's. This year the plan was to open gifts at their house and come back to spend time with Mom. Later that evening we were supposed to go back to Dad's for dinner. It seemed like a lot of unnecessary movement.

We arrived back at my mother's house at around 1:00. She was sitting on the living room couch, nursing a beer. He eyes were watery and sad, and she refused to talk to us.

"What's the matter, Mom?" Annie asked, concerned.

"Do you think it's fun for me to sit here by myself on Christmas while you're off the whole day with your father?"

"Oh, for God's sake, Mom! How the fuck do you think we feel?" Annie screamed. "Do you think we like being shuffled around like orphans on Christmas day? You and Dad set this whole fucking thing up, and now you're crying about it! Well, I'm sick of it! This is the last time I come home for Christmas!" she said, bursting into tears.

The rest of my sisters followed, and my mother finally broke down and cried as well. I didn't know what to do with myself, so I locked myself in my study. All three of my sisters decided to go back to my father's, and my mother drank herself senseless. This would be my last Christmas at home as well.

At school, once Christmas break was over, we were required

to declare our senior electives. I went to see my guidance counselor, Mr. Dexter. He looked terrible; he was dying of leukemia, and the chemotherapy turned his face bright red and made his skin peel. I felt bad for him. The freshman English teacher, Mrs. Holston, was offering a creative writing class, and of course I signed up. Two English electives were offered: Modern American Literature and a course on comedy offered by Mr. Vargas. The comedy class sounded fun, and I signed up for that as well. I saw him later that day.

"Drew! How are you? Did you have a good Christmas?"

"Yes, I did," I lied.

"I read your story. Do you have some time?"

"Yeah, I've got a few minutes."

"Take a walk with me," he said. We went down to the auditorium at the far end of the school. Mr. Vargas opened a little storage room with a key and turned on the light. The place was cluttered with props and costumes and my story was sitting on a desk at the far end of the room.

"Have a seat," he said, shutting the door. He picked up my short story and sat down in a chair next to me. "This is a good story, Drew."

"Thank you." Why did he need to bring me here to talk to me about my story?

"Your erotic descriptions were very nice. Have you done a lot of erotic writing?"

"No, not really." I felt tense and wanted to leave.

"When I was in college I did quite a bit of erotic writing. I enjoy writing it as much as reading it. When I was in college I had quite a few interesting experiences. A friend and I were taking a shower together once. He touched me and I touched him. It was no big deal. In fact, it was a real turn-on," he said, putting his hand on my thigh.

"I'm not into this at all," I said, standing up. I took my story from him and left, ashen-faced and disgusted. One of my classmates saw me as I was walking down the hall. She was a cheerleader and was pretty involved in the drama club.

"What happened?" she asked, seeing the mortified look on my face.

"Ask Mr. Vargas," I said with contempt.

"Did he do something bad?"

"No, he didn't. Leave me alone."

"Drew, you're not the only one," she said.

I stopped dead in my tracks. "What do you mean?"

"He touched you, didn't he?"

"Yeah, and he told me he was gay. So what," I said, walking away.

Later that day rumors were flying around school that Mr. Vargas was gay. The rumors must have gotten back to him because after English class he told me that I had to have a note if I was ever late to class again, and that if I missed a single homework assignment he'd flunk me. I had no recourse and it was too late to get out of his class. There was no way to fight him; he was the head of the English department, and my grades were just a shade above passing. Even if I tried to fight him I'd never get the support of my parents; in fact, my family problems would probably be used against me.

The rest of the teachers scowled at me when I walked by. Suddenly I was the most hated student in school. My creative writing teacher was probably the only exception. Anyone who had her for freshman English class feared her. She was so austere looking, with her dark, wavy hair pulled smartly back into a bun. Most of the classes consisted of basic writing exercises on how to describe a boat sailing across a lake or something to that effect. I enjoyed the exercises—they were basic, but I liked the challenge of describing a scene on demand.

It wasn't until we were required to turn in our first attempt at a story when things started to turn around. I turned in "Harmony House". I had made some revisions as a result of the class, so I didn't feel bad about submitting a previous work. The truth was I didn't care. It was my best work so far, and I was tired. The day our stories were due I plopped the manuscript on her desk with a resounding thud. It was typewritten, double-spaced, without a single mistake by now. I had whittled it down from twenty-three pages to seventeen, condensing my language and tightening the plot wherever I could.

The following day I was called down to Mr. Dexter's office. Mrs. Holston sat primly in her chair with my story, her white sweater buttoned all the way to her neck. Mr. Dexter looked bewildered.

"Drew, did you write this story?" she asked.

"What kind of question is that?" I asked, preparing myself for all-out battle. I was sick of being bullied by my teachers.

"It's unusual for someone your age to submit something like this," she said.

"Of course it's my work. I've been working on it for months."

"Drew, your writing is phenomenal. It's hard to believe someone so young can produce something so good. You have obviously spent a lot of time writing."

"I've been writing almost everyday since I was fifteen. It's what I want to do most with my life."

"Drew, I know talent when I see it, and I hate to see it go to waste. Have you started applying for colleges?"

"Why the hell does everyone care if I go to college suddenly? Mr. Dexter thinks I would be better off being a grease

244

monkey!"

"Well, Drew, I understand your anger," Mr. Dexter said. "But your grades gave us absolutely no indication of your abilities."

"I've done fairly well in English class," I said, defensively.

"Yes, but you are in danger of being held back if there isn't some improvement in the rest of your grades. Your grade-point average is just above failing."

"So I won't be going to Harvard. I can live with it. What's your point?"

"The point is, Drew, you should go to college. There are some programs that I can help you get into that will foster your writing abilities," Mrs. Holston said.

"But you won't get in if you fail out of school," said Mr. Dexter. "I'm wondering if we should hold you back a year to give you a chance to bring your grades up."

I was horrified. "I'd cut my wrists and blow my head off before I'd stay here another year."

Mr. Dexter and Mrs. Holston looked at me wide-eyed with their mouths open.

"These are your grades for the year," Mr. Dexter said, showing me a chart listing nothing but D's and a few F's. I felt pretty embarrassed seeing my academic record displayed so bluntly. "You need to get at least two B's to graduate and at least one A to get your grades high enough to get into anywhere besides community college."

"Drew, have you spoken to your parents about college?" Mrs. Holston asked.

"No."

"Have you shown your parents any of your writing?"

"My mother has seen some of it. She's the one that made me take typing lessons."

Mrs. Holston nodded at me and smiled. "And every teacher can thank her for it. It's nice to see students turn in such well-typed work. You should talk to them about colleges. I can help you pick a good program, but you are going to have to get your grades up. I'd be happy to give you a reference. Do you have any other work?"

"I have tons of work. I write all the time."

"Bring in your three best stories, and we'll start building your portfolio," she said.

"You have one of them. I can bring you some others, as long as you're not offended by the material."

She waved her hand at me and smiled. "I can guarantee I won't be offended by the material."

"Well, I have a couple other stories to show you, and I'll work on my grades."

"I hope you do," Mr. Dexter said. "You've had a tough road. I'd like to see you get a break."

"Thank you. Thank you both," I said. "Is that it for now?"

"Yes. I think so," Mrs. Holston said. "I'll see you in class."

I got up to leave. English class started in less than twenty minutes, so I took a walk outside. Spring was coming, and the trees were starting to bud. I had no idea how I was going to pull two B's. Mrs. Holston's class was a guaranteed A, but Mr. Vargas was going to be a problem. The man hated me now, and nothing I could do would change that. Most of my other teachers felt the same way.

I started spending my free time in the library studying. Mr. Vargas's class was a breeze. It was really a drama class; we watched comedy videos and talked about comic devices. When papers were due I always turned them in early, taking extra time to ensure my grammar and spelling were perfect. Nonetheless, he always returned them with acerbic comments all over them.

Mrs. Holston and I met once a week in the library to go through my stories. She had a lot of good comments. At first I didn't take her criticism very well. She didn't come from the kind of background I did, and she didn't relate immediately to my work as easily as some people. After awhile her perspective helped me think more objectively about my own.

Toward the end of April I started seeing dramatic improvements in my grades. One afternoon I came home and found my mother sitting on the couch with Aunt Tess. I hadn't seen her in ages. She was wearing one of her floppy straw hats, and she looked like she had been gardening all day.

"Your mother tells me your writing is getting better all the time," she said as I walked in the door.

"I'm working hard at it, Aunt Tess. It's going really well."

"I think I found the perfect writing program for you," my mother said with a big grin.

"You did?"

"I called an old friend of mine, Jim Brown, in New York. He's a top literary agent. He used to be an editor at the paper where I worked. I told him all about you."

"Did you tell him how badly I'm doing in school?"

"I did, but I also told him how gifted you are. He wanted to see some of your work. I sent him 'Harmony House'. I'm sure you wouldn't mind."

"What did he say?" I asked, too shocked to believe Mom would do something like that.

"He recommended you to a creative-writing program in England."

"You're kidding! What program?"

"It's sponsored by Antioch International in Yellow Springs, Ohio. It's a good school. The program is at Oxford."

"You're joking! What's the catch?" I was so happy I couldn't contain myself.

"The catch is you have to get some good references from your teachers. His reference means a lot, but you need to have at least three teachers pulling for you to make up for your grades." At this point I could count at least two.

"Mom, that's wonderful!" I said, throwing my arms around her. I didn't know where she found the wherewithal to pull off something like this. She already had the application and school catalogue.

"Make sure you fill this out right away. You are going to have to write an essay. Read the guidelines and get it done as soon as possible. It's getting late," she said.

"I will, Mom. I promise."

"Congratulations, Dear," Aunt Tess said, pulling me to her and kissing me on the cheek.

"I'm not in yet, Aunt Tess."

"I'm not worried about it, Sweetheart. Your kind of talent never goes unnoticed."

"We'll see," I said. "If you don't mind, I'm going to go look this stuff over."

"Help yourself, Dear. And best of luck," Aunt Tess said as I went into the study to read through the brochure.

The program was an intensive summer seminar for creative writers. Those who qualified would be matriculated into a yearlong program in London. I couldn't believe it was happening. I read through the application carefully and began filling it out. That was the easy part—the essay, now that required some thought. The topic was open, so I decided to write a brief synopsis of my travels through Europe and how they affected my outlook on life.

The next day I found Mrs. Holston and showed her the catalogue.

"This sounds wonderful," she said, sitting back in her chair and smiling. "I'd be happy to give you a reference. How soon do you need it?"

"In another week or so. I have to get the application in soon."

"It's no problem," she said. "If anyone deserves it, it's you."

The only other teacher I could count on was my junior year English teacher. I only had him for one semester, but I had shown him one of my stories. He recommended me to the advanced English classes for my senior year. I found him in his office and approached him on the topic.

"Mrs. Holston tells me your writing has come a long way, Drew. I'm happy to help you out."

"Thank you, Sir. I appreciate it a lot. It's my one shot out of here."

"Use it well. Most people don't get chances like this."

"I will. Thank you."

The weather turned warmer, the semester was coming to an end, and everyone talked about which colleges had accepted them. Some people asked me where I had applied to, but I didn't say anything to anyone. Toward the end of May we were all required to read our stories in creative-writing class. Most stories were five or six pages long without much substance. I asked Mrs. Holston which story I should read.

"Read whichever one you want."

"Can I read 'Harmony House'?"

"You can, but there won't be any time for feedback. Can you read that much so quickly?"

"It's a lot. Maybe I should read something else."

"No, read 'Harmony House'. It's your favorite story."

The next class Mrs. Holston introduced my story. "Drew's story, 'Harmony House', is rather long, but I'm sure you'll find it entertaining. Go ahead Drew," she said, nodding at me.

I read my story almost from memory. I had worked on it for nearly a year and a half, and I knew every intonation perfectly. Every line of dialogue was burned indelibly into my brain, and I made each character come alive as I read. Between the joint efforts of Mrs. Holston, my mother, Mr. Vargas, and hours and hours of refinement, the story was honed to its bare essentials. I finished reading just before the period ended.

When done, I looked up at everyone for the first time. They all stared at me with disbelief. Finally, a girl from my math class spoke. Attractive and busty, she had never before given me the time of day. "Drew, I just want to tell you that was a great story."

"Thank you," I said, beaming with pride. The bell sounded, ending the period and everyone got out of their seats. Mrs. Holston smiled. She knew how satisfied I felt.

Finally the day came when I arrived home from school to find my mother handing me a letter from Antioch College. I ripped open the envelope impatiently. I had been accepted! My mother was so happy for me, she insisted my father go out and buy me a new and better typewriter as a reward.

After final exams Mr. Vargas gave me my grade for the semester—a D minus. I was enraged. I didn't expect to get a good grade but certainly didn't expect to get hit that hard.

"You can't do this! I never missed a single class and I completed every assignment!"

"Well, Drew, in my estimation your work didn't warrant a higher grade."

"I will fight this, you prick. I'm going to go see Mr. Dexter and I will bring my mother in. I am not going to let you get away with this."

"You do that, Drew. And I'll look forward to meeting your mother."

I went down to see Mr. Dexter and told him what happened;

we went over my grades for the semester. Despite my English grade I was going to graduate anyway. I had managed to get a B+ in Economics and an A- in History. Combined with the A I got in Creative Writing my grade-point average was high enough to finish. I decided to fight him anyway just out of principle, and Mr. Dexter scheduled an appointment for Mr. Vargas and me to meet in his office next week. On the appointed day I showed up without my mother. I never even told her what happened.

"Have a seat, Drew," Mr. Dexter said.

"No thanks, this won't take long."

"Where's your mother? You told me you were going to bring your mother. So where is she?" Mr. Vargas asked, his eyes filled with spite.

"I don't need my mother to handle this, you prick. What little you had to offer, I learned. You are nothing but a nasty, little pervert with a chip on his shoulder. You don't have the talent to do anything substantial with your life, so you thought you'd go after me. Well, fuck you! I won. You can't touch me now. School is over, and I'm still going to Oxford."

"Jesus, Drew!" Mr. Dexter said. "You have no shame!"

I simply looked at him. The man was clueless about what really happened between Mr. Vargas and me.

"I'm sorry for you, Mr. Dexter. I don't mean to offend you, but some things have to be said."

"Not like that!" he yelled.

"It was the only way," I said, leaving his office.

I went outside. I could see Mr. Vargas and Mr. Dexter through the window. Mr. Vargas leaned against the wall, looking as though he had endured a terrible blow to his ego. He was acting, but I didn't care. He didn't matter to me anymore; nobody here mattered to me. I was leaving, and I had no intentions of ever coming back.

Chapter 11

I grabbed a cab from the airport to London Station, and had barely enough time to catch my train. The big brownstone buildings we passed had ornate carvings of gargoyles on the cornices, reminding me of some of the older cathedrals I had seen in New York. As the train departed, the houses became smaller and closer together, but were eventually replaced with rolling green hills.

An hour later we pulled into Oxford. It was nothing like I imagined. I had expected to see young, brilliant scholars roaming about, but most of the students were gone for the summer holidays and the streets were all but deserted.

I took a cab from the train station, and peered out the window at the passing scenery with excitement and nervousness. I could hardly believe I was here. The English took their gardens seriously, and even the tiny cottages that lined the narrow cobblestone streets were resplendent with colorful flowerbeds.

Plater College, the school where I would be studying for the summer, was nestled in a rural area behind a low wall atop a steep hill above the town center. The old brownstone buildings that made up the university campus were daunting and austere with a small administrative office, a cafeteria, a couple of classroom buildings, and a two-story dormitory.

A tall man with a soft voice greeted me when I arrived. "You must be Drew Smith," he said, shaking my hand. "My name is Michael Vespi, the program director. I've been waiting to meet you. You're the youngest writer we've ever had in our program."

"Really?"

"Yep. Let me show you to your room," he said, offering to carry my typewriter.

I followed him down to the dormitory. My room was small, but had a well-lighted desk and looked comfortable. "There will be an orientation meeting in the dining hall at 5:00. Why don't you get settled and we'll see you later," he said, leaving.

I unpacked my typewriter, put it on my desk, and looked out the sliding-glass window over the courtyard. Lush, green grass covered the area between the buildings where a couple of students were throwing a Frisbee to each other. It was pleasant here, and the climate seemed identical to home. I unpacked my suitcase and shoved it underneath my bed. I had a bit of time, so I sat down and wrote Alexandra a brief letter on my new typewriter, telling her about my new school.

That evening all us met in the dining hall for dinner where we were served sausages and potatoes—typical English food. When everyone was seated Michael stood up.

"Welcome to Antioch's Summer Seminar for Creative Writing," he said. "My name is Michael Vespi, and this is my third year teaching this seminar. I just want to go over a few details before we go around the room and introduce ourselves. Some of you are new to your craft, and some of you are seasoned professionals. We'll all be working together, and hopefully by the end of the summer we'll have taken our skills to a whole new level. Toward that end, we have outlined a course syllabus that should suit all of your needs. I will be meeting with each of you personally to tailor your program to your individual goals and skills. Our guest lecturer this year will be none other than the esteemed novelist, Margaret Drabble."

Everyone applauded. From the reaction of the others I gathered she must be someone important. The participants' ages ranged from the early twenties to the mid-fifties. Most everyone was American, but a couple of French girls were attending as well.

We went around the room and introduced ourselves. Betsy, a rail-thin girl with silky blond hair, wrote for a newspaper, but wanted to be a poet. A speechwriter named John from Washington, D.C. was here to write his first novel. David, a young man from Brazil with kinky strawberry-blond hair that fell down to his shoulders, was writing a play about the carnival in Rio de Janeiro. Robert was working on his Master's degree, and wanted to be a fantasy writer. Almost everyone had done a substantial amount of writing in some form or another. Finally, it came to my turn to speak.

"Hi, my name is Drew Smith, and I come from New Jersey. I just finished high school, and I want to be a writer." I felt so green in comparison to everyone else.

"All right, Drew," said Betsy. "You're in the right place."

"Well, then," said Michael. "Here are the classes and the course syllabi. Why don't you all read through them carefully and we'll talk about it tomorrow during your interviews. In the meantime, you'll find that the town of Oxford is pretty quiet in the summer, but there are a lot of good places to go. The problem is getting there. I suggest you rent bicycles and ride like most fine, English folk do. There's a bike shop in the center of town. For those of you who need to do research, there's a small library here, but we have library privileges at Corpus Christie College for the summer should you need to do more extensive research."

I felt out of place being so young—listening to everyone discussing their writing careers intimidated me. Michael came up to me a little later. He smiled at me and asked how I was doing.

"Who is Margaret Drabble?" I asked quietly.

"She's a famous English novelist. Her books are quite popular here. I recommend you read one or two of them before she starts her lectures."

I nodded.

He asked me to drop by his office the next afternoon to register for classes.

The next morning I was out of bed early. Breakfast consisted of scrambled eggs, toast, and sausages. A group of people was going down to town to buy some supplies. I walked with them down the steep path to town. It was quiet, and the cobblestone side streets were devoid of traffic. The town center was filled with rustic shops that sold stationary, books and souvenirs. We found the bike shop and I rented an old, three-speed, which was solid and moved pretty fast.

We rode down a path along the river Thames, marveling at the medieval spires of cathedrals and college buildings poking through the thick, green canopies of tall trees. The small cottages that lined the streets looked rustic and comfortable, and I enjoyed the ride. Peddling up the steep hill to school was too difficult for most of us, so we got off our bikes and walked the rest of the way.

I read through the course descriptions. The summer session was divided into two halves: June and July, with a week break in between. The courses were evenly split between fiction and poetry. I enjoyed writing poetry, and wondered if I should take a class. That afternoon I met with Michael where I signed up for some fiction writing courses.

That evening after dinner we drove to town in the school van. On a small, cobblestone side street was a beer garden beneath a tent where local townies drank and played darts. We sat in the evening air on picnic benches, drinking warm beer and exchanging stories about where we were from.

The speechwriter, John, had been in the Vietnam War. He had seen a lot of action, and his greatest wish was to write the Great American Novel about some of his horrifying experiences.

Betsy came from a small town in Indiana, where her father

255

owned a consortium of newspapers. She had been writing ever since she could remember, but really wanted nothing more than to write poetry the rest of her life. She said she had to fight for years with her father to get time off to attend this seminar.

Everyone else had either just finished college or was in the process of getting their Master's degrees. I didn't have much to say, although people were somewhat intrigued by my experiences in Switzerland.

When we got back some of us met in the common room and talked. John shared one of his poems—a long ballad about the decline of democracy which everyone enjoyed.

"I have a poem," I said, almost in a whisper.

"Go ahead and read it," Betsy said, looking up at me and smiling.

"I have to go get it. It's in my room," I said, feeling a little embarrassed. I found my poem in a binder just for my poetry, and went back to where everyone was sitting. "It's called 'Stormy Nights'."

Warmth of
familiar blankets on
cold, rainy nights with
fluttering expectations in
the cool down of the softest pillow
the night is somehow less menacing now

Wind against the window it
shakes the leaves of trees with
unpredictable forces of nature that
bends wills and shapes futures in
a blink of an eye.

I looked up at everyone when I finished reading.

"Did you write that, Drew?" John asked, smugly.

I was surprised he'd ask me that, but was also flattered. "Yes, I wrote it just before I came here."

"It's good, but you'll get over it," Betsy said with a slight sneer.

Her words stung, and I wondered what she meant by them. Maybe I would get over what I was feeling, but I certainly didn't like being mocked, and just sat quietly the rest of the night.

Introduction to Creative Writing started early in the morning, and was taught by Michael. Only a few younger, less seasoned writers took the class. The writing exercises we were given were much more complicated than Mrs. Holston's; instead of simply describing a scene we were required to describe it from different angles, using point-of-view to move in and out like a television camera.

Michael was big on James Joyce, and he constantly referred to passages in Joyce's novels for examples on how to use voice. He was passionate about writing technique. The exercises were difficult, and I found the critique from my classmates harsh at times. I was pretty sensitive about my writing.

When we weren't in class, we stayed in our rooms with the curtains drawn, pounding out prose, constantly working on perfecting our technique. I was happy with my progress. On weekends we went to concerts or the theatre in town.

Just before midsummer break I got a phone call from Alexandra. She invited me to Rome for the week. I got off the phone and ran outside into the pouring rain, my heart pounding with excitement. I skipped around in a circle, splashing water from a puddle in all directions, and yelped with glee.

"What's going on?" David, the playwright from Brazil asked.

"I'm going to see an old girlfriend."

257

"Well, I'm happy for you. I hope you have better luck than Robert."

"Why? What happened to Robert?"

"He's a mess. We went to go pick up his wife at the train station and she wasn't there. When he called to find out what happened, her father told him she wasn't coming and she was going to have the marriage annulled."

"That's awful! Why would she do that?"

"She barely knew him when they married. Apparently he met her just before he came over here. He told her she was the one and that they were destined to spend the rest of their lives together. They got married and he gave her all his money. She was supposed to come to England to meet him and live happily ever after."

"Why the hell would he do something like that? And why would she agree? The whole thing sounds kind of weird." I said.

"She was only seventeen. She didn't know better. He should have known."

Later that day I saw Robert sitting in the common room. His bloodshot eyes were filled with tears and his hands shook slightly as he puffed on his cigarette. He was a good writer; his prose was very poetic and filled with passion. He was forced to leave the program to find the woman who had taken him to the cleaners. We all shook hands with him and said goodbye.

Betsy just shook her head and clucked her tongue. "These passionate artists are always getting into trouble," she said.

"I thought what he did was kind of romantic," I said.

"Yeah, right up until the point she got hold of her senses and took off with all his money."

"What the hell made you so bitter?" I asked.

"You'll see," she said, sneering at me. "You've been kicked around a lot in life, but nothing tears you up like love."

258

Perhaps she was right, though rather insensitive. Robert was a nice guy, and he didn't deserve to be shafted so badly.

The session ended, and I took the first train to London. Because the school shut down for the week, my parents had given me some spending money for a hotel. I decided it was best not to tell them I was going to Rome. It would have taken two days to get there by train, so I flew.

Alexandra was waiting for me at the terminal. Her hair was still long, dark and thick, and her eyes were as deep and beautiful as ever. I had to fight like hell not to break into a run when I saw her. She wore a black pair of slacks and a thin cotton top. She gave me a big smile and I took her in my arms.

"Alexandra, my God! It's so good to see you," I said, inhaling the sweet scent of her hair.

"You too, Drew. You look good."

"Thank you," I said, bending down to kiss her, but surprisingly, she offered me her cheek.

"How's the writing going?"

"It's really good. This program is wonderful. I can't tell you how much I've learned."

"Why don't we get going? You can tell me all about it in the car."

We left the terminal and walked to the parking lot. I was happy to find Rome wasn't as hot as the last time I was here. Alexandra led us to a bright-red Fiat convertible.

"Nice car," I said.

"It was my father's. I drive it now."

"How is your mother doing?"

"Oeuf! You don't want to know," she said. "She remembers you well. She's looking forward to seeing you."

I frowned. "I'll bet she is."

"Oh, you don't need to worry about that. It's ancient

259

history. She's forgiven you by now."

I didn't want to ask about Collalto, but I was curious about where she was living. As we drove through the south of Rome and headed towards Frascati, a small town east of the city, I reached across the seat and took her hand in mine. She squeezed my hand gently, and then pulled her hand away.

"So I'll bet you have lots of new stories by now," Alexandra said.

"You would think so, but I haven't had the time to work on stories. We do nothing but writing exercises. Next session we're going to work on stories."

"What kind of exercises?" she asked.

I told her all about the things we were learning, describing in detail the importance of voice.

"It sounds interesting," said Alexandra. "I'll bet it has done wonders for your writing."

"I hope so. I've worked my ass off this summer."

"Do you have a girlfriend?" she asked.

"A girlfriend? Me? No, I don't have a girlfriend." Taken off-guard by her question, I braced myself for what was next. "What about you? Do you have a boyfriend?"

She shook her head and smiled. "Are you ready for this?"

"I suppose so," I replied, terrified at what she might say.

"I was engaged to be married. But we just broke it off."

"You're kidding! Why didn't you tell me about this before?"

"I was going to write you, but I didn't know what to say."

"You just tell me. You just say, 'Drew, I met someone new and I'm getting married.'"

"I was going to, but we broke it off."

"Who is he?"

"His name is Paolo. He's going to law school. He comes from a very important family in Rome. His father is a very

260

famous lawyer."

"How long were you seeing him?" I asked, doing my best to control my hurt.

"About a year. His father was my father's lawyer. They were very good friends. I met him at his father's office while going over my father's estate."

"So what happened?"

"Well, things were good for a year, but he decided to go to law school in Naples, and I wanted to stay in Rome."

I sat up in my seat and looked over at her. "You broke off your engagement over that? You could have gone with him."

"I didn't want to. And besides, his family was putting so much pressure on me. Things were moving too quickly."

"Do you love him?"

"Yes, I love him, but I'm just not ready for marriage. It's too much for me right now."

"You could have postponed the engagement if you needed more time. Was he upset when you broke it off?"

She shook her head and laughed. "He was furious. I gave him back all the rings he had given me, and he threw them into the ocean. 'Now what the hell am I supposed to do with these?' he told me. His father was even angrier and told me someday I would regret what I did."

"I can imagine. You broke his son's heart. Where is he now?"

"He's in Naples."

"Nothing tears you up like love," I said, wistfully.

"What was that?"

"Nothing."

Oddly, I felt worse for Paolo than I did for her. Alexandra didn't seem too torn up over the relationship. In fact, I got the sense she was relieved. Although I wanted the best for her, I was also hoping we could simply pick up where we had left off. We were silent for a few minutes as we left the busy streets of Rome and headed into the rolling foothills of Frascati. I studied her tanned face for a moment. Alexandra saw me gazing at her and smiled. "I'm sorry, Drew. I was going to tell you. I didn't mean to hurt you."

I did my best not to show my disappointment. She pulled off the main road and headed up a long, steep road to a large, white villa surrounded by olive trees and bougainvillea. The white-washed exterior was chipped and peeling, but it had nice, big windows and looked airy. The fountain in the front courtyard was filled with algae and overgrown with lily pads.

She stopped the car and taking my bag and typewriter in hand, I followed her inside. The interior was simple and elegant with large wooden beams traversing the ceilings, while the walls were unadorned and painted white. I recognized some of the furniture from the castle. Alexandra said the house had been in her family a long time. The main salon was covered with drop cloths, and all sorts of tools sat in buckets on the floor.

"I've been working my butt off restoring this place," Alexandra said.

"You? I'm impressed, it looks like quite a project."

"You have no idea. This place was a disaster when we moved in. I've scraped so many walls my hands are ruined for the rest of my life."

Alexandra showed me to a bedroom upstairs. Two huge windows overlooked a small, brick courtyard. I walked over to one of the windows and looked outside. The bricks were covered with moss. Beyond the courtyard was a large olive grove that extended the length of the property.

"Alexandra, this place has so much potential. It reminds me a little bit of the house where I grew up. When we first moved in it was practically unlivable. My mother and father worked on the place for almost an entire year to get it looking as good as it did."

"I admire that," she said. "I think you appreciate your house more when you put that kind of effort into it. Let me show you around," she said, taking my arm.

The kitchen stove was new, and so was the sink and cabinets. It was nicely done.

"I did all this myself," she told me.

"You did the cabinets too?"

"I had someone make them and install them, but I designed them. I also ripped out most of the old stuff and did the plaster and painting on my own."

"Wow! Where did you learn all that?"

"It's not so hard," she said. "It's actually kind of fun. Hard work keeps me going."

She led me through the house. The rooms that had been refurbished looked really beautiful, and were in stark contrast with rest. She had started with the more important rooms and was working her way through the entire house.

"Alexandra, what can I do to help?" I asked.

"You don't want to spend your vacation working." she replied, laughing

"It would be fun. I want to help."

"If you insist. There's a ton of work."

She showed me the garden. She said the olives were good, but the trees hadn't been pruned in years. Alexandra put her arm in mine, and we walked through rows of trees. Orange blossoms and jasmine grew wild throughout the shrubs, giving the air a delicious smell. She picked an orange blossom off one of the bushes and held it to my nose. The scent overwhelmed me. I wanted to kiss her but she was elusive, always staying one step out of reach.

We went back to the house. Her mother had just arrived. She reminded me of my mother in some ways; her eyes had that same glazed look in them, only my mother's eyes were filled with anger, hers were filled with sadness. She had aged quite a bit, and her disheveled, gray hair hung loosely in her face.

"Hello, Signora Cavalletti. How are you?"

"Drew, could you help me with these bags? They are just too heavy for me," she said.

"Yes, of course." I reached into the back seat of the car loaded with groceries.

"It's okay. Leave them. The maid will get them," Alexandra said.

Her mother had already gone inside, and a young woman came out to get the groceries. I left the bags where they were. Alexandra may have lost the castle, but things didn't seem so bad. Winning and losing was only a question of degrees.

"Your mother looks good, Alexandra."

She frowned and looked away. "Drew, we can go out for dinner tonight, or we can stay here and cook."

"It's your call, Alexandra. I'm happy doing either."

"Let's go out. I don't feel like cooking tonight, and the maid leaves at 5:00. Are you hungry? You probably haven't eaten since breakfast."

"A little."

"Come into the kitchen. I'll make you a panino," she said, and I followed her inside.

"You know, I haven't had one of those since I was in Rome. Remember?"

"No. When did we eat paninos?"

"When we left the Vatican. You and I sat in a little bar and drank bottled water and you ordered a panino for me."

"Ah, yes! I do remember that. It seems so long ago. You

264

have a good memory."

"For me it was like yesterday. Those were some of the happiest times of my life."

"I've thought about writing," she said.

"That's wonderful. I'm sure you'd be great. What would you want to write?"

"I don't have your imagination, but I love literature. I think I'd like to be a translator."

"A translator," I said, rubbing my chin. "That suits you fine. You write really well, and you've mastered so many languages. Have you finished your studies in Switzerland?"

"Yes, I'm going to college next year at the University of Padova. I'm going to study French Literature."

"That's wonderful. They take their literature seriously. How's Claudio doing?"

"Fine."

She finished making the panino and put it down in front of me. I munched on the sandwich happily. She sat down across from and frowned. "I'm not the same girl you knew at *Ecole des Roches*. So much has changed."

"Life has changed. You are still the same girl I knew when I was just fifteen. You are as beautiful as ever."

"Thank you, I don't feel so beautiful these days. What I meant is that things between us have changed. What we had when we were teenagers was wonderful, but we are both older now."

"We're still friends, aren't we?"

"I hope so. That's the one thing I will always treasure."

"Well then, now that that's settled, can we move on?" I asked, trying my very best not to show my disappointment. I was still in love, but pushed my feelings aside the best I could.

"Drew, I'm so sorry for what you have been through," she said, squeezing my hand. "It's really awful, but I think things will be better for you now. You have a fantastic opportunity in front of you, and I know you are going to do well."

"It's been pretty rough, but I think the worst of it is over."

Her mother sat down between us. "Alexandra, can't we do something about the living room? I'm getting so tired of seeing it such a state."

"I'm working on it. We're going out tonight. Is there any-place special you want to go?"

"Oh! We should tell Claudio. He'll want to go," she said.

"Yes, Mother."

"Where is he?" I asked. Alexandra tapped me gently beneath the table with her foot, and I realized something was amiss. Her mother frowned and brushed the loose strands of her hair out of her face.

"I'm going to show Drew around Frascati before dinner. Can I get you anything?"

"Could you stop at the bakery and bring me some of those pastries I like so well?"

"Sure," she said, getting up to leave.

I followed her out to the car. She handed me the keys.

"Do you want to drive?"

"Hell, yes!" I got in the car and adjusted the seat. The car roared when I turned on the ignition. "So what's the deal with Claudio?" I asked, shifting into first gear. The car lurched forward when I stepped on the gas.

"I'm really disappointed in him. He moved out right after my father died, and he hasn't helped at all. To make matters worse, my mother is giving him control over most of the estate, and he won't even talk to her anymore unless it concerns money."

"Which way do I turn?" I asked.

"Make a left. I'll show you the aqueducts then we'll stop off at the bakery."

I dropped the car into a lower gear before the next turn. It hugged the road and sped through the turn. "So how did your brother get control over the entire estate?"

"Basically she just gave it to him. When my father died, a society was started from his estate with three separate shares. Claudio and I have equal shares, and my mother has the controlling share. She makes all the decisions, but he is the one who is benefiting. She does whatever he tells her. He takes most of the money and gives us barely enough to survive."

"And your mother doesn't realize what's going on?"

Alexandra shook her head and shrugged. "My mother doesn't know where she is half the time. Haven't you noticed?"

"She seems pretty out of it. Is she on some sort of medication?"

"No. That's the scary part. She probably should be."

"Have you tried getting her professional help?"

"She refuses any kind of help, and she won't listen to anyone."

"Have you tried talking to Claudio?"

She sighed. "Many, many times. I told him there was enough for everyone, and that he didn't need to be so greedy, but he won't listen. Make a right."

I enjoyed driving through the rolling hills of Frascati. Some of the old estates we drove past reminded me of the southern mansions I had seen in Louisiana, but these were parchment colored and looked Mediterranean and less formal. Alexandra said they were now mostly museums. The ancient Roman aqueduct cut through the hills like the Great Wall of China. It was a remarkable bit of engineering. I pulled the car over to the side of the road. We got out and walked beneath one of the great arches. Despite being overgrown with moss, the stone structure was still intact and looked solid.

"Alexandra, I don't understand. Your brother is living in luxury from the money your mother controls, and he won't do anything to help?"

"That's pretty much how it is," she said, looking directly into my eyes.

"What a bastard. Can't you fight him?"

"There is nothing I can do. It's my mother's decision. She's allowing this to happen."

"But why?"

"Because he is her son, and he's the oldest in the family. She just wants to give her responsibility to him. It's really crazy because he doesn't give a damn about us." Her voice quavered a bit.

"I'm sorry, Alexandra," I said, wrapping my arms around her. She did not hug me back, and I felt her pulling away. I had to fight the urge to sulk.

"Why don't we go to town and get the pastries my mother wanted. They are delicious."

"No problem," I said, heading for the car. She directed me to the center of town. Most of the buildings in Frascati had been built at the turn of the Eighteenth century. The architecture wasn't as ornate as some I had seen in Rome, but its classical influence was unpretentious and beautiful. We went inside a small bakery. The sweet smell of fresh-baked bread permeated the shop. Alexandra ordered a couple loaves and an assortment of pastries.

"We'll have these tomorrow morning for breakfast. You'll love them," she said.

That evening the three of us went out. Alexandra had changed into a cotton skirt and a thin blouse. Her figure was a bit fuller than I remembered; her breasts seemed larger and heavier, but she was fit from all the physical labor she had been doing. I barely quelled my desire for her.

He mother had also changed for dinner, but her hair was still mussed and her makeup didn't seem right. We went to a small place near the town center. It wasn't very fancy, and the longer I knew Alexandra the more I realized she didn't like fancy. She appreciated fine things, but stayed away from glamour.

I helped her mother into her chair and waited for Alexandra to sit. The waiter started to clear the extra place setting, but Alexandra's mother stopped him.

"My son will be joining us shortly," she said.

"*Certo, Signora.*"

Alexandra ignored her. I sat quietly, wondering what to do next.

"Tell me, Drew. What are you doing with yourself?" her mother asked politely.

"Well, I'm going to school at Oxford for the summer. I'm in a creative-writing program."

"Yes, you're a writer. I remember now. How's your dear aunt doing? I remember her so well."

"Aunt Tess? She's doing fine. I think she'd be jealous if she knew I was here with both of you right now."

"Your aunt is a real saint," said Alexandra.

"I haven't seen much of her lately. We sort of drifted apart."

"I'm sorry to hear that," said Alexandra's mother.

"Yes, well, I think she was more upset about what happened in Switzerland than both my parents combined."

"It's no big deal," said Alexandra.

"*Signora*, I never did apologize for what happened. Things happened so quickly, and then life sort of fell apart for a while. But I am deeply sorry for what happened."

"Drew, it was a long time ago. You kids were lucky you didn't get into more trouble, but I remember what it was like to be so in love," she said, her eyes filled with wistful sadness.

269

"True love lasts a lifetime," I said with a sigh.

"Spoken like a true Italian," her mother said, squeezing my hand. Alexandra cocked her head and smiled. Even if her mother was a bit crackers I had no problems connecting with her. I had enough experience at dealing with crazies, and I considered her tame stuff compared to some I knew. Even so, I was surprised by how much her attitude had softened, and realized what she needed most was attention; she was in terrible pain.

"Frascati is also known as the City of Wine," Alexandra said. "The wine is wonderful here. You'll have to try some."

We ordered a bottle and *Signora* Cavalletti insisted that Claudio's glass be filled as well. She expected him to appear at any moment, as if he were away making a phone call or something. Dinner was good, and afterward we finished the wine and talked. Alexandra's mother and I chatted endlessly about everything. She had moments of enchanting enlightenment. I found her fascinating.

After dinner Alexandra took my arm and we went home. Her mother turned in early, and Alexandra and I talked in the kitchen.

"You and my mother get along surprisingly well," she said.

"She doesn't seem like such a bad woman. She seems pretty unhappy though."

"She brings most of her unhappiness on herself. She has the power to make herself happy, but she won't use it."

"Has she gotten better or worse since we were in Switzerland?"

She put her hand under her chin and leaned her elbow on the table. "That's an interesting question. When my father first died she was unable to function. After the first year she seemed to be doing okay, but she just refuses to take any responsibility. And the decisions she makes are just insane. She has destroyed a

270

fortune, and she won't listen to anyone, least of all me."

"She seems pretty reasonable, all things considered."

"She can hold a conversation; just don't ask her to make any sound decisions. It's very frustrating," she said, folding her arms on the table.

"What are you going to do?"

"I don't know. I'm going to finish college and leave Rome. I can't stay here anymore, it's too painful. I can't sit here and watch my brother live like a king while my mother throws her life away."

"Where are you going to go?"

"I don't know, yet. Right now I'm going to bed. Are you sure you want to work tomorrow on the house? I can't imagine it would be very much fun for you," she said, standing up.

"Yes, I'm sure. We can start early and do something fun later in the afternoon."

I followed her upstairs. When we got to the landing she kissed me on the cheek.

"Good night, Drew. Sleep well," she said, closing her door.

I stood on the landing a moment, wondering if I should go to her; she could have at least given me a decent kiss. Could I handle being here because of the way I felt? I had an urge to leave the next morning, but that would seem too childish. I went to bed.

The next morning I got up early. Alexandra stood at the kitchen counter wearing an old pair of jeans and a t-shirt, squeezing oranges. Her mother was sitting at the kitchen table in her bathrobe, eating pastries and chocolate.

Alexandra smiled. "Good morning, Drew. Do you want a cappuccino?"

"Please."

"Help yourself to some chocolate and pastries," she said,

handing me a glass of orange juice. I heard the espresso machine running, and then the loud hissing of milk being steamed. She served me a cappuccino in a large cup and made one for herself. I missed cappuccinos. English coffee was no better than American, and the English drank so much tea my back teeth were floating in it at times.

After breakfast Alexandra and I started work. The living room was pretty large with high ceilings and nice detail in the moldings. Drop cloths covered most of the furniture. The oak floor needed to be refinished. The walls were cracked and peeling and the windows looked like they needed to be replaced.

"Where do you want to start?" I asked.

"Why don't you start scraping the walls and I'll start sanding the trim."

We worked hard all morning. Parts of the wall came off in chunks. Apparently the roof leaked and the plaster had been saturated with water, leaving it soft and crumbly. I concentrated on scraping until the room was finished. Pieces of plaster and paint lay in piles on the floor. By lunchtime my hands were raw and tingling.

Alexandra went into the kitchen to help her mother make lunch. I swept up all the debris. The room looked terrible now, but would be gorgeous when we were finished. The maid set the table for us and we sat down to eat. We were both covered with dust. The food was simple—spaghetti in oil and garlic with fresh bread and a salad. It wasn't quite the fare I remembered eating at the castle, but it was good.

After lunch Alexandra showed me how to mix plaster, and I carefully patched the pockmarks in the wall. The plaster dried quickly, leaving little time to get it smooth. It would require some sanding.

"Nice job, Drew," Alexandra said, running her hand over

the wall.

"Thanks." I got off the ladder and walked over to the window. The sill was cracked and rotting. "What are you going to do about these windows? They are in terrible shape."

"I have a carpenter coming to replace them. I'd do it myself, but I just don't have the tools."

"It's probably best. Windows can be tricky, and they need to be done right. What about the floor?"

"What about it?"

"It's beautiful, but it needs to be refinished. I once saw my father sand the floor of our house with an electric sander. It's not that hard. You just need to be sure you follow the grain of the wood and don't sand too deep."

"Those cost a fortune," she said.

"Can't you rent one? That's what my father did."

"I never thought of that," she said squatting down to run her hand over the wood. "I wouldn't know where to rent something like that. Maybe someplace in Rome? I'll look in the phone book. Let's stop for now; I think we've done enough for one day."

My hands and arms were covered in plaster. "Is this stuff hard to get off?"

"You probably don't want to let it dry too long. Why don't you take a shower and I'll see if I can find a place to rent a sander?"

The shower felt good, and I changed into a clean pair of jeans and a plain white shirt. I waited for Alexandra in the kitchen. Her mother was sitting idly at the kitchen table, thumbing through a magazine. She looked up at me and smiled.

"You know, Drew, now that you're all grown up you remind me of an American my late husband knew. He used to come to Italy quite often. You met my husband, didn't you?"

"Yes, I did. He was a wonderful man."

273

"Yes, he was. I miss him terribly. Claudio is just like him. He's going to be a very important man someday."

"Yes, I'm sure he will. What about Alexandra? She has quite a bit of spirit."

She shook her head and frowned. "Yes, we had high hopes for her. She was going to join the Foreign Service. We were grooming her to be a diplomat. She would have done very, very well."

"She still can. Her life is not over, *Signora*."

"She doesn't want it. She only wants to do what she wants to do. All my plans fell to the wayside—the language schools and training have all gone to waste," she said, tossing her magazine on the table in disgust.

"I'm sorry, *Signora*. I don't see it that way. I've known Alexandra a long time. She is brilliant, hardworking, and strong. She will do whatever she sets her mind to."

Her mother looked out the kitchen window with deep sadness. "She would have been a very good diplomat. All the most influential people in Rome thought she was so charming."

"Yes, I can see how they would," I replied, realizing then that she only saw Alexandra as an extension of her dreams, and now that her life had been shattered, Alexandra didn't count for much anymore.

Alexandra came downstairs, fresh out of the shower. She was wearing a simple cotton sundress and sandals. "Drew, I found a place in Rome that rents the machine we need. Do you want to come with me to pick it up?"

"Sure, I'd love to."

"We'll see you later, Mom."

Alexandra handed me the keys and we headed toward Rome. The weather was perfect—not too hot with a soft breeze. The summer insects buzzed in the grass by the side of the road. The wind tousled her dark hair and pulled at the edge of her dress.

274

Her legs were still just as beautiful as I remembered. Almost instinctively I wanted to put my hand on her thigh, and found it difficult to control my urge to touch her.

"Tomorrow morning we'll paint and then in the afternoon we can start sanding the floor."

"I don't think that's a good idea, Alexandra. Sanding the floor raises an amazing amount of dust. I would wait a day for the paint to dry before I started sanding."

"Do you think so? I hate to make a trip for nothing. We'll stop by to look at the store. Maybe we can reserve the machine for the day after tomorrow."

Alexandra directed me to a little side street in a commercial area of Rome. The store was dark and dirty. All kinds of power equipment littered the floor and hung from the walls. A group of unshaven men sat around a desk in the back playing cards. Alexandra made quite a splash when she walked through the door. The sun streamed through the greasy window, illuminating the silhouette of her legs through her dress, and the men leered at her as she stood in the middle of the room.

"*Bongiorno, Signora,*" said one of the men, getting out of his chair. His t-shirt was streaked with yellow stains, and his gut hung over his belt. Alexandra spoke to him in Italian for several minutes, and then two men were loading the sander into the back of the car.

"*Grazie, Signore. Ci vediamo,*" she said.

"What happened?" I asked.

"They let me have the sander for three days for the price of one."

"That doesn't surprise me. You have very persuasive legs."

She smiled. "I know a nice *gelateria* nearby. Why don't we go get some?"

"*Gelateria?*"

"Gelato. Ice cream. The Swiss are famous for their chocolate, and Italians for their ice cream. This is the month when all the towns in Italy have competitions to see who makes the best."

"That sounds good," I said. We walked through narrow side streets to a small *piazza* where a small ice cream store with a red and green awning sat. Underneath the awning were some wrought-iron tables and chairs. On the other side of the *piazza* was a long flight of stone steps leading to an old church. We went inside and stood at the counter. A machine was slowly cranking away at a sealed vat.

"That's where they make the ice cream," said Alexandra.

A young girl in her early twenties stood behind the counter. She had pretty green eyes and wavy blond hair. Her athletic figure rippled beneath her uniform, and her firm, high breasts pushed against the thin material. I noticed her staring at me. I stared back.

"*Bongiourno*," I said.

"*Bongiourno*. Can I help you?" she asked in broken English.

Alexandra noticed the way she looked at me and stroked my arm. "We'd like to try some of your *spumoni*," she said.

"Large or small?"

"Large for him, and I'll take a small. And could we have some water, please?"

I watched her as she bent down to scoop the ice cream out of the cardboard containers in the freezer. Her thin, white uniform rode up the back of her legs, revealing the muscular shape of her thighs. When she was finished she put the ice cream on a tray on the counter.

"I've got it, Alexandra," I said, pulling out my wallet. The girl took the money from me and smiled. Her eyes were the prettiest green, and her nipples pushed through the lace of her bra. It gave me an erection. She noticed and blushed. Alexandra picked up the tray and went to a table outside. I waited for my change.

276

She placed it in my hand and smiled.

"*Grazie,*" I said.

"*Prego,*" she replied. We gazed into each others eyes for a second or two with animalistic desire, and then she turned away.

Alexandra was watching from the table outside. I blushed; coming on to a woman while accompanying another was bad form, even if our relationship was now platonic.

I went outside and sat down. Alexandra handed me my ice cream, and I opened her water for her.

"Is this okay here?" she asked.

"Yes, it's fine."

"If you want we can sit inside. You could talk to the ice cream girl."

I simply smiled. I didn't get the sense that she was really jealous, but from my experience women had an odd tendency to be possessive, even with men they didn't want. Her reaction reassured me she still had feelings for me.

"I'm happy sitting here talking to you, Alexandra."

A group of nuns walked up the street in pairs. A group of young boys climbed the top of the church steps and waited for them to pass. As they did the boys heaved water balloons at them. The nuns shrieked as the balloons shattered on their heads. They were soaked, and the boys hollered as they ran away.

"My God! Did you see that?" I exclaimed.

"Hoodlums," said Alexandra. "Young people all over Italy are rebelling against the church."

"You have to admit, the church has been pretty repressive. People just want to have fun. "

"Did you know women are burning their bras in northern Italy? There's a big women's movement growing."

"They started doing that in America ten years ago," I said.

"Yes, but Italy has always been behind America in those

277

kind of things."

"I find it strange that Italy leads the world in fashion design, yet it is so far behind in so many other areas. I sometimes wonder if the Italian fashion sense comes out of their sexual frustration. The church has done a number on a lot of people's heads."

Alexandra cocked her head and smiled. "I've always felt that way," she said. "It's one of the reasons why I never followed fashion as closely as some of my friends."

"Yes, it's one of the things I admired most about you. I also remember you telling your mother about your lack of interest in clothes. She was so exasperated."

"I remember that," said Alexandra. "I never really lived up to her expectations."

"Oh, well. At least you're not well-dressed and sexually frustrated."

Alexandra laughed. "How do you like the ice cream?" she asked.

"It's delicious. It reminds me a little of the stuff we used to make. My father once brought home an old-fashioned ice cream maker. We had to crank it by hand, and as it started to freeze it got harder to operate. The first couple of times it tasted awful, but once we got the hang of it, it tasted great."

"That sounds like a nice memory."

"There were quite a few nice ones. I can't say it was all bad, although it seemed to get worse the older we got."

"Well, things will only get better for you now," she said, squeezing my hand. I finished my ice cream and wiped my mouth. Alexandra turned her chair to face the sun, and put her feet up on the chair across from me. Her legs were tan and smooth. She didn't shave, but her hair was so silky and light it wasn't noticeable.

"So what happened with you and Paolo?" I asked.

"I already told you. There's not much to tell."

"Not much to tell? Alexandra, you were engaged to be married. How can you say there's not much to tell?"

"Drew, I really didn't know him very well. I met him that Christmas after we got kicked out of school. He asked me out a few times and we started dating. He came to Switzerland to visit during holidays, and we started getting serious last summer. He asked me to marry him just before Christmas."

"But if you weren't sure why did you say yes?"

"I was confused. His family was putting so much pressure on me. I couldn't handle it."

"But you told me you love him."

"I do love him! But not enough to marry him. I cannot marry just because it's convenient. He's a wonderful boy, but he's just not for me."

"I don't mean to pry, Alexandra, but this news really took me by surprise. I had no idea."

"It's okay, Drew. I have no secrets from you. Like I told you, I was going to tell you, but things fell apart."

"It's okay, Alexandra. I'm just disappointed, that's all."

"Disappointed? Why?" she asked.

"Forget it. Why don't we get going?"

"No," she said, putting her hand on my arm. "Tell me what's wrong."

"Alexandra, I still have feelings for you. They never really died. The whole time during high school I thought of nothing but you. It was your memory that helped me survive."

My head began to ache from holding back my tears, and the compassion in her big, brown eyes didn't help.

"Drew, I am so sorry," she said, rubbing my arm. "We were just kids. It was so long ago. I don't feel the same anymore."

279

"It hasn't been that long, Alexandra. It's only been a year and a half!"

"A year and a half and a lifetime ago, so much has changed. We have changed, and so have our lives. I still love you, but it's not the same burning passion I had when we were kids."

"But you still love me?"

"Yes, Drew, but I am not in love."

"Alexandra, we have to get out of here. I can't handle this anymore."

"Are you okay?"

"Yes, I'm fine," I said standing up. My head was pounding from too much emotion. When I got to my feet my head spun. I lost my balance and fell back in my chair.

"Drew!" cried Alexandra. She grabbed hold of my arm and helped me up. "Let's get you home."

She held onto my arm and led me back to the car. I felt weak and disoriented. She took the keys from me and we headed back to Frascati. The facades of the buildings seemed to blend together, and the sounds of the street echoed in my head. I could feel my mind disconnecting from my body, and I lie back in my seat and slowly shut down. All the years of pain I endured started to overtake my body, and by the time we got home I was nearly numb.

"Drew, are you sure you are okay?"

"I just need to lie down." I got out of the car slowly. My stomach was queasy and my muscles didn't respond correctly. I went upstairs and got into bed.

Alexandra was sitting on the edge of my bed when I awoke, and I thought I was dreaming for a moment or two. I blinked my eyes in the darkness. She stroked my hair, and I wrapped my arms around her legs.

"What time is it?" I asked.

280

"It's after ten. You must be hungry. You've been sleeping almost two days. I've been worried sick about you."

Then I remembered what happened, and felt the pain returning.

"Do you want to eat something?" she asked.

"In a bit," I replied. I slipped my arm around her waist and pulled her down to me. She kicked off her shoes, got under the covers, and wrapped herself around my body. I felt comfortable and warm, and I held onto her tightly. We lay there several minutes and drifted off to sleep.

Later that night she got out of bed and stripped out of her clothes. It had been so long since I had felt her skin next to mine. I wanted to make love to her but I was just too tired. She pulled off my underwear and slid down between my legs. I was practically powerless as I felt my orgasm rising. I was too spent to reciprocate.

"It's okay, Drew," she said. She put her arms around me and we went back to sleep.

I awoke the next morning feeling groggy. Alexandra's naked body was wrapped around me like a snake. Raindrops tapped softly on the window. I caressed the small of her back, and she pushed her hips against mine.

"Good morning," she said, as she began to wake.

"Good morning," I said. I ran my hand down the curve of her breasts, feeling her erect nipples beneath my fingertips. I kissed her shoulders and neck, and she pulled me on top of her. I made love to her for as long as I could, until at last I couldn't hold back any longer. I lay on top of her for quite awhile until my stomach rumbled loudly.

Alexandra laughed. "It's been days since you've eaten. You must be starving."

"I'm getting pretty hungry."

281

"Why don't you take a shower and get dressed, Mr. Smith. I'll make us some breakfast."

I went downstairs after my morning shower. The living room was nearly finished. The walls had been sanded and painted, and a carpenter had ripped out the old windows and was busy replacing them with new ones. He nodded at me when he saw me and continued working. Alexandra had kept herself busy while I was asleep.

"The room looks wonderful!" I said, walking into the kitchen.

"Welcome back to the living," said her mother. "Are you feeling better?"

"Yes, thank you. I feel like Rip Van Winkle."

"Who's that?" asked Alexandra.

"Oh, it's an American folktale about a lazy man who fell asleep in the Catskill Mountains and slept for twenty years after drinking a magic potion."

"Sounds like an interesting story," said her mother.

Alexandra put an extra-large glass of orange juice in front of me and began making cappuccinos. I looked forward to having some caffeine in my system. I had a dull headache from too much sleep, and the caffeine would help clear out the cotton between my ears. A big basket of croissants and pastries sat in the center of the table. I helped myself to some and sipped at my coffee.

Alexandra sat down next to me. Where did we stand? Last night felt wonderful, as well as this morning. What made her change her mind? I was afraid to bring up the subject; I was simply happy to feel her in my arms again, even if it was a temporary situation.

After breakfast we went into the living room. The carpenter was nearly finished framing in the new windows, and he made

282

a lot of racket as he drove in the nails with his hammer. The floor sander sat in the corner of the room. A thick, yellow extension cord was neatly draped over the handles.

"When do you plan on sanding the floor?"

"As soon as the carpenter is finished. Can you help me move this furniture?" asked Alexandra.

"Where do you want it?"

"We'll move it into the foyer for now," she said.

I helped her carry out the furniture. According to Alexandra the dining room was her next project. It wasn't in as bad shape as the living room—it just needed a fresh coat of paint. We couldn't do much else until the carpenter was finished. Alexandra spoke with him briefly. He told her he'd be done by lunch.

Alexandra took my arm and we walked in the garden. The rain had stopped and the sun was breaking through the clouds. The air was heavy with the heavenly smell of jasmine. We walked all they way down to the bottom of the hill through the olive trees to a small, wooden fence that overlooked the town of Frascati. We leaned our elbows on the fence. Parchment-colored, old houses with ample verandas were sprinkled across the countryside, overlooking the town.

"It's nice here," I said.

"Yes, I like it. But I wish I could see water instead of buildings. I really love the sea."

"We live pretty close to the ocean. It's nice, but I don't live for the beach like some people do."

"I love the beach, but only because I love seeing the water. I love seeing beautiful things. I don't think I could stand it if I was surrounded by ugliness."

"Where would you like to live if you had your way?" I asked.

"I don't know. There are so many beautiful places in the world, but I would want to stay in Italy. I would love to live in

Taormina. Do you know where it is?"

"Yes. Aunt Tess was there. She did some beautiful paintings of the area."

"She told me she was there. It really is the most gorgeous place. I would love to have a house there someday."

"Maybe someday you will," I said. "I believe you can do anything you want." She put her arm around me and kissed me on the cheek.

Alexandra, I'm a little confused," I said.

"About what?"

"Last night."

"Drew, you've been through too much pain. I did what I did because I care about you. It was the best way I knew how to help you," she said.

"I have to admit, it helped a lot," I said, taking her in my arms.

"Drew, you need to understand I really enjoy sex with you, and I love you as a friend, but I am not in love."

What she told me didn't seem to matter. Feeling her in my arms made me so excited. She unbuttoned my pants and caressed me as I unbuttoned hers. The grass was too wet to lie down in, so she turned her back to me and leaned over the fence. It was the most wonderful sex I ever had. When we were finished I turned her to me and kissed her.

"Thank you," I said.

"It's my pleasure," she said, caressing my chest.

We walked hand-in-hand back to the house. Alexandra helped her mother in the kitchen, and I went to the living room to see how the carpenter was doing. He was putting on the trim. I swept the floor while he worked and then studied the sander.

In a small bag were belts of sandpaper of varying grades. The floor wasn't scarred or stained. It just needed to be stripped and refinished. I chose a light grade, knowing from experience that the sander could eat through the wood pretty quickly. I began to fiddle with the belt, trying to get it on the rollers. I wasn't having much success.

"*Non, non. Fai cosi*," said the carpenter. He took the belt from my hands and turned it around. I had it on backward. Then he took a monkey wrench from his bag and loosened a nut on the side of the sander. The belt slipped on easily. He tightened the nut and the belt pulled taught over the rollers.

"*Ecco!*" he said, smiling.

"*Grazie*," I said.

"*Prego*," he replied, returning to his work.

I carefully removed the floor molding from the walls and stacked it in the foyer when Alexandra called me to lunch. She had made linguini with a white clam sauce. It smelled good.

"Alexandra, where did you learn to cook so well?"

"Cooking is not so hard, and I don't mind doing it. It doesn't take much time if you are organized. I can put together a decent meal pretty quickly."

After lunch Alexandra and I went back to work. She painted the window trim on the outside of the house while I sanded the floor. I worked my way up and down the room, one plank at a time, being careful not to lean on the sander and allow the machine to do most of the work. The machine roared loudly and raised a thick cloud of sawdust. I took off my t-shirt and wrapped it around my face to keep from choking to death. When finished I bent down and ran my hand across the wood. Although the paper wasn't very coarse, the wood was rough; it would need another pass with a finer grain.

"This looks beautiful," said Alexandra, coming into the room.

"It's not done yet," I said, turning the machine on its side.

285

I dug a wrench out of a toolbox nearby and loosened the belt. I fitted the belt with the finest paper on the machine. "This should bring out the natural grain in the wood," I said.

Alexandra watched as I worked my way down the floor, being careful to follow the grain of the wood. When I was done I stood back to admire my work. The floor looked good. I went outside to get some air. Alexandra was putting the finishing touches on the last window. She had done a nice job. I helped her clean the brushes when she was through and put away the paint. The sun was just beginning to set when we finished.

"What now?" I asked.

"What do you want to do?"

"I don't know. We should probably get all that dust off the floor. It's not good to leave the floor unfinished too long. Even a dirty pair of shoes will leave ugly marks."

"Do you think we should finish it tonight?"

"It's probably a good idea. Do you have any floor finish?"

"Yes, the people who rented me the machine sold me some."

"If we do it together we can finish the first coat before dinner."

I started sweeping the sawdust into piles and scooping it into the trash. Alexandra found a vacuum and sucked up all the loose dirt and remaining sawdust. She opened a can of polyurethane, and we started at one end of the room and worked our way toward the door. Night had fallen by the time we were finished. The floor looked beautiful, and I felt proud.

I took Alexandra out to dinner. We went to a small, crowded *trattoria* not far from the house. We sat at a long, wooden table covered with plain, brown paper next to strangers. Baskets of bread sat on the table, and people just helped themselves. We were the only ones speaking English.

Dinner was served in a copper skillet. The waiter placed it

between us in the middle of the table. The food was good, and there was plenty of it. Afterward we went to a little bar in town and had a cappuccino. I enjoyed sitting outside and talking in the warm, night air. People strolled by leisurely. I was reminded vaguely of Rumson—only the people here were much more fashionable. The men wore pleated slacks and polo shirts and the women wore elegant summer dresses or brightly colored pants.

When we got back, I followed Alexandra up the stairs. She kissed me on the cheek and said goodnight.

"Aren't you going to stay with me?" I asked, taking her hand.

"I don't know if that's such a good idea, Drew."

"What's not good about it?" I asked, placing her hand between my legs. She laughed and ran her hand over my erection. As we kissed I undid the buttons on her blouse. She took my hand and we went to her room.

I awoke the next morning with Alexandra's body entwined around mine.

"Good morning," said Alexandra.

"Good morning," I said, getting on top of her. Her mother came shuffling up the stairs. I jumped out of bed and ran into the bathroom. Alexandra scooped up my clothes and put them in the tub. She slipped into a nighty just before her mother got to the door. I got dressed quietly while Alexandra spoke with her mother. I was beginning to pick up some words, although I didn't understand what they were saying. Her mother left and Alexandra opened the door.

"What did she want?" I asked.

"Nothing. She just wanted to complain about the house."

Alexandra's bathroom was large with black and white tile. A big window overlooked the tub, and an old pedestal sink stood next to the toilet. Alexandra stood in front of the sink and began brushing her teeth. The thin, silk nighty barely concealed her skin. I sat on the toilet and watched. Her breasts moved back and forth as she brushed, and I could see her ass as she bent over the sink. Finally I got behind her and unzipped my pants.

"Can't I finish brushing my teeth?"

"You sure can," I said, wrapping my hands around her hips. I think Alexandra loved sex more than I did. I never had to ask for it, and she often seduced me. I considered it one of her best qualities.

After breakfast Alexandra started painting the dining room, and I put a second coat of polyurethane on the living room floor. Her mother stood outside and watched me work. She had pinned her hair up into a bun, but it looked like a bird's nest on top of her head. Loose strands hung in her face, and her blue shirt clashed with her pants.

"What do you think, *Signora*?"

"I was wondering about the windows," she said.

"What about them?"

"I was wondering what kind of curtains Claudio's wife would like."

"Claudio is married?" I asked.

"No."

"Oh! Well, then. When he gets married you'll have to ask her."

"Yes, I'll do that," she said, walking away.

I finished the floor and cleaned my brush. Alexandra had already finished one wall. Her hair was spotted with white paint. She looked cute. I told her about the conversation I had with her mother.

"Oh, yes, she already pictures Claudio married," she said.

"Is he even dating?"

"Yes, he's dating. He has a girlfriend. I don't like her."

"Why not?"

"She's only interested in his money. Claudio used to talk to me about her before we stopped talking. I think she is manipulative and dishonest, but he won't listen."

"Why do you say that?"

"Because she's always trying to get him to spend money on her, and she has been bugging him for years to marry her."

"Are they going to get married?"

"Probably. She says she is pregnant by him."

"You think she is trying to trick him?" I asked.

"That's what I think. She's a real bitch."

"Is she pretty?"

"Yes, she's very pretty, but she doesn't come from a very good family. They are constantly pushing her to marry him just so they can have a more comfortable life."

"Does he love her?" I asked.

"I don't think so. Maybe he did in the beginning, but not anymore. I think she got pregnant just so she wouldn't lose him."

"That's terrible! I can't imagine marrying someone under those circumstances."

"The sad part is he will probably marry her out of his own sense of honor."

"Well, maybe things will work out in the long run," I said.

"I hope so—for his sake. I could never marry a man just for his money. I think she's disgusting."

"Maybe she loves him. It doesn't have to be just about money," I said.

Alexandra gave me one of her curious looks. She had a tendency to see things in black and white sometimes. Other times she was amazingly insightful. I helped her clean brushes and rollers.

"After lunch we should take the sander back," she said.

"Sounds good. As long as you let me drive."

"Are you hungry?" she asked.

"Yes."

"That's a stupid question. You're always hungry. I'll start lunch," she said going into the kitchen. "Why don't you get cleaned up?"

I jumped into the shower and put on some clean clothes. After lunch we loaded the sander into the trunk of her car. Alexandra handed me the keys and we started toward Rome. We dropped off the sander at the rental place and Alexandra paid him.

"Is there anything special you want to do this afternoon?" she asked, taking my hand.

"There is so much of Rome I never got to see the last time I was here. What happened to your farm?"

"We still own the land, but the stables are gone."

"What about your parents' little cottage in the woods?"

"It's still there, although I don't think anyone has been there in ages. I'm sure it's a mess."

"I'd like to see it again. It's one of my happiest memories."

"I don't know if that's such a good idea, Drew. It would be painful for me to go back there. I don't think I could. I agree that we had a wonderful time there when we were young, but that was the place where my parents went when they were healthy and in love. I prefer to leave that memory alone."

"I understand," I said, kissing her forehead.

She took me on a quick sightseeing tour around Rome. She was no longer very affectionate, and only let me hold her hand as if making a gesture of capitulation. The closeness we had as kids was not the same; that magical feeling of adventure we shared seemed to be missing. I knew she had tender feelings for me, but we had an invisible wall between us that I could not get past. I

290

would run into it whenever I tried to display my tenderness for her, or tell her how I felt. My words seemed to bounce off her and fall lifeless at her feet. At times I felt as though I were doing something wrong, and so I chose my words carefully, and tried not to be too affectionate. But I was still so in love with her, and caressed her arms awkwardly, wishing she'd respond. I never knew whether to stay or leave. I had one more day before I had to be back at school, and in a way I was relieved.

My last day there I helped Alexandra put the finishing touches on the living room and dining room. The downstairs was nearly done. I felt good about contributing to the restoration of the house, as though I had left a piece of myself there. The living room floor glowed as if brand new, and the walls were clean and smooth. Our final chore was to move the furniture back in and remove the drop cloths. We arranged the furniture to give the room a homey and warm look. Alexandra was grateful for my help; that evening she took me out to nice restaurant in Rome.

The morning of my departure she drove me to the airport. I said goodbye to her mother and packed my things in the car. Alexandra drove this time. We drove silently through Rome until we approached the airport.

"Work well when you get back to school, Drew."

"I intend to," I said.

"What are your plans when the summer is over?" she asked.

"I am going to matriculate into the London program."

"That sounds wonderful. London is beautiful."

"We won't be that far from each other. We can see each other on weekends and holidays."

Alexandra took a deep breath and sighed. The moment was portentous, and I braced myself.

"Drew, I'd love to see you, but I don't want to lead you on. I love you as a friend, but I am not in love with you. You deserve

291

so much more. You need to find a woman who can love you the way you deserve to be loved."

"Alexandra, you are the love of my life. I can't imagine loving anyone else."

She parked the car in the lot and took my hand. "Drew, I will always be there for you if you need me, but I can't give you the kind of love you deserve."

The pain I had been suppressing started rising to my throat. It lodged in my chest and burned like a hot coal. "Alexandra, perhaps I should go on by myself. Thank you for everything," I said, kissing her on the cheek.

"Drew—" she said, but then stopped short. She got out of the car and opened the trunk. I reached in and grabbed my things, and she put her arms around me and gave me a hug.

I walked to the terminal and fought back my tears. Now I couldn't leave Rome fast enough. I sat in the terminal waiting for my flight to board. I tried to understand what had happened between us, but I couldn't comprehend it all. If she didn't love me why was the sex so damn good? I fought back my tears the entire flight back to London.

Chapter 12

Being accepted into the London program was a bitter-sweet moment. I expected to be much happier about it, but I took the news in stride. I had some time to kill before the fall classes began. The campus was located in Angel, in the North Eastern part of London. Michael told me finding a place was difficult, especially when all the students were returning from the summer holidays. He suggested I find someone who wanted to share a flat or inquire about a bedsit.

"What's a bedsit?" I asked.

"That's where you rent a furnished room in a house. Normally you share the bath with the other tenants. Usually each room has a little kitchenette and you pay for your heat by putting fifty pence in a gas meter. Staying warm gets expensive in the winter, but the rent is not bad. You'd be better off finding a flat. I suggest you get a place in a youth hostel until you find someplace more permanent."

I found a youth hostel near Piccadilly Circus my first day in London. It cost next to nothing to stay there, and kids from all over the world were crammed into tiny rooms filled with bunk beds. Most everyone there was backpacking through Europe. I locked my typewriter and bags into a locker assigned to me. I would have been happy staying there indefinitely, but guests were limited to one week stays to keep vagrants from setting up permanent residencies.

I scanned the papers for shares I might be able to afford. Everything in Central London was way out of my price range. Even shares in Angel were pretty pricey. The few I places I looked at were tiny, and at least ten people stood in line to look at the same place. Someone suggested I start looking further north. Finally I came upon a bedsit in Hampstead Heath that wasn't too outrageous.

Getting there wasn't easy. I had to transfer twice on the tube. The London Underground was fairly easy to get around in. I loved the way the British always waited patiently in neat lines to buy their tokens. Only the French and Americans occasionally jumped the line to get to the booth first. Nobody ever said anything, but they shook their heads and clucked their tongues disapprovingly. I had to take the Piccadilly Line from Piccadilly Circus to the Northern Line, get off at Hampstead and take the National Rail over to Hampstead Heath.

The area was mostly working-class residential. Brownstone row houses lined the streets. Much of the area had been heavily bombed during WWII and a few buildings were left in ruins as a testament to those times. Their burned-out shells broke the charming residential skyline with dark and jagged edges. I finally found the address and rang the bell. A man from India opened the door. I introduced myself and he showed me in.

A thin, bearded man, he wore a cotton tunic and a turban. He and his wife lived in the apartment on the first floor. He managed the building. He led me up an old, winding stair case to the second floor. At the top of the landing was a pay phone. The room he showed me was at the front of the house, overlooking the quiet street. I liked it. Two great windows let in plenty of light. A table and two chairs sat in front of one of the windows. At the front of the room to the right was a kitchenette, which was comprised of simply two electric burners and a sink. A small refrigerator was neatly tucked beneath the counter. The bed was old with a cast-iron frame. The mattress seemed a bit lumpy, and the springs creaked when I sat on it, but I had slept on worse. Next to the bed was a small gas heater mounted on the wall with a place to insert coins, just as Michael had described.

294

The bathroom was at the end of the hall outside. No shower as I had hoped, but instead a big cast-iron tub with a shower attachment. The bathroom was clean.

"How many people live here?" I asked.

"There are three on this floor and two downstairs," he answered. "Almost everyone here works fulltime. You will probably only see them at night. What do you do?" he asked.

"I'm a student. I study creative writing."

"The rent is 150 quid per month, payable on the first. We'll also need a deposit."

I did some quick math in my head—almost $250 per month—not unreasonable.

"I'll take it," I said.

He took me to his apartment to fill out some papers. His wife was busy cooking something in the kitchen. She watched me from the corner of her eye while I filled out the application. When I finished I gave him 300 pounds and he handed me the keys.

"There is a place to do laundry down the street to your right, and you can buy groceries at a market two streets over."

I went back to the youth hostel to pick up my things. I arrived back at my new home well after 5:00. Laughter and music filtered from the open door next to mine, and a few moments later two women came out to greet me.

"Oh, hello," one of them said. "We heard someone new moved in. Welcome. My name is Helen, and this is Nan."

"How do you do," I said, shaking their hands. Helen was much older than Nan. She looked to be in her late thirties. Her frizzy, blond hair sat on the side of her head like a thatch. She had a mild overbite, and her large front teeth had a wide gap between them. Nan looked to be in her mid-twenties, and was almost as tall as I. She wore her light-brown hair in a bob, and had pretty, blue eyes. Their accents were not British. I asked them about it.

"We're from Australia," Nan said. "We came to England for work. We're both nurses in a hospital nearby. What do you do, Yank?"

"Yank?"

"It's an expression for an American. You're the first one that's stayed here."

"I'm a writer. I'm going to school starting in the fall."

"A writer!" said Helen. "As in novels and such?"

"I haven't written any novels yet, but I hope to someday. I spent the summer at Oxford, learning the elements of fiction writing."

"How wonderful!" exclaimed Helen. "We have a potentially famous person in our midst."

I laughed. "I hope so, although I've heard most writers don't make much money. Some never get published."

"Are you any good?" asked Nan.

"Yeah, so I've been told, but it's too early to tell. I've only written short stories. I've never tried to write anything more substantial."

"Well, good luck to you, Yank," said Nan. "Why don't you join us for tea? We were about to have a cup."

"I'd love to, thanks," I said, following the women to Nan's room. Her place looked like an older version of a college dormitory room. A silk scarf was draped over the lamp next to her bed, illuminating the room with a soft, seductive glow, and her stockings were hanging to dry from the edge of her sink. Her uniform was draped over the door of her closet. She wasn't messy, but she looked as though she barely found time to do any cleaning. They served me tea and cookies and we talked until about 8:00 pm. Helen excused herself to get ready for bed. She lived across the hall from Nan. They both got up very early.

"It was a pleasure meeting both of you. I hope to do this

again," I said.

"Oh, sure," said Helen. "You'll see us tomorrow after work."

Later that night I called my father. It took a while for the operator to get through.

"Hello? Dad? How are you?"

"I'm fine, Drew. Did you find a place yet?"

"Yes. I'm living in a bedsit in Hampstead Heath. It's nice. I'm not that far from school."

"How much money are you going to need each month?" I calculated. My rent was about $250 a month, and food would cost at least another hundred, transportation to school would be another fifty, heat another fifty and then there were various miscellaneous expenses that would inevitably pop up.

"I think $650 a month should do it, Dad."

"I'll send you a check each month. I suggest you open up a bank account there so you can make deposits. Study hard."

"I'll do that, Dad. Thanks," I said, hanging up the phone.

That night before going to bed I unpacked my suitcase and typewriter. I had some time to kill before starting school. My options were limited; almost all my money was spent on moving. I set up my typewriter on the table next to the window and thought about my next project. Why not try to write a novel? I had an idea in mind; I wanted to write about my parents before their marriage went bad. Bits of their lives floated around in my memory, and I wanted to write it all down and piece together what happened. Not the entire story was unhappy. According to my mother they had many happy years between them.

The next morning I went down to Lloyd's Bank of London and opened a checking account, and then went to the supermarket to buy some groceries. I didn't have a lot to spend, so I bought just a few things to keep from going hungry. I'd have to make do until my father sent his first check. Later I sat down to a

297

cup of hot tea and started writing. I wrote most of the day, taking a short break for lunch. Late that afternoon a knock rapped on my door. It was Helen and Nan. Nan was still wearing her uniform. She wasn't especially pretty, but she had nice legs. Helen had already changed into a t-shirt and blue jeans.

"Hello Drew," said Helen. "We've been listening to your typewriter ever since we got home. We thought we'd invite you over for tea, if you're not too busy."

"No, not at all. I'll be right there. Just give me a moment to finish this one thought," I said.

I finished and went to Nan's room. Her door was ajar, and I could see her in the mirror. Helen was sitting on the bed talking while Nan got out of her uniform. She was wearing thin, cotton panties and a lace bra. Her figure was curvy and full, with large, soft breasts. I waited outside the door for her to slip into some jeans and an old sweatshirt before knocking on the door.

"Come in," said Nan.

"How are you, ladies?" I asked, taking a chair.

"We're fine," said Helen. "How was your day?"

"Busy. I spent most of it writing. I've decided it's time to start that novel I've always wanted to write."

"That's wonderful," said Helen. "What's it about?"

"It's about my parents."

"Most writers write about themselves at first. It's very cathartic," said Nan.

"I have to write what I know. I haven't really experienced all that much yet."

"You'll have to let us read some of your work," said Helen.

"I'd love to," I said, getting out of my chair. I went to my room, picked out "Harmony House," went back to Nan's room, and handed Helen my story. "This one I consider my best," I said.

"'Harmony House'. I like that title," said Helen. "Mind if I have a go at this?"

"No, not at all. It's kind of weird in parts."

Helen sat back on the bed and began reading while Nan and I talked. I kept my eye on Helen as she read. She seemed engrossed in the story—always a promising sign.

"We were going to cook some dinner. Would you like to have dinner with us, Yank?" Nan asked.

"I'd love to. Thank you."

"We're not having anything fancy. Just chicken and rice," she said.

"I don't think fancy is actually possible in a kitchen this small," I said.

"You'd be surprised what I can throw together in here. I've whipped up some pretty good meals. Carrots okay?" she asked, reaching into the refrigerator.

"Carrots are fine. Anything I can do to help?" I asked

"I've got it under control. *Ta*," she said.

"*Ta*?" I asked.

"*Ta*," she replied. "It means thank you in Australia."

"Oh, it sounded like you were saying goodbye. How do like living in England?"

"It's okay. It's a bit cold in the winter, but it's not bad. The English are a lot different than we are."

"How so?" I asked.

"Well, in England you are defined by where you come from, but in Australia you are defined by where you are," she said, peeling carrots and cutting them into pieces.

"What do you mean by that?" I asked.

"Here we go," said Helen, rolling her eyes from her corner on the bed. She was sitting with her back to the wall and my manuscript propped on her knees.

"What I mean is that people respect more the man who has inherited millions of dollars than the man who has recently made millions from nothing. In Australia it's the other way around."

"New Money versus old money, it's the same in America. The old money frowns upon the new money. It's a question of aristocracy. People who have new money are considered gauche."

"Well, I think it's stupid, Yank," she said with one hand on her hip. "They should respect the man that's made his own money, rather than the bloke who's done nothing to earn it except have the good fortune to be born into the right family."

"I agree to an extent, but I think the real difference in old and new money is the attitude towards it. I think people with new money need to flaunt it with showy cars and overbuilt houses. People from old money simply understand that it's there and don't need to flaunt it as much."

"Yes, the attitude is most certainly the biggest difference. Some of these rich, old snobs I've had to deal with made me want to kill them," she said, banging a pot of water down on the stove.

"She's talking about some of the people she did private care for before she got her job in the hospital," said Helen. "Some of them treated her pretty badly."

"And what's wrong with enjoying your money if you have it?" asked Nan.

"There's nothing wrong with enjoying your money, but if your only purpose for buying a big house is to show people how rich you are then that's gauche."

Nan and I continued talking about new money versus old, and Helen continued reading. When she was finished she put all the papers back in order and handed me the manuscript. "This is quite good, Drew."

"Thank you."

"Yeah? Is he any good, Helen?" asked Nan.

"Yes, he's quite good. You should have a read," she said.

"I'll do that. You mind leaving it with me? I'll read it tonight before bed."

"No, not at all."

Helen got off the bed and set the table. Nan's place was smaller than mine, and with the three of us it was crowded but cozy. Dinner was tasty. She sautéed some chicken breasts in spices and butter, and then made gravy for the rice.

Helen and Nan told me all about how they came to London from Sydney after finishing college. They had to work at least a year doing private care before they could get jobs in the hospital where they now worked. Both women had to be up very early in the morning, so we called it a night. I went back to my room and continued writing. There was no television, which was probably for the best; I had no distractions.

During the day I wrote as much as I could. The girls arrived home at about 4:00. It was a nice time for me to take a break, and we usually had tea. Nan told me she liked my story. We got along well, and I liked her sarcastic wit. Helen was much more reserved, although I found her to be pleasant.

That Sunday Nan asked me if I'd like to go to Hyde Park with her and Helen. It was a beautiful day, and I had been cooped up most of the week.

"You will enjoy this," said Nan. "Every Sunday at Speaker's Corner you can hear people harangue about anything they want."

"What do you mean?"

"You'll see," she said.

The three of us took the Underground to Hyde Park Corner. It was a bright, sunny day. The leaves hadn't begun to turn yet, but the season was just beginning to change. I had walked

301

through Hyde Park before, but I didn't know what Nan was talking about. Near Marble Arch, standing on little wooden crates, about a dozen men were screaming at the top of their lungs. Crowds of people stood around them. The ones who were more interesting drew bigger crowds.

"Did you ever wonder where the expression 'To get up on one's soapbox comes from?" asked Nan.

"I never actually thought about it, but now that you mention it—"

"There you have it," she said, gesturing with her hand. "People stand on soapboxes every Sunday and harangue on any subject they want. It's one of the ways Brits exercise their right to free speech."

We walked over to one of the larger crowds. A man in his early thirties was yelling at the crowd about England's policies toward Ireland. He had quite a few hecklers in the crowd. His speech was quite topical, given that the IRA had just blown up a Harrods store right near Kensington Park. Seven people had died, and another twenty-three were injured. London was in pretty bad shape. The unemployment rate had reached an all-time high, and for the first time in London's history, Bobbies were issued firearms. It seemed the whole country was exploding. Labor unions all across England were going on strike. The first week I moved to London there was a baker's strike, and Londoners queued up in front of grocery stores to stock up on bread. Now the electric company announced a strike, and scheduled brown-outs all over the city. People had a lot to talk about, and Hyde Park corner was just the place to do it.

Given the explosive nature of some of the harangues, I thought there would be much more that just heckling going on.

"This is one of Briton's oldest traditions," explained Helen. "People normally don't get too far out of line."

We moved from crowd to crowd, listening to what people had to say. The discourses were on almost every topic from politics to sex. A few lost souls stood on their boxes and talked craziness to themselves. Occasionally someone would stop to listen for a couple of seconds before shaking their head and moving on. The better orators had been doing this awhile.

Later that day we stopped at a street vendor for some fish and chips. British fast food was worse than American; the grease from the deep-fried fish filets saturated the newspaper it was wrapped in. How is it the entire British Empire didn't simply die of heart disease? The hardest thing to stomach in England was undoubtedly the food, and I never could develop a taste for it. But the best part about London was the ethnic variety. You could get any kind of food you wanted—from Caribbean to Far Eastern. We sat on a park bench, eating our lunch and watching the passersby.

Late that afternoon we headed home. Helen offered to cook dinner, and Nan and I went to buy groceries.

"What are you in the mood to eat, Yank?" she asked.

"I don't know. My stomach is a bit touchy from lunch."

"Too greasy for you, eh? How about a macaroni and tuna salad?"

I nodded. We picked up a box of pasta and a couple cans of tuna. I offered to pay.

"*Ta*," she said. "When we get back I'll make you some tea. It will settle your stomach."

We gave Helen the groceries and sat on the bed while she cooked. Nan and I began to flirt. When dinner was ready we sat at the table and talked casually. I felt Nan's leg wrap around my own. After dinner Helen went to bed, and I went back to my room.

A few minutes later Nan knocked on my door. I opened

the door and let her in. We kissed. Within minutes we were both undressed and in bed. We made love twice, but I wasn't used to going to bed so early, and was up half the night tossing and turning. I liked Nan, but the chemistry between us wasn't very strong. I kept thinking about Alexandra, and how good it felt to hold her next to me. It didn't feel the same with Nan, and I lay next to her trying not to move around too much. When I finally fell asleep it seemed only minutes later when the alarm went off. I lay in bed and watched her get dressed.

"I'd better get out of here before Helen wakes up," she said.

"I'll see you later," I said, giving her a kiss. It was still dark out. I couldn't imagine having to get up so early everyday for work. My head ached and my eyes were puffy from lack of sleep, so I went back to bed.

I awakened after 10:00. I made myself a cup of coffee and drew a bath. It was nice having the house to myself. I sat in the tub for at least an hour before I finally dressed.

The mailman came, and I ran downstairs to see if my check had come. A postcard from Alexandra showed pictures of the antique archways of Padova. She wrote to thank me for helping with the house, and to give me her new address and phone number. I tore open the envelope from Browning Seals International, Inc. and found a check enclosed in a blank piece of paper. It was for only $350.00.

There was a mistake. I couldn't live on that each month. I went to the pay phone and called my father collect. He refused to accept the charges. I decided to call him direct. This time he hung up on me. I couldn't believe it. How was I going to make ends meet? I could cover the rent, but I wasn't sure I could buy food and heat. I sat down to calculate how much it would cost to get to school each week. I couldn't do it on this allowance, and school started in just a few days. My only option was to go out and get a job.

I went down to the bank and deposited my check. It would take at least a week to clear. Afterward I walked around the neighborhood to find work. The only experience I had was in restaurants. At the very least I could get some extra money washing dishes. I spent most of the day applying for jobs everywhere I could. Every place I applied turned me down. Nobody would consider me without proper working papers, especially now when England was in such dire straights. At the end of the day I went home tired and discouraged. When I got there Nan and Helen had already arrived.

"Did you have school today?" asked Helen.

"No. School doesn't start until next Wednesday. I was out sightseeing," I said.

"Did you see anything good?" asked Nan.

"I saw London Bridge and Big Ben." I didn't want to tell them what had happened, but I was pretty agitated.

They made me a cup of tea and we sat and talked about the brown-outs that were afflicting the city. Soon our area would be affected, and we hoped the strike would be resolved before that.

Later that night Nan came and knocked on my door. She was wearing only her bathrobe. She slipped it off and got into bed.

"I thought I'd come over and warm you up a bit," she said.

"That's very considerate," I said. I got out of my clothes quickly and got in bed next to her.

With her it was just sex. In fact, sometimes I felt we had almost nothing at all in common. I found it difficult to express any sort of tenderness towards her during our love making, and I discovered that sex meant more to me than just going through the motions. Sex without passion made me feel guilty, as if I were

were not being true to my partner or myself, but I did my best to conceal what I was feeling to avoid hurting her. Besides, our relationship was young, and I wanted to give things a chance.

Registration for fall classes started that Wednesday. I went down to school and signed up for my classes. Given that I was entering as a freshman I had to take mostly core requirements and only one creative writing class. I scheduled as many classes as I could on the same day to avoid the travel costs. I would have to go twice a week.

As October progressed the nights got colder. Finally, the brown-outs hit our neighborhood, and everyone lit candles. We made the best of the situation. Local restaurants had romantic candlelight dinners. The mood was festive for the first couple days, but not having electricity was an amazing inconvenience, and all of London breathed a sigh of relief when the strike was finally resolved.

On mornings when I didn't have to be at school, I continued looking for work. It was becoming futile: I couldn't get even the most menial job. Nan and I drifted apart. I knew she was disappointed, and I missed the friendship we once enjoyed, but I was so broke I could barely function, and I was ashamed to tell her how bad things were. Each night I made a choice between eating and heat. I had cut back my diet to only rice and beans, and I counted every penny and did my best to make things last, but on some nights it was so cold I couldn't stand it, and I fed the gas meter just enough money to keep warm, knowing that I would have to go without a meal later in the week.

One Saturday night Nan and Helen asked me if I'd like to go out to a club. I accepted the invitation. Later we were introduced to a young man a couple years older than I. He was Nan's date, and he had a car. David worked in a bank. I felt slightly out of place, and Nan gloated as we drove down to Knightsbridge to an after-hours club. The cover charge was five pounds. I wasn't expecting to pay a cover charge, and was forced to admit that I didn't have any money.

"Why would you go out if you didn't have any money?" asked Nan.

"I didn't expect to drink. I though it would be fun just to get out."

"I'll lend you twenty quid for now. You can pay me back," she said.

"Thank you," I told her, taking the money. I knew if I spent that much I would not be able to eat for a week. The place was crowded and smoky. Nan and her friend found a table near the back. It was more of a lounge than a night club. A tiny dance floor, surrounded by mirrors, was in the back, but mostly the place was filled with overstuffed couches and chairs. It would have been cozy if the music weren't so loud. Later that night I told Helen what was going on.

"Drew, why didn't you say anything?" she asked.

"I don't know. I thought I could find a job or something."

"Drew, you can't get a job here. Whatever jobs that might be available are reserved only for members of the European common market. Even if I lost my job I would probably have to go back to Australia. Things are really bad now."

I ran my fingers through my hair and sighed. "Don't I know it."

"What are you going to do?"

"I can't stay here anymore. I'm going to starve or freeze to death. I have a friend in Italy that will help me out. I'm going to drop out of school and stay with her for awhile."

"I don't think dropping out of school is such a good idea, Drew."

"What choice do I have?"

307

"Can't you talk to someone else in the family?"

"No, not really, my father controls the money, and my mother just drinks."

"Can't the school help you out?"

"I don't know. I can't stay here anymore. I'm going to take what's left of my money, buy a train ticket, and get out of here," I said. "My friend will help me get settled. I've known her since I was fifteen."

I was tired. My ears were pounding from the music being played so loud. David and Nan dropped Helen and me off at the house, and they continued back to his place. It felt a little strange, but I wasn't terribly hurt; I was just happy to get into bed, and I even had a few coins for heat.

I woke up late the next morning, and the room was cold. I got dressed quickly and called the number Alexandra had given me. Another girl answered the phone.

"*Pronto?*"

I didn't know what to say at first. I thought of speaking French, but chose English instead.

"Hello. Is Alexandra there, please?"

"*Sì*, One moment please."

"Hello?" said Alexandra. The sound of her voice put me at ease.

"Alexandra. It's Drew. How are you?"

"Drew! You got my post card. How are you?"

"I'm fine. Listen, I need to come see you. I was thinking of taking the train to Padova tomorrow."

"Tomorrow? Drew, I'd love to see you but I'm in the middle of school. Can't we make it some other time?"

"Alexandra, I'm in trouble. I'm completely broke and my father cut me off."

"What do you mean, cut you off?"

"I mean he is barely giving me enough money to live. I can pay my rent but I can't afford food or heat, let alone transportation to school. I can't take any more of this."

"Can't you find a job?" she asked.

"Believe me I have tried. I've applied everywhere, but people are demonstrating in the streets because the unemployment is so bad."

"Yes, I've read about it in the news, but things are not much better here. I'd even say they are worse. I don't see how coming here is going to help you. Have you tried talking to your father?"

"He won't take my calls. I called him twice. The first time he refused to accept the charges, and the second time he just hung up."

"Well, Drew, you can come to Padova, but you can't stay with me. I have a roommate, and it would not be fair to her. I have some friends here that might be able to put you up."

"I appreciate that, Alexandra. I'll call you when I get to Italy. Thank you."

She didn't sound too thrilled about the idea of me coming to Italy, but it beat the hell out of starving to death in London. Later that day I found a cheap luggage store and bought a backpack. I was not going to lug a big suitcase around Europe anymore. I packed only the essentials and gave the rest to goodwill. I had too many clothes anyway.

The next morning I went down to the bank and closed my account. I had just enough money for my train ticket and some food. My train left that afternoon. I went back to my room, tidied up a bit and turned in my key. I didn't bother telling anyone at school what I was about to do. Nobody there really knew me anyway. I had attended only two weeks of classes, and had skipped a week because I was too broke to afford transportation.

I picked up my typewriter and backpack and headed toward Waterloo Station. Padova was a long way away, and I wondered what was in store for me now. By the time anybody figured out I was missing, I would be long gone. I found an empty seat by the window. The train pulled out and I stared at the scenery. London was beautiful, but the weather was raw. Although I enjoyed London, it was not one of my favorite cities, and I was happy when our train was ferried into France.

Chapter 13

I was dead tired when the train pulled into Padova. Most of the train ride I wondered if what I was doing made even a bit of sense. It was too late now; I was already committed. I picked up my backpack and typewriter and stepped off the train. Having grown used to the warmer climates of Rome and Frascati, I didn't expect it to be so cold, and wished I had a warm jacket. I found a pay phone outside and dialed Alexandra's number.

"Pronto," she said.

"Alexandra, it's Drew. How are you?"

"I'm fine, thank you. Where are you?" she asked.

"I'm at the train station. I just got in."

"Welcome back to Italy. There's a little bar across the street from where you are. Do you see it?"

"Yes. Is it the one with the red awning?"

"I think so. It's called Sbarra Stazione."

"Ah, yes. You want me to wait there for you?"

"If you could, please. I will be by to pick you up in about an hour."

"Okay. I'll look forward to seeing you."

"You too," she said. "I'll see you later."

I walked across the street to the bar. The town seemed pretty spread out. The buildings were not as ornate as those in Rome, but the rustic, antique look gave them a lot of charm. Many of the buildings had heavy, wooden doors with ornate, cast-iron hardware, and I could only imagine what lay beyond them. The bronze domes of various cathedrals glittered across the sky-line. I went inside and sat down.

"May I help you?" asked a young man behind the bar.

"Could I have a cappuccino, please."

"Certainly. Are you an American?" he asked.

"Yes."

"Are you just visiting, or are you going to school here?"

"I'm just visiting. Are there many Americans here?" I asked.

"There's a few. Many Americans come here for the medical school."

"There's a medical school here?"

"Oh, yes. It's one of the oldest in Europe." He put the cappuccino in front of me along with a napkin and a spoon. "Enjoy," he said.

"Thank you."

I sipped my coffee and waited impatiently for Alexandra to arrive. As much as I wanted to see her I felt just as nervous. I didn't like showing up at her door penniless and forlorn, but didn't know where else to go. I had managed to stuff my hurt feelings from our last encounter deep inside me, and didn't know how I'd react once we saw each other again.

The sky grew cloudy, and it got really cold. I rummaged through my backpack for anything warm and found a thick, cotton t-shirt to wear underneath my shirt. I went to the bathroom and put it on. When I came out I saw Alexandra's car. A tall, thin man with dark hair and brown eyes was driving. He got out of the car and opened the door for her. He was very well dressed with wool trousers and a plush, thick sweater.

Alexandra got out of the car and came inside. "Hello, Drew!" she said, kissing me on both cheeks.

"Hi! It's good to see you. Sorry about giving you such short notice, but I was really in a jam."

"No problem. Are you okay?"

"I'm a little short on money. And I don't have any winter clothes."

"Don't worry about that. I will loan you some money, and

313

tomorrow I'll take you shopping."

"Thank you, Alexandra. You have no idea how much I appreciate your help."

Alexandra's friend came inside a few moments later.

"Drew, I'd like to introduce you to my friend, Gianfranco. Gianfranco, this is my friend, Drew."

I shook his hand and said hello. He was much taller than I; at least as tall as my father, and he had the most beautiful smile. His nose was finely chiseled and his eyes dark and big. He had perfect lips atop a strong chin, and his smile created little dimples in his cheeks.

From the way they looked at each other it seemed as though they were pretty intimate.

"*Ciao.* It is nice to meet you," he said in broken English.

"Is this all you brought?" asked Alexandra, pointing to my backpack and typewriter. She looked around for the rest of my luggage.

"Yes. I decided to travel light."

"Why don't we get going. Gianfranco has a cousin who is going to school here. He has an extra room he can put you in."

"Thank you."

I picked up my things and put them in the car. Alexandra got in the back and I sat next to Gianfranco. He enjoyed driving the car at least as much as I did, but he seemed a bit crazy behind the wheel. He drove really fast and weaved through the traffic as if he were untouchable. Not far from the station we came to a large *piazza* in front of a long building with an arcade three stories high, supported by ornate arches and columns. The arcade was crowded with people and shops.

"This is *Piazza della Frutta*," said Alexandra. That building you see is the *Palazzo della Ragione*. On weekends there is an open-air market here."

We drove through the center of town. The streets were narrow and Alexandra's tiny car shook violently on the cobblestones. We finally left the city center and headed north toward the suburbs on a two-lane road that followed along a canal. The buildings here were much more modern.

"Alexandra, did you finally finish the house?" I asked.

"Most of it. But I never got to the bathrooms."

"Oh, well. They were not in the worst of shape."

"No, but it doesn't matter anymore. I probably won't go back there."

"I'm sorry, Alexandra. Are things okay?"

"Yes, things are fine. Claudio is getting married next month," she said.

"Well, that's certainly news. Where's the wedding going to be?"

"In Rome. My mother is giving him and his family the house."

"*Che stronza*," said Gianfranco. Until now he hadn't said anything.

"What does that mean?" I asked.

"You don't want to know," replied Alexandra.

We stopped at an apartment complex with automatic sliding-glass doors that opened into the lobby. Gianfranco had a key for the inner door, and we took the elevator to the fifth floor. At the end of the hall was a big, double door. He opened it and let us in.

A large room opened up in front of the foyer. It was meant to be a living room but had been converted to a bedroom. Befitting the most famous of porn stars, a king-sized bed was tucked in the corner on a homemade platform fitted with plush carpeting and string lights. Mounted on the headboard was a control panel with all sorts of switches and knobs. Apparently the owner had automated most everything in his bedroom—from the stereo to the Venetian blinds that shaded the large picture window overlooking the narrow, raised canal.

We went into the kitchen where four boys my age were preparing dinner. One was cutting up garlic cloves, another preparing a salad, and another was stirring tomato sauce in a large, shallow skillet.

"Gianfranco, Alexandra! *Ciao!*" said a boy with dark, curly hair and glasses. He kissed Alexandra on both cheeks. To my surprise he also kissed Gianfranco.

"Drew, this is Gianfranco's cousin, Claudio," said Alexandra. His thin, dark hair hung in ringlets over his forehead. He was quite beautiful really. He had dark, brown eyes like his cousin's, but seemed so effeminate and gentle.

"Nice to meet you," I said.

He said something to me in Italian.

"He doesn't speak English," said Alexandra.

In fact, none of them did. I was introduced to each of them. All of them were engineering students from Messina in Sicily, and each had dark hair and olive skin.

They showed me to a tiny, windowless spare room with a small bed. Next to the bed was a chair and a little card table. It wasn't much, but I was grateful to have it.

Claudio took my arm and showed me around the apartment. I figured out pretty quickly the large bedroom was his. Down the hall was Sonny's room. Sonny was tall and gangly with thick glasses. He seemed very nice. Next to his room in the corner was Vincenzo's room. Vincenzo was about my height. Much more reserved than the others, he had dark, green eyes and a chipped tooth. Franco's room was right across the hall. He was even shorter than Claudio, although not as slight, and seemed rather shy. All of them had drafting tables in their rooms, and piles of books.

Everyone gathered in Claudio's room while Alexandra and Gianfranco finished cooking. Sonny spoke only a smattering of English, but not enough to say anything substantial. I tried a little French with them, but that was nearly as useless as English, and realized I'd have to learn Italian if we were ever going to communicate at all. Finally the boys conversed with each other, and I sat politely and listened. Alexandra and Gianfranco laughed and talked in the kitchen, so I excused myself to join them.

Alexandra was finishing the sauce while Gianfranco put the pasta into a big pot of boiling water. They didn't see me come in at first. I sat down at the kitchen table and watched. She put her arm around his waist and stroked his back, and I felt a wave of pain shoot through my body. Gianfranco saw me and nodded. Alexandra turned around. She looked startled at having been found out so quickly, and I could tell she knew what I was feeling, but also knew it didn't matter. Did Gianfranco know our history?

"Are you hungry, Drew?"

"You know me, Alexandra. I'm always hungry."

"We'll be eating in a few minutes," she said.

She took some plates and glasses out of the cupboard and began setting the table. I smelled her hair as she leaned over me, and nearly choked on my pain. Gianfranco was so handsome, and I could understand the attraction. She also laughed a lot with him, and he was always joking and smiling. I did my best to swallow back the hurt.

Dinner was called, and we all sat together in the tiny kitchen, eating pasta and salad. The conversation was in Italian, and I was clueless about what was going on. Claudio seemed to dominate the conversation. His demeanor was so easy and charming. He was magnetic, and people just gravitated to him. I liked him, even if we couldn't say more than two words to each other. Gianfranco didn't say much, but when he did everyone laughed. I wished

316

desperately to be able to speak Italian.

After dinner we talked for awhile at the kitchen table while Alexandra cleaned the dishes. When she was done, she started getting ready to leave. Gianfranco went into the room where I was staying and grabbed a change of clothes from a suitcase. He noticed me looking at him and went about his business. This was his room, and now I felt even more uncomfortable. He put his clothes in a paper bag and went into the foyer.

"Drew, I'll call you tomorrow," said Alexandra. "Tomorrow afternoon I'll take you shopping."

"Thank you, Alexandra. I'll see you tomorrow. Goodnight, Gianfranco," I said, shaking his hand. "It was nice meeting you."

They left and I sat in Claudio's room for awhile. Claudio tried hard to communicate with me. He found an Italian/English dictionary and looked up words, and then had me read them back to him. He managed to get across that he was a third-year engineering student. He showed me a map of Sicily and pointed out Messina. I had seen pictures; it looked like a nice place to live. Later that night a young girl came to visit. Claudio explained Antonella was his girlfriend.

She was thin and cute, with light-blond hair and blue eyes—nothing at all like the young girls I had seen in southern Italy. Claudio and Antonella said goodnight, and I went into my room and lay on the small bed. Gianfranco's suitcase sat conspicuously in the corner, but I was too tired to think about all that now and drifted off to sleep.

Sonny was in the kitchen brewing an espresso in one of those octagonal coffee makers when I awakened.

"*Café?*" he asked.

"*Grazie,*" I said. When the coffee finished brewing he poured some into two little cups. He put three big spoons of sugar in his coffee. After tasting my espresso I understood why, and he laughed at the face I made.

"*Ha bisogno di zucchero,*" he said, handing me the sugar bowl. Although I didn't understand exactly what he said, I knew exactly what he meant.

"*Zucchero,*" I said. "*Molto zucchero.*"

He laughed. I went to my room and grabbed the dictionary. I tied to explain to him I was writer through pointing out words, but he didn't get it until I showed him my typewriter and a couple of manuscripts. I expected everyone to be off at school, going to classes and such, but they stayed in their rooms and studied all morning. I set up my typewriter on the kitchen table and continued working on my novel.

Claudio and Antonella came out to watch. I took long pauses between sentences, planning how I wanted to craft my paragraph, and in a flurry of keystrokes I pounded out the words in short bursts of passion. Claudio found it amusing; Antonella didn't seem too impressed.

Later that morning Alexandra called. She told me she would be over to get me before lunch so we could get our shopping done before the stores closed for siesta. I took a quick shower and dressed.

Alexandra and Gianfranco arrived just after 11:00. Gianfranco greeted me politely and went to talk to his cousin.

"Are you ready?" asked Alexandra.

"Yes."

We took the elevator down to the lobby. Alexandra's car was sitting out front. She asked me if I wanted to drive. I declined. It wasn't my place to sit behind the wheel of her car anymore. She knew what I was feeling, and I knew sooner or later we would have a conversation about it. I wasn't going to initiate the discussion; I had enough problems.

We drove into the center of town. Alexandra found a place to park not far from the *piazza* she showed me yesterday.

I followed her down a narrow side street filled with boutiques. We entered a small men's store. The saleswoman showed me some warm winter coats. I tried on several. Finally I looked to Alexandra for her advice. Her tastes were always expensive. She picked out a beautiful, suede-leather jacket with thick, fleece lining. I also noticed it but declined to take it off the rack, not wanting to seem too rapacious.

"Put this on," she said.

The suede was soft and thick. The jacket enveloped me when I put it on, and the fleece felt warm and comfortable.

"Alexandra, this jacket is gorgeous."

"It looks beautiful on you," she said.

"You think so?" I asked, admiring myself in the mirror. Did she still find me attractive? "I can't accept this," I said, taking it off.

"Why not?"

"It's too expensive. You don't need to spend so much."

"Oh, please. Take the jacket. It will keep you warm."

"Thank you, Alexandra," I said, putting it back on and zipping it up. It felt so luxurious.

She picked out a couple of wool sweaters.

"Try these on," she said.

They fit perfectly.

"Do you like them?" I asked.

"It's not for me to decide. You are the one who has to wear them."

"I like them," I said.

"Then we'll take both."

The saleslady rang up our purchases. I wore the coat out of the store and carried the sweaters in two big boxes, happy to be warm. The narrow street was crowded with pedestrians, and small cars headed down the road toward *Piazza dei Signori*. A large fountain was in the middle of the square, where groups of students sat and talked. Alexandra took me to a nice restaurant at the foot of the *piazza*. We sat at a small table in the corner.

"Thank you for the clothes, Alexandra."

"It's nothing. It's my pleasure," she said. "Drew, why don't you stay here a couple of weeks and then go back to London? The school will understand if you explain what happened."

"I don't know, Alexandra. I don't know if I can go back. I don't even have a place to live there anymore. And then there's my father. He's the reason I'm in this mess to begin with."

"But can't you reason with him? I'm sure if you talked to him now he'd be willing to listen."

"Alexandra, I'm finished with him. I don't want his money."

"But what are you going to do?" she asked.

"I don't know. I am going to find a job and finish my novel."

"What kind of work are you going to do? You don't even speak Italian."

"I'll find something. I don't have much of a choice. I'm not going back."

Alexandra sighed. My mind was made up, and she wasn't happy about it. "I'll ask around and see what I can find," she said, finally.

"Thank you, Alexandra."

She ordered lunch for both of us. I felt helpless but determined. Alexandra frowned and shook her head. I knew she didn't agree with what I was doing, but I didn't care. I talked to her about my novel, and how well the writing was going. Just before lunch was served I finally asked about Gianfranco.

"He's here visiting his cousin and some friends from Messina," she said.

"You mean he doesn't go to school with you?"

"No. He doesn't go to school."

Well! Alexandra put so much importance on education and knowledge. Their relationship couldn't possibly be serious…

"So, he doesn't live here," I said.

"No. Not yet. He's moving up here next month."

"Oh," I said. "Is he going to stay with Claudio?"

"No. We are getting an apartment together."

I tried hard not to wince.

"Are you in love?" I asked.

"Very much so," she said.

"I'm happy for you, Alexandra. He seems like a nice guy."

"Thank you, Drew."

"What does he do?" I asked, breaking a piece of bread, hoping she didn't notice my hands shaking.

"He can do a lot of things. He wants to be an artist. He's moving up here to find work."

"Well, I wish him lots of luck," I said.

We kept the conversation relatively casual. The more I looked at her the more I loved her, even if I knew I had to let her go, and I could feel my pain turning to anger like a slow-growing cancer.

We drove back to Claudio's apartment in silence. I felt like a fish that had just been gutted. Underneath all the pain and anger was nothing but cavernous emptiness. I swallowed it back and did my best not to show my feelings. I loved her for her kindness, and hated her for not loving me. I felt ridiculous wearing the expensive jacket she had bought for me, but without it I'd freeze. When we got back to the apartment she didn't go up; instead she waited downstairs for Gianfranco to join her.

"Drew, I have some money if you need it," she said.

"No thank you," I said. "You have done enough already."

The elevator doors opened Gianfranco walked out. He seemed so easy going and carefree. I walked by him without even acknowledging him; no matter what, I'd never like him. Beneath his good looks was something so deceptive and arrogant. When I got upstairs everyone admired my new jacket. I put my sweater boxes in the corner, not sure I'd ever wear them.

I was really upset when I got back, and to make matters worse, Claudio kept shouting the same words over and over at me, as if raising his voice would help me catch his meaning. It got to be a bit nerve-wracking. With his help I wrote down the words he repeated in my journal and then looked them up in the dictionary. The words I really needed to remember I wrote out several times.

Money was getting really tight, and I needed to find work. Antonella knew an English couple who was looking for someone to do light housework. She took me to their apartment. They lived in a third-floor walkup in an old building near *Piazza dei Signori*. She taught English at the university, and he was a translator. Both in their early thirties, his name was John and hers, Sara. She was short and stocky with a small, round face. She had a button nose and blue eyes that were obscured by thick wire-framed glasses.

John was not much taller. He was a good-looking man, with a solid jaw and rugged features. He had a big, bushy moustache. Sara took me around the apartment and showed me what needed to be done. The place was a mess. They were both so busy they had no time to clean.

"Can you handle this?" she asked.

"Yes, I think I can manage," I replied.

"Oh, good! You can start tomorrow. I'll be needing you three times a week. Can you cook," she asked?

"It's not my area of expertise, but I can throw together

something basic when necessary."

"That's more than I can do. Perfect. Where are you from, Drew?"

"Originally New Jersey."

"You came all the way here from New Jersey?"

"Actually I was in London before I made it over here."

"What were you doing in London?" she asked.

"Going to school. I was studying creative writing. I came to Italy to write."

"How wonderful! This is a great place to write."

"Can you type?" asked John.

"Yes. I can type quite well. I even have my own typewriter."

"Fantastic! I hate typing. I'll pay you extra to transcribe my manuscripts."

"That sounds great. I could use the extra money."

Antonella and I took the bus back to the apartment. Claudio was walking around in silk pajamas and a bathrobe. He never seemed to study. Sonny stayed in his room most of the day with the door closed. He emerged only for lunch and then went back to his books until at least 3:00 or 4:00. After dinner he was back at his desk. He worked harder than everyone else. Vincenzo usually stopped just before lunch, and Franco stayed in his room almost all the time. He was bit of an enigma. He didn't say much, and everyone teased him about his girlfriend and the size of his cock. Apparently he was very well-endowed. He kept a picture of his girlfriend on his desk. Her dark hair and big, brown eyes gave made her look broody. Everyone talked about how jealous she was, as if he were going out with scores of other women. One day he shocked all of us when he played a guitar solo from a Led Zeppelin song without missing a single note. He was an amazing guitarist.

All these boys were gifted in one way or another, but Claudio was the most brilliant. Sonny explained that Claudio got perfect grades, but he only studied an hour or two a day. The rest of the time he made love to Antonella. They had an odd relationship. Antonella was his concubine. When they weren't making love they were wrestling around the bed or the apartment. She didn't talk much; at least not to me, but she was fiercely devoted to him. He was devoted to her—in his own peculiar way—but his true love was back in Messina.

The next morning I got up early to go to my job. The bus was crowded with people on their way to work. I listened to the conversations around me and began picking out words. I got off at my stop and walked to the building where my employers lived. They let me in when I buzzed.

"I'd like you to start in the bathroom," said Sara. "I put a bucket of cleaning supplies in there for you."

"Okay," I said, taking off my jacket.

The bathroom was large with an old tile floor. It looked as though it hadn't been cleaned in months. The bathtub was an old-fashioned, cast-iron type that stood on ornate feet. The inside was stained with rust and soap scum. The sink was just as old and ornate, and makeup and facial accoutrements cluttered the top. The toilet had been recently cleaned, probably as a courtesy to me.

I decided to start with the bathtub; it would require the most work. I put on a pair of rubber gloves and doused the interior with cleaning powder. I scrubbed nearly all morning until I had eradicated every stain. It looked almost new. After rinsing it out I doused it with bleach to make it was as white as possible.

The sink was my next project. I put all the makeup in a paper bag and then cleaned out the medicine cabinet. Once emptied, I wiped it down and put everything back in perfect order. Then I scrubbed the sink, the floor, the walls, and the toilet. I scrubbed and scrubbed until my shoulders were sore. Around noon Sara and John stood in the doorway amazed.

"I hope you don't mind, I reorganized all your makeup," I said, flipping open the medicine cabinet. Her lipstick and nail polish were organized by color. His things were near the top because he was taller, and hers were on the bottom, within easy reach. "Would it be too much trouble if you could manage to keep things tidy?"

"We'll do our best," said Sara. "My word! I don't think I've ever seen the bathroom so clean."

"Cleaning is not so hard. You just need to be organized. I rather enjoy it, although I'm not so sure I'd want to do this for the rest of my life."

"Well, you're rather brilliant at it," said John. "I can't wait to see what you do to the bedroom."

"I'm afraid to look at it."

"It's not so bad," said Sara. "It's just a bit cluttered."

"Well, maybe I should start with the kitchen before I tackle anything else."

"Can it wait until next time? It's starting to get late," said Sara.

"What time is it?" I asked.

"It's going on 1:00. Most people take a break for the rest of the afternoon. Being an American you're probably not used to it."

"No. I guess not. Most Americans work their asses off from 9:00 until 5:00."

"The pace is a little slower in Italy," said John. "But if you're looking to keep working I have a manuscript you can type."

"Sure, I'd love to," I said.

"It's pretty technical. It's a scientific paper written by one of the professors," he said, going into his office. "They have to

325

publish in English because that's the standard in the medical community," he said from the next room. He shuffled some papers together and came out carrying a folder stuffed with handwritten notes. "Well, here it is," he said, handing me the folder.

I read through his writing. For the most part it was legible, but there were a lot of scientific symbols and formulas.

"What do I do about the formulas?" I asked.

"I usually handle it with subscripts and superscripts. I just wing it the best I can. Can your typewriter do subscripts?"

"I think so. It's a pretty brilliant machine. It's an Olivetti."

"Good," said John. "When do you think you can have it done?"

"Let me take it home and start working on it, and I'll give you a call later."

"Well, then. Thank you for doing such an excellent job," said Sara. She reached into her pocketbook and paid me for the day's work. "We'll hear from you later?"

"Yes, thank you. Talk to you soon."

I ran down the stairs feeling good about myself. I had enough money to buy some typing paper and typewriter ribbons. Sara directed me to an office supply store under the arcade at *Piazza della Frutta*. It was not that far from the train station. Only some tobacco shops and a few bars were still open. To my disappointment, the office supply store had already closed for *siesta*.

I wasn't going to wait around for it to open, so I decided to head back. Across the *piazza* I saw Alexandra and Gianfranco standing under the arcade. She was in his arms and they were kissing each other playfully. I couldn't stand to watch, but I was frozen. I wanted her to notice me, even if I knew it would make things more uncomfortable. I thought I saw her look toward me, but I turned around abruptly and walked away. Inside myself I prayed she'd come after me, but knew she wouldn't. She had let me go, and as much as I tried, I couldn't deal with that knowledge. I ran down the street in tears, not knowing what else to do with the pain that was coursing through my body.

I ran all the way to the train station. When I stopped my lungs were hurting and I was sweating. I was out of shape, but running made me feel better. I couldn't get the image of Alexandra and Gianfranco out of my head. How insanely jealous I was of him! He walked around with his fancy clothes as if he were better than everyone else. I hated him.

Later that afternoon I took the bus back home. I set up my typewriter in the kitchen and took a look at the manuscript John had given me. The first few pages were just introductory material, but the remainder was mostly formulas and mathematical expressions. I looked at the instructions that came with my typewriter. Creating a subscript wasn't so difficult. A little knob on the side of the carriage could be turned to advance or reverse the paper as needed. I practiced writing a few formulas. The work was tedious, and I wondered if I should charge extra for the additional effort. Finally I inserted a fresh sheet of paper and pounded away at the keys.

Claudio came in and looked over my shoulder. He was always fascinated by my typewriter.

"*Che fai,* Drew?" he said, picking up the manuscript. I understood almost nothing about what I was transcribing. I just knew it had to do with physics and thermodynamics. Claudio waved the manuscript above his head and ran around the apartment yelling in Italian. I understood some of what he was saying. Within minutes everyone was in the kitchen going through the handwritten pages. The author of the paper was one of their professors. Apparently he was famous at the university. My roommates didn't understand any of the English, but got very excited about some of the equations. For me it was just the opposite: I understood absolutely nothing about the math, and could barely comprehend the parts that were in English.

After much effort they understood that I was being paid to type the manuscript, which my employer had given me after it had been translated. After all the excitement died down, Claudio thumbed through the manuscript once more. I could see him working through the equations in his mind. After a bit he simply nodded and clapped me on the back.

"*Buon lavoro*, Drew," he said, going back to his room.

I continued working until dinner. The formulas were difficult to transcribe, but not impossible. After getting the hang of it I realized how long it was going to take, and called John to apprise him of my progress.

The next morning I woke up early. Most everyone slept late except for Sonny. Because my room was outside the kitchen, the rich smell of coffee being made always woke me. Sonny and I sat in the kitchen together each morning, and he'd show me how to conjugate a new verb. After breakfast I sat with his paper, looking up words and writing them in my journal.

After studying the newspaper, I set up my typewriter and began working on my novel. I figured I could write until lunch, and then finish transcribing John's manuscript later that afternoon. I was busy writing when Alexandra and Gianfranco came in. The glow on her face was unmistakable. She was wearing a faded pair of jeans and a nice sweater. Gianfranco simply nodded at me and went to talk to Claudio. Alexandra sat down next to me. She fingered my manuscript with interest. I hadn't gotten very far yet, but the story was starting to take shape. I put my hand on it and slid it out of reach.

"It's a work in progress," I said.

"It's okay. I understand. How are things going, Drew?"

"Fine. Things are going okay," I said.

"I hear you found a job. Congratulations."

"It's not very glamorous, but it's a start."

"I'm happy for you. Is it full time?"

"No. It's three days a week, but I also do some typing when needed. I'm working on a manuscript now."

"Well, if you are still looking for work, I found something for you in a pizzeria on the other side of town. It's not far from where I live."

"I've never seen where you live," I said coldly.

My tone didn't faze her. "I talked with the owner, and he'd like to meet you."

"When?" I asked.

"This afternoon, if you are available."

"I don't have any plans," I said. "What time?"

"He doesn't open for business until 7:00, but he begins work at 5:00. He asked me to bring you in then."

"Okay. I have experience working in a pizzeria. I worked in one during high school."

She smiled. "Really?"

"Yes. The owner was from Naples. His name was Anniello. He taught me how to make pasta."

"That's wonderful. Then you will be a fast learner," she said. "Why don't I pick you up at 4:30?"

"That will be fine. Thank you, Alexandra."

"I'll leave you to your work," she said.

As she stood up I noticed the curve of her thighs. She still took my breath away. I tried to concentrate on my writing, but all I could think about was her. She talked with Claudio and Gianfranco in the other room. Gianfranco went into my bedroom and started moving things around. I got up to see what was going on. He opened his suitcase and took out a dark, blue shirt, laid it on the bed, and pulled off the shirt he was wearing. His

329

body was thin and strong. He wasn't an athlete, that was apparent, but he was naturally lean. As he bent over I noticed some deep scars on his back. They were cross-hatched and uneven, as if he had been whipped repeatedly with a belt.

He looked at me and smirked, as if he were proud of his scars and had earned the right to wear them. I was speechless. How had he gotten them? I left the room and went back to my writing.

A few minutes later Alexandra popped in to say goodbye. "I'll see you later, Drew. *Buon lavoro.*"

"*Grazie, ci vediamo,*" I replied.

"Bravo! Your Italian is getting better," she said.

"You'd be surprised. I study every morning."

I showed her my journal, which by now was half-filled with verb conjugations and vocabulary words. I still had trouble putting together complete sentences, but was beginning to understand more and more. My background in French helped, as well as the fact that my roommates didn't speak English.

She leafed through my journal and handed it back to me. "I think I have some books that may help you. I'll bring them by later if I can find them."

"Thank you, Alexandra. I'll see you later."

Gianfranco gave me a half salute as they left. I didn't have much to say to him, but the scars on his back made him much more enigmatic. Later that morning Claudio sauntered into the kitchen for some water. He was wearing his silk bathrobe, and Antonella was lying in his bed, nestled beneath the covers. He watched me type for a few minutes and went back to his room. I could hear them laughing and frolicking in the bed. He may not take his studies very seriously, but he certainly had a good time. I continued writing until lunch.

All four boys came out of their rooms at around 12:30.

330

Claudio usually made the sauce, and everyone else pitched in. Today I volunteered to cook. Nobody believed I could, but everyone was amazed when I flashed several large tomatoes and deftly removed their skins. Claudio made the sauce from canned tomatoes. I crushed the tomatoes in the pan and added some oil and spices. As the sauce reduced I added a bit more oil and some fresh vegetables.

Claudio took a taste. "*Incredibile! Il fa la cucina molto bene!*"

Vincenzo asked me where I learned to cook. I explained the best I could my job in the pizzeria with Anniello. When lunch was ready we all sat down together. It was like a family. Very rarely one of them made other plans, and generally they all did things together. They had all known each other since they were kids. I was the only outsider, but they were so warm and kind I didn't feel that way.

After lunch Alexandra called to tell me she was on her way over. When she rang the bell I grabbed my jacket and headed downstairs to greet her.

"*Boca lupo*," said Antonella.

I didn't know what she meant by it, and I asked Alexandra about it.

"Mouth of the wolf," she said. "It means good luck in Italian."

"In America we say break a leg. It's kind of the same thing."

"You Americans have some strange expressions."

"And you Italians don't?"

She laughed. It was the first time since I had been back in Italy we had joked together. We drove toward the center of town, and she parked the car near the university. The campus buildings were made of old, worn brownstone, and the walls and arches were so antiquated I was surprised the buildings still stood. The sidewalk was crowded with young people.

"My apartment is right over there," she said, pointing towards an old building with ornate balustrades and tall windows. "This is *Palazzo del Bò*. Over there is *Café Pedrocchi*. It's very famous in Italy. Many writers and artists go there. You'd like the place. I'll take you there later."

We headed down a small side street and came to the pizzeria. Alexandra knocked on the door. About ten tables were in the front, and a large pizza oven was in the back.

A bald, thin man in his late fifties came to let us in. "Alexandra! *Bienvenuto!*"

Alexandra introduced me to him. His name was Marcello. "*Parla Italiano?*" he asked her.

"*Non molto, ma io capisco abistanza bene,*" I replied.

"*Benissimo!*" he said.

He started rattling off in Italian. I tried to keep up, but quickly became lost. My Italian wasn't conversational yet. Alexandra translated. He showed me the kitchen. He wanted me to work Thursday through Saturday. My job was to top the pizzas when the orders came in, and then he'd throw them in the oven. When the pizzas were ready he would send them back to me, and I would cut them into slices and his wife would take them to the tables.

Outside he showed me a large woodpile. He made the pizzas in an old-fashioned brick oven. He told me the secret of his success was to use only aged cedar. He had already started stoking the oven, and the smell of burning cedar was pungent. I agreed to start my job that Thursday at 5:00.

"He makes the best pizzas in Italy," she said as we were leaving.

"I can believe it. Aged cedar? I've never even seen a brick oven. I can only imagine how good the pizza is."

"You'll find out. Just be careful to not eat too much. I'd

hate to see you become fat. I've already put on some extra weight from eating there too much."

"I've never seen you look better, Alexandra."

"Thank you, Drew. I wish it were true. Gianfranco and I eat out too much."

I didn't say anything. Just hearing his name mentioned hurt. We walked down the crowded street and came to *Café Pedrocchi*.

"Let me buy you a coffee," she said.

We went inside. The place was filled with young people. An ornate walnut bar stretched the length of the wall near the door, and the floor was made of marble. Works of art from local artists adorned the walls, and in the back was a sitting room and library. We sat at a small table near the window overlooking the cobblestone street.

"What would you like?" she asked.

"A cappuccino would be fine, thank you."

"You Americans—always drinking cappuccinos," she said, shaking her head. Her hair fell across her shoulders.

"What's wrong with cappuccinos?"

"Cappuccinos are for the morning. In the afternoon we drink just coffee or tea."

"I like cappuccinos."

"Yes, so does Gianfranco. He drinks them all the time."

"How are things going with him," I asked, realizing that ignoring the fact that he existed was futile.

She smiled and nodded. "Things are good. We'll be going down to Rome next week to my brother's wedding."

"Has your mother met him?"

"Yes, but only briefly. She came up here to visit and we took her out to dinner."

"How did she like him?"

"She didn't, but that matters next to nothing to me."

"Alexandra, I noticed that Gianfranco has some pretty deep scars on his back. How did he get them?"

Her cheeks flushed ever so slightly. "Gianfranco has had a pretty hard life," she said. "He comes from a very poor family in Messina. His father was a drunk and used to beat him with a belt almost everyday until he was old enough to defend himself."

"I know what that feels like," I said. Although my father didn't beat me everyday until I bled, I understood the fear and anger.

"In order to make the experience even more painful and horrifying he soaked the belt in salt water and dried it in the sun everyday."

"Jesus! How the hell did he survive?"

"People adjust. It's amazing what you can learn to tolerate."

"Poor bastard. It probably left a few more scars than just the ones on his back."

"He seems to have come out of it okay. People react to things in different ways."

"I suppose you're right," I said.

I felt guilty. Compared to what Gianfranco had been through I didn't have all that much to complain about. The news explained a lot about his attitude. Regardless, I still didn't like him, and in some ways this information made me dislike him even more. Alexandra had a thing for tortured artists, and Gianfranco seemed to have way more scars than I did.

"Where are you going to move to?" I asked.

"You mean Gianfranco and me?"

"Yes."

"We are going to stay where we are. My roommate is getting another place. She wants to live by herself."

"So, when's he officially moving in?" I asked, sipping the

334

foamy cream from the top of my cappuccino.

"After the wedding. We are going down to Messina for a week, and then he'll be with me up here."

"I hope it works out for you, Alexandra. Have you met his family before?"

"I met his sister. This will be the first time I'll have met both his parents."

"Are you nervous?"

She shook her head and frowned. "No, not really. I don't know how I will react, knowing what his father did to him. I don't expect it to be the most pleasant experience."

"Probably not. They don't sound like very kind people."

"His family reminds me of how hard people can be from that area."

"Harshness is everywhere, and it doesn't have to be just among poor people. Some of the most psychotic people I've ever met have lots of money."

"Yes, my mother is living proof of that," she said.

I didn't say anything. I really didn't consider her mother very psychotic. Still, I could understand Alexandra's anger—she had twice the brains and motivation than her brother. She could have done a fantastic job running her father's estate, but her mother gave all her power to Claudio. To grow up with so much and then have it all taken away...

I sipped my cappuccino while she drank her tea. We talked for awhile about the differences between Northern and Southern Italy. Her hair fell in long, dark tresses across her shoulders, and she sat up straight in her chair with perfect posture, even if she were relaxed. I loved her shape, and no matter what I could not quell my desire for her.

"Are you ready? I need to study before I've lost the entire day."

335

"Yes, I'm ready. Thanks for the coffee, Alexandra," I said, helping her with her coat. "By the way, how's school going?"

"Oeuf! All I do is read. I love literature, and I'm lucky I read fast, but between all the books we read and the papers we have to write, I'm wondering if I will enjoy literature the way I used to," she said.

We left the café and went out into the street. Occasional snowflakes swirled around in the cold evening air. Alexandra took me home.

"Thank you for your help," I said, getting out of the car.

"Perhaps we'll see you in the restaurant sometime."

"Perhaps, although I'll probably be in the kitchen."

I went upstairs and found everyone already preparing dinner. I went to my room and continued typing John's manuscript. There was still a lot to do, and I would probably be up late. I worked until dinner, and continued afterward until 1:00 am. Everyone else had gone to sleep, but at least I had gotten the job done. Before going to bed I thought about Alexandra. I could not be angry with her after the way she helped me, but the more she helped the more I loved her, and I would never accept that she didn't love me back.

That Thursday I showed up at the pizzeria at the appointed time.

"*Buona sera,* Drew," Marcello said. He took me out back. A big pile of evenly cut logs was stacked against the wall. He picked out about ten of them and threw them on the ground.

"I need you to split these like this," he said, showing me some pieces that had been split into neat quarters. Splitting wood was something I had a lot of experience with. It took me almost an hour to split all the logs. I was sweating and tired when finished. Marcello had me stack what I could in a big, metal hopper next to the oven. The rest I stacked outside.

336

Marcello placed some wood on a slow-burning pile of logs at the back of the oven. It took awhile to get the oven hot enough to cook the pizza. Behind him, on a small stainless-steel table, he showed me how to set up the toppings for the incoming orders. His wife, Lucia, had been prepping vegetables and cutting up pieces of salami and pepperoni. She put them in shallow pans and placed them toward the back of the table.

Marcello showed me how to load the dough into the pan. The pizza he made was much smaller and thicker than Anniello's.

When the doors opened for business I wasn't expecting the place to fill up so quickly. Within minutes every table was full. Lucia went from table to table taking orders. She brought them into the back and placed them on a rack in front of me. Beyond the fact that her writing was nearly illegible, the orders were in Italian, and I understood next to nothing.

Lucia explained the orders to me and pointed to the different toppings on the menu. She showed me how to top the pizzas, sprinkling the ingredients evenly across the surface. When they were ready I carried the pans over to Marcello. He slid the pans into the oven on a large, wooden spatula. Marcello stood in front of the oven, holding a can of olive oil in one hand and his wooden spatula in the other. He reminded me of the Tin Man from the Wizard of Oz. His face and uniform were covered with sweat. He squirted oil on the pizzas every few minutes, causing the flames from the fire to jump.

When the pizza crusts were golden brown he pulled them out of the oven and sent them back to us. Lucia showed me how to cut them evenly, and she carried them to the customers. The dough smelled sweet and delicious, and the various toppings made my mouth water. Later that evening a line of people overflowed out the door. The place was packed, and it was only Thursday night.

"What's it like on the weekends?" I asked Lucia in broken Italian.

"It's crazy. It doesn't stop until closing." I remembered what Anniello had told me about the pizza business—about keeping your overhead down and watching your expenses. If that were true, Marcello was making a killing. At around 9:30 the orders finally stopped flooding in. Most everyone was busy laughing and eating pizza.

"*Ai fame?*" asked Lucia.

The pace was so fast I hadn't thought about eating. She told me to top a pizza for myself. I put generous amounts of pepperoni on it and sent it out to Marcello. When it was ready he sent it back to me and I cut it into slices. I had never tasted pizza so good; the crust was light and chewy, and the tomato sauce had a tangy, sweet flavor. The olive oil made it rather rich, if not somewhat messy, but it tasted so good I could have eaten another. I don't ever recall tasting pizza so good. Alexandra was serious when she said that Marcello made the best pizza in Italy.

At about 10:00 we got another small rush, and then late-night customers trickled in until closing. I helped Lucia wash all the pizza dishes and put away the food. It was a crazy night; Anniello's was never this busy. I was exhausted by the time we finally left, and tomorrow I had to be up early to clean John and Sara's house. When I got home I was covered in oil and grease, but was too tired to care and went right to sleep.

I was groggy when I woke up the next morning, but the Italian habits agreed with me. I took a long nap after lunch before going back to Marcello's that evening. The place was so packed I never stopped moving. By the end of the night I barely found the strength to get home. Saturday night was even crazier, and I was glad when Sunday finally came.

Sundays were always fun because on weekends there were

lots of open-air markets in different *piazzas*. In *Piazza della Frutta,* we bought fresh vegetables and fruit, but my favorite place to go was at *Prato della Valle*. On the third Sunday of every month all the local artists, students and crafts people sold their wears at a flea market.

All of us piled into Claudio's tiny Citroen and drove across town. *Prato della Valle* was a large oval square surrounded by a channel. Standing on pedestals around the channel were statues of famous artists and cultural figures. If one needed anything cheap this was the place to be.

Claudio had a passion for shoes and fine men's cologne. His closet was stuffed with them, and he always smelled divine. I enjoyed his narcissistic tendencies. It was unusual to see them in a man who wasn't gay.

Claudio put his arm in mine and we walked through the square. "Drew, it's time you started dressing like an Italian," he said. We found a booth that sold discounted men's wear. Claudio found a black pair of pleated wool pants and a matching belt.

"Will these even fit?" I asked.

"You can try them on over there," said a salesgirl, pointing to a small, makeshift dressing room fashioned from a thin, black curtain. I put them on and showed Claudio. He pulled at the waist to make sure there was enough room, and then turned me around to check how they fit in the back. They fit fine, although I wasn't used to the crotch being cut so high, but that was how most Italian men wore their clothes. Claudio picked out several pairs of shoes and asked which ones I liked. All of them had heels a quarter inch taller than I would have normally worn, but it worked out okay because the cuffs on my pants were nearly dragging on the ground. I chose a handsome black pair with a simple gold clasp. I put them on and felt as if I had just stepped off the set of Saturday Night Fever.

Claudio took a step back and admired his work. "*Che bello*," he said. "But we need to get you a decent shirt."

We picked out a plain white shirt that was tightly fitted. Trying to walk with high-heels was awkward at first. Claudio laughed as he watched me lurch around. When Vincenzo saw me he doubled over in hysterics. I felt completely ridiculous until the salesgirl smiled at me. I changed out of my new clothes and paid for them.

We went home and everyone disappeared into their rooms to study for finals. I was going to have the apartment to myself during Christmas break. Claudio told me I could have his room while he was away.

The morning they left Claudio kissed me on the cheek. "Be good, Drew. And call your mother for Christmas. She is probably worried sick about you."

"*Grazie*. Merry Christmas," I replied.

Almost three months had passed since I had disappeared from London, and I wondered if my parents had even looked for me. I had thought about calling them before, but wanted to establish myself before I did. Things were okay; my job at the pizzeria was going well, and I was no longer cleaning for John and Sara. Instead, John gave me more manuscripts to type, and Sara referred me to some of her students for private tutoring.

The University of Padova's medical school was world renowned. But most of the students couldn't get jobs once they graduated. Consequently everyone wanted to take the medical boards in America once they finished school, but to do so they needed to learn English. Eventually I had a steady stream of students, all of whom had varying degrees of proficiency with the language.

I found that teaching English as a second language was much more difficult than I thought, and turned to Sara for help.

She recommended some books for me to use and helped me create a lesson plan. For some, learning English was next to impossible, and required endless amounts of patience. For others, learning a new language was easy, and they were speaking new phases quickly. Regardless of my students' abilities, I found teaching to be rewarding.

Gianfranco and Alexandra stopped by the apartment, carrying a shopping bag filled with Christmas gifts. "These are for you," she said.

"Alexandra, I am completely embarrassed. I didn't get anything for you," I said.

"Don't worry about that, Drew. I don't want anything. You are still trying to get things together. There is some food in there. You might want to put it in the refrigerator. Let me help," she said, going into the kitchen.

I put the kettle on for some tea. "Where are you going for Christmas, Alexandra?"

"We're going to the Maldives Islands for a couple of weeks," she replied.

"That sounds nice, Alexandra. Are you working, Gianfranco?" I asked.

Gianfranco just nodded and took a chair.

"Gianfranco and I have started a small business," said Alexandra.

"Wow! Where do you find the time with school?" I asked.

"That's the beauty. I make *tiramisu*. It doesn't require much time—just a few hours each night in the kitchen and Gianfranco sells it to the local restaurants while I'm in school."

I shook my head and smiled. Alexandra was so enterprising. "Are you making good money?"

"We're doing pretty well. It's a good side business," she said.

"After Christmas I'm going to set up a booth at *Piazza della Frutta* and sell it on the weekends," said Gianfranco.

"I hope it works out well for you. How was your brother's wedding, Alexandra?"

"The ceremony was nice, but I can't stand my brother's wife and her family. It was as if they couldn't wait for the ceremony to be over so that they could all move into the house. My poor mother has no idea what she is in for."

"She deserves what she gets," said Gianfranco.

"I'm sorry, Alexandra. It must hurt," I said.

Alexandra took a seat and smoothed back her hair. "It hurts, but I'll survive," she said. Her chocolate-brown eyes were slightly downcast and her eyebrows knitted, but I knew how strong she was, and was sure she would come out on top.

I poured the tea and sat down at the table.

"We can't stay too long," said Alexandra. "We have other errands to run before we leave for vacation."

"When are you leaving?"

"Tomorrow morning," she said. "Do you have any plans for Christmas?"

"Stay here and do some writing. I'll also be working in the pizzeria."

"Marcello says you are doing very well. We stopped in for dinner last Wednesday. How's the writing going?"

"It's going well," I said. Actually the writing wasn't going well at all. Although I wrote everyday, I was beginning to lose my focus. Writing a novel was more difficult than I thought, and I was becoming daunted by such an ambitious endeavor.

Alexandra finished her tea and got up to leave. "Have a good Christmas, Drew," she said, kissing me on the cheek.

"Thank you, Alexandra. You too."

I shook hands with Gianfranco and showed them to the

door. Tomorrow they would be on a plane headed to a tropical paradise. I could imagine how much fun they were going to have, and I envied Gianfranco for his good fortune. I went into the kitchen and found the bag that Alexandra had brought me. I saw two large boxes wrapped in bright paper and a smaller one at the bottom. Christmas was not for another week. Should I wait?

I sat on Claudio's bed and shook the boxes next to my ear. They didn't make much noise—they had to be clothes. The little box at the bottom looked delicate, and I thought best not to give it a shake. I put the gifts at the foot of the bed. I decided to wait until Christmas morning to open them.

It was lonely in the apartment without everyone around. I missed having breakfast with Sonny and watching Claudio's foppery when he finally decided to get dressed. Even the restaurant was slow, and as Christmas approached the idea of spending Christmas with my family became more appealing. I wondered how my sisters were doing.

On Christmas Eve I walked down to an international phone center. I had to wait several minutes for an available line. I prepaid for fifteen minutes, giving me enough time to say what I needed. The operator waived me to an available booth when my call finally got through. The phone rang four times before it picked up.

"Hello?" It was Julie.

"Julie? It's Drew. How are you?"

"Drew? My, God! Drew! We thought you were dead. Where are you?"

"I'm in Italy."

"Are you okay?"

"Yes, I'm fine. Everything is okay."

"Why the hell didn't you tell anyone you were leaving? Nobody knew what happened to you!"

343

"Did anyone bother looking?" I asked.

"Yes! The school called when you stopped showing up for classes, and Dad filed a missing-persons report. The girls you were living with in London told the police you took off but didn't know where you went."

I thought about it a second or two. Both Helen and Nan knew I went to Italy, and I doubt they would have lied to the police. I guess my father decided he'd let me go once he knew I wasn't dead or in the hospital.

"Is Mom there?" I asked Julie.

"I'll go get her," she said. "Mom! Mom! It's Drew! He's on the telephone!"

A few moments later I heard my mother's voice. "Drew? Where are you?"

"I'm in Italy, Mom."

"Are you okay?"

"Yes, I'm fine."

"What are you doing in Italy?" she asked.

"I'm tutoring English to medical students at the University of Padova."

"Where is that?"

"It's about twenty minutes south of Venice by train," I said.

"Are you going to stay there?"

"I'll be here for awhile, Mom."

"What about school?" she asked.

"I'm not ready for school. Besides, I'm getting a good education right here. I'm living with four Sicilian boys who don't speak English, and I'm learning Italian. I'm also writing a novel. It's going really well."

"I'm happy for you, Dear. Would you like to speak to the rest of your sisters?"

"Sure!"

"Let me get your address first," she said. "Julie, go get me a pen and a piece of paper."

I dictated my address and phone number.

"You be good," she said.

"I will, Mom. Merry Christmas."

"Merry Christmas, Dear. I love you."

She handed me back to Julie. "Are you with Alexandra?"

"Sort of. We're no longer together. We're friends. She has a new boyfriend now."

"I'm sorry, Drew. That must be hard. Are you okay?"

"Yes, I'm fine. That's the way life goes sometimes."

"Well, here, let me pass you to Annie. Bye Drew!"

"Bye Julie."

I spoke to each of my sisters in turn, but then heard the phone beep, signaling that my time was up, and we were cut off. I left the phone booth and headed home. The buses were on some crazy holiday schedule, so I ended up walking. It didn't really snow here, but it was bitterly cold. The sky was dark and a strong wind pelted my jacket with occasional rain drops. I heard it was nice in the summertime, and I looked forward to seeing some warmer weather.

I was freezing by the time I got home. The lights of Christmas tress blinked and glittered through the windows of other people's apartments, and I grew more homesick. But I didn't miss home as much as I missed Alexandra, and wished more than anything I could be with her on her little tropical island. I lay down on Claudio's bed and cried. That night I ate some of the food Alexandra had brought over and went to bed early.

The next morning I slept in. Claudio's bed was comfortable, and I had so much fun playing with all the little controls he had built into the headboard. One knob rotated the levelers of the blinds, another opened and closed them, another controlled the strip lights that were built into the platform the bed was on, and the rest controlled the stereo.

I made myself some coffee, heated up some milk, and put the milk and coffee in a bowl. On the counter some day-old rolls were crusty and hard. I crumbled them into the bowl, making a poor man's breakfast. It was like eating oatmeal with a kick. Claudio called it *zuppa*.

I took my bowl back to Claudio's room and sat on the bed with Alexandra's gifts. The first box I opened contained a fine, dark-blue silk shirt. It fit perfectly, and the silk felt so luxurious against my skin. The next gift was a dark-blue cashmere vest with a v-neck collar. It would look perfect with a white shirt. The last gift I was almost afraid to open. The box was long and narrow with dark green wrapping paper and a red ribbon. I opened it carefully. Inside was a handcrafted, sterling silver pen. It looked expensive. A small note was at the bottom of the box: "For jotting all your wonderful thoughts… Merry Christmas. Alexandra."

The gifts were wonderful but they made me even sadder. I wished I could have opened them with her. With not much to do on Christmas day, I set up my typewriter on Claudio's desk and continued writing. The words came to me slowly and the characters felt wooden and forced. My work didn't have any direction; I just told the story on the fly, not really knowing where it was going. Writing about my father was especially hard. I didn't really understand who he was, and I was afraid to find out.

My mother was much easier. I could identify with her feelings of abandonment and pain. Her character was full of color, but my father remained in the background like an omniscient chimera, manipulating the people and events around him. I was frustrated with my inability to portray him, and didn't feel my writing was very honest. Nonetheless, I felt it was my duty to keep on, so I struggled with it the best I could.

I was glad to see everyone come back from vacation, although I was going to miss staying in Claudio's room. They arrived on a Sunday, full of laughter and chatter.

Claudio kissed me on both cheeks when he saw me. "How was your Christmas, Drew?"

"It was okay. I called my parents. They were surprised to hear from me."

"That's wonderful. The most important thing in life is family," he said. "How are they doing?"

"Fine."

"And your father?"

"I didn't talk to him. I called my mother."

"I brought you something for Christmas," he said, going to his room. He opened his travel bag and pulled out a box of cologne. It was one he liked to wear. Not very strong, it had a pleasant, citrus smell. I showed him all the gifts Alexandra gave me. He liked the shirt the most.

"She's a really nice girl. How long have you known her?"

"Since I was fifteen," I replied. "I met her in Switzerland. We went to school together."

"Was there something between you two before? You seem to be very much in love with her."

I was surprised he didn't know more about our history, given that his cousin was living with her now. "She was my first love," I said.

"And you still love her?"

"I'll always love her. It can't be helped."

Claudio pursed his lips and shook his head. "Drew, she is not in love with you. You have to accept it. When you came to Italy and were waiting at the train station, she and Gianfranco were in his room making love. She made you wait for an hour before picking you up."

His words hurt. "I called her at her house," I protested.

"She came over here first. Women are real bitches with men they don't want. It's just a fact of life," he said.

"It's true. I've seen my sisters rip men to pieces."

He stroked the back of my neck and kissed my cheek. "But that doesn't mean she doesn't love you as a friend. She's a good woman, but you are going to have to move on."

"I really don't have a choice, do I? After all, she's living with Gianfranco. She's in love with him now."

"You understand it up here," he said, tapping his forehead. "But it's here where you have to let go," he said, placing his hand on my chest. "I know by the way you look at her. She's a beautiful woman and she has a lot to offer, but she can only give you a small piece of her heart."

"Has she talked to you about this?" I asked.

"She doesn't have to, Drew. It's all in your eyes. Eventually you will let go one way or another. You are lucky she is kind. My woman would just cut your heart open and walk away while you bled to death on the floor. She's taken good care of you and has been very generous, despite the protests of my cousin."

"What's the deal with him?" I asked. "He doesn't seem like the kind of man she'd fall for."

"Ah, Gianfranco. Love is blind, Drew. I've known Gianfranco all my life. He doesn't come from a good family. He could do so much but he's lazy. He's always been that way. He thinks the world owes him a living. He's lucky he's found a woman like Alexandra. Without her he'd be nothing."

Hearing Claudio speak that way about his own cousin surprised me. It justified my animosity toward him.

Later that week I got a call from her. She and Gianfranco had just gotten back from vacation. She said she had a wonderful time.

"How was your Christmas?" she asked.

"It was good, Alexandra. Thank you for the gifts. They were beautiful."

"You are welcome, Drew. Are things okay?"

"Things are fine. I talked to my mother."

"Good! How was it? I'll bet she was happy to hear from you."

"I think my sisters missed me more than she did. She sounded almost cold, as if she were upset with me or something. We didn't talk very long."

"I'm sure she misses you. What about your father? Did you talk to him?"

"No, but I'm sure I'll hear from him eventually."

"I'm sure he misses you too. Well, I just called to check in on you and see how you are doing."

"Thanks, Alexandra. I'm doing fine. I got you a Christmas gift while you were away. Can I drop by tomorrow and give it to you?"

"Drew, you didn't have to do that."

"I wanted to. Especially after all the beautiful things you gave me. Besides, I've never seen where you live."

We made arrangements, and the next day Claudio inspected my clothes carefully. I wore the pants and shirt we had bought, and then put on the sweater Alexandra had given me.

"*Bellino*," he said, adjusting my sweater. "*Cos'ai la?*" he asked, pointing to my crotch. "*Potates?*"

I laughed. Although I was becoming more comfortable dressing like an Italian, I always felt a bit ridiculous. Most Americans wouldn't be caught dead in these clothes. I had bought Alexandra a first edition of Flaubert's Madame Bovary from an antique book dealer. It cost me a fortune. I wrapped it carefully in tissue and wrote a nice note in Italian with the pen she gave me. I slipped the note inside the binder and wrapped the book in a colorful Christmas paper.

The weather was nice; at least not as dreary as it had been the last few weeks. Feeling good, I decided to walk. It was a fairly long ways, but the weather was sunny and warm. I finally arrived at her apartment and rang the bell.

"I'm on the second floor. Apartment 2b," she said, buzzing me in.

I pushed open the door and went upstairs. The stairs were wide with a brass railing. Her door was large and heavy. She opened it before I arrived.

"Drew! *Come stai?*"

"*Bene, molto bene,*" I said, kissing her on both cheeks.

"Come in, come in," she said.

Their apartment wasn't as luxurious as I had expected, but it was spacious. The living room was large with high ceilings. An old-fashioned fan dangled in the center of the room. They were lucky to have a corner apartment. Four big French doors on each wall opened onto a narrow terrace, overlooking the cobblestone street. Gianfranco and three of his friends sat on a large, white sofa, drinking beer. He nodded at me and shook my hand when I came in. His friends looked a bit rough. Alexandra introduced me to them and showed me around the apartment.

She took me into the kitchen. The appliances were new and there was plenty of space. It was much nicer than ours. In the middle of the room was a simple wood table. It looked like an antique. Their bedroom was roomy with two huge windows. The bed was fitted with fine linens and a big, soft duvet. Seeing her bed made me squirm, as if I were invading her privacy just by looking at it.

Alexandra preferred a beautiful view of nature rather than fancy curtains and overbearing furniture. I liked her taste: it was understated and simple.

I sat down in a big armchair near the couch and listened to Gianfranco brag about the new car they were about to buy—a Mercedes sedan with leather seats and a hand-finished wooden dashboard. I wasn't really included in the conversation, and eventually I went into the kitchen to see how Alexandra was doing. She was busy preparing dinner.

"I'm not interrupting, am I? I didn't know you'd be entertaining guests."

"I didn't either," she said. "They just dropped by."

"You're buying a new car?" I asked.

"Yes."

"What are you going to do with the Fiat? That's a great car."

"Gianfranco totaled it," she said.

"My God! Were you in the car?"

"No. I was at school. He was making a delivery. The car was filled with *tiramisu*. It was quite a mess."

"What happened?"

"He went around a corner too fast and lost control. The car slammed into the side of a building."

"He's lucky to have walked away from it," I said. Gianfranco's driving was reckless and crazy. I had known people like him before; his attitude behind the wheel reflected his irresponsibility and lack of respect for others. I saw it so clearly, and couldn't understand why Alexandra didn't see it as well.

Alexandra prepared a plate of vegetables and dip and carried it out to the living room. Gianfranco's friends were just as rude to her as they were to me. One of them handed her his empty beer bottle and told her to get him another as if she were a common servant. Alexandra obeyed without a word. It wasn't like her. Gianfranco treated her like a ghost when he was with his friends.

I finally decided to present my gift to her. I handed it to her in front of everyone.

"Merry Christmas," I said.

She un-wrapped the gift slowly and peeled away the layers of tissue.

"Madame Bovary!" she said.

"It's a first edition," I said proudly. "I got it from an antique book dealer in town."

"It's beautiful! Thank you!"

She opened the cover and my note slipped out. She quickly read it, put it in her shirt pocket, and handed the book to Gianfranco. He flipped through the pages briefly and gave it back to her. His friends were even surlier toward me than before. I didn't care; Alexandra liked it, and that was all that mattered. She put the book on the top shelf of her bookcase in the bedroom.

Although Gianfranco wasn't completely obvious, I knew I wasn't welcome for dinner. I could tell Alexandra wasn't in the mood to cook for all his friends, but she went into the kitchen anyway and finished preparing dinner.

I went into the kitchen a few moments later. "I have to get going," I told her.

"You don't want to stay for dinner?" she asked.

"I'd love to, but I have another manuscript to type before tomorrow."

"Thanks for the wonderful gift. It was nice seeing you," she said, kissing me on the cheek.

She walked me to the door, and I waved to Gianfranco and his friends as I left. I breathed a sigh of relief when I got outside. Gianfranco and his friends made me uncomfortable. Night was falling and the air got colder. I decided to stop in *Café Pedrocchi* for a cappuccino before going home. I sat at the bar. Most everyone was either reading or talking about literature, art, or philosophy. I began to wonder if dropping out of school was the right decision. I was living a lie; I had no business being in Italy. My writing wasn't really progressing, and unless I got back into school I would never go anywhere. I paid my tab and started home. It was nearly 8:00 pm when I arrived.

"Drew, call your father," Claudio said.

"Why? What's the matter?"

"I don't know. He said it's an emergency."

"Can I use the phone here? I'll call him collect."

"Yes, it's no problem," said Claudio.

Claudio let me use his room to make the call. It took a few minutes to get through.

"Dad, it's Drew. How are you?"

"I'm fine. How are you?"

"I'm fine, Dad. What's going on? You asked me to call."

"It's your mother. She's not doing too well."

"Why? What's going on?"

"They found a tumor in her lung. She went in to have a bronchoscopy to check things out, but things didn't go well."

"What happened?"

"Well, they ruptured the tumor and she nearly died."

"Christ! Is she okay?"

"Nobody knows. She's been in a coma since this morning. Her doctor said she had a major stroke. She may not come out of it. If you want to see her now is the time."

"Shit! I'm coming home. I'll call you when I get to New York," I said.

"All right, I'll see you when you get here," he said, hanging up the phone.

I went into the kitchen where everyone was busy preparing dinner. All the color drained out of my face, and I felt light-headed as I sat down in a chair with a heavy groan.

"What happened?" asked Claudio.

My vocabulary wasn't good enough to explain every detail, but they got the point.

"I need to go home," I said. I did a quick inventory of all the money I had saved—not enough for a plane ticket. That night I called Sara and John and told them what happened. Sara said she would take my students, and John offered to come by and pick up his manuscript tomorrow morning. I called Alexandra and told her the news.

"Drew, I'm so sorry. Is there anything I can do?"

"Could you tell Marcello what happened for me and tell him thank you for everything?"

"Yes, of course. When are you leaving?"

"I don't know yet. I haven't even found a flight. I just found all this out a few minutes ago."

"Call me when you have more information," she said.

"I will. Goodnight."

I spent the next hour calling various airlines, trying to find the cheapest, fastest way home. The next flight was tomorrow morning with a connecting flight from Paris. I booked it, even though I was a couple hundred dollars short. Claudio offered to lend me some money. I called Alexandra back and told her my situation.

"What time does your flight leave?" she asked.

"Seven am."

"I'd offer to take you to the airport but we don't have a car."

"Then I guess this is goodbye," I said, wincing at the finality.

"For now. Please let me know how things are going."

"I will, Alexandra. You take care."

"You too, Drew. Goodbye," she said.

That night I didn't sleep. I was up the entire night packing. My hands shook slightly the entire time, and at first I wasn't sure if I was scared or sad. My backpack was stuffed with clothes and manuscripts. The next morning everyone drove me to the airport. Claudio kissed me and hugged me goodbye. I was going to miss him the most. Sonny shook my hand and asked me to write. One by one we all said our goodbyes, and I headed toward the terminal to purchase my ticket. It would be a long flight home, and I hoped I would make it on time.

Chapter 14

After arriving at JFK I took the shuttle into the city and grabbed a train to Red Bank. The bitter cold nipped my ears and it was snowing like crazy. I had not seen so much snow in years. I sat on the train and watched the storm swirl past my window. Someone told me this was the fourth snow storm that winter, and some parked cars were barely visible beneath the huge drifts that threatened to engulf them.

The train station wasn't very far from the hospital. The street lights were merely splotches of light in the driving storm. I found a pay phone and called my father. Joan answered the phone.

"Hi Joan. It's Drew. I'm in Red Bank."

"Oh, hello Drew, you can't come here. We're having a party tonight."

"Is my father there?" I asked.

"He's taking a bath," she said.

"Well, just tell him I arrived," I said, hanging up the phone.

I could not believe that conversation just took place. God, I hated that woman. The wind howled around me, and not a soul was in sight. It was too cold to walk, so I grabbed a cab. The receptionist directed me to the intensive care unit.

"Take those elevators over there to the fifth floor," she said, pointing to a bank of elevators down the hall. The receptionist at the ICU stopped me at the door.

"I'm going to see my mother, Martha Smith," I said.

"Oh, yes. Your family is expecting you. She's in unit ten."

I passed through two large, swinging doors into a room lined with glass-walled cubicles. In the center of the room was some sort of control center where nurses sat watching monitors. I saw my sisters through the window of one of the rooms.

My mother had been intubated, and all sorts of hoses were stuffed down her throat. Various tubes were stuck in her arms and her vital signs beeped and flashed across several monitors.

All three of my sisters were sitting around the bed. They looked shell-shocked and tired, as if they hadn't slept in days. Their eyes were puffy from crying and the seriousness of their expressions was disturbing. They all watched her as if she were going to suddenly snap out of her trance and say something.

"Hi," I said.

"Drew! Welcome home!" they all said. Julie threw her arms around me and gave me a hug.

"How's she doing?" I asked.

"It's too early to say," said Gretchen. "Did you just arrive?"

I put down my backpack and typewriter. "I came straight from the airport. I feel like I haven't slept in days."

"You must be starving. Why don't we all go eat? Mom's not going anywhere," said Gretchen.

Annie shot her a dirty look. "I'm going to stay here with Mom," she said.

"Annie, we've been here all day. Mom won't mind if we leave her for half a second to go eat," said Julie. Everyone had taken leave of their senses. They were probably just overtired and over-stressed.

"Where are we going to eat? Have you seen the way it's snowing?" I asked.

"Isn't it awful? This weather is almost appropriate for the occasion. There's always the cafeteria," said Gretchen.

"Hospital food? I just got off the worst flight of my life. The last thing I want is hospital food."

"There's a Chinese restaurant on Broad Street," said Julie.

"I remember that place. I used to eat there sometimes when I was in high school," I said.

"Is that okay with you, Annie?" asked Gretchen.

"I guess so," she answered, letting go of Mom's hand.

It was snowing even harder than before. The restaurant was a short walk from where we were, but none of us wanted to brave the storm. Instead, we piled into my mother's Buick. We headed down the snow-covered street to the restaurant—a tiny little place in the middle of Broad Street. It was the only place open. Gretchen parked the car as close to the sidewalk as she could. The roads had just been plowed, pushing the snow into a deep bank on the side of the street, and we all climbed over the bank.

We were the only customers there. The entire staff was sitting at a large table enjoying a big meal. I felt almost as though we were intruding. We were seated at a booth near the window.

"So, what the hell happened?" I asked. "I spoke to Mom not more than two weeks ago."

"She had the flu," said Julie. "Her doctor noticed something wrong and decided to do a chest x-ray. That's when they found the tumor. A few days later they scheduled her for a biopsy and then all this shit happened."

"What happened during the biopsy?"

"They stuck a tube down her throat to get a better look at the tumor and ruptured it. She nearly bled to death right there on the table and then coded. They cracked her sternum trying to resuscitate to her," said Julie. "They managed to save her life, but then she had a stroke and went into a coma."

"Holy shit! Is it definitely malignant?" I asked.

Gretchen lowered her voice. "It's small-cell cancer," she said.

"What's the difference?" I asked.

"Small-cell cancer is the kind you get from smoking," said Gretchen. Tears welled up in her eyes as she shook her head. "It's deadlier than other types of lung cancer and spreads a lot faster."

"What's the prognosis?" I asked.

"Who the hell knows," said Julie. "None of these doctors can tell us a damn thing."

"Is she going to live?" I asked.

"Nobody knows yet," said Gretchen. "We just have to wait. She may never come out of the coma."

"Christ, this is not exactly what I wanted to come home to," I said.

"Shut the fuck up, you stupid asshole," said Annie.

"Give him a break, Annie. He just got off the goddamn plane," said Gretchen.

"Speaking of which, I called Dad when I got in. Joan told me not to come over because they were having a party."

"Are you serious?" asked Julie, raising her lip in disgust.

"What a fucking bitch!" said Gretchen.

"Has Dad been at all supportive?" I asked.

"He's been okay. He hasn't done a whole lot, but then what can he do," Julie said.

"He could keep his stupid wife on a shorter leash," Annie said.

We all laughed. When Annie wanted to be funny she was hysterical.

After dinner we decided to call it a night. Tired and emotionally drained, we drove back to Mom's house through the storm. The only cars on the road were snow plows.

"Dad is having a party in this?" I asked.

"It's their annual Christmas dinner. People love going to it," Julie said.

"Neither rain nor sleet nor deaths in the family," I said.

"It's just like Dad," Gretchen said. "He can be so damn inappropriate sometimes."

359

Mom's house was at least warm. She had acquired a couple of dogs from the SPCA since I had left—both of which were mangy, little mutts with odd personalities. From their behavior I guessed they were abused or neglected puppies. One looked like a cross between a Scottish terrier and a collie, and the other looked like she had a bit of Labrador Retriever in her. They both snarled and barked at me. The retriever bared her teeth at me as if she were smiling and circled around my feet, never getting too close. I got the feeling she was flirting.

Exhausted, we went straight to bed. The next morning we got up early to go to the hospital. The snow had stopped, although it was still overcast and windy outside. Giant snowdrifts had nearly engulfed our front porch, and I spent a few minutes shoveling a path down the stairs.

I felt groggy and tired when we got to the hospital, and the edginess in my sisters was almost electric. Thankfully we were not besieged by endless visitors.

We camped out around her bed and simply waited for something to happen. Every so often her eyelids would twitch and she would move her head slightly, but the doctor told us this was natural. We debated whether she could feel anything, and we took turns holding her hand and stroking her hair. Annie insisted she was in pain, and there were times when I agreed with her.

I grew tired of watching every one of Mom's facial movements, so I went down to the cafeteria to get some coffee and a muffin. It was still pretty early and the only people around were the hospital staff. Most everyone was wearing white, and I felt out of place in my wool pants and silk shirt. My heels clacked on the floor conspicuously, and people eyed me curiously as I walked down the hall.

I took my breakfast back upstairs. My father had dropped in to check on things before going to work. The plant wasn't that far from the hospital anyway.

He looked at me and laughed when he saw me. "Hello Drew. Welcome home," he said.

"Thanks, Dad. How was your party?"

"It was nice. We had a great turnout despite the snow storm. How was Italy?"

"It was great, Dad. How about we talk about it later?" I asked.

"Sure…of course," he replied. "Has her doctor made her morning rounds?" he asked Gretchen.

"Not yet," she replied. "She's usually here at around ten."

"Well, call me if there's any change. I have to get to work," he said.

"Bye, Dad," my sisters all chimed.

"Drew, why don't you come by the plant around lunch time so we can catch up," he said.

"Sure. I'll see you later, Dad."

I sat in the only available chair and sipped my coffee and nibbled at my muffin. Mom's heart rate suddenly became more erratic. Two nurses came in to see what was happening.

"She's regaining consciousness," said one nurse to the other. "Call her doctor." I saw my mother's eyes open and the nurses asked us to leave the room. We stood outside with our faces pressed against the window while they checked her vital signs. Mom's doctor came in.

"When did she come out of it?" she asked.

"Just a few minutes ago. Her vital signs are stable."

"Let's get her off the respirator," her doctor said.

The nurses held her while the doctor unhooked several tubes from the machine. She grabbed the hose from the base near her mouth and wrenched it out of her throat. My mother coughed for several minutes as she regained consciousness. When the doctor was certain she was stable, we were allowed back in the room.

My mother burst into tears when she saw us. "Where's my husband?" was the first thing she asked.

I felt truly sorry for her—after all this time and all that had happened she was still in love with my father. Gretchen got on the phone and called him. He said he'd be right down.

When he arrived my mother smiled at him and took his hand. "David!" she cried, bursting into tears again. "I've had the most terrible dream. I didn't know if I'd see you again."

"Likewise," said my father, trying to make light of the situation.

My mother's memory was scrambled from her ordeal. My father went along with it. It was the first time in years I had seen any kind of tenderness between them.

Later that day she was given every kind of test imaginable. The stroke had paralyzed the left side of her body. She could no longer walk. Her doctor said she might be able regain some mobility in her arm, but her cancer was a much higher priority and needed to be dealt with immediately.

She was finally moved out of the ICU and into a regular room. Hospitals were no longer the places of care and professionalism that I remembered. The nurses had been replaced by untrained assistants who complained most of the time about being overworked. We couldn't even get one to change the sheets when necessary, and Gretchen and Julie had to do it themselves.

My mother's memory came back to her, and she was angry about what happened. She found a lawyer to sue the doctor who had botched the procedure and put her in a wheelchair. The doctor understandably spent a good deal of time backpedaling to cover his tracks. We got her out of the hospital as quickly as possible.

Getting up and down the stairs was no longer possible for

her, so we got her a hospital bed and set it up in what used to be our study. My father came over periodically to install additional electrical outlets and an air purifier. Whenever he dropped by my mother's face would light up. He usually stopped by in the mornings on his way to work, or on his way home.

Julie knew about a specialist in Philadelphia. We drove her down to see him. After his initial examination he said her only chance was to remove her lung. We wasted no time, and she was admitted as fast as they would take her. The morning she was admitted I dropped her dogs off at Uncle Frank's house and then headed toward the New Jersey Turnpike. I got lost at least twice trying to find the entrance to the turnpike, which put her in a foul mood. I pulled into a service station to get directions.

"How the hell can you get lost going to Philadelphia?" she snapped.

"I haven't been around here in ages, Mom."

"Christ, you are such a fuck up," she said.

"Thanks, Mom. I'd say I've done all right, all things considered."

"I don't consider being a college dropout as doing alright."

"Listen, Mom, it's been a real struggle so I don't want to hear it."

"Stuggle my ass! You were handed every opportunity on a silver platter. You just blew it."

"Do you honestly believe that, Mom? We were just kids. We had our guts ripped out of us by you and Dad. Between your drinking and Dad's abusiveness, we're all lucky to be alive. I don't want to hear anymore of your shit, so shut the fuck up and let me drive you down to Philadelphia so we can save your miserable life!"

We didn't say another word the entire way down. Right after she was admitted the Eastern Seaboard was besieged with yet another snowstorm. This one was even more violent than the last, and the amount snow it dumped on us made it nearly impossible to get around.

The surgery took only a few hours, and she was out of the hospital in just two weeks. Her progress was monitored carefully. Finally the doctor came to her and told her how lucky she was; they had gotten all of it just in time. Despite that she was put on chemotherapy to prevent a relapse. Now all she had to do was work on getting some mobility back in her arm. Her chances of walking again were slim to none.

She was too fragile for us to drive her home in her car, so we arranged to have her driven in a private ambulance. The insurance didn't cover it, but my father offered to pay. We found the best physical therapist we could as soon as we got home. Everyday we watched my mother struggle to bring movement into her hand. Her affliction left her arm twisted and her fingers slightly curled. We called it her claw, and as part of her therapy we had to straighten the fingers in her hand to keep the muscles from contracting too tightly. She had a large knot in her shoulders and neck and was in a lot of pain. When she wanted attention she would offer us her mangled hand.

"Give me a massage, will you, Dear?" she would ask.

Of course, none of us could refuse her, especially since she just narrowly escaped death, but none of us enjoyed touching her lifeless, stiff hand either.

Despite that, her determination was Herculean, and she never stopped trying to bring her arm back to life. Her progress was slow, and at first I didn't think she'd ever be able to use her hand again, but after a couple of months she was able to get her fingers around a small, rubber ball. Her therapist was always full of encouragement. With time she was able to hold the ball in her crooked fingers and inch her arm across her chest.

She insisted that we never leave her alone, so we took turns watching her. She complained constantly about losing her independence, and we had to fetch things for her whenever she wanted. It got to the point where we were afraid to be around lest she make us massage her claw or run endless errands, no matter how trivial they were. Even her therapist told her she would have to start learning to do things on her own again, but she held on to her handicap as tightly as she could.

Every two weeks she had to be taken to the hospital for her chemotherapy sessions. She hated the thought of losing all her hair. Although the deep auburn had left her years ago, she had an amazing mane of white hair. Most of it fell slowly away until all that was left were a few loose strands. She refused to wear a wig, opting for scarves or a hat.

The snow never stopped that winter. When we weren't being pounded with snow storm after snow storm, it was bitterly cold. Despite the weather my mother's spirits seemed to get better, and she looked forward to the spring. It was always her favorite time of year.

March was even harsher than February, and we were hit with one more mammoth snow storm, the day after which Julie and I drove Mom down to the hospital for her treatments. That was when her doctor gave her the news. Her cancer was back. It had metastasized, and a tumor the size of a grapefruit was wrapped around her heart. There was nothing anyone could do. She had less than six months to live.

She took the news well and resigned herself to dying as if she were making her last great swan song. The doctor told her that chemo was optional; it might prolong her life a little while and slow the growth of the tumor, but the end was inevitable. She decided not to continue chemo, and we arranged to get her hospice care. The pain was unbearable at times. She was given liberal amounts of morphine, which only made her temper more vicious. She threw things and cursed at the nurses she didn't like, and we had to talk them out of quitting several times.

In the final weeks my father and Joan stopped by. Joan fidgeted nervously, and I knew the last place she wanted to be was at my mother's deathbed, but she did her best to be gracious.

"Promise me you'll be good to my children," my mother said to her.

"Of course," said Joan. "I promise." I knew it was a promise she would never keep, and the fact that my mother had to even ask her for her promise only made her more pitiable.

My mother withered away rather quickly. She was skin and bones. The tumors in her chest were now protruding through her porcelain skin, and she looked increasingly fragile. She told us her biggest regret was all the years of drinking she had done, and how it destroyed our lives. She asked our forgiveness.

My father came over one last time to say goodbye. My mother insisted that we dress her properly and put some makeup on her. My father sat in a chair next to her bed and held her hand.

"David, Smith money goes to Smith children. Do you understand?" she asked.

"Yes, of course. That's the way it should be," he said.

"I'm sorry I couldn't be the wife you wanted," she said.

"Don't worry about that now. It's all water under the bridge."

"Take care of our children."

"They'll be taken care of. You rest now," he said, kissing her on the forehead. My mother smiled. That simple gesture was her dying wish.

The next week she drifted in and out of consciousness until finally she just slipped away. It was a warm May morning when she died. Uncle Frank and Aunt Tess came over with a bottle of champagne and we drank a toast in her honor. That night I went to a bar in Sea Bright and got smashed. My sisters all stayed home and cried. I knew I wouldn't miss her, and in a way felt as though a huge burden had been lifted from my shoulders. I loved my mother but she was way too destructive and had always been a toxic element in my life. Glad she was gone, I felt guilty about not feeling guilty, and so for the first time in months I drank.

That night I had the time of my life. I met a young girl while playing pool. She couldn't have been a day over eighteen. When she asked me how I was doing I simply told her I hadn't a clue because my mother had just died that morning and I was way too tired to deal with it now. Later that night she took me home and fucked me senseless. I never saw her again, but I'm certain it was the best lay either of us ever had.

I was surprised by how many people showed up at her funeral. Despite her alcoholism she had a lot of friends. The service was short, and her eulogy was right to the point—the priest didn't mince his words. He said that Betty Smith was the angriest woman he had ever known, but through her anger was immense kindness and love for God. She was finally at peace in the Lord's Garden.

After the funeral I found myself completely burned out and without direction. I had no job to go back to, and was too tired to write. During the final months of my mother's illness, I managed most of her finances, although Gretchen was given power of attorney to pay the bills. My mother didn't have a lot of money. She had a bit of cash in her checking account and some retirement funds. Gretchen had liquidated the smaller ones to keep the house going.

After the funeral Gretchen took off with her check book and credit cards and went on a shopping spree. She spent all the cash immediately, and then went to Sears and bought a new washer and dryer with the credit cards. I discovered it when the statements came to the house. I called her as soon as I could.

"Gretchen, what the hell are you doing?" I asked.

"What are you talking about?"

"You're spending our inheritance! You can't do that. Mom's money should have been frozen as soon as she died."

"Listen, after the shit we've been through I'm entitled to some money."

"But it's our money. When were you going to tell us that you had gone a shopping spree? After all the money was gone?"

"I have power of attorney. I can do what I want."

"No you can't! What you are doing is illegal. Cease and desist, you crazy bitch!"

She hung up and continued spending as much as she could. I called the credit card companies and my mother's lawyer to get her money frozen before she burned through it all. Uncle Frank was the executor of the estate. When I told him what was happening he just laughed.

"So, Gretchen has gone off the deep end? Well, don't worry about it. Whatever damage she incurs will be deducted from her share of the estate. But you might want get your mother's credit cards away from her before she does too much damage. It's going to be a couple days before we can get those accounts closed."

That night I drove to Philadelphia to take the credit cards away. Gretchen lived in a small house by herself in the suburbs. I pounded on her front door until she opened it. Her eyes had a wild look in them and her red hair was completely disheveled.

"Give me the credit cards," I said.

"Fine, take them. I can't handle this anymore." She found her purse and took out all my mother's credit cards. "I was trying to establish some credit for myself," she said.

"By committing fraud? That's a great way to do it! You can

368

tack your credit rating to the bottom of your rap sheet. What the hell is the matter with you?"

"Fuck off, and get out of my house," she said.

"Fine. Goodnight."

I left and she slammed the door behind me. She was really out of her mind, but despite my anger I was concerned for her. Out of all of us I considered her the weakest. Perhaps because she was the oldest in the family she was broken the worst, but I always considered Julie to have it harder than anyone else, only because she was the youngest. Gretchen simply wasn't good at fighting her demons, and it was only a question of time before they got the better of her.

We had a heated discussion over what to do with the house. I wanted to sell it as quickly as possible, but Julie wanted to keep it so we could have a place to come home to. The mortgage would take at least ten years to pay off.

"Who's going to pay to keep the place running?" I asked.

"We could split the expenses," she replied.

"Julie, forget it," said Annie. "Let's just sell the house and get the hell out of Rumson. Why the hell would you want to stay here anyway?"

"I like Rumson. I wouldn't mind staying here. How about if I buy you all out?"

"With what?" I asked. "You don't have any money! And what would you do here? You'd end up becoming Mom."

Julie looked at me with so much rage I thought for a second she was going to claw my eyes out. Instead, she simply got in her car and left. She and Annie went down to Philadelphia, where my sisters had somehow transplanted themselves. It started with Annie; she went to Tyler School of Art, then Julie, and finally Gretchen. They all lived within easy driving distance of each other. How they managed to get along in the same city without killing each other was nothing short of a miracle.

With nowhere to go, I stayed in the house that summer and took care of things. I could have stayed in my mother's room, but instead I slept in my old room; I couldn't handle being in her bed, and waking up in my old bed brought back bitter-sweet memories of my high school days.

Most of the time I was alone, and I spent my time going through my mother's things. In the back of her closet was a big box of photos of when we were kids. I sat on the floor and went through them. When we were really young we looked happy and normal. The pictures of the farm in Lincroft before we moved to Rumson interested me the most. My mother was so beautiful back then—her hair was the deepest auburn and her features were so finely chiseled. She looked happy in those years. My father always looked serious in pictures, but he was so handsome then that he could have been a movie star.

Despite how we looked, my earliest memories were strangely unhappy, and I wasn't sure why. I remembered the time my father gave us baskets of live chicks for Easter to put in our duck pond, but by the end of the day the snapping turtles had devoured every last one. My sisters were traumatized for years. When young, I followed my father around the house like he was my greatest hero, but he was always too busy and never had time for me. I learned sadness at an early age.

Up in the rafters of the garage I found an old box with some of my personal belongings. Inside were some knick-knacks and old things that still had some special significance. At the bottom of the box I found my yearbook from *Ecole des Roches*. It was dusty and dirty, but aside from that it had survived fairly well. I took it inside and cleaned it up. I flipped through the pages until I found Alexandra's picture. Her long, dark hair was straight down. She had a slight smile, and her big, brown eyes had a hint of playfulness. I could feel the pain welling up in my throat. How she was doing? I hadn't heard from her since I left Italy, and I thought about calling or writing her quick letter, but then thought it best to simply let her go. I wrapped the yearbook in brown paper and put it in a box with rest of my keepsakes.

Aunt Tess came by later that morning. I hadn't seen her since the funeral. She was wearing a pair of draw-sting pants and a straw hat. She had been painting, and her easel was stuffed in the back of her station wagon.

"How are you making out, Drew?" she asked, kissing me on the cheek.

"I'm okay, Aunt Tess. Would you like some coffee?"

She looked around the kitchen and saw what a mess it was. "I'll make it, Sweetheart. Why don't you just relax?" She made the coffee and then started on the dishes that were piled in the sink. "So where do you and Alexandra stand?" she asked.

Her question took me off guard. "We're no longer together. She's with someone else."

Aunt Tess turned around to look at me, her eyes filled with compassion. "You two were never destined for each other," she said. "You two are worlds apart. How's her mother doing?"

"She's a mess. She never really recovered after her husband died."

"I'm sorry to hear that. It's got to be tough on Alexandra. Is she okay?"

"She's doing alright," I said with a deep sigh.

Aunt Tess kissed me on the cheek. "Poor Drew. You've been through a hell of a lot. Your mother would be proud to see how well you are coming along."

"Do you think? I don't feel so proud."

"Your mother was always proud of you, but her demons didn't always let her show it. Listen, Sweetheart. You need to let

371

this all go and start fresh. What are your plans?"

"I have no idea, Aunt Tess. I was thinking of going out to California."

"That's what Roy did. Just be careful. He got mixed up with the wrong people and started doing drugs."

"Don't worry, Aunt Tess. That won't happen to me."

"I hope not, Dear. You're young and strong. Now is the time for you to make something out of yourself. Listen, I need to get back to take care of some things at home. Give me a call if you need anything," she said, patting my cheek and kissing me.

Summer was in full swing. Occasionally I would see Dad and Joan on their way to the beach to eat a picnic dinner. I was never invited. I felt like a stranger here, as if I didn't belong. I didn't go to the tennis club anymore. Mom had some old manuscripts in her office, which I sat down to read. The writing was awful, but she had a computer, which fascinated me. In a big box next to her computer were some large floppy disks. I had no idea how to use the damn thing, but I found a manual and started reading. The tutorials were simple enough to follow. At first the computer was so cryptic, and the DOS commands intimidated me, but after a while I figured out how to work with the operating system.

When I became more comfortable with some of the basics I started teaching myself WordPerfect. I soon realized how powerful some of the editing features were. Well! The ability to copy and paste blocks of text made the use of a typewriter completely obsolete. Mom had a small dot-matrix printer that made a big racket when I used it, and the output wasn't all that nice, but it was still better than using my typewriter. The computer would simply have to go to me.

In the late afternoons I sat on the front porch and drank coffee. The neighborhood was quiet. I watched the day wind down in the warm afternoon sun. My father's convertible came around the corner. Somehow his Firebird remained untouched by the harsh New Jersey weather. He spent a lot of money keeping it in mint condition, and only drove it during the summer.

He parked in front of the house and came up on the porch. He was wearing his summer work clothes—khaki pants, a button-down shirt, and a tie.

"Hello, Drew," he said.

"Hi, Dad."

"Well, you've kept the place up pretty well."

"It's not that hard. Uncle Frank says it needs a bit of work before we can sell it. Any idea when we can put this place on the market?"

"It shouldn't be too long now. This place should sell pretty quickly. In the meantime I have an idea that could get you kids some money immediately."

"Oh, yeah? What did you have in mind?" I asked, not really believing him.

"Each of you kids has a share in the real estate at Browning Seals International, Inc. We set it up for you when you were children. I'd like to buy you out. I'd pay you $534.57 cents each month for the next 20 years. It would give you an income and I would get a tax break."

I scratched my head and smoothed back my hair. The proposition sounded good. I was jobless and broke; at least this would ensure I had an income for awhile until I got on my feet.

"Have you talked this over with everyone else?"

"Not yet. I wanted to get you all together before I presented it. I just wanted to hear your thoughts on the subject."

"It sounds interesting. How much is the plant worth?"

"You all just own a small piece of the land, as well as Uncle Frank's wife. It's not worth a whole lot. The benefit would be a tax break for me and income for you."

"Well, I'll talk it over with Gretchen, Annie, and Julie and see what they think."

"Okay, my accountant is working on some numbers. I should have something in writing by the end of the week. How are things going otherwise?"

"Things are fine, Dad."

"We'll get together soon for some tennis."

He got back in his car and drove away. Was his proposal legitimate? When it came to money he could be a real snake. Later that week we all got a letter from his attorney with an agreement to sell our shares in the company. The agreement was long. My sisters didn't know what to make of it at first. Annie and Julie decided it was best to talk to Uncle Frank about it.

They came up that weekend, and we all went over to his house for lunch. We sat out on the veranda and watched the powerboats zip up and down the river below his house while eating lobster-salad sandwiches in the warm, afternoon sun. Uncle Frank's broad face was red from the heat and from doing yard work in the sun all morning. Julie had mailed him a copy of the agreement, and it sat on the table in front of him.

"Well, on the surface there's nothing wrong with what he's proposing," he said. "But you have to understand how this thing came about. When you kids were just babies, your father and I came up with the idea for this company. Neither of us had any money. Your father came up with most of the capital by borrowing money from the trust funds your grandfather setup for you. He agreed to lend your father the money so long as you all got a piece of the company. What your father is proposing is to buy out your shares with your own money. Eventually those partnerships will start paying out pretty generous dividends."

"How much is the land worth?" asked Annie.

He picked up the contract and ran his hands down the creases. "It's not worth a whole lot now, but in a few years that will change. Who knows what it's going to be worth twenty years from now. From the way this area is growing it could be worth a fortune. My advice is not to sell."

"What's his real motivation behind all this?" asked Annie.

"That's obvious. It's money. You know your father tried to get control of Browning Seals International, Inc. years ago. At the time your parents were still married. He tried to buyout the other partners' shares, but the way he did it was pretty damn sneaky. I didn't know about it until almost too late. Sandy and I put a stop to it before the deal was signed."

"He says it's so he can get a tax write off," I said.

"Tax write off? Hell, if anything it will only increase his taxes. He just wants control of that land. He's banking on the idea that the property is going to be worth a fortune by the time he retires."

"What do you think, Uncle Frank?" Julie asked.

"Well, there's a couple of problems we're facing. The land is sitting on top of a potential environmental disaster. The previous tenants stored their oil tanks underground. That's illegal now. In order to comply with the new laws we had to dig the tanks up. In the process we discovered one of them leaked. We're running tests to see what kind of damage there is. If the damage is severe enough the cleanup could cost us a fortune which, of course, would devalue the land. The other problem is the demographics in the area. The plant is not in very a desirable part of town, but that will probably change. It's close to the train station and the area will probably be gentrified in the next ten years."

"What kind of risk is there with that environmental problem?" I asked.

"It really depends how much oil has leaked into the ground.

If the EPA got wind of what's going on they'd order the contaminated soil excavated, which would cost a fortune. We're looking at alternative methods to do the cleanup. But first we need to figure out how bad it is."

"Who's in charge of all that?" I asked.

"Who else—your father," replied Uncle Frank, dropping the papers on the table in front of him. "It explains why he's dragging his feet on all this."

"You'd think he'd want to know," said Annie. "Especially considering what he's proposing."

"Why do you think he didn't tell us about it?" I asked her.

"He probably knows something. This has been going on for months. He's had all kinds of consultants come in and look at the place, but so far we haven't seen any of their findings. Your aunt Sandy is a shareholder, and she's been chewing at the bit trying to find out what the hell is going on."

Uncle Frank said Mom's estate would take at least a year to settle. Her illness accrued significant debt, but there would be plenty to cover that once the house was sold. He thought the house would get a good price because of its location near the bridge, and it was in pretty good shape for its age.

That weekend we had dinner with my father and Joan. Joan made a tuna and pasta salad, and we drank a white wine with dinner. At first we didn't talk about his proposal; instead we discussed my mother's house. My father graciously offered to help out with some of the repairs. Paying for the repairs out of the estate would have meant using the last of my mother's retirement funds, leaving us with no cash until the house was sold.

The subject of the contracts came up after dinner. Joan had cleared our plates and served a desert of vanilla ice cream and warm fudge.

"So, Dad, you've made us an interesting proposal," said Annie, looking up at him to see how he'd react.

"Well, I think it's a good deal for you kids," said my father.

"What's the total payout?" asked Julie.

"It would be about $300,000.00 at the end of the contract, when you figure in the interest charges."

"It sounds like a good deal," I said. "What's the deal with the environmental problems?"

He looked over at me and blushed slightly. "You're talking about the oil spill from the previous owners?"

"Yeah," I replied.

"Well, one of the oil tanks had a crack in it, causing a slow leak. It must have been there a while because when we pulled the tank out of the ground the whole thing split open, dumping whatever oil was left into the ground."

"How much was there?" asked Annie.

"The tank wasn't full, but there was enough to make a pretty big mess. But the real problem was that leak. Who knows how much oil has seeped into the ground all these years. If it contaminated the water table then we've got real problems."

"How long will it take to figure out how much damage was done?" asked Julie.

"Well, the preliminary findings show the damage to be contained near the surface, but we're still trying to get an exact measurement of how much oil was spilled. Depending on how deep and how much damage there is will determine what needs to be done."

"So what's in it for you?" asked Annie.

"Well, for me it's a tax write off," he replied.

"How is it a tax write off?" she asked.

"Well, I'd be the one responsible for the cleanup. You kids would be free of that complication. And then I'd be able to write the losses off. The money you got every month for the next twenty years would help keep you all going."

I would be forty-four by the time the contract was paid out. By then I should be fairly well established. The deal was enticing, but Annie and Julie were not convinced. With Uncle Frank's help they got a lawyer to look at the contracts more closely. The lawyer told them that the land was undervalued, and that there was no provision in the agreement to protect them should my father go bankrupt. Annie went back to my father and told him she'd sign the agreement if he'd be willing to sign a promissory note. He refused, and she went back to Philadelphia with Julie.

I didn't hear from them for a couple of weeks. My father stopped by after work one afternoon upset and angry. He showed me a letter Annie had written him. The letter simply said that she never trusted him, and why should she trust him now? By not signing the promissory note, he was not showing any good faith. Both she and Julie refused to sell their shares. Gretchen had already signed the agreement and sent it back.

"What are you going to do, Drew?"

I scratched my head and rubbed my chin. The income would definitely help. "I'm going to sell," I replied.

The next morning I went down to my father's office and had the agreement notarized. I knew in my heart I probably shouldn't sell, but the thought of being penniless was just too much. I still wanted to finish college, and the money would give me enough of a cushion to allow me to go back to school. Payments would begin on the first of next month.

The day after I received my first check I took off. I headed out to California in my mother's old car with only a few of my belongings. I had heard that schools were practically free out there once you established residency. Now that my entire life had been turned to scars and bad memories, I had no choice but to rebuild from scratch.

Chapter 15

My wife and I sat nervously in our lawyer's office as he read the closing agreement. She held our son Christopher in her arms while he cooed and squirmed. She was three months pregnant with our second child. I had known my lawyer even before I met my wife. He was a shrewd man, not much older than I, who specialized in retirement planning.

"You realize they want a six-month close on the house," he said.

"Yes. That seems awfully long," I replied.

"It also presents a problem. Most banks will only give you a mortgage commitment for three months. After that you have to reapply. If the rates go up you are stuck."

"Is there anything we can do about it?" asked Mariana.

"Well, there are some things we can do that will require some delicate timing. According to New York law, you have ninety days to come up with the financing after the agreement is signed. After that you forfeit your down payment. If we apply for the loan at the last minute the mortgage commitment might extend past the closing."

"What happens if we don't get the loan?" I asked.

"We'll cross that bridge when we get to it," he said. "How's your credit?"

"I have some blemishes from about ten years ago for being late on a couple of student-loan payments, but everything is current now."

"Do you have credit, Mariana?" he asked.

"Everything I have is from him," she said, squeezing my hand.

"How much money did you make last year?" he asked me.

"Just over 100,000 dollars. It's been up and down, but lately the market has been good. I'll probably do better this year."

"He's done very well since we've been married," said Mariana. Christopher had his hands wrapped around the gold cross dangling from her neck. Her long, dark hair was pulled back into a pony tail.

"So, what are you doing now? You're a computer programmer, right?"

"Yes. I write custom software for different companies."

"Boy, you're in the right business. The IT sector is really booming."

"Things are good. I have too much work. I keep raising my rates and they keep paying them."

"Nothing wrong with that! I'd like to be in your position. I guess the world just doesn't need another greedy lawyer."

I laughed, and Christopher turned his head at me and gurgled.

"Have your parents met their grandchild?" Nat asked Mariana.

"No, not yet. My father would never leave Colombia. My mother was here once before Christopher was born, and I think she'll be back to visit with me and my sisters."

"I'll bet she's anxious to meet her grandson," he said.

"She can't get enough pictures. She's always asking for more pictures."

"Do you know where you are going to go for the loan?" asked Nat.

"My grandmother said I should use her bank," I said. "They already sent me the loan application."

"How much of a down payment are you going to make?"

"I was hoping to put down twenty percent to avoid paying PMI," I said.

"What's PMI?" asked Mariana.

"Private mortgage insurance," explained Nat. "Banks ask you to pay insurance on top of the mortgage to ensure they get paid if you default on the loan. Often banks will waive the PMI if you can manage to come up with twenty percent of the loan."

"Do we have that?" Mariana asked.

"I think so. It's going to be tight. Coming up with 40,000 dollars is going to leave us a little short for other expenses, but it's worth the expense in the long run."

"Anything helps. If you can manage to double up on your mortgage payments during the first year your interest payments are reduced exponentially. Why don't you fill out your loan application tonight, and I'll get the rest of the paperwork started."

"Thanks, Nat," I said, shaking his hand.

"My pleasure. Bye, Mariana," he said.

"Bye, Nat. Thank you," she said, gathering up Christopher's things. I took Christopher from her while she packed up his bottles, binkies and blankets. He was all smiles and gurgles. Mariana was a bit upset with me because the first words out of his mouth this morning were "Daddy" instead of "Mommy". To make matters worse, he uttered them in a crowded diner in front of a group of people while she was holding him in her lap.

"Here, take your baby," she said, handing him to me in disgust. Everyone laughed. It was a proud moment for me, I have to admit. Christopher was the spitting image of me. He even looked exactly like I did when I was a baby. Mariana was very insecure about it. Mariana was South American, and many people assumed she was the babysitter when they saw her pushing our son around in the stroller. On several occasions people thought the credit cards she used were stolen because they had my name on them.

I strapped Christopher into his car seat, and inspected the

results of Mariana's latest car accident. This was the third one in two years. The first one happened just before we were married. She was driving my car. It wasn't her fault—a guy in a Jeep ran out in front of her. She didn't even have time to stop. The car was totaled, and her knee was blown out. She had to have it surgically reconstructed.

She got a check for $20,000 from the insurance settlement, which certainly helped with getting our new home. The rest of the settlement came in structured payments, which helped pay the utility bills. I used part of the money to pay off some debts, and the rest I put into a mutual fund. The other two accidents were just plain carelessness. My insurance rates were ridiculously high, yet she insisted that she have a new car to drive. I bought her a Toyota Corolla, and I drove an old, used one. Somehow I always managed to make my monthly expenses.

"Can we drive by the house again," she asked.

"Do we have to? I have work to do. The house isn't going anywhere."

"Oh, please, please, my blue-blood *Gringo*" she said, smiling and cooing. She called me her blue-blood *Gringo* after seeing how my father lived. She was intimidated by my Grandmother's house, but, strangely, everyone in the family adored her. Joan especially liked her, and she was always talking to her about recipes and such.

"All right," I said. "We'll drive by one more time."

Instead of driving east down 287 towards White Plains, I headed over the Tappan Zee bridge into Rockland County where we would be moving soon. The bridge traffic was awful, and most people didn't like Rockland County for that reason, but the real estate values in Westchester were simply out of my price range.

Besides, Mariana insisted that we get a house with a decent-sized yard for our children to play in. I was content living in

383

a new townhouse in a good school district, but once I showed her what a townhouse was she would have nothing to do with it. It had to be a house with a yard, and not too small either.

I headed north on the Palisades Parkway until we came to New Hempstead. Our new home was on a long side street off a main thoroughfare. The current owner told me an express bus stopped at the end of the street to pick up people to go to the city. The commute wasn't bad; it took forty-five minutes.

We both knew we had found our house when we saw it. A split-level ranch with a large family room that had been added next to the kitchen, it was situated on nearly three quarters of an acre with lots of trees. A long porch extended the length of the house, and the backyard was private because of a thick, woody area separating us from the next street.

What I liked most was the fireplace. None of the other houses we looked at in our price range had one, and having a fireplace reminded me of our old house in Rumson. The kitchen was in good shape, although the appliances were pretty old. A small dining room adjoined the kitchen. A nice-sized family area was on the split level before going up the stairs. The house was built in 1957—the year I was born—which I thought to be a good omen. A small office with a Murphy bed was next to the foyer. I especially liked the office; it had a large picture window overlooking the front yard and was a perfect place for me to work.

"Well, this is where we are going to live," I said, as we approached the house.

"I love it," said Mariana. "Do you think we made a mistake moving so far from Westchester?"

"Westchester is right over the bridge!"

"Yes, but I'm pretty far from my sisters," she said.

"You don't even like your sisters."

She looked out the window and scowled. "That's not true. I'm not like you and the way you treat your family. We fight sometimes, but we stay together."

"What do you mean, the way I treat my family?"

"I'm ashamed at the way you treat your father. He doesn't deserve to be treated that way."

"You have no idea what you're talking about," I said. "He's a prick. I don't like him."

"He's your father. I had problems with my mother growing up, but I've forgiven her."

"Your mother left for Colombia a week before Christopher was born. And for no good reason except she wanted to go home! What kind of mother does that to her daughter?"

"My mother is like a child. My sisters told her she should go home and take care of my father, so she did what she was told."

"Your sisters didn't think you might need your mother around while you were giving birth to your first child? I'm sorry, Mariana, but I think it was awful. She apologized to me before she left. She knew what she was doing was wrong. Didn't it hurt at all?"

"Yes, it hurt, but I don't let it run my life like your feelings towards your father runs you. Sometimes I wonder why you married me. There are times I think you married me just to prove to your father you could get married."

"Do we have to go through this again? I'm so sick of fighting with you," I said, turning the car around.

"No man ever disrespected me the way you did that night you called me a bitch. My father never cursed my mother. I should have left you then."

"Mariana, I came to you and told you how much I can afford to get us a house, and you told me it wasn't good enough.

How the hell did you expect me to react? You're lucky I didn't leave. I was really tempted."

"Well, it's not too late," she said.

"Yes, it is. We just signed a contract to buy a house—unless you don't mind throwing away forty grand," I said with disgust.

"Just remember," she said, staring out the window, "if it wasn't for me and the money I got from the accident we couldn't get the house."

"That's not true. I'll admit the money helped, but I had enough in savings. I'm worried about keeping up with all the expenses. It would really help if you went out and got a job when Christopher gets a little older."

She looked over at me and frowned. "My father never sent my mother out to work," she said.

"Mariana, you haven't worked a day since we've been married. The world doesn't owe you a living."

"When you met me we had almost nothing. Now look at all we have. I think I've helped improve you life."

I didn't say anything. When we met I was living in a small, comfortable apartment and worked only when I wanted. In the two years since we've been married I nearly quadrupled my income. But I wasn't happy. I met Mariana at a real low point in my life. She worked at the local gas station. When I first saw her she was wearing a short, blue skirt and was dancing salsa. She danced really well, and I couldn't take my eyes off her pretty form as she shimmied across the dance floor. She was thin and athletic—with strong legs and shapely arms. She was very Indian looking, and her smile was amazing—it lit up her entire face.

Her English was terrible, and my Spanish even worse, but we started dating anyway. I was lonely and tired, having just moved to White Plains, and I didn't know a soul. Although she had come to this country with a valid visa, it was about to expire. In an effort to help I got her a good immigration lawyer. The lawyer explained that the immigration laws had just gotten stricter, and the administration was cracking down on illegal aliens. The only way for her to stay in the country was for us to get married. And we had to do it before her visa expired.

My friends were skeptical of the whole situation, and Nat suggested getting a prenuptial agreement, but the immigration lawyer advised against it.

"That's the first thing they check for," she said.

Against the advice of my friends and my own better judgment, we were married in a small, civil ceremony. None of her sisters came to the ceremony. In fact, I never even met them until after the wedding. She came from a family of fifteen, eight of whom were women. At least four of them lived in the area, but Mariana didn't get along with them. That didn't matter to me. I understood family problems, and knew she came from a rough family. She was a good woman, and I was convinced that she loved me. I wasn't in love with her, but I cared about her deeply. I was willing to gamble that our love would grow with time.

It didn't. Our marriage was becoming a hellish nightmare.

The beginning of the end started the night I pre-qualified myself for a home mortgage on the internet. I went to Mariana and told her I could afford an $180,000 dollar home.

"One hundred eighty dollars! That's all? You can't buy shit for that much. I won't live in a house that cheap," she said.

I was in so much shock I didn't know how to react. I worked so hard and saved religiously so we could move out of our apartment. "Mariana, you can get a decent house for that money. Maybe not in Westchester, but it's not a bad start."

"No way! I won't live in a house that cheap. My kids need to have a yard," she said.

I sunk to my knees on the floor, took her hand, and looked

up at her. "Mariana, please tell me you are proud of me and all that I have done for this family," I pleaded.

She simply pulled her hand away and went into the bedroom. We had a terrible fight afterward, and she nearly walked out. I knew then what a terrible mistake I had made, but out of my sense of responsibility for my son I decided to stay in the marriage.

My heart wasn't into buying our house, but I went through motions to keep the peace. I was beginning to shut down. All my passion and zest for living was starting to die, and I put my energies into the software I wrote, which kept me mesmerized in front of my computer for hours on end. Mariana and I just had nothing in common, and there was no communication between us at all— much less sex. Our marriage was loveless and harsh.

I had mixed feelings when I found out Mariana was pregnant again. Having another child was a huge mistake, but what was done was done. Mariana told me she wouldn't stop having children until she had a girl and a boy. When we found out she was having a girl I was very relieved—I could finally hang up my spurs.

That night I filled out the loan application and sent it off to the bank. A few days later I got a call from my grandmother's banker.

"Drew! How are you? My name is John O'Connor. I'm your grandmother's account manager."

"Did you get my loan application?"

"Yes, I did. I've assigned a loan officer from our Private Clients Group to work with you. His name is Nick Presario. He'll give you a call in a couple of days."

"Okay. Thank you," I said.

"So, Drew. What do you do?" he asked.

"I'm a software engineer. I write custom applications for people."

"Do you work for yourself?"

"Yes. I have a small consulting firm called DataDesign Solutions."

"Very good. I'll update your file with that information."

"You have a file on me?" I asked.

"Nothing substantial. I just keep information on all the grandchildren."

"Oh, well, if you want you can go to my website and learn more about what I do. Do you have an e-mail address? "

"Yes. I'd be happy to look at your website. Here's my e-mail address…"

"Hold on, let me get a pen." I wrote down his address, and put it next to my keyboard.

"Well, it was good talking to you, Drew. If you need anything or have any questions give me a call. Nick is a good man. He'll take care of you."

"Thank you for calling," I said.

It was an odd conversation, but I didn't think much of it. A few days later the guy called.

"Drew, my name is Nick Presario. I've been assigned to handle your loan application."

"Hi. Is everything complete?"

"Yes, everything is fine. We don't usually do home loans this small, but everything is in order."

"I should tell you up front that I have a couple blemishes on my credit record."

"Well, Drew, your credit is not important to us," he said.

"What do you mean?" I asked. I thought he was joking. No bank in its right mind would give out a $200,000 loan without knowing your credit history.

"What I mean is that you are dealing with the Private Clients Group. I can't say that your loan is one hundred percent guaranteed, but I will say there is no way you will be denied the loan at this time."

"Oh! Well, that's good to know," I said. My mind started racing. Either my grandmother had guaranteed the loan for me, or something was going on that I didn't know about. Considering how my family felt about money I decided to keep quiet and see what developed.

"All right, Drew. I'll start the process for the loan application."

"That reminds me. The owners of the house want a six-month close. How long is the mortgage commitment good for?"

"Three months. Is that a problem?"

"Well, my lawyer told me if we waited until the last minute to put the application in we can time it so the mortgage commitment spans the closing date."

"We could do that," he said. "But the interest rates are the lowest they've been in years. I would apply now while the rates are good."

"But won't we have to reapply for the loan after the commitment has expired?"

"I wouldn't worry about it. If the rates go up I'm sure the bank would be willing to buy the extra points."

Now I knew something was up, but I had no clue what. I had struggled and scraped to get by without any help from anyone for so many years, I could hardly believe all this was happening.

"Well, thank you. I don't know what to say."

"Just relax and we'll take care of everything."

"What about the deposit?"

"How much of a deposit did you want to make?"

"Well, I'm prepared to put down twenty percent to avoid paying PMI."

"You won't be required to pay PMI. If you want to put down twenty percent to lower your monthly payments that's fine, but I suggest you put down ten percent and use the rest of the money for something else."

Now I was flabbergasted. What was happening was unheard of, but still I kept my mouth shut. John O'Connor had sent me down an application for a checking account with the Private Clients Group. Along with it came a credit card with a $25,000 line of credit. I was not going to breathe a word of this to anyone, especially Mariana. About three weeks later Nick called me back. My loan had been approved.

Finally I couldn't stand it anymore. "Nick, I'm just a regular guy trying to make a living. Why is the bank extending me so much preferential treatment?"

"Well, Drew, because your name is on a big piece of your grandmother's money, and when you hit it big, we want to make sure we have your business going forward."

I couldn't believe he just told me that.

"How big is big?" I asked.

"I'm not at liberty to say, Drew. But I will tell you that to qualify for Private Client status at our bank you have to have at least one million dollars in liquid assets."

I nearly dropped the phone. That was too much information. My father had told us that most of her money was gone. None of us expected to get anything. I could never tell a soul. It was my trump card.

"Thank you, Nick. Thanks for everything."

"My pleasure, Drew. Give us a call when you are ready to get your next house."

"I will. Thanks again."

I sat in front of my computer and tried to go back to work. I couldn't. The thought of being a millionaire was too much.

How would I use the money? I had been sitting on an idea for a software venture that could make millions. Before I went independent I worked at an HMO for Medicaid and low-income families. It was a lucrative, specialized market that tried to shoehorn commercial systems into their business model. It never worked smoothly. The government was constantly changing the rules, and the big commercial systems were not flexible enough to handle the changes.

My idea was to create a modular, client-server system and have all the business rules data driven. My old boss, an ex-boxer named Mikhail from Russia, constantly talked about it. He had been in the business for years and knew most of the major pieces. He always said the biggest hurdle would be finding a business analyst who knew enough to write the requirements. He admitted that if it were done right it would make a fortune.

I had the technical skills to pull it off, but didn't know the business well enough. With enough money those problems could be solved. Mikhail was getting ready to retire. He knew some people that could help us with the requirements. I decided to give him a call and see how serious he was about helping me write the software.

"Mikhail! How are you?"

"Drew? It's good to hear from you! What's new? How's business?"

"Business is good. I'm staying busy. Mikhail, remember how we used to talk about writing our own software system?"

"Yes. Why? You want to become a billionaire?"

I laughed. Mikhail hated the system the company was using, but nothing better was available.

"I think it's time we start thinking seriously about putting together our own company."

"Did you find an investor?"

"Not quite. Please keep this quiet. You are the only guy I can trust with this information. I just found out that I have quite a bit of money in my name. It would be more than enough to start a company."

"You're a lucky boy. Is the money available now?"

"No. I just found out about it. I don't think I'm even supposed to know. My grandmother's bank told me this morning."

"It's your inheritance?" he asked.

"Yes, but my grandmother is ninety-six years old. Now is the time to start planning, but we need to do it quietly. I don't want people to find out about this in case the money doesn't come through for some reason."

"All right, but we need to hire someone who knows the business from every angle. I can find people who have experience in various aspects of the business, but we need someone who understands how everything ties together."

"Do you know anyone like that?"

"Yes. She works for the company that sold us our first system. If we could get her we would be set."

"Do you know how to get hold of her?"

"Yeah, but I wouldn't contact her until we're ready to offer her something solid. She won't work for free, I guarantee that. How do you intend to write the system?"

"I'd leverage the skills that we have. I'd use SQL Server on the backend and Visual FoxPro on the front. It would be a three-tier model, with all the business logic in the middle tier. The database would be simply a repository, and the front end would be as light as possible."

"You could use FoxPro for your data," he said.

"I wouldn't want to. SQL Server is faster and more stable. Some people might not buy the system if it were written strictly with FoxPro."

"You're probably right. Why don't you get back to me in a couple of weeks? I'll start sketching some rough designs."

"Thanks, Mikhail. I guess this means you're interested?"

"Yes, of course I'm interested—as long as we have the resources to make sure we succeed."

"That's why I'm calling, Mikhail. I wanted to tell you I always liked your idea, and I think we could build something solid."

"We'll both retire multi-millionaires," he said.

I quietly started writing a business plan for our company. Mikhail was a really gifted programmer; he had taught me a lot. His skills were outdated, but his understanding of the concepts was unshakable. Between the two of us we could create an exceptional product. He was much smarter than I when it came to business analysis, but my technical skills were far more advanced.

That summer we closed on our house. Nat told me to make sure I brought enough checks. The lawyers did most of the talking while I sat there and wrote check after check. At the end of it all nearly my entire life savings was spent.

Mariana was all smiles.

"We bought a house," she said.

For better or worse, I thought. Moving day wasn't so bad. Mariana wanted to get some of her friends to help us to save money, but I insisted on using a professional. It would be faster and easier. The last thing I wanted was to lug furniture around all day. And besides, Mariana would have been useless as pregnant as she was. We packed everything up in the boxes they gave us, and the next day they came and moved us within just a few hours. It was all so civilized.

I let Mariana arrange the house the way she wanted. My only demand was that the office was mine to do with the way I wanted.

"I don't want your ugly desk in there," she said.

"I like my desk."

"You're not going to put that ugly bookcase in there are you?"

"Yes! It goes with the desk. Look, I need a place to work and this is perfect."

"Why don't you put your office in the little dining room next to the kitchen?"

"Mariana, I don't understand. Why don't you want me to have my own space? If I put my office in there I'll never have any privacy."

"Because that room is so charming. It would make a perfect spare bedroom."

"Forget it, Mariana. You're not moving any of your sisters in here. I need a private place to work so I can pay for all this and that's the end of it!"

"Who said I wanted to move my sisters in here? They would never want to live with a crazy *gringo* like you! But you promised me I could do what I wanted with the house."

"You can. Just not with my office."

"But your office is part of the house."

"Think of my office as not part of the house, but somewhere I go to work each day."

"But it's so close to the front door. People can see how messy you are. You better keep it clean."

"Fine, I will," I said, shutting the door. I think she just didn't want me to have my own space. Business was good enough I could probably get an office out of the house. I couldn't stand her constant nagging, but for now I needed to work at home to save money. At times I couldn't stand being around her. The only way to keep her out of my hair was to give her money so she could go shopping.

Thankfully she didn't spend a lot of money on clothes. A

gifted seamstress, she made almost everything she wore. The best investment I ever made was to buy her a good sewing machine. But what she didn't spend on clothes she spent in other ways. I constantly asked her to watch how she spent money, but money to her didn't seem to have any value. Her credit card debts were killing me.

At three in the morning our daughter was born. It was an easy childbirth, unlike Christopher's, which took almost seventeen hours. We named her Victoria. She was beautiful.

My father and Joan came for a visit that summer. It was the first time I had seen him in months. They only lived an hour and a half away, but I hated going down there. Joan didn't have one picture of Christopher in her house, so every Christmas I sent them a nice photo of him in a good frame just to spite her. They always ended up in the bottom drawer of an old chest in her hallway.

They were coming over on Sunday. Mariana wanted to barbecue. I went out and bought some spare ribs the night before so she could marinate them. That morning she was out of bed early cleaning the house from top to bottom. She handed me a brush and a bucket.

"Go outside and wash the windows," she said.

"Wash the windows? Are you out of your mind? They're not even dirty!"

"Just do it. I won't have your father visiting us with the house looking like this."

Just to appease her I scrubbed all the windows and the patio in back while she ran around the house in a panic with her mop and a bucketful of rags and assorted cleaning products. The house reeked of disinfectant by the time she was done.

We barely had time to wash ourselves when my father showed up. Every inch of the house had been washed and scrubbed. My father seemed impressed with the house. I don't think he expected it to be so big. He certainly didn't expect to see so much property, and gaped over the expansive lawn. Mariana gave them a tour of the house. Afterward, she and Joan went outside to look at the garden while my father and I talked in my office.

"Congratulations on the house. You've done well for yourself, Drew."

"All things considered, I've done pretty well," I replied.

"You know your grandmother is not doing very well," he said.

"I heard. Is she okay?"

"She's in good health, but her short-term memory is gone. She can remember things from years ago, but she can't remember what she did from one day to the next. I've been going up to see her quite often."

"Give her my love. When I get a chance I'll go up to visit."

"I'm going up there next week. I'll be meeting with John O'Connor," he added.

I froze. Something wasn't right, and I braced myself. "Oh, yeah? What about?" I asked.

"Well, your grandmother never did any estate planning. I'm going to try to salvage what's left of her money before it all gets eaten up by taxes."

He was lying. When it came to money my grandmother didn't fool around. She wasn't the kind of woman to sit on her money and never do anything with it.

"What do you mean by what's left of her money?" I asked.

"You know she has had a fulltime staff of nurses taking care of her the last year. All those expenses ate up most of her money,"

Again I didn't believe him. My grandmother had a nice

397

yearly income that she barely used—she never lived beyond her means. Home nursing care was expensive, but she had plenty of money and could afford it. I got the sense he was trying to find out how much I knew. Obviously he was going to start moving money around. Now was the time to throw my cards on the table.

"I speak to John O'Connor quite often too. He's my relationship manager."

"What do you mean, your relationship manager," my father said, laughing.

"I'm a private client," I replied, showing him my bank card. The words 'Private Clients Group' was stamped on the bottom in gold letters.

My father looked at it and handed it back to me. "Well, I'm not even a private client," he said.

Now I knew something was up.

"Membership has its privileges," I said.

"Oh, yeah? Like what," said my father.

"Nothing much. I just don't need to pay any fees, and I get a preferred rate on credit cards and things."

"Being a private client doesn't mean anything," my father said with a snort. "That's just something the bank did for you because of Grandma."

"Really? So I guess we're not getting as much as we thought."

"No. I'm only getting a million and a half. Aunt Gracie is getting another million. And Uncle Herman is getting a million. All the grandchildren will get 50,000 dollars."

"Is that right?" I asked. I felt my cheeks flush and the tips of my ears burned. "That's not what I was told by the bank."

"What did the bank tell you?" he asked. He shifted his stance nervously and cleared his throat. Obviously I knew more than he had hoped.

"They told me my name was on a big piece of Grandma's

money," I said.

"Who told you that?"

"Nick Presario did. After I got the loan," I replied.

"He's not you grandmother's banker. John O'Connor is!"

"He's affiliated with the Private Clients Group. I'm sure he knows something about it."

"He obviously confused you with me."

"I doubt it, Dad. Besides, they don't give a Private Clients account to just anyone. He was pretty specific about what he was saying."

His eyes squinted with rage, and his jaw tightened. "They were just extending you a favor because of your grandmother's wealth!"

"That's bullshit! Do you have any idea the terms of the loan? They didn't even check my credit! Banks don't do that unless you have money behind you. Grandma isn't responsible for the loan. I am!"

"Look, it's not your money and besides, it's none of your goddamn business!"

"Well, Dad, I might be inclined to agree with you if the bank hadn't made it my business!"

Mariana and Joan ran inside to see what was going on. For the first time in my life I could have killed my father. I had to restrain myself from picking up a heavy object and bludgeoning him to death. He felt the same way.

"What's going on?" asked Mariana. She could see how enraged we were. My father went outside with Joan, and Mariana shut the door of the office.

"Nothing is going on," I said. "I can't talk about it now."

"I can see the anger in your eyes. Don't tell me nothing is going on."

"I don't want to talk about it now!" I said.

"I can't believe you'd start a fight with you father after he drove all this way to see us!"

"What makes you think I was the one who started it?"

She stamped her foot on the floor. "Because I know what goes on in that crazy brain of yours. Don't you think I can see all the anger in you? You've lost all your friends, and now your own family doesn't want to talk to you. I'm the only person in your life who is still here. I try to understand you, but you are just too angry."

I looked at her in shock. It was the first time she had said anything to me that made even a lick of sense. She was right about my anger. It had destroyed a lot of friendships, and it was the main reason why I decided to work as an independent consultant. But she missed the bigger picture. She would never believe what my father was doing, or all the things he had done. For her, he was a charming, old man who didn't deserve my anger.

"Look, I'm going outside to start the barbecue. Come out when you are ready, but I don't want you to start fighting again. Okay?"

She left the room and I sat down for a moment to collect myself. Finally I went outside to join everyone on the patio. Mariana was busy barbecuing spareribs and corn on the cob. My father and Joan were sitting at our brand-new, teak picnic table that Mariana insisted she had to have. It cost me a fortune, but it looked good. Everyone sat at the table stiffly and tried to make small talk. Joan avoided any conversation with me.

Lunch was tense, and I did my best to be cordial. My father was better at it than I was. He once told me the one thing he disliked most about me was my manners. He might be right, but I always considered him to be a well-mannered prick.

After lunch Joan went inside to help Mariana with the dishes while we sat outside in the sun. Christopher was crawling around in the grass while Victoria napped in her basinet in the living room.

"You know your Seal Ring checks will be ending soon," he said to me after lunch.

"Thanks for reminding me, Dad."

"I was thinking of giving you back your shares."

"That's very generous of you. Did you ever resolve all those problems with the pollution in the ground?"

"Perhaps this is not a good time to talk about it," he said.

"Perhaps not."

My guess was that the problem was still there. I couldn't see why he'd give me back my shares in the company unless there was some sort of gain for him. I just didn't trust him. A few years after my father bought me out, those shares started producing dividends amounting to almost $700.00 per month. My father used my own money to buy me out. I never forgave him for that.

Joan came outside. "Are you ready? We'd better get going if we want to get home at a decent hour," she said.

They said goodbye and left as quickly as possible. Afterward Mariana and I had another fight. She wanted to know what my father and I were fighting about. I tried to explain to her what my father was doing. She didn't believe me. She didn't think my father was capable of any of the things I said he did. It became a major rift in our marriage. I just couldn't talk to her at all.

All this commotion about the money and our inheritance had ruined my concentration. Mariana said she was worried I would never be able to let it go. I was obsessed with stopping my father from doing anymore damage to my sisters and me. We had suffered enough. I had a long talk with Aunt Gracie about it.

"Look, Aunt Gracie. You were never around to see all that was happening in our family, but trust me when I tell you my father doesn't have our best interests at heart."

"Drew, your sisters all seemed to have gotten over it. Why can't you?"

"Gotten over it? How do you get over what we went through? And besides, none of us have really gotten over anything. Gretchen can barely function."

"Drew, I'm sorry you went through all this. But that doesn't change the way things are."

"Then I guess I won't be a millionaire after all."

"Most people aren't, Drew. But if there is anything I can do to help you and Mariana out, don't hesitate to call."

"Thanks Aunt Gracie. Take care."

I didn't believe anyone anymore. I had always been the bastard stepchild who could never do anything right. I believed my grandmother's bank before I believed my father and my aunt. But going to my grandmother would have been suicide. She would have been deeply offended if I asked her questions about her money.

Mariana and I continued to fight over it. She thought I was being paranoid and unreasonable. She had no idea how manipulative my father could be. By now the whole thing was out in the open.

My heart was breaking. I didn't know if I were doing the right thing anymore. One thing for sure—I was no longer afraid of my father, even if he were more powerful than I was. He could squash me whenever he wanted. I had to let it go. It was doubtful I would ever know the truth about what happened to my inheritance.

Chapter 16

The biggest event of the year for database programmers was coming up this September in San Diego. Mariana wanted to come, but it wasn't practical with the children. Besides, this wasn't going to be a vacation; I would be attending seminars most of the time. I looked forward to the time away from her and everything else that was going on in my life.

On Tuesday morning, the second day of the conference, I turned on my T.V. to catch the morning news. One of the towers of the World Trade Center was on fire. People were jumping from the top floors of the building to escape the inferno. I soon learned that a jet had slammed into the side of the tower. I watched in disbelief as another plane flew low over the horizon and slammed into the second tower. At first I thought I was watching a reenactment, but then realized what was happening: New York was under attack.

I ran downstairs to the hotel lobby. Several televisions had been set up and people were crowded around them. Moments later another plane slammed into the Pentagon, and then another crashed in Pennsylvania. We all watched together as the towers burned and collapsed. Never in my life would I have thought something so awful was possible.

I went back to my room and tried to get hold of Mariana. She couldn't stop crying.

"When are you coming home?" she asked.

"I don't know yet. All flights are cancelled. Do you know if Annie is okay?"

"Yes. Your father called. She saw the whole thing from her apartment."

"She must be shell-shocked. I'll give her a call. I'll let you know when I'm coming home when I have more information. Try not to watch too much T.V. It will only make you feel worse."

"I can't help it. I can't turn if off. How can people be so evil?" she asked.

"I don't know, Mariana. One thing for sure our country will never be the same. Things are different now. I'll give you a call later."

Getting home took more than a week. I had to drive all the way to L.A. to get a flight. When I got home things had changed more than I thought. I no longer cared about my father and his money. We never even spoke after the disaster. Worse, all my biggest clients cancelled their projects. Work started to dry up, and I was going broke. Mariana didn't want to hear it. She demanded that I continue giving her the same money she was accustomed to receiving.

"Mariana, I don't have any money," I tried to explain.

"You always have money!"

"Not anymore. I have no work. I'm going to have to go out and get a job."

"But you always said you had more work than you could handle."

"Not anymore. Nobody is doing any more development. The country is going into a recession. I have one project left that I'm finishing for a smaller client. After that, I don't know what's going to happen."

I sat in my office the next couple of weeks and made phone call after phone call. Work had just stopped. I began polishing my resume and started looking for a regular job. I was beginning to panic. My Seal Ring checks were going to stop in a couple of months, and I would have no more income. One morning I was sitting in my office when the phone rang.

404

"May I speak to Drew Smith, please," said a woman on the other end. The call sounded long distance.

"This is he."

"Drew. This is Alexandra Cavalletti. How are you?"

"Alexandra! My God! It's been twenty years! How did you get my number?"

"Classmates.com. Your website is in your profile. I found your number there. When I realized you lived in New York I called to see if you are okay."

"Yes, I'm fine. My God! This is quite a surprise. I can't believe it's you!"

"Is this a good time?"

"Yes, it's fine," I said. Mariana was at her kickboxing class for at least another hour.

"When I heard the news about the World Trade Center I got really worried. Your website said your business is based in New York City."

"Things are okay, Alexandra. It hurt my business pretty bad, but my friends and family are fine."

"Are you still writing, Drew?"

"I haven't written anything in years, Alexandra. I work in computers now."

"I'm sorry to hear that. You're a really good writer. Perhaps you could write in your spare time?"

"Maybe. I have a feeling I'm going to have plenty of it. What about you? The last time I saw you, you were hot and heavy with Gianfranco."

"That's a long story," she said. "We moved to Switzerland together and had four children."

"That's wonderful! How are things going?"

"We haven't been together for years, Drew. He moved back to Italy."

"I'm sorry. Are you divorced?"

"We were never married," she replied.

It didn't strike me as odd that she should have four children out of wedlock. It was just like her. "So, how do you like Switzerland?" I asked.

"Switzerland is wonderful for business, but I spend most of my time in Spain. The children all go to school here. I go to Switzerland to work when I need to."

"It sounds to me like you have done well for yourself. Where in Spain do you live?"

"On a little island off the coast of Barcelona called Ibiza. Have you heard of it?"

"Yes! I've heard it's beautiful. It's a real party place."

"Not where we live. We live out in the country. I have a beautiful view of the ocean."

"That's what you always wanted, Alexandra."

"What about you? Are you married?"

"Yes, I've been married about five years. I have a son, Christopher. He just turned three. And my daughter, Victoria, will be two soon."

"Congratulations, Drew. I'm happy for you."

"Tell me about your children."

"I have three daughters and a son. Lucia is the oldest. She just turned Twelve. Then comes Anna. She is ten. Paula is eight and Giuseppe is seven. They are very happy children."

"That's wonderful. Do they see their father at all?"

"No. I wouldn't want them to."

"Oh," was all I could muster, realizing this was an issue we probably shouldn't talk about just yet.

"Listen, Drew. This phone call is going to cost a fortune. Is the e-mail address on your website a good place to write you?"

"Yes. I would love to hear more about you. There is so

much to catch up on. It's been so many years. Can you send me some pictures?"

"I don't have too many, but I'll send you what I have."

She gave me her address and phone number in Spain.

Not more than twenty minutes after we hung up I received an e-mail from her. Attached were some pictures of the children in her garden. They were beautiful. They were a nice mix between her and Gianfranco. The house was big. She lived on a high bluff, overlooking the Mediterranean, with the emerald-colored sea in the background. It looked peaceful.

I wrote her what I had been through for the last twenty years. The writing was cathartic. I described in detail how loveless my marriage had become, and how materialistic Mariana was. It was the most writing I had done since college. The words just poured out of me, and the release felt good. I sent off my e-mail and went for a walk. Hearing from Alexandra revived all kinds of unexpected feelings. Was she involved with anyone?

The next morning she sent me her response. She compared Mariana to Gianfranco. Apparently after college they moved to Neuchatel and restored old buildings, turning them into rental properties. She did most of the work while Gianfranco reaped all the benefits. I wasn't surprised.

The final straw was when she decided to open a restaurant. She was pregnant with their fourth child, and he wasn't around to help. He was always off getting stoned with his friends. She told me she would run home in the middle of work to feed the kids while he was sleeping with another woman. Her family pleaded with him to take more responsibility, but he wouldn't. He couldn't deal with being a father and the fact that his girlfriend had become so successful. He was constantly getting into car accidents.

When she finally cut him off financially he went crazy. One night he held a gun to her head and threatened to kill her.

Reading those words tore my heart open. I knew there was something off about him, but I didn't think he was capable of all that. Her family offered him a large sum of money to get started somewhere else. He took the money and squandered it and then complained it wasn't enough. He finally left Switzerland and went back to Messina to live with his father. She said she hadn't seen him since and was afraid to because of the children.

She had another man in her life, but he didn't love her. She and her children lived a comfortable, easy life in Ibiza, and her biggest fear was losing what she had. Her e-mail really touched a nerve. What became of her mother and brother? I decided to call her later that morning when Mariana was out.

"Alexandra, I just finished reading your e-mail. I'm in shock! How did you manage to survive?"

"Things are not so bad anymore, Drew. I'm a very lucky woman. I have a beautiful house and wonderful, healthy children. We live quite well here, although I miss Italy."

"You can't go back?"

"No, there's too much sadness there for me now. I could never live in Rome after what happened with my mother and brother. If I were going to live anywhere I'd want to live in Taormina, but Gianfranco lives in Messina, which is not so far away. I'd be too afraid he'd find me and maybe hurt the children."

"What about your mother? How is she doing?"

"She's much worse, Drew. She's living in a home for poor people while my brother and his family are living like royalty."

"Can't you do anything for her? She's your mother, Alexandra."

"Drew, I can't. She has really destroyed a lot. I have no pity for her. If I brought her into my life it would just be too destructive. I have enough keeping my home together."

"I know how that feels, Alexandra. When my mother died

it was almost a relief. I took care of her at the end. I'm glad I did, but if I had children at the time it would have been a different story. It took a lot out of me."

"Drew, your e-mail really disturbed me. A lot of what you told me about Mariana reminded me of Gianfranco. All he cared about was having an easy, comfortable life. I worked and he took. That's what Mariana is doing to you. You need to put a stop to it."

"I've tried, Alexandra. I've put her on a budget, but she keeps applying for new credit cards and I keep paying them. It's killing me."

"Why can't she work?"

"She has the baby," I replied.

"Oh, please. I hate hearing that excuse. I had four children and I still worked. I've also managed to become very successful."

"Alexandra, not every woman can be like you."

"No, but everyone should try to pull their weight in life. I used to have a woman who worked for me. When I met her she was poor. Her husband had left her with two children and no money. She cleaned my house until she saved enough money to open her own business. She is doing well now. I respect people like that. I really hate people who do nothing but take."

"She takes, but she's not a bad woman. She's just materialistic. It's part of who she is."

"Drew, it's your marriage. People get married for all sorts of reasons. Some do it for comfort or security, others for love. You and I have a lot in common. We both got involved in relationships for the wrong reasons."

"Perhaps you are right, Alexandra. I can't even lie to myself anymore. I haven't been in love with Mariana for at least two years. I can't even bring myself to have sex with her anymore. The idea makes me sick."

"Oh, Drew. I'm so sorry. Nothing is worse than being in a

relationship like that. Can't you two try to work things out? Sometimes you can stay in a marriage as friends."

"Alexandra, the more I think about her the more I dislike her. We can't talk about anything. It's like we are from completely different planets. Just to keep the peace I give her money, but I don't have much more of that anymore."

"Have you talked to her about it?"

"I've tried, but everything turns into a big fight. At one point I tried to get her into marriage counseling, but she refused to go. She told me all the problems were my fault. I ended up going by myself."

She sighed heavily. "That's a cultural thing. Most people from South America are like that. Does she come from an educated family?"

"No. In fact, I don't think her mother knows how to read or write."

"It must be hard for you, Drew. How have you managed to handle it?"

"I've shut down, Alexandra. I concentrate on work and making money, but even that's going sour. Since September 11th all the work has dried up."

"It's the same thing in Switzerland. I know a lot of people who had to change careers or get regular jobs because the work has stopped."

"Has it affected you?"

"No, not really. People always need to rent apartments."

"What about your restaurant?"

"I closed that years ago. I made so much money with the restaurant, but the work got to be too much. It's never ending. What you wrote me about your father and your inheritance reminded me so much of my mother. It's scary how much we have in common."

"That's not over yet. I guess I'll never know the truth about all that until my grandmother dies. My father has done a lot of damage, Alexandra. He really broke my heart."

"Drew, it would be in your best interest to reconcile with him. He has all the power. You might not be able to stop him from taking your inheritance, but if he loves his grandchildren, he could really help them."

"You've gotten smarter over the years. Tell me about this guy you've been seeing."

"Sergio?" She sighed softly. "He's the most difficult man I've ever known. He lives in Taormina. I've been seeing him on and off for about five years. He's the only man I've ever wanted to marry, but he doesn't want me."

"Why not?"

"I don't know, Drew. He tells me he loves me, but when he comes to visit he gets angry if I don't pay enough attention to him. He tells me I'm raising my children all wrong. Once he came to visit and got so angry with me for taking a business call during dinner that we didn't talk for a month."

"Alexandra, he sounds like a real primadonna. What are you doing with someone like that? It doesn't sound like you at all."

"He is a primadonna, but he has some worthy qualities. He's very honest, and he has unswerving integrity."

"What does he do?"

"He's an editor. He's very famous in his field. He only works with the best writers."

"Another artist. At least this one is successful at it. Where did you meet him?"

"In Rome. His parents were friends with my mother. His father used to be quite famous. You've heard of *Bernulli* water?"

"Yes. That's who he is? Sergio Bernulli?"

"Yes, but he has nothing to do with that anymore. When his mother died his father remarried. He didn't take care of the business and things started going bad. When he died he left all his money to his new wife, and Sergio got nothing. He's quite sensitive about it."

"I don't blame him. It probably explains a lot of his behavior. Are you still in love with him?"

"I don't know anymore, Drew. I still love him, but it's been some time now since we've been together. It's foolish of me to hold onto him any longer."

"Maybe we can help each other, Alexandra. I need a vacation. Would it be all right if I come for a visit?"

"Drew, you are welcome any time. When were you thinking of coming?"

"I'm not sure yet. Let me make some arrangements and I'll get back to you. Maybe in a couple of weeks."

"Will you be bringing Mariana?"

"I don't think that's such a good idea. In fact, it's probably not a good idea I tell her where I'm going. It would cause too many problems."

"Drew, you are welcome to come visit, but I don't want to give you the wrong impression—"

"Don't worry, Alexandra. I just need to get away for awhile. It's been so many years since I've seen you. I can't wait to see your beautiful face again."

"Well, it's not so beautiful anymore. I've aged quite a bit, and having four children hasn't helped."

"Oh, please, Alexandra. You're scaring me."

Mariana pulled into the driveway. She got out and unloaded several large shopping bags.

"Mariana is home. I'd better get off the phone. I'll talk to you soon."

"Thank you for calling, Drew."

"Goodbye, Alexandra."

I went outside to see how much Mariana had spent.

"Macy's was having a sale," she said when she saw my face turn red. "And I saved another ten percent because I put it on my Macy's Card."

I rummaged through the bags. "Mariana, how much did you spend?"

"We needed new sheets, and the price was so good."

I finally found the receipt in the bag. She had spent almost $350.00 on the best sheets in stock. "Mariana we can't afford this!"

"With all the discounts I'm saving you money."

"It only applies if you can pay off the balance each month. The interest rates are killing me. You can't do this anymore!"

"But you love sleeping on good sheets," she said.

"Yes, but we don't need them. I told you we're almost broke. We need to spend only on necessities until the money starts coming in again."

"When is that going to be?"

"I don't know. Hopefully soon. I'm meeting with a new client in a couple of weeks."

I was telling a half-truth. I was going to meet with a new client, but it wasn't for another month. I needed to find an excuse to get away for awhile. Even if I wanted to go somewhere on my own, Mariana would never stand for it. As much as she complained about all my bad habits, she couldn't stand me having time for myself. She wasn't jealous; she knew I wouldn't cheat, but she couldn't handle not being a part of every aspect of my world.

I booked a flight to Barcelona for the following week. Alexandra graciously paid for the flight from Barcelona to Ibiza.

I told Mariana I was flying to San Francisco to spend a week helping write the software requirements for someone I had worked with before. She didn't complain, although she was nervous about me flying so soon after September 11th.

I was a nervous wreck the entire flight. I didn't know how I'd feel when I saw her. I had nearly forgotten her after so many years, but hearing her voice revived so many feelings I thought were lost forever.

Barcelona was much nicer than I thought. My connection didn't leave for another hour, and I wandered briefly around the city. People in Barcelona took their art seriously. A huge sculpture in the shape of big, red clothespin sat in the middle of an intersection, and various sculptures by prominent modern artists were sprinkled throughout the town. The town wasn't built up, but was very charming.

The plane ride to Ibiza took just over an hour. As we approached the island the azure color of the water stood out along the rocky shores. An old, medieval city, enclosed by an imposing wall, was on the northern part of the island. A tall, rugged peak rose up in the center of the island, ending at a huge television antenna. Winding roads weaved through the great bluffs that overlooked the water. In the higher areas, nestled in the rocks and trees, white-washed houses with softly curved arches and swimming pools overlooked the sea. I was certain Alexandra lived in one of them.

When the plane landed I went outside and saw Alexandra surrounded by her four children. She had aged quite a bit, but she still took my breath away. She didn't seem as tall as I remembered, but she was never that tall to begin with. Her hair, once so dark and long, was now cut shoulder length and streaked with gray. Little wrinkles surrounded her plump mouth and chocolate-brown eyes. She obviously spent a lot of time in the sun. Still thin and strong, she put her arms around me and gave me a gentle hug.

"Alexandra, you look even more beautiful now," I said.

"It's good to see you, Drew. These are my children," she said, gesturing to a row of innocent-looking creatures. One by one we were introduced. They were all very well-mannered and full of smiles. Alexandra had raised them well. The children helped carry my bags as we walked to her car, a Mercedes station wagon. All her children spoke French. The school they attended was French, even though they were living in Spain. Alexandra spoke to them in Italian, but they always replied in French. It was a blessing I understood both languages, although I had forgotten so much.

"The house is not far," she said.

We drove down a long, straight road away from town, and then drove up a winding road through the bluffs. Most of the houses were obscured from view through the tall pine trees and security fences. The children sang together in the back. It was a tender moment, and I sat back and smiled. We came to a small village with a single road passing through it. I could see the ocean. The outline of a tiny island glistened in the horizon. The road made a sharp, right turn and headed toward an old monastery on a hill.

"One of these days that's where I'm going to live," she said.

"I don't think so, Alexandra. Not if I can help it." She gave me a hint of a smile. To our right was a small seafood restaurant.

"This place is not very good, but it's useful," she said.

We continued until the pavement ended. At the end of the road, at the last gate to the left, was the entrance to her driveway. Her son, Giuseppe, whom she called Papi, popped out of the back and opened the wooden gate. A small gazebo overlooked the edge of the bluff. Further down was the main house. The

415

children all got out of the car and ran down the driveway before us. We followed behind them as they laughed and yelled. Pine needles blanketed the stones in the driveway. The place had a cool, tranquil feeling.

The house was bigger than I expected. The spacious garden was well-tended by Alexandra and her children. It was her hobby. A large swimming pool was in front of the house, and to the side was a nice yard with an old, twisted tree. It looked as though it would topple at any moment. Alexandra took my arm and led me down a flight of stone steps next to the pool. She took me to the edge of the property to show me the *miradors*. Each afforded a different view of the sea. I was speechless at the amazing beauty. The beach was far below us, but the water was everywhere.

"Let me show you the house," she said. She took my arm and we headed up the hill. Underneath the pool were the laundry and a separate room. "Nico lives in there," she said.

"Who is Nico?"

"He's one of my *au-pairs*. He helps with the driving and takes care of the property."

The front porch, made with terracotta tiles, had a round, glass table with comfortable, wicker chairs on it. Several large pots filled with white and purple daisies sat on either side of the front door.

She led me inside and we were greeted by her help. Two *au-pairs* helped with the children, and another young girl did the cleaning and helped in the kitchen.

"You will be staying in Lucia's room," said Alexandra. She led me down a long corridor past the dining room toward the back of the house. The room nearest the garage was where I would be staying. Lucia had picked fresh flowers for me and put them on the nightstand. I set down my bags and looked at the five of them. They smiled back at me. Her children seemed so curious about me. How much did they know? According to Alexandra she told them everything.

Alexandra showed me around the rest of the house. Her bedroom was round and the bed had been molded into the wall from the same cement-like materials as the rest of the house. The room had no sharp edges. A French window opened onto a little porch that overlooked the sea. On the far wall was a small fireplace.

The room next to her bedroom had been made into an office. Huge windows afforded a panoramic view of the sea. Next to that room was the bathroom. It was not as impressive as the rest of the house but it was nice. Off to the side was a large, walk-in closet.

On top of her bureau I noticed a photograph of a stern-looking man.

"Who is that?" I asked.

"That's Sergio," she said.

"Oh!" I stared at the photo a few moments longer, trying to get an idea of what sort of man he was. Tall and thin with dark, piercing eyes, he wore a pair of pleated trousers and a button-down shirt. He looked so serious.

Night was falling, and a purplish haze hung in the horizon. It was colder than I expected, and I realized I didn't bring proper clothes.

"You must be hungry," said Alexandra. "We're going out tonight."

"Would it be okay if I took a shower? I've been on planes all day. I won't be long."

"Take your time," she said. "I'll show you where the shower is."

The shower felt good, and I changed into something casual yet smart. Alexandra took us to the "useful" restaurant down the road. The children asked endless questions about where I was from and how we met.

"I knew your mother when she was a little girl," I told them.

"My mother said you were in love when you were young," said Papi, grinning at us and laughing.

"It's true. Your mother was my first love," I answered. I expected Alexandra to be a little embarrassed, but she wasn't.

"Did you kiss my mother when she was young?" he asked, teasing us.

"Papi, *non devi fare cosi*," said Alexandra.

"It's okay, Alexandra. It brings back many fond memories. So much has happened since we were young. I'm really happy you've done so well for yourself. How did you manage to do it?"

"Well," she said, sweeping back her hair, "In the beginning it was difficult. When we moved to Switzerland we had almost no money. I got the idea to renovate old houses and turn them into apartments. I borrowed some money from my mother and went to a bank to get a loan. Once we got the loan I used that to go to another bank and get another one."

"Isn't that illegal?"

"Not in Switzerland. It's just really risky. We bought two houses. It was very stressful in the beginning because we were under so much pressure to payback the loans. To make matters worse, I couldn't get Gianfranco to do any work. He would not show up for appointments, and he spent almost everything we had. He thought it perfectly okay to sleep until 10:00 am when we had workmen waiting to start their jobs. We nearly went bankrupt a couple of times."

"Alexandra, I never understood how you could end up with a loser like him. Even when I met him in Padova I knew what a schmuck he was."

She sighed and put her elbows on the table. "Drew, my spirit was so broken by all that I went through I just went to the first friendly face that would accept me. In the beginning we had a lot of fun. Things started to go really bad after Lucia was born. It really isn't so hard to explain. If you asked yourself why you married Mariana you'd probably tell me something similar."

I nodded. "It's true. I had been through so many bad relationships and my spirit was so badly battered I ended up with Mariana because I never thought I'd meet anyone and I didn't want to be alone. It's the biggest mistake I've ever made, and I've made a few."

"Yes, but you can correct it if that's what you really want. There will be consequences because of your children. It's a shame you didn't realize all this before you had children together. You should really think about trying to work things out."

I shook my head and sighed. "Alexandra, I can't. The thought of staying with her makes me sick. The marriage is over. Even the marriage counselor told me to get out of the marriage. I didn't want to accept it at first but I knew he was right. Mariana and I have nothing in common and her family treats me like dirt."

"Gianfranco's family did the same to me," said Alexandra. "They would come to visit and were always so rude. I've really come to appreciate my upbringing. The older I get the more traditional I've become. I am very traditional and Italian at heart. The thought of my children being exposed to Gianfranco's family and all their bad manners makes me glad we're not together anymore."

"Given how you feel about manners, I'm surprised you would tolerate someone like Sergio. His antics seem very ill-mannered."

"He's not really. He just has a bad temper. You described him perfectly when you called him a primadonna, but he's very aristocratic. He's almost too formal, and I don't think it would be good for the children, even though I know he loves them. He's a very difficult man, but the older I get the more understanding I become."

Who was this man who had her so twisted up? He seemed so self-absorbed and temperamental. I never understand why she loved the men she did, especially because of the way I loved her. It didn't seem fair.

The children ate their fish happily while Alexandra and I talked. It was late, and the children had to be at school tomorrow, so we went home and put them to bed. Each of them had drawn pictures for me with crayons and put them on my pillow. I leafed through them and smiled. Alexandra wished me goodnight and went upstairs. I lay on my bed and watched the thick, bright stars through my window and realized I was falling in love with her all over again.

I woke up rather late the next morning to the sound of Alexandra pounding away on her keyboard. She typed quickly. Her *au-pair* offered me a cappuccino when I finally emerged from my bedroom. Alexandra came downstairs. She was wrapped in a soft, cotton bathrobe that covered a silky, white nightgown.

"I was waiting for you to get up to have breakfast with you," she said.

"You didn't have to wait, Alexandra."

"*Voulez-vous un cappuccino, Signora?*" asked her au-pair.

"*Oui, Merci*, Claire," she replied.

"How many languages are spoken in this house?" I asked.

"It depends who's around. The maid speaks Spanish. She's from the island. Nico is from Argentina. He speaks some English, but he mostly speaks Spanish. The children speak French with me and Claire, and Spanish with Nico. I speak Italian to the children, even if they refuse to speak it back to me. It gets a little

420

confusing at times. How's your Spanish?"

"It's good. I learned quite a bit with Mariana and her family, although the accent is different here."

"Here they speak Catalan. It's a mixture between French, Spanish, and a few other languages. My Spanish teacher taught me a little bit, but it's a difficult language to learn."

Alexandra put together a plate of chocolates and cookies and we took our cappuccinos out to the porch. It was a beautiful day, and she put her feet up on the chair next to mine and turned her face to the sun. Her toes were short and stubby, even if her legs were nice. She had short fingers and strong hands, and endless amounts of energy, even if she seemed relaxed. I liked the gray in her hair; she looked distinguished.

"Eventually I am going to have to move off this island," she said, biting into a piece of chocolate.

"Why?"

"There are no good schools here, and I need to put down some roots for the children."

"What about Switzerland?"

"It's too cold. It's a wonderful place for making money, but I want to live somewhere warm. I've been thinking about the south of France."

"Alexandra, why don't you just go back to Italy? There are other places besides Rome and Taormina."

She shook her head and frowned. "I can't go back, Drew. I'd be too afraid for the children. There are two things I'll never forgive Sergio for: he never helped me move back to Italy, and he never gave me children. He could have protected me and the children from Gianfranco, but he just didn't want to."

"What the hell do you want more children for? Four is not enough?"

"I love children, Drew. You know, Sergio always said that

he wanted to be a great builder, but he has built nothing with his life. Nothing. No children, no love, nothing. He will be quite alone. Nobody can stay with him because he is so difficult. So many women have fallen in love with him and found he was just too difficult to stay with. One woman, a very well-know journalist in Italy, was so heart-broken and angry with him she wrote a book about him. It was very accurate too."

"When was the last time you saw him?"

"It's been several months," she said. "He still writes and calls occasionally. But his e-mails are as difficult as he is."

"Why are you so in love with a man who makes your life miserable?" I asked. It was a rhetorical question. I already knew the answer.

"Because when you love you just love. You can't force it as much as you can stop it."

In a way I felt bad for her. She was feeling the way I felt for the longest time.

"What do you want to do today, Drew?"

"I'm at your disposal, Alexandra. I'd like to see some of your enchanting Island."

"Well, let me get dressed, and I'll take you to see some of the nicer beaches. I'm taking you to lunch at my favorite *chiringuito*. Have you ever been to one?"

"No. What is it?"

"In Ibiza people will put some tables and chairs on the beach and open a restaurant right there in the sand. They make the most wonderful seafood. Have you ever had *paella*?"

"No," I replied again.

"It's different seafood stir-fried in a skillet with rice. It's very popular here. You'll enjoy it. Let me get dressed and we'll get going," she said, getting up.

Her robe flowed behind her. She looked so elegant now.

Although some may argue she hadn't aged very well, I could see beyond her wrinkles. Her eyes were still filled with passion, if not a little more sadness than before. She was the most beautiful woman I had ever known.

A young man in his early twenties came walking down the driveway with a newspaper and a shopping bag. "Hello, my name is Nico," he said. His English wasn't bad; it was better than my Spanish.

"Nice to meet you, Nico. My name is Drew," I said, shaking his hand. He put the paper and bag in the kitchen, and then went outside. I watched him as he skimmed the leaves from the pool. He seemed like an amiable young man.

Alexandra came downstairs in a pair of jeans and t-shirt. She talked with Nico in the garden for several minutes, giving him his chores for the day. It took several minutes, and Nico fidgeted impatiently throughout the conversation. She finally finished and we headed toward the car.

"Would you like to drive?" she asked, handing me the keys.

"I'd love to," I replied.

Driving her Mercedes was such a pleasure, but the car was out of gas.

"Alexandra. We'd better get to a gas station quickly."

"Damn, Nico!" she said. "He always does this. He never tells me when the car needs gas, and then brings it home when it's almost empty. He's really irresponsible."

"Tell him not to do it anymore."

"I've talked to him about it several times, but he doesn't seem to listen. You know once he ran out of gas and walked all the way back home to tell me what happened. I had to take a cab to get gas for the car. I was really angry."

I shook my head and frowned. "Alexandra, it's unacceptable that he should do that. You need to be firm with him. What if there were an emergency with your children and you can't use the car because there is no gas?"

"You are right. I'll talk to him again later."

We found a gas station just in time. The car was sputtering as I drove up to the pump. After filling the tank, Alexandra took me around the island to her favorite places. The roads in Ibiza were always questionable—one never knew from day to day whether a road would still be there or not. A good storm could take a paved road and turn it to mud. The roads leading down to the beach were always made of dirt. The beaches Alexandra showed me were rocky with small stretches of sand. Few people were on the beach; it was still too cold for most tourists.

Later that day she took me down a long, dirt road to a little shack on the beach for lunch.

"So, this is a *chiringuito?*" I asked.

"Yes, every year a new one pops up. This one has been here for a while. It's one of my favorites."

She ordered lunch for us. The waiter brought a basket of bread with a garlic dip. It was delicious. Lunch was served in a cast-iron skillet filled with seafood and rice. The water was not more than twenty yards from where we were sitting. Although still winter, the sun was warm. Alexandra and I talked about how much she loved it here, and what a shame it was she would have to move.

"Are you still in touch with anyone from school?" I asked.

"Yes. Laurence and I have remained friends. She lives in Sweden with her husband and children. What about you?"

"I've lost touch with just about everyone. Through the years I never stopped thinking about Axel, and I often wonder what happened to him. You remember him, don't you?"

"Of course I do. You were so upset he never wrote you back. Did you ever find out what happened to him?" she asked.

"Nope. He just disappeared."

"I'll bet you could find him again if you tried."

"I would love to find Axel again," I said. "He was the closest thing I ever had to a brother."

After lunch we went to go pick up the children. The school was down a small, dirt lane off the main road just outside of town. The children were playing in the school yard with several others. We gathered them up and took them home. The girls skipped around in the yard together while Papi played football with Nico in the grass by the pool. I sat on the front porch and watched. Nico was quite good at the game, and was patient about teaching Papi proper footwork.

That night the children were fed in the kitchen by themselves, and Alexandra took me out to dinner. We went to a small place out in the country. Only one other couple was there. Although not her favorite, I found the restaurant to be charming. In the corner a large fireplace burned driftwood from the beach, and the food was good. We sat next to the fire after dinner and shared a bottle of wine.

"Alexandra, did Gianfranco really try to kill you?"

"I don't know, Drew. He was desperate and afraid of being alone. He had no education or skills. When we first split up he said he didn't know how he'd survive. I told him to go get a job waiting tables."

"Did he?"

"No. He grew a ponytail and calls himself an artist. My lawyer told me he sold the last house he owned. It's a shame. He had four in his name. If he had kept them he would have had a nice income, but he sold them just so he could have fast money."

"How many properties do you have?"

"Twenty. I also own a couple of office buildings and four parking lots. The parking lots are in the children's names."

I was shocked. I would never ask her how much she was worth, but it was obvious she was a millionaire several times over.

I shook my head. "Jesus, Alexandra, you've built a lot. You must be really proud of yourself."

"I've done well, and I'm lucky to have such a comfortable life. I've always wanted to be a great builder. My father was a great builder. Some people build, other people destroy. Gianfranco and my mother have destroyed a lot."

"Your father would be proud of you, Alexandra. If he is watching I know he is proud."

"Thank you, Drew. You are so sweet," she said, squeezing my hand. "You know, the biggest difference between you and Sergio is that you are so sweet and he is so harsh. He says he loves me but I don't why he would say that when he's so critical all the time."

"Alexandra, it sounds to me like your relationship with him is over. You need to move on."

"Yes, I know you are right, Drew. But it's such a shame. He threw away so much love. It's a waste, really."

"To squander love is always a waste. True love happens maybe once or twice a lifetime. Beyond that it's just about filling in the blanks," I said, topping off our glasses.

"You're right. Besides you, Sergio and Gianfranco, there haven't been any other men in my life."

"Really? Well, to be honest with you, Alexandra, I never fell out of love with you. I still love you like I loved you when I was sixteen."

Alexandra pursed her lips slightly and cocked her head. Her eyes were moist with tenderness, and I didn't know what to do with myself. I wanted her so badly, but this was not the time.

She paid the check and we went home, both a little drunk. Alexandra checked in on her children. We stood in the kitchen

426

and drank some water before bed. She mentioned something about being exhausted and started upstairs. Without thinking I grabbed her arm and kissed her. The kiss was spontaneous and passionate. She kissed me back.

"Drew, it's been so long since I've been with another man besides Sergio. I don't know if I can," she said.

I knew she could. I knew her body well, even if it had been twenty years. I put my hand between her legs and caressed her. She took me upstairs. She stood in front of her bed and let me undress her. Her body was still so beautiful. Her breasts were not as full and firm as I remembered, but that was to be expected after four children. We made love furiously most of the night. Afterward we curled up together under her duvet and fell asleep.

The next morning I felt her stir. It was a cloudy, cold day. She turned toward me and kissed me the way she used to do when we were younger. Funny how some habits never changed.

"I don't remember you being so good in bed," she told me playfully the next morning.

"I've had some good teachers over the years."

"Well! Good for you," she said.

"I would have hoped it was good for you as well!" I said, teasing her.

"It was amazing," she said, kissing me.

"Really?"

"Unbelievable," she said.

"Did Sergio please you the way I do?" I asked.

"Sergio is a great lover, but he doesn't come close to you. He considers himself such a great kisser, but his kisses are hard like he is. Yours are so soft. You know, I used to think about the softness of your lips at times."

"Really?"

"Yes. And you are very comfortable. When we fell asleep

together last night I woke up in your arms because I felt so comfortable. You cuddle so well. I used to have to chase Sergio around the bed."

"He doesn't sound very affectionate."

"He is in his own way. But he doesn't have your tenderness. If I could just take the two of you and put you together I would have the perfect man."

I was beginning to hate this man. She went downstairs to see her children off to school, and I waited for her in bed. Sergio's picture stared at me from across the room. His ghost hung over me like a dark cloud, but I was determined she would forget about him while we were together.

After several minutes the voices of the children disappeared. Alexandra thudded up the stairs, carrying a tray filled with coffee, biscuits, chocolate and fresh-squeezed orange juice. She set the tray on the bed and took off her robe. We sat naked together, drinking coffee and eating.

When we were done I decided to show her what twenty years of experience had taught me. I went down on her so passionately I thought she was going to pass out. When I thought she had enough I got up to go to the bathroom. She was still in the throes of her orgasm when I was done. I watched from the foot of the bed in amazement as she lay on her side and moaned into a pillow. I never had that effect on a woman before.

She rolled onto her back and threw the pillow at me. "You bastard!" she said.

I laughed. I still had at least two more orgasms left in me and got back into bed and made love to her until lunch. Exhausted, we took a leisurely bath together and finally went downstairs. Alexandra looked satisfied and happy. Her skin glowed and we giggled like school kids. Her staff didn't know what to say. I was starving. Alexandra made me a sandwich.

"Will you be getting the children?" asked Nico.

"Would you mind picking them up for me?" asked Alexandra.

"It's past 3:00," said Nico.

"I'm aware of the time," said Alexandra.

I laughed. Nico had a subtle sense of humor, although I don't think Alexandra appreciated it. I ate my sandwich happily while Alexandra talked with her staff. She had bragged to me about what a great lover Sergio was, but after last night and today I had ruined her in bed for him.

When the children got home they sensed something was different, although they were not sure what. We thought it best not to say anything, even if we couldn't help our actions. The way we looked at each other, and the subtle caresses we made when we brushed against each other spoke volumes. The children watched us like hawks, wondering what was going on. The only other man in their lives besides their father was Sergio, even if they hadn't seen him in months.

Alexandra took me out to dinner again. This time we went to a small restaurant in the center of town. Finding parking was difficult, and I could imagine what it was like in the summertime. Alexandra said you couldn't get a cab if you tried in the middle of the busy season. Throughout the entire evening we stared into each other's eyes with tenderness.

"Drew, I'm falling in love with you," she said.

I nearly started to cry. All those years of lovelessness had taken their toll. Alexandra was the only real tenderness left from my youth. Being here with her like this was like a dream come true.

"You were always in my heart, Alexandra. There were times when I would look at our year book from *Ecole des Roches* and *Prés Fleuris* and stop at your picture and wonder how you were. It was hard to let you go."

"I'm so sorry, Drew," she said, taking my hand. "We have been through so much, haven't we? It's amazing we survived."

"I think my battles have just begun. This stuff with my father really broke my heart."

She shook her head and frowned. "Drew, how do you know your father is trying to take your inheritance?"

"I don't know for sure. I only know what the bank told me. It's an issue of trust. You know for years after I finished college I really hoped I could work at the factory with my father. He kept promising me a job but he never delivered. He told me the partners had made a decision years ago that the families wouldn't work at the factory. But all the other partners' sons were working there."

"Why would you want to work there anyway after all you've been through with him?" she asked.

I sighed heavily. "I don't know. Approval? I loved him, and I thought we could have a relationship. Anyway, I stopped trying when he told me the partners never made provisions for their retirement, and that if I bought out his partnership I could work there."

"How would you pay for it?" she asked, laughing. Only Alexandra could see the humor in it.

"Well, that's the good part. He said he'd take it out of my salary."

"Oh, so you'd work for nothing so you could finance your father's golden years," she said, shaking her head.

"Exactly. But that's not all. It goes on and on. I just don't trust him. I never did. I feel he swindled me out of my shares of the company."

She nodded. "I remember you wrote me about that. He never lied to you. You sold your shares willingly."

"Yeah, but I feel like he took advantage of my trust. He

430

had to know how much that real estate was going to be worth. All my life I've felt as though I had to protect myself from him."

"It reminds me so much of my mother. You know, I am taking both her and my brother to court in Rome this summer."

"Court? Why?"

"Because it's not right that my brother should get everything. Sergio talked me into doing it for the children."

"I don't know if that's such a good idea, Alexandra. You have plenty. Can't you just walk away and be happy?"

"It's a matter of principle," she said. "Both she and my brother have destroyed so much, and it's not right his children should get everything."

That night I followed Alexandra up to her room. She and I got in bed together. It was a cool, clear night, and the full moon hung over the sea and illuminated the bedroom with an eerie, incandescent glow. Alexandra got on top of me. She looked so pretty in the moonlight.

"Would you consider having a child with me?" she asked.

"Are you serious?"

"Yes."

"You know how much I love you, Alexandra. I think we would have a beautiful child together. But don't you think we should wait a bit?"

"I don't have a lot of time, Drew. I am forty-four years old. It won't be long before nature decides for me."

"It would be complicated. I already have two babies, and you have your children." I said.

"We could work it out. It wouldn't be that difficult. You could move here, or I could come to the States."

"You would do that?"

"Yes, I think it would be good for the children."

"All right, when did you want to start trying?" I asked.

"How about now," she said, slipping out of her nightgown. We made love gently in the moonlight. For me it was almost a religious experience. I had never felt so wonderful. Being with her it was unlike any other woman I had ever been with. Something about us seemed to click so well. I had never been so deeply in love.

The rest of that week Alexandra took me all around the island. We made love at least three or four times a day. Sometimes she would throw a blanket in the back of the car and drive to a deserted beach where we would sleep naked in the sun. It was her favorite pastime. I have to admit, I loved it too, especially after sex. But what I liked most was when we woke up in each other's arms. The first thing we did when we woke up together was have sex.

Later that week, Alexandra and I sat in her office. Her children were playing at our feet with her jewelry. She kept it in a small safe in the back of her closet, but the safe was not very secure. It was made of thin sheet-metal and could easily be compromised. She usually hid her jewelry when she left the island. Most of it was handmade from the highest quality gold and precious stones. She designed most of it herself. A jewelry maker she worked with in Messina did excellent work. Her children were draped with gold necklaces and diamond rings the size of acorns.

I lay back on the couch and watched her children play among her jewelry. Alexandra picked up each piece one at a time and draped them on my chest, telling me the story behind each one. She picked up a set of gold bracelets that were embedded with multicolored stones in a very handsome design.

"These stones are not worth much, but when I was working in the restaurant an American woman saw me wearing this set and offered me 25,000 dollars for it."

"You're kidding! Why didn't you sell them?"

"I did! And then I had some more made!"

I laughed. Alexandra had an amazing talent for making money. She told me she spent a year buying and selling corporate bonds and made a small fortune. She said there were thousands of ways to make money.

"Alexandra, all this has to be worth almost a million dollars. Shouldn't you keep it in a more secure place?"

"I don't trust the banks in Spain, and this safe is fine for when we are here."

"Can't you get something more secure?"

"Not in Ibiza. Maybe somewhere else, but I am not so worried. I've never had a problem." Alexandra smiled at me and pulled a little necklace from the bottom of the pile. "Do you remember this?" she asked.

"Oh, my God! That's the locket I gave you when we were fifteen. I can't believe you still have it!"

"I still wear it sometimes," she said.

I opened it up and read the inscription: *Ti amerò sempre –* Drew.

"Can I put it on you?" I asked.

"Sure," she said.

I got on my knees and placed the locket around her neck. "Words well spoken that still remain true," I said, kissing her gently.

She kissed me back and her children all giggled. That weekend the children came upstairs and found me in bed with their mother. Each of them reacted differently, and the girls demanded a conference straight away. I could hear them talking in the kitchen.

"Is he going to be our father?" asked Paula.

"It's too early to say," answered Alexandra.

"What about Sergio?" asked Papi.

"Sergio and I are friends," she answered.

433

"Don't worry, Mama. I won't tell him," said Papi.

"Well, thank you, Papi," said Alexandra, laughing.

"Are you in love with him?" asked Paula.

"I love him, but I don't know yet if I'm in love." An honest answer, but not the one I wanted to hear.

"Well, if you are not, then I think it's disgusting," said Paula. I laughed. She was a real firecracker. Funny the way children see things in black and white.

Alexandra and I were leaving the island on the same day. She and the children were going to go to Switzerland so she could take care of some business. Although the children were going to lose a week of school, she never went anywhere without them. She had a morbid fear of flying and decided that if the plane was going to go down, she wanted her children with her so they would not have to be alone.

She and I had talked about her fear one night. The children hated being pulled out of school whenever she needed to travel, but according to her, if she died, Gianfranco would get custody of the children and all of their money. The last thing she wanted was for that to happen. She said that the only way to protect them was to get married. Sergio had asked her to marry him on a couple of occasions, but she said his proposals were half-hearted attempts over the phone. She wanted to be courted properly. I didn't understand their relationship at all.

Alexandra decided she wanted to drive to Switzerland. A ferry left the island in the evening and arrived in Barcelona the next day. Before departing she gave me all her jewelry in a plastic garbage bag.

"Drew, could you please find a place in the garden and bury this for me?"

"Will it be okay like that?"

"Yes, it will be fine," she said.

We didn't have a lot of time. The boat was leaving soon and the children hadn't finished packing. I found a place in the garden where I thought the ground was soft and began digging. The bag was big and the hole had to be fairly deep. Nico came outside to see what I was doing. It must have looked as though I was burying a body or something. Having seen more than he thought he should, he went back inside. I covered the hole and spread some pine needles on top to make it look natural. I felt a little ridiculous burying all her jewelry in her back yard, but she insisted that's what all Italian women did.

Alexandra drove like a maniac down to the harbor. We managed to get onboard with seconds to spare. Nico and the maid stayed behind to take care of the house, and Claire took a plane to Switzerland to spend some time with her family before rejoining Alexandra and the children.

She had booked two cabins: one for us and one for the children. Papi did not want to sleep with his sisters, and he insisted on sleeping in our cabin.

"No, Papi. Sleep with your sisters tonight," Alexandra said.

"No! I don't want to sleep with them!" he yelled.

"It's okay, Alexandra. He can stay with us." I felt bad for him. He was the youngest in a family of headstrong women. How he managed to hold his own at all was beyond me. He did very well, even if he acted out quite a bit. He mostly took out his frustration on poor Claire by never listening to her. I could see her frustration, as well as Papi's. He ran next door to get his suitcase.

"You know, he really needs a father figure," I said.

"Yes, well, he has a lot of friends at school, and Nico spends a lot of time with him."

"He needs someone who can teach him how to be a man. Nico is an *au-pair*. He's really not a proper father for him."

"I was really hoping Sergio could have been their father, but the more I think about it I realize he's just too harsh. Children are like small animals; they need tenderness."

"Like me?" I asked, teasing her.

"You are very tender," she said, stroking my hair. "My only problem with you is that you are a little too *sauvage*."

"*Sauvage*? What do you mean *sauvage*?"

"Your manners," she said. "You are little too rough for me."

I felt as though I had been slapped across the face, especially after the wonderful time we spent together.

"Manners can be improved, and besides, I've had a pretty rough life."

"Manners are an attitude. It's part of who you are. Either you are refined or your not," she said.

"What the hell are you talking about?"

"I'm not sure if it's the difference in our cultures or you are just not aware of what you are doing, but even my children mentioned your bad manners."

"Can you be a little more specific?"

"Yes. When we were at dinner the other night you poured yourself some water before offering any to Lucia or me. You were at a table with two ladies. You always help the women before yourself."

"It was an oversight, Alexandra. I can certainly improve my table manners."

"It's not just that, Drew. It's a question of sensitivity. Good manners mean being sensitive towards another person."

"I'm always sensitive towards others!"

"Yes, you are sensitive, but you lack the refinement I look for in a man."

"Are you saying this is a deal breaker?" I asked.

"No. I am saying that this could be a problem for me."

I breathed a sigh of relief. "Well, Alexandra, I'll do what I can to improve my manners, but you have to realize even though I understand what good manners are, my world was all about survival when I was growing up."

"This is what I am talking about, Drew. When I was with Gianfranco I put up with all his bad manners because I had been cast out of my family and everything I loved. But I had been brought up with good manners; it's part of who I am."

"Fine, Alexandra. I will work on my manners, and you will help. Believe it or not I've always felt that my lack of manners has held me back in many ways. My father once told me that one of the things he disapproved of the most were my lack of manners."

"What can I do to help?" she asked.

"Tell me when I am not following proper etiquette."

"All right, but just as long as you won't be defensive when I correct you."

"I won't be defensive, but try to be gentle. There is no need to belittle me."

That night Papi went to sleep beneath our bunk. Alexandra and I slept in the one above him. He complained that if we had sex the bed might collapse on him, but I was so shaken by our conversation sex was the last thing on my mind. I held Alexandra in my arms and wondered what was going to happen between us. Before falling asleep, I asked her if she loved me.

"I am not in love. I need more time to figure out how I feel. I don't know if I can get Sergio out of my heart. I still love him very much. How would you feel if I went to visit him one last time just to find out if we can actually make our relationship work?"

"How would I feel? I would feel terrible, but I wouldn't try to stop you either. If that's what you really want there's nothing I

437

can say or do to stop you anyway."

"I don't know if he'll even have me," she said.

"Then you are wasting your time, Alexandra. Do you think you are pregnant?" I asked.

"I don't know. Maybe."

"We had a lot of unprotected sex. It wouldn't surprise me," I said, turning away.

She put her arms around me and held me close. "I will see my doctor when I get to Switzerland. We need to talk more about this."

"Do you still want to have a baby?" I asked.

"Yes, I think so."

Now I was confused. Why would she want my baby if she didn't love me? I fell asleep with a huge lump in my throat. It had been a wonderful week until now. Alexandra really rattled me, and on top of everything else I dreaded going home and having to deal with Mariana. I knew for sure I couldn't stay married to her anymore. I woke up that night frightened and upset.

"Drew, what's the matter?" asked Alexandra, sitting up in bed.

"I think my world is coming apart," I said. "I know my marriage is over, and everything I have built is ashes."

"Drew, you have to be strong. Mariana takes. She's a real bitch. You don't need that. Just get out and start over."

"I'm going to get reamed on this one," I said.

"Only if you let her. You have to show her who the boss is. That's what I did with Gianfranco. I simply cut him off and kicked him out of my life."

"It's different when you are married. And she has two small children. I feel so guilty about what I'm doing to my family."

"You can't think of it like that. Mariana is a bitch. All she cares about is money, but she could care less about how hard you

438

have worked for it. All she does is take. If you loved her it would be different, but it's obvious you don't. So you have to take care of yourself."

"I don't know, Alexandra. My whole world is spinning apart right now. I can't think straight."

She held me close. "It's okay, Drew," she said, kissing me. "Everything is going to be fine. You just need to be strong."

We made love gently and quietly to not wake up Papi. In the morning, we had a quick breakfast in Barcelona, and then Alexandra dropped me at the airport. Our goodbye was brief, and as I walked to my terminal I didn't know where I stood with her. It seemed I always felt that way with her.

I knew something was wrong as soon as I got home. Mariana was standing in the kitchen washing dishes. Her face turned scarlet when I walked through the door.

"How was your business trip?" she asked.

"It was good," I said. "I got a lot done."

"I'll bet. So who is Alexandra?"

I knew I'd been had, and decided it was best to tell the truth.

"She's an old friend. I've known her since I was fifteen. How do you know about her?"

"I have my ways," she said.

"What ways?"

"I read your e-mail."

I panicked. I locked my computer before I left. She must have known my password, but I don't remember ever giving it to her.

"Listen, Mariana, whatever you're thinking I want you to know that she and I are good friends."

"Oh, bullshit, Drew! From what I read you two are already in love. So, are you in love with her?"

439

"Yes, I am. I've been in love with her all my life."

She folded the dishtowel and hung it on the oven door. "Well then, I guess the marriage is over," she said.

"It's been over for a long time, Mariana. I can't live like this anymore."

"Fine, then you need to move out."

"I will, Mariana. Tomorrow I am going to see my lawyer and get a separation agreement."

Mariana went upstairs and shut the bedroom door. She was pretty angry, but she didn't react as badly as I expected. The first thing I did was change all my passwords. I wrote Alexandra an e-mail and explained what had happened. That night I slept in my office. I didn't sleep very well. The next morning Mariana was out of the house like a shot. I got a call from Alexandra as soon as she got my e-mail.

"How did she find out?" asked Alexandra.

"She says she read my e-mail, but I didn't think she knew the password to my computer."

"So what's going to happen?"

"I'm moving out, Alexandra. I'm going to go see my lawyer as soon as I can."

"Drew, are you sure that's a good idea? Perhaps you two can work things out. It's not too late, and you have two small children to think about."

"Alexandra, I can't live like this anymore. I just don't love her. It wouldn't be so bad if we could only communicate, but we can't even do that."

"Things are going to get rough for you, but you are a big, strong man. I know you can handle it."

"I'll let you know what happens," I said. "Thanks for calling."

Later that day I went to see my lawyer. I explained the situation. My lawyer told me that Mariana could sue for divorce if she wanted on the grounds of adultery. I told my lawyer that I wanted a fair separation agreement. She could never afford the house on her own, and I couldn't afford to keep her in it by myself. I proposed that we sell the house and that I use my share of the equity to get her into something cheaper. I was willing to give her maintenance and, of course, child support.

"What about a move-out date?" asked my lawyer.

"That's a problem. I'm broke. I can't afford to move out until I start generating some income. The house is big enough we can live under the same roof without killing each other, even if it will be very uncomfortable."

"I'll start working this up," she said.

Later that day I told Mariana about my plans. She listened quietly until I had finished.

"Sell the house? I don't think so. Where am I going to go? And what about the children?"

"Mariana, I can't afford this house, and neither can you. I am willing to help you get into something more affordable, but I just need a little time to get back on my feet."

"When are you planning to move out?" she asked.

"As soon as possible."

"I want you out of here now."

"Mariana, I can't go. I don't have any money or any work. If you throw me out now, you will destroy a lot. Just be patient until I get another job."

That night I wrote Alexandra. She told me I had a good plan. Mariana became obsessively jealous of my computer. Whenever she heard me typing on my keyboard, she got furious.

"I am tired of listening to you stay up all night writing love letters to your girlfriend."

"I'm not writing love letters. I'm either working or trying to find work."

I lied. Alexandra and I were writing each other three times a day. Although I was trying to find work, I was too distraught to concentrate. All I could think about was her. The pressure was killing me.

Mariana insisted on redoing the downstairs bathroom because Christopher was allergic to mold. The shower pan leaked and the mold was growing up the wall. Although we couldn't afford it I agreed we needed to get the work done, especially if we were going to sell the house.

"Mariana, the only money we have is in Christopher's trust fund. I am willing to use a small part of it because he is the one who will benefit, but we have to do this cheaply."

"I will take care of it," she said. "My sister has a Colombian friend who specializes in bathroom and kitchen remodels."

I was a little skeptical. A few days later a construction worker showed up. He measured the bathroom and talked with us. Mariana wanted to rip out the window and all kinds of other nonsense. We talked her out of it. A few days later he came by with a quote for the work. It would cost about $4,000.00. I could live with that amount, and gave him the go ahead.

As the work progressed he kept running into more problems, and, of course, Mariana had to have the best fixtures and tile. To top it all off, several months ago we planned on taking a vacation together with some of her friends in Puerto Rico. The tickets were already paid, and Mariana insisted on going. I couldn't afford it, and refused to go. She demanded that I pay for her trip and stay home with the children. In the meantime, the bathroom ended up costing more than $7,000.00. I told her if she went to Puerto Rico I was going to Spain.

"If you go to Spain you won't have a place to live when you get back."

"Then don't go to Puerto Rico," I said.

"I deserve a vacation after all this."

"Deserve has nothing to do with it. We can't afford it. How are you going to pay for it?"

"I will put it on the credit card."

"Jesus, Mariana! That card is nearly maxed out. We'll never pay it off."

"I don't give a shit. I'm taking a vacation."

"Fine, but don't expect me to stay here and suffer."

That afternoon I wrote Alexandra and told her what was happening. She called me. I had a portable phone that I took into the backyard for most of our conversations.

"Alexandra, I can't take the pressure. I want to come see you."

"Drew, I don't think that's a good idea if it's going to cause you more problems."

"More problems! How many more problems can I have? I just finished paying for a bathroom I can't afford. My wife is hell-bent on spending every last dime we have, and I'm in love with a woman who lives in a different country. I can't take it anymore. I need to come see you."

"You are welcome here anytime, but I don't want you to put yourself into more trouble."

"I'm already in trouble, Alexandra. This shit is killing me."

"She is really a bitch, Drew. You need to be careful of her. It sounds to me like she is a lot stronger than you."

"I don't know if she's stronger, but she's definitely angry. She's going to rip me to pieces whether I go or not. That's obvious."

"When were you thinking of coming?"

"On your birthday, of course. You didn't think I forgot after all these years?"

"You are sweet, but I don't pay too much attention to those things."

"I think it's only right that we celebrate your forty-fifth birthday together. I'll let you know when I have booked a flight."

That evening I found a direct flight from New York to Barcelona. I got a good deal. I e-mailed Alexandra my itinerary, and again she graciously booked me a flight from Barcelona to Ibiza.

Mariana was furious, but I refused to back down. If she was going to Puerto Rico, I was going to Spain. A few days before my departure, I sent Alexandra a dozen roses for her birthday. I timed it so they would arrive when I did. Mariana left with the kids the same day I did. Thankfully her flight was earlier than mine.

I arrived in Ibiza in the middle of a huge Birthday party. It was her daughter's birthday as well. Kids ran around the house most of the afternoon. Alexandra and I snuck away to her bedroom to make love. We had to tie the door shut to keep the kids from coming in, but we were so wild with desire we couldn't help ourselves.

Later that night when things had settled down, Alexandra and I sat in her office and talked.

"I told Sergio about us," she said.

"Really? How did he take it?"

"He took it well. You know I was really hoping he would come around, but he didn't."

"What do you mean?"

"I mean that I was hoping that the thought of losing me would open his eyes and he would try to work things out."

"Alexandra, how the hell is that supposed to make me feel?"

Her eyes were wide with surprise. "What do you mean?"

"I mean I feel completely used. Why would you even tell me something like that?"

"It's just a fact, like discussing the weather."

The tips of my ears started to burn. "Discussing the weather! We are talking about my feelings. I'm in love with you, and you use me to get back at your ex-boyfriend!"

"It's not like that. I was just stating a fact. I had hoped he would have come around. It has nothing to do with my feelings for you."

"That just makes me feel like second best, Alexandra. It's not right, and I'm really angry."

"It's not like that, Drew. I have to be honest. At least appreciate me for that."

"I'm real appreciative, thanks!"

"Drew, Sergio and I share so much in our Italian past. He comes from the same background as I do. With him I feel so comfortable, but with you I feel so alone."

I was speechless. Why didn't she tell me all this before? I didn't quite now how to react. I sat in her office chair in my underwear and t-shirt. She was sitting on the small flight of steps leading to her bedroom. I could see her panties beneath her short sundress.

Despite the pain, my erection poked through my shorts. She slipped off her panties and sat on top of me. Perhaps it was the emotional situation, or the position we were in—or even a combination of the two—but it was the most amazing sex we ever had. Afterward we went to bed. I couldn't deal with the pain, so I pushed it away like I always did.

For most of the week Alexandra and I had constant sex—all of it unprotected. We had sex almost everywhere—in the yard, on the bathroom floor, on the beach, and in the kitchen. I did my best to mind my manners. At one point Lucia came to us and asked us to please keep the door close because of all the noise we made.

Later that week, Nico had cut down a large pine tree outside his window because it blocked his view. The trees in Ibiza were protected government property. She had to tell her landlord what had happened. She was already having problems with him because he was allowing other people to use her electricity and she was paying for it. The case was in court.

Nico was already on shaky ground because he had dug up her jewelry that I had buried before she left for Switzerland the last time I was there. Alexandra had found out because Nico's sister sent her an e-mail saying her brother wasn't responsible for anything that might happen to it.

"Alexandra, he was probably just curious about what I had buried. Was anything missing?"

"No, but I had my lawyer come and collect it. He had him sign a note that nothing was missing."

"I don't think he's dishonest. If he were going to steal it, he would not have told his sister. I think he dug it up and panicked when he discovered what was buried. Hell, I would have done the same."

"I still don't trust him," she said. "And he is lazy. I asked him to finish a lot of work in the garden when I was in Switzerland, and when I got back a lot wasn't done. He is typical of so many South Americans I've met. He only thinks of himself and complains when things don't go well. He spends all his money at the disco and complains when he is broke."

"He's twenty-two years old. I doubt I could live out here like that without entertainment. He needs to go out."

"He also smokes. It's something I am very against. He hides it well, but I went into his room for some things and found his cigarettes. His room stinks of them."

"I don't know what to say about that, Alexandra. He doesn't smoke in front of the children, but those are the rules of your house, and he has to obey them. At least his room is underneath the pool and not in the main house."

"When Nico cut down that tree he caused a lot of problems. Now the landlord is trying to have me prosecuted for destroying public property."

"Are you going to fire him?" I asked.

"I'm thinking about it. I've had enough of his bad manners and surely attitude."

"Why don't you let me talk to him first?"

"Please."

That evening before dinner I walked with Nico in the garden. We sat down on one of the *miradors* and watched the sunset. The evening air was cold, and the sun hung like big, orange ball over the ocean.

"Nico, *Signora* Cavalletti is not all that hard to please. You just need to do what she wants."

He shrugged. "But she expects so much for so little. I never have enough money, and I work all the time."

"But you have a pretty good situation here. The food is good, you have a beautiful place to live, and the family is wonderful."

"Yes, I love the children, but I don't have any time for myself. And *Signora* is not very friendly. She never smiles."

"She smiles a lot when she is pleased. You just need to learn how to please her. When she tells you to do something simply make sure you get it done. If it's too much do as much as you can, but make sure you always have something to show her at the end of the day."

"I do!" he said. "Look around. See all the things I have done. She just expects so much."

"Nico, I haven't been here that long, but I see how you move. Your style is very easygoing and relaxed. Hers is go, go, go. She accomplishes a lot in very little time, and she expects others

447

to do the same. It may not be fair but that's how it is."

"I will try to work harder," he said.

"Oh, and be careful about the cigarettes. She knows all about them."

"Thank you," he said.

The next couple days Nico worked hard. Alexandra and I purchased a chain saw and Nico and I took apart the tree he had cut down. He had thrown it over the side of the bluff, and getting to it was dangerous. I managed to cut the tree into pieces pretty quickly, and the two of us disposed of it. It took most of the afternoon.

Nonetheless, later that week, Alexandra had enough of Nico, and she fired him one afternoon while her children listened to them fighting outside her office. The discussion was loud, but mostly in Spanish, so I only understood bits and pieces. Nico left the next morning. It was tearful and hard for the rest of the staff. The children didn't know what to say, but they stood by their mother, who was always and forever at their side.

Nico gathered up his bags and loaded them into a waiting cab. It was especially hard for Papi; he had lost yet another surrogate father. He and Nico spent a lot of time together playing football and other games. Even so, I also stood by Alexandra. This was her house, and I loved her.

Alexandra told me that Sergio had never been to visit her in Spain. He had made several trips to Switzerland in the course of their relationship, and she used to fly quite often to Italy. I couldn't believe he would not come see her in such a beautiful place, but according to her, one of the reasons why she loved him the way she did was because he didn't give a hoot about her money. He never wanted anything from her—including her, so it seemed to me. Her ideal man just didn't love her, and it vexed her to no end. She talked endlessly about it, and I listened patiently to all the gory details. Meanwhile, his picture still glared at me from across the room.

Alexandra's banker had negotiated the purchase of a new office building, and she wanted to thank him properly. The next time we went food shopping, she asked me what I thought would be a good gift for him.

"I don't know," I said. "When you buy someone a gift it should be something personal; something you know they will appreciate. Does he drink?"

"I think so," she answered.

"Why don't you get him something like a bottle of Chivas Regal or some chocolate, if you don't think he would like that."

"Sometimes I feel so alone with you," she said, throwing up her hands in disgust. "A well-mannered person would never buy a gift like Chivas Regal."

"Why the hell not? He's just your banker. He's not your goddamn father!"

"Because he can get something like that anywhere. When you get a gift for someone you always get something unique that they wouldn't normally be able to get, like a bottle of wine from the area."

"Then why the hell did you ask me, Alexandra?"

I walked out and went to the car. She was taking all this too far. If she felt so alone with me and so comfortable with him, why was I here and he wasn't? I got the sense she was trying to get rid of me, and I wondered why we were trying so hard to get her pregnant. The situation twisted me up inside, and I didn't know how to react. I didn't get angry for fear of losing her, which was probably a mistake. Instead I kept calm and tried to please her. After all, a well-mannered man never loses his temper.

As I was leaving I had those same mixed feelings about where we stood. Alexandra said we should try to make the best of our differences. She was willing to give things a try. I wasn't so sure, but I was so in love I didn't want to let her go. She talked about the possibility of moving to the States for a year with the children so we could get to know each other better. I didn't know if she was serious, but she insisted she was.

Alexandra scheduled her trip back to Switzerland to coincide with my flight home. We all left for the airport together. Alexandra kissed me goodbye at my gate, and then continued to her own with all her children in tow.

Mariana was home before me. I got home late at night, and went straight to bed. Exhausted and emotionally battered, I was confused about Alexandra's intentions. The next morning Mariana asked me if I had a place to go.

"Not yet," I replied.

"Fine, I will take care of this myself," she said. She left with the children and I went through the mail. The bills were piling up. Mariana and I managed to keep away from each other while I continued trying to find work. Alexandra and I wrote each other every day. She made it clear she wasn't in love, but refused to discuss how she felt. I read her e-mails carefully, reading between each line to see what she was feeling. One night a couple of weeks later she told me she got her period. I guess I was relieved, but the idea of having a child with her intrigued me somehow.

One night a couple of weeks later a policeman showed up at my door. He handed me a temporary order of restraint. I had to be out of the house in less than a week.

"I told you I'd fix this problem," said Mariana.

"Jesus, Mariana, do you have any idea what you have done? You are throwing me out of the house when I'm flat broke! How am I supposed to take care of you and the kids when I'm homeless?"

450

"I don't believe any of that shit about your separation agreement. I just want you out."

"Jesus, Mariana. You are shooting yourself in the foot. I can't do anything for you if I'm on the streets with no money. I have nowhere to go."

"Well, you better find someplace quick."

I called my lawyer and told her what was happening. We had to be in court in a few days. When I told Alexandra what happened she called me immediately.

"Drew, she's stupid! She's going to lose everything. You need to get custody of your children."

"What are you talking about, Alexandra?"

"Drew, do you really want an uneducated, greedy woman like that raising your children?"

"She's a good mother, Alexandra. She takes good care of them."

"It's your life, but I would not let a woman like that raise my children. She may bathe them and feed them but they will grow up with her values. As a parent it's your responsibility to give them the best you can. You have more education than she does. If you get custody of your children she will have to leave, not you."

"It's not that simple, and besides, I can't focus on that now. My survival is at stake."

"You have to focus on it now. If you don't you might regret it later. She is trying to destroy you and you have to fight back."

"What the hell do you want me to do?"

"Destroy her before she destroys you!"

"Alexandra, I can't. She is the mother of my children. She has a lot of problems but she is not all evil. And I can't focus on that now. It's too much. I am going to be homeless in less than a week."

451

"You are going to fight it in court, right?"

"Yes, I'm going to fight it in court. But my lawyer said that this is how wives get their husbands out of the house."

A couple days later I faced Mariana in court. She told the judge stories about how I threatened to kill her if she didn't shut the hell up about my girlfriend. Even the judge knew she was lying. My lawyer brought up the point that I had initiated a fair and generous separation agreement. The judge cut me a break and allowed me an extra week. He recommended I not try to fight it because the laws were very strict about domestic violence, and my reputation would be at stake. My lawyer agreed. After the hearing Mariana left the room in tears. She was more hurt than anything else, and she walked by my lawyer and me in a huff.

"How long have you been so detached from your wife?" my lawyer asked.

"Is it that obvious?"

"Yes. You watched her walk out of here without a shred of emotion."

"I've felt this way for about three years," I replied.

"That's rough. I'm sorry. Well, you'd better get out of the house."

"I can't believe she did this. I didn't think she would."

"Why would you think that?" she asked.

"I don't know. I thought she'd understand that I didn't love her and would believe me when I told her that I would take care of her."

"It wasn't enough. She wants it all. And she wants to make sure you get nothing."

"But she's the one that will lose. She can't afford that place, and I can't afford to keep her in it."

"Do you have a place to go?"

"Not yet."

452

"Well you better find a place quick," she said.

The next two weeks I scoured the area trying to find a room for rent. The judge ordered me to pay $1,107.00 in child support payments and continue the health insurance, which was an additional $700.00 a month. I couldn't find anything on such short notice, and none of my sisters would take me in. They all thought I was a monster for what I did to my wife. I finally called Aunt Tess.

"How are you making out, Dear?" she asked.

"Not so well. The judge ordered me out of the house, and I've got nowhere to go."

"Well, I'd ask you to stay here but Shelly is coming up with the baby, and we don't have room for you. Why don't you give your aunt Gracie a call? You're a Smith; she should help."

The thought of staying up in Rochester with my father's sister was more appalling than being on the streets. "It's okay, Aunt Tess. I'll be fine."

"Drew, it's none of my business, but I have to tell you how disappointed I am, even if I understand what you're going through. I've always thought with my heart instead of my head, but you have no business leaving your wife with two small children for some childhood flame in another country."

"It's more complicated than that, Aunt Tess. Mariana and I have been having problems for a long, long time."

"Have you and Mariana really tried to work things out? I'd hate to see you do something you regret."

"Aunt Tess, we have nothing in common, and Alexandra means the world to me."

"Well, just make sure you do what's right," she said.

On my moving day I grabbed everything I could of my personal belongings and loaded them into my car. I rented a storage facility and moved into a residence hotel in the city. My lawyer recommended I liquidate my retirement savings to keep myself going. The senior partner let me set up my computer in a spare office just so I would have a place to go. I was speechless at their generosity.

As a favor, Alexandra shipped them a huge box of Swiss chocolate. We continued writing each other every day, and she called when she could. I was finally offered a job in Queens. We had talked about me coming to Spain to work on a software project that could possibly make some money, but it was a huge risk. She was willing to help.

"Alexandra, I have to ask you. Do you want me to come to Spain?"

"It's not what I want, Drew. That decision has to be yours. I would be glad to have you, but if I told you to come and things didn't work out you would blame me for it."

"That doesn't sound very reassuring, Alexandra. If I were to go to Spain I would want to go there because I love you. It's a huge risk for me, but I am not willing to risk everything for nothing."

"Life is full of risks, Drew. I would be happy to have you, but you need to do what's best for you."

Now I was really confused, and finally talked to my lawyer about it.

"Stay here and finish the divorce," she said. "You need to stand on your own, otherwise you will end up being a kept man, completely at her mercy. She's made it clear she doesn't love you, so you should focus on your life and your children."

That was all I needed to hear. I was so heartbroken I couldn't stop crying when I wrote Alexandra of my decision. I wanted to be with her more than anything in the world.

Alexandra was disappointed. I think she wanted me to come, but it was too big a risk for me. If she had told me she loved me

I would have been on the first plane; instead she put all the responsibility on my shoulders. I accepted the job in Queens and eventually moved into a charming little apartment in an old Tudor house in a quiet neighborhood. I had no furniture. My landlord, an old lady with a huge heart, felt bad for me and gave me a mattress to sleep on.

A few days later Mariana's lawyer informed us that she was suing for divorce on the grounds of adultery. Things were about to get ugly. I sat in my lawyer's office while she tried to negotiate terms with him on the telephone. Her lawyer wasn't going to budge.

"Well, there is the matter of the house," she said. "My client can't afford to pay the mortgage."

My lawyer frowned and shook her head.

"What do you mean the mortgage is not an issue?

Another pause.

"How long has his father been paying the mortgage?"

What the hell was going on? She finally got off the phone and told me that my father was picking up all the expenses of the house. I was stunned. He would pay to keep Mariana and the kids in the house, but he wouldn't help me directly. It didn't matter; he was helping anyway, even if I didn't trust him. At least the kids would have a place to live, and we wouldn't lose the house in a foreclosure.

"Who's paying for her lawyer?" I asked, knowing Mariana didn't have any money of her own.

"Apparently your father is," she said, looking somewhat surprised herself.

I wasn't surprised at all. The man would not be satisfied until he saw me completely destroyed, and I knew he had gone out of his way to find Mariana the best divorce lawyer money could buy. No wonder I was getting reamed.

I hated my job, but it was convenient—less than ten minutes from where I lived. Alexandra and I continued writing each other everyday. The phone calls stopped, but our e-mails were long and passionate. She complained constantly about how difficult her life was without Nico. She couldn't find anyone to replace him and had to do all the driving herself. She also worked around the clock whenever she went to Switzerland. I didn't know how she did it. I told her I still wanted to come to Spain, but didn't want to abrogate my financial responsibilities to my family. I tried my hardest to get an independent contract that would allow me to work anywhere, but nothing was available. I was lucky to have a job, crummy as it was.

That summer she went to Rome to face her mother and brother in court. I offered to go with her. She refused; she said she wanted to go alone, and besides, I would have lost my job. I was still on probation, having been there less than a month. She e-mailed me after it was over. She had lost the case. The judge told her she should be a better daughter and take care of her mother. It was the first time she had seen her brother in years. He just sat there as if he were bored. He could have destroyed her if he wanted. She was responsible for paying the annual fees for some of the expenses of the society. He could have made things so expensive for her she would have been bankrupt. Her mother simply looked at her daughter with sadness, wondering why all this was happening. Alexandra was heartbroken. She had expected Sergio to come offer support, but he never showed.

As the summer progressed, so did my frustration. Alexandra and I were writing each other three times a day. She would tell me about how she would sunbathe naked on her veranda, and how much she missed my kisses. I wanted desperately to be with her, but I was trapped in my job and the endless expenses. I had huge debts from my divorce, and every bit of extra money I had went

456

toward paying them off. Mariana couldn't afford car insurance and the other expenses with the house, so I ended up paying for them as well. I lived like a monk with no furniture or any kind of luxuries. Everyone told me I was an idiot for paying all that, but she could never do it on her own with two small children.

I thought about what Alexandra had said about finding Axel, and decided to give it a try. I was certain he no longer lived in Greece, but his father was famous by now. I contacted some webmasters at some of his fan club sites, and asked if they knew the whereabouts of Marianne and her son.

A few days later one of them wrote back, informing me that Marianne had remarried and was living in Oslo. He gave me her married name and birth date. I sent a letter with only that information on the envelope. Several weeks later I received a reply:

Dear Drew,

Your letter reached me today. I just returned from Hydra. I remember you, and so does Axel. Axel has been very sick, but he's on his feet. I will forward your letter to him and help him contact you. Axel visited his father the year after you left Switzerland. He was given LSD at a party and somehow never came through. He was only fifteen at the time. He is living in the country with good helpers. Music is very important to him. I will talk to him tomorrow.

So good to hear from you after all these years.

All good things,

Marianne

Upon reading her letter I collapsed to my knees and sobbed. I must have cried for at least fifteen minutes. Axel was the best part of my childhood memories, and I couldn't believe what had happened. If I had know sooner I could have done something,

457

but now there was nothing to be done. I wrote Marianne and told her I'd visit as soon as I could.

Later I found out Aunt Gracie and my father decided to put Mariana through school. She was studying accounting and computers, and was in the honors program. I was proud of her. She told me the only way to pay back my family's generosity was to get good grades. I helped her with the computer when I came to see the children on Saturdays.

Alexandra and I schemed of ways for us to be together. I only got two weeks vacation per year, but I wasn't eligible to take any for another six months. One day she called me from Ibiza.

"I have an idea," she said. "Why don't we open a restaurant here? You could run it, as long as I don't have to be too involved."

"That's a great idea! How soon do you think we could pull that together?"

"It takes forever to get things done in Spain. It's not like Switzerland. You have to go through so much red tape."

"But we could get it done, right?"

"Yes, I think so. But I have to ask you a question, and I need you to be honest with me."

"What is it, Alexandra?"

"If you came to Spain and went into business with me, and I fell in love with another man, how would you react?"

I couldn't believe she was asking me this question. It was another emotional slap in the face. "I'd be devastated, Alexandra. What do you think? I'm in love with you, and you keep me hanging on, but I don't know why."

"Well, Drew, I need more time to understand my feelings. It's only right, especially at our age."

"That's all well and good, Alexandra. But why would I want to leave my children and move to another country for a woman who is talking about leaving me for another man?"

"I'm offering you a good opportunity. It would be good for you to live in a beautiful place and run your own business."

"I agree it would be wonderful—if we could do it together. We could be a good team. I could help you with your children and your work in Switzerland. At the same time I would have enough money to meet my financial obligations. That's important to me. I have so much to give you, if you would only allow me."

"I don't need a man, Drew. I want one. That's the difference between you and me. I am not going to bring you into my life just to make myself more comfortable. If I brought you into my life it would be simply because I love you."

"Are you saying you don't love me, Alexandra?"

"I'm saying I could never leave my family the way you did just because I wanted to be with another person. You live your life the way you want, and if things mesh then you spend your time together, but you never simply move in with someone just to make yourself more comfortable."

"Alexandra, that's bullshit! I love you with all my heart. If I moved to Spain it would be simply to help you and love you. Eventually I would find my own niche because that's who I am. It may take me some time but it would most certainly happen."

"Drew, I wouldn't want you to move here for me. If you did it would have to be strictly for you. I don't want that responsibility."

"It seems to me you have a problem with responsibility, Alexandra."

"It's not true! I am responsible for me and my children. I work hard to give them a better life. I would rather eat potatoes for the rest of my life than live off of somebody else. I could be like your lovely wife Mariana, and accept money from your family to go to school and do nothing."

459

"That's not fair! Mariana came to this country with nothing. English is her second language. She is going to school so she can become more independent and be a better mother!"

"I'm sorry. I could never do that. I was taught to be independent and strong."

"I think you are a little hard on her. She's had a tough life, and things have been pretty painful.

"Mariana has not lost as much as I have. She came from nothing, so she doesn't know what it's like to lose. I was supposed to live a life of luxury, and now I have to work for everything I have."

I couldn't believe she just said that, and didn't quite know how to respond. I never remembered her being so arrogant. "Pain is pain, no matter who is feeling it, Alexandra. When we were trying so hard to get you pregnant, what was that all about?"

"I think you put too much importance on that."

"Too much importance! We had unprotected sex three times a day for three weeks. I practically wore my dick off trying to get you pregnant! What the hell was that about?"

"I was sad about Sergio," she admitted.

"So, all this was about Sergio. You could have gotten pregnant with any man in the world. Why did you choose my dick?"

"Because you loved me, and I have feelings for you."

"But you don't love me."

"No, I don't love you," she said.

"How am I supposed to feel, Alexandra? What am I supposed to do?"

"I don't know, Drew. That's up to you. I can only be honest with you and tell you that I still love Sergio. I can't get him out of my heart. You might be able to leave your wife and children for another woman just like that, but for me love is much deeper."

Something about her was not right. Perhaps all the pain

she had been through in her life made her this way. She might never be right. She put so much emotion into a man who didn't love her.

"All this was about Sergio. Jesus, Alexandra, I feel like an idiot. You've really broken my heart."

"I'm sorry, Drew. I tried to love you but I couldn't. I was really hoping Sergio would come take me home. I'm hoping he still does."

"I hope so too, Alexandra."

I hung up the phone. My life was in ruins. I went downstairs and found my landlord in her kitchen. She and I drank a cup of tea together and I told her the entire story.

She put her hand on her cheek and shook her head. "Jesus, Drew, you've been through a lot. What are you going to do? You need to find yourself a hobby. Get this stuff off your mind. If you stick around here and do nothing you'll drive yourself crazy. Do you have any hobbies?"

"I like to write, although I haven't done any in ages."

"That's a wonderful idea! You should write a book."

"I have a great story even if it's so twisted most people would never believe it."

"Well that's what you should do. It will help you put all this in perspective."

"I think you are right. I've always wanted to write a book."

"Well, get upstairs and start writing!" she said.

I went upstairs and sat in front of my computer. The story was there in front of me, waiting to be told. I started typing.

About the Author

James Weil has lived in four different countries and speaks four languages. He has travelled extensively throughout Europe and the United States. He is a self-taught computer programmer and worked his way up to the title Senior Programmer/Analyst.

He currently works for the State of New York as a software engineer in New York City and lives in Flushing, Queens. When he is not writing he is constantly looking for his next great read.

Also available from Dailey Swan Publishing

Mystery/Suspense

Revenge by JH Hardy	$12.95
Deadline! by Paula Tutman	$15.95
Deadline!! Second Block by Paula Tutman	$15.95
The Acorn Dossier by William Beecher	$14.95
The Transyvania Connection by Garrison Walters	$14.95
Duper's Fork (Prisoners of War) by Andrew Winter	$14.95
Duper's Fork (Prisoners of Greed) by Andrew Winter	$14.95
Duper's Fork (Prisoners of fear) by Andrew Winter	$14.95
Charlie 9-Lives by E. H. Davis	$14.95
Doc Be Nimble by Allen Parsley	$14.95

Non-Fiction

Chicken Noodle News by John Baker	$15.95
Are You Fascinated by Ken Tucker	$10.95
My Husband Made a Man Outta Me by Dr. Cecile Forte	$12.95

www.daileyswanpublishing.com